Unofficial & Deniable

John Gordon Davis was born in Rhodesia and brought up in South Africa. He went to school in the Transkei, and was a student at Rhodes University in the Eastern Cape. He took a degree in Political Science before moving on to the University of South Africa, Pretoria, from which he qualified as a lawyer while serving as a judge's clerk. He spent his university vacations as a deckhand with the British and Dutch merchant navies. After a spell as a miner in Ontario he returned to courtroom work in Rhodesia as an assistant public prosecutor before becoming crown counsel. He was later appointed to the same position in Hong Kong.

The international success of his first novel, *Hold My Hand I'm Dying*, allowed him to take up writing full time. His recent novels include *The Land God Made in Anger*, *Roots of Outrage* and *The Year of Dangerous Loving*.

'This is the New South Africa – and the sins of the past come home to roost in this exhilarating novel of intrigue and courtroom drama. John Gordon Davis puts together a highly satisfying blend of history, politics, romance and adventure. He has a feel for Africa, and in particular South Africa and its people . . . immaculate research. With a fast-moving plot this becomes a most satisfying thriller. Anyone who lived through the Apartheid era, the developments swinging South Africa to a working democracy and who witnessed the Truth and Reconciliation Commission, will realize just how plausible his story is. What a story! What a climax! And what a twist!'

The Citizen

By John Gordon Davis

Hold My Hand I'm Dying
Cape of Storms
Years of the Hungry Tiger
Taller Than Trees
Leviathan
Typhoon
Fear No Evil
Seize the Reckless Wind
A Woman Involved
The Land God Made in Anger
Talk to Me Tenderly, Tell Me Lies
Roots of Outrage
The Year of Dangerous Loving
Unofficial & Deniable

Non-fiction
Operation Rhino
Hong Kong Through the Looking Glass

JOHN GORDON DAVIS

UNOFFICIAL & DENIABLE

HarperCollins*Publishers*

HarperCollins*Publishers*
77–85 Fulham Palace Road,
Hammersmith, London W6 8JB

www.fireandwater.com

This paperback edition 2000
1 3 5 7 9 10 8 6 4 2

First published in Great Britain by
HarperCollins*Publishers* 1999

ISBN 0 00 651262 3

Typeset in Meridien by
Palimpsest Book Production Limited, Polmont, Stirlingshire

Printed and bound in Great Britain by
Clays Ltd, St Ives plc

To Tana and David Hilton-Barber

PROLOGUE

Andy Meyer, the junior officer on watch in the US Coast Guard station, remembered the yacht dropping anchor in the open channel of St Thomas, American Virgin Islands, in the small hours of that September morning in 1996 because it was not flying a flag. Four hours later, just before dawn, he noticed the yacht steaming out of the channel towards the nearby British Virgin Islands. Meyer hoped the skipper knew what he was doing – there were rocky waters ahead, best navigated in daylight, and technically he should have registered his arrival in American waters before departing. Meyer decided to make an entry in the Log, just to show he had done some work.

The sun was up when the yacht, *Rosemary*, anchored in the big open bay of Road Town, Tortola, the sleepy little capital of the nearby British Virgin Islands, but it is established by Immigration Department records that it was not until three o'clock that afternoon that the skipper, Sinclair Jonathan Harker, reported his arrival. He appeared, according to Mrs Doris Johnston, the chief immigration officer, to have been drinking; he was nervous, unshaven, wild-looking. He gave his last port of call as Nassau, Bahamas, and produced a crew list certifying that only he and his wife Josephine were aboard. He presented Josephine's passport, along with his own, but Mrs Johnston told him that Josephine had to report in person. Mrs Johnston then demanded his Nassau port clearance certificate: Harker said he had not known he needed such a document before leaving the Bahamas. Mrs Johnston told him in no uncertain terms that he would have to return to Nassau to get it.

Harker then left Mrs Johnston's indignant presence, went

to the American Express office and telephoned Josephine's insurance company in New York advising them of her death and asking what procedures he had to follow. He then sent a fax to her attorney, asking the same question, then another to her father, Denys Valentine, in Boston, reporting his daughter's death, saying he would telephone as soon as he had composed himself. Then, instead of heading to the police station to report her death, he returned to his boat and proceeded to drink a bottle of rum.

At noon the next day a police party went out to his boat, alerted by Mrs Doris Johnston who had complained to them that Josephine Harker still had not reported to Immigration Department. The Commissioner of Police, Joshua Humphrey, found Harker sitting in the saloon of his yacht, ashen, starting on a new bottle of rum. Harker looked up and said:

'I want to report a person missing on the high seas . . .'

Joshua Humphrey, portly, black, with forty years' experience, suspected immediately that Sinclair Jonathan Harker was guilty as *sin*; '*Sin-clear* Harker the *sinful* sailor,' he dubbed him. And when he went into Jack Harker's history and learned that he had been a career officer in the Rhodesian army battling freedom-fighters until the bitter end of that long, nasty, bush war, he was *sure*. But when he learned that, at the end of that war, Harker had been snapped up by the South African Defence Force to fight in their bush war in Angola against the ANC guerrillas and the Cuban army, Commissioner Joshua Humphrey, a devout Africanist, was downright *convinced* of his guilt.

'An' what you bin doin' since you stopped being a soldier for apartheid, *Major* Harker?'

'A publisher. And I was never a soldier *for* apartheid – I was a soldier *against* communism.'

Joshua Humphrey found the distinction a metaphysical one but decided not to argue. 'A *publisher*? How does a military man become a publisher, sir? Where?'

'In New York. Commissioner, I'm very traumatized and I feel your attitude is persecutory.'

'In New *York*, huh?'

The Commissioner was smart enough to know his lack of real experience. It was a relief to share responsibility and telephone the US Coast Guard in St Thomas and ask, as a favour, whether an officer experienced in investigations on the high seas would come over to take a look at this case.

The Virgin Islands, with balmy turquoise bays and white beaches, interlaced with exotic coral reefs, are very beautiful, possibly the best real estate in the world, but commercially they are good for little more than offshore banking and tourism. Named for their unspoilt beauty, they were colonized by Great Britain and Denmark as bases from which to battle the Spaniards and the pirates who plagued the merchantmen carrying the spoils of the New World back to Europe. Sugar plantations were developed, but the problem was labour: the tropical heat made the cane fields unworkable by white men; they simply did not have the sweat-glands for hard work in such a climate. The solution was black labour – for over two hundred years British and American slaving ships sailed to West Africa and brought back their cargoes of human beings to be sold as slaves to the plantation owners. The Virgins, like all the islands arcing across the Caribbean Sea, prospered, despite a series of rebellions by slaves which were ruthlessly suppressed. But then came the Abolition of Slavery Act in Great Britain which decreed that all slaves throughout the British Empire be freed at midnight on 31 December 1834.

Thus the basic economy of the Caribbean was dislocated: the plantation owners returned to Europe, the cane fields went to ruin, the erstwhile slaves scratched a subsistence living. Denmark sold her share of the Virgin Islands to the United States of America; the British hung on to their share

3

of the islands until the Wind of Change swept Africa, whereupon she granted independence to all her colonies. But, unlike the newly independent African states, the Caribbean islanders spoke no African language, the only culture they knew was that of their colonial masters and they clung to that. Joshua Humphrey, Commissioner of Police, great grandson of slaves, was proud of his British heritage. He had something very important in common with Lieutenant-Commander Albert Smith of the US Coast Guard: both were proud to be black descendants of slaves, determined to show they could do their jobs as well as any white man, and both deeply resented South Africans because of their former politics. And now here sat a South African, a former senior officer in the South African army, with a story of his American wife's mysterious disappearance.

'Where exactly did this take place, Major?' Smith asked, his pen poised.

Harker took a note from his pocket with trembly fingers. He handed it across the desk. 'Those are the coordinates I got from my satellite-navigator when I woke up and found Josephine missing.'

Smith consulted a chart on the desk. He carefully marked in the coordinates with a parallel ruler.

'But,' he said, 'that means she disappeared south east of Florida, in American waters.'

'I thought they were international waters.'

Smith smiled. 'Come on, Major, you're a military man who can read maps, you know enough law to know where's "high seas" and where's territorial waters.' He paused for a response, then continued: 'But no matter what you *thought*, why didn't you sail back to Florida, back to Miami or Key West to report to the police? They were less than two hundred miles away, and the winds would have been in your favour. Why did you go a thousand miles or more, *against* the wind, into the Atlantic, all the way to the Virgin Islands to report?'

Harker wiped a hand down his gaunt face. 'I just didn't think of it. I was distraught. Exhausted . . . We were heading for the Virgin Islands when this accident happened and I just carried on.'

Smith sat back. 'So seven days later you arrived here. What time was that?'

'About eight o'clock in the morning.'

'And this was your first stop in the Virgins?'

'Yes.'

'Well,' Smith said with satisfaction, 'it was recorded by our Coast Guard station that you stopped in the American Virgins for several hours the night before last.'

'Oh,' Harker said, 'that. But I only anchored, I didn't go ashore.'

'But you "stopped",' Humphrey insisted. 'Why did you not go ashore, to the police, to report Josephine's disappearance?'

Harker closed his eyes. 'Because,' he said tensely, 'I needed to sleep.'

'So why didn't you go ashore to report *after* you slept?'

'Because it was still dark. I thought it better to wait until daylight when senior police officers would be at work, not juniors on night duty.'

Humphrey smirked. Smith said: 'Not because you thought the US Virgins police might be more efficient and therefore more dangerous to you? Seeing Josephine was American and she disappeared in American waters off an American boat.'

Harker's nerves were ragged. 'No. And I've told you I thought she'd been lost in international waters.'

Both officials smirked. 'But you reached Tortola at about eight o'clock that morning,' Smith said. 'Yet you didn't report to this police station at all – they came to your boat, the next day. Only *then* did you report anything.' Smith looked at him. 'How come, Major?'

'Because I was exhausted after my ordeal – seven days at sea alone. I needed to sleep some more.'

5

'But,' Smith said, 'Mr Humphrey says you had been drinking when he went out to your boat.'

'When I woke up I had a few drinks. To pull myself together before reporting.'

'But what *did* you do yesterday, when you arrived?'

Harker closed his eyes. 'I sent a fax to Josephine's father from the American Express office, informing him of her death.'

'Why didn't you telephone?'

'Because,' Harker said tensely, 'of the emotion. I wanted him to be informed before I telephoned and we all burst into tears.'

'I see . . .' Smith nodded. 'Not because you didn't want to answer awkward questions? And then you returned to your boat to rest?'

Harker hesitated an instant. 'Yes.'

Smith smiled. 'Not so, Major. You made another phone call. American Express gave us the number. Who to?'

Harker closed his eyes again, sick in his guts. 'I forgot. To Josephine's insurance company.'

Humphrey's face creased in theatrical wonder: 'But how can you forget? And why, Major? What was the hurry? Why was that more important than reporting her death to *me*, the police?'

'I was in the American Express offices, I had the facilities available, I simply took the opportunity to do the responsible thing.'

Humphrey snorted. 'An' what did you ask the insurance company?'

'I simply reported Josephine's death.'

'You didn't ask how to collect the insurance?'

Harker hesitated. 'No. I mean I simply asked what formalities were required of me generally.'

'Formalities? For what?'

Harker sighed.

'Formalities to wind up her estate. Affidavits, death certificates, police reports and so on?' Smith suggested.

Harker hesitated, then sighed. 'Yes.'

'In other words,' Humphrey said, 'how to satisfy the insurance company that they had to pay up.'

'And how much insurance did you have on Josephine, Major?' Smith asked.

'None,' Harker said shakily. 'She insured her own life. She paid the premiums.'

'And who was the beneficiary?'

'Her estate.'

'And who was the beneficiary of her estate under her will?'

Harker took a deep breath. 'As far as I know, some of her relations, and her father. And me. Mostly me, but I don't know the amounts.'

'You don't *know*?'

'A will is a private matter, isn't it?' Harker rasped angrily.

Silence. Then: 'And you? Who is the beneficiary under your will?'

'Josephine. She gets everything.'

'Did she know?'

Harker closed his eyes. 'Yes. When we got married and decided to do this trip around the world we both made new wills in each other's favour.'

'And where *is* her will?'

'With her attorney, in New York. As is mine.'

'And did you advise her attorney of her death when you were at American Express?'

Harker sighed. 'Yes.'

'Why didn't you tell us earlier?'

'I forgot that detail.'

'Oh, you forgot. Like you forgot to mention that you advised her insurance company?' Smith smiled. 'And how long have you and Josephine been together?'

'Over seven years.'

'And did she work?'

'She was a writer. She published under her maiden name, Josephine Valentine.'

7

Smith looked at Humphrey. 'You mean *the* Josephine Valentine? Who wrote that book about South Africa: *Outrage*?'

'Right.'

Smith and Humphrey glared at each other. 'So your wife was a wealthy woman?' Smith asked.

Harker shifted. 'Well off, yes.'

'And you, Major?'

'I published her books, or rather my company did, Harvest House. So I'm well off too.' He added shakily: 'So why the hell am I suspected of murdering her? Why would I kill the goose that lays the golden eggs?'

Smith smiled grimly. 'Nobody's accusing you yet, Major. And we will ask the questions, if you please. But tell me – was your relationship happy?'

'Very.'

Smith frowned. 'But how did she feel about your military history? Fighting for apartheid, against the freedom forces of Nelson Mandela – she was very anti-South Africa in her books.'

'She understood that I never regarded myself as fighting *for* apartheid. I was a professional soldier fighting against the Cuban army, Russia's surrogates in Africa who were helping the illegal communist regime of Angola fight the Angola freedom forces. The South African army was supporting those freedom fighters, and so was America, because it was no secret that the Cubans also intended to overrun South Africa and turn it into another communist state. *That's* what I was fighting against.'

'But,' Humphrey said, 'that also meant you were fighting *for* apartheid. And against the ANC who had bases in Angola.'

Harker dragged his hand down his face. 'I knew apartheid was going to collapse soon. The greater evil was if the Cubans and Russians overran South Africa, taking the Cape Sea Route. The communists could already control Suez any time they wanted. Next to go would have been the Panama

Canal. Then the communists would have had the whole world sewn up. So the important thing was to defeat the Cuban army in Angola, drive them out of Africa.'

'But you and your famous wife never quarrelled about this?'

'No.'

'So when did you settle in America?'

Harker said tensely: 'In 1986 I was wounded, and invalided out of the army. First I went to England and became involved in publishing. I came to America in 1987 and took over Harvest House. In 1988 I met Josephine and later started publishing her books. And we've lived happily ever after. Okay?' He closed his eyes. 'And now I want to go back to my boat and sleep.'

Humphrey said, 'No, we've impounded your boat, Major, while the forensic scientist examines it, takes photographs and so on. You'll have to sleep in a hotel tonight. So please tell us again what happened that night Josephine disappeared.'

Harker opened his eyes. 'Jesus. I've told you twice.'

'Again, please.'

'Look, evidently you suspect me. So I want a lawyer.'

Smith smiled. 'Why do you want a lawyer if you're innocent, Major? Why are you scared of just telling us again what happened, if you're telling the truth?'

Harker took a deep, tense breath. 'You can't put me to the expense of a hotel when I have my own boat.'

'Okay,' Humphrey smiled, 'so I offer you a bed in the cells instead. It's up to you. But I would be grateful if you came back here at noon tomorrow to resume our discussion. And I would be grateful for your passport, please . . .'

Harker had left his boat at anchor in the bay: now, on emerging from the police station, he found it chained to the government jetty, under guard. Policemen were aboard. He collected some things and checked into the Ambrosia boarding house.

At ten o'clock the next morning Jack Harker was arrested

at the aerodrome attempting to board a flight to the French island of Guadeloupe. In his baggage was a .25 Browning pistol. His South African passport had been surrendered to Humphrey: he was using an expired passport which the police had not known he possessed. On his return to the police station he was further interrogated; finally he was formally charged with the murder of Josephine Valentine Harker.

A week later he was extradited to Florida to face trial.

PART I

The Back-story

1

In those days of apartheid many accidental deaths occurred in police custody – black suspects fell down stairs and cracked their skulls, or slipped on soap in the showers, or sometimes even threw themselves out of upper windows in a reckless attempt to escape. There was always an official inquest, as the law required, but the magistrate very seldom found anything suspicious, anything indicating reprehensible interrogation techniques by the police. The inquest into the death of Steve Biko, for example, evoked no judicial censure even though Biko was driven naked through the night, a thousand miles, in the back of an open truck, to a police hospital after he had sustained a fractured skull when he fell against a wall whilst irrationally attacking his police interrogators. In those days these accidental deaths were attributed by most of the white public to a few 'bad apples' in the police, though the frequency suggested that there must be a lot of them, but not too many questions were asked and there were no hard facts to gainsay police explanations.

Then deaths began to befall the apartheid government's enemies outside the country, which were clearly not accidental: Professor Ruth First, wife of the leader of the South African Communist Party, was killed by a parcel bomb in Mozambique; Jeanette Schoon, wife of an anti-apartheid activist, was blown to bits, together with her little daughter, by another parcel bomb in Angola; Dulcie September died in a hail of bullets in Paris as she opened the offices of the African National Congress; Dr Albie Sachs, anti-apartheid activist, had his arm blown off by a car-bomb in Mozambique; Advocate Anton Lubowski, another anti-apartheid politician, was gunned down outside his home in Namibia on the eve of his country's independence from South Africa. The press, particularly the international press, argued that the pattern of these murders suggested they were the work of the South African government, but this was hotly denied. But then there were a number of explosions: at the London headquarters of the African National Congress, and at Cosatu House in Johannesburg, headquarters of the Congress of South African Trade Unions. Khotso House, also in Johannesburg, the headquarters of the South African Council of Churches, was bombed; Khanya House, headquarters of the South African Bishops' Conference in Pretoria, was set on fire. Who were the people committing all these crimes? The government blamed it all on black political rivalry and 'Godless communists'; others blamed it on those bad apples in the police; only a few believed it was government policy to murder and destroy its enemies and their property, and they largely kept their mouths shut because of the security police. For those were the days of the Brezhnev Doctrine, the Cold War in which Africa was the major battleground, most of Africa being communist-sponsored one-party dictatorships, the era of the Total Onslaught Total Strategy, the total strategy to combat the total onslaught of the ungodly communist forces of darkness bent on overthrowing Western democracy and the Godly principles of apartheid. The security police could detain anyone for 180 days without trial, and then another 180 days immediately afterwards, and then another, and so on until, in the words of the Minister of Justice, 'the far side of eternity'. There was freedom of speech in parliament but precious little outside; radio and television were government-controlled, the press had to watch its step and foreign journalists who wrote unkindly about apartheid were unceremoniously deported.

And one of those deported was the beautiful Josephine Valentine.

* * *

Major Jack Harker had heard of her for years – the legendary heart-throb Josephine Valentine, the long-legged American blonde with the dazzling smile who collected wars and war heroes, the beautiful busty photo-journalist in sweat-stained khaki who always managed to wangle a helicopter ride into battle-zones denied to others by using charms pressmen don't possess. She had a formidable and exotic reputation which lost nothing in the telling: while it was not true that she had been a high-priced hooker in New York, as alleged by certain members of the press, it was probably true that she always managed to be in the right place at the right time to get her spectacular pictures by screwing the right officer. It was said of her that she collected war heroes – but 'warriors' would have been a better word. She never had a lengthy relationship with her conquests: she used them, thanked them and left them with a broken heart.

Her war photographs made her famous: Harker had seen her name in many magazines over the years, read many a piece by her, seen many of her hair-raising pictures. Ms Valentine had shown up in Rhodesia during the long bush war, leaping out of helicopters with her cameras into operational zones, 'screwing her way into the front lines' to get her photographs; then she had been seen on the other side of the Zambezi amongst the black terrorists; and she was always popping up in the Middle East in the Arab–Israeli conflict. It seemed that wherever there was a war Josephine Valentine was there, charming her way into more stories; she was big buddies with the heavyweights of both sides. Military men all over the world knew about her, particularly in Africa; many had seen her, met her, entertained her, fantasized about her. Jack Harker was intrigued by what he knew of her and not a little frustrated that he seemed to be one of the few military men who had never set eyes on her. A dozen times she had left the bar, mess, bunker, trench, helicopter moments before he arrived.

And then, in 1986, when he finally encountered her in the Battle of Bassinga she was covered in blood, half naked, her teeth bared as she furiously tried to fire an AK47 automatic rifle at him.

The Battle of Bassinga in Angola was Jack Harker's 'century', the hundredth battle of his military career, the hundredth time he had leapt into action, heart pounding, to do or die. It was also one of the worst battles: a parachute jump at a dangerously low level, at night, right over the target area, which was a camp holding thousands of terrorists and their Cuban advisors, all armed with billions of dollars worth of the latest Russian military hardware with which to liberate southern Africa from the capitalist yoke. The aircraft came in low in the hopes of avoiding the terrorists' radar but the groundfire started up before they were over the drop-zone. Harker led from the front and he was first out of the aircraft, plummeting through thin air with his heart in his mouth, and he was the first casualty of the operation – a bullet got him through the shoulder as he pulled his parachute's rip-cord: he was covered in blood by the time he crash-landed in a tree on the wrong side of the river. He extricated himself with great difficulty and strong language, stuffed a wad of emergency dressing deep into the wound and forded the river with more strong language.

All battles are bad but this seemed Jack Harker's worst ever. He was awarded a medal for it, but he did not have coherent memories of it. He remembered the cacophony, the screams and the gunfire, the flames leaping, the shadows racing, remembered stumbling, lurching, the bullets whistling about him, blood flooding down his chest into his trousers no matter how deep into the wound he rammed the wad of cotton wool with his finger; he remembered storming the water tower, staggering up the ladder to destroy the machine-gun nest that was causing so much havoc, storming a Russian tank and throwing a hand-grenade down the hatch, he remembered the sun coming up on the cacophony of gunfire and smoke and flames and the stink of blood and cordite; he remembered being pinned down for a long time by a barrage of automatic fire coming from a concrete building on the edge of the parade ground, two of his men being mowed down as they tried to storm the building; he remembered scrambling up and running at the doorway.

The battle had been going on for an hour, the sun was up now, the camp strewn with bodies, the earth muddy with blood. Harker lurched across the parade ground, doubled up, rasping, trying to run flat out but finding he could only stagger, and he crashed against the wall beside the door. He leant there a moment, gasping, trying to get his breath, to clear his head, and he was about to burst through the doorway, gun blazing, when he heard a woman cry in English, *'You bastards . . .'* Harker lurched into the room, his rifle at his hip – and stared.

Josephine Valentine was clad only in white panties; she had her back to him, her blonde hair in a pony-tail, crouched at the window, wrestling with the jammed mechanism of an AK47, sobbing, *'You bastards . . .'* On the floor behind her sprawled the half naked body of a Cuban officer, blood flooding from his back. Beside him crouched a black soldier, holding a rifle in one hand, shaking the body with the other; then he saw Harker, his eyes widened in terror, he raised his gun and Harker shot him. The soldier crashed against the wall, dead, and Josephine turned wildly and saw Harker. Her beautiful face was creased in anguish, her wild blue eyes widened in terror at seeing him; she flung the useless rifle aside, collapsed on to her knees beside the dead black soldier and screamed: *'He's only a boy!'* She snatched up his weapon, *'Only a toy gun, he carved it!'* She flung it at Harker, then she scrambled frantically to the dead Cuban and grabbed at his pistol holster.

'Leave that gun!' Harker shouted.

'You killed my man!' she shrieked and swung the big pistol on Harker and pulled the trigger. There was a deafening

bang and the force of the bullet knocked him backwards across the room, his thigh shattered. He crashed into the wall, shocked, and then saw her turn the pistol on herself. In a wild dramatic movement she thrust the muzzle against her naked left breast, her mouth contorted in anguish as she howled, *'You killed him . . .'* She pulled the trigger and the blow of it knocked her off her knees, on to her back.

2

'Publishing,' said General Tanner, head of Military Intelligence, when he visited Harker in hospital on the South West African border, 'is excellent cover for an espionage agent.'

Harker frowned. 'Are you saying she was a spy?'

The general smiled. 'I've changed the subject, I'm talking about you now. But yes, Josephine Valentine is a spy of a kind, fraternizing with the enemy. All photo-journalists are spies because they sneak up on you, take their forbidden pictures and flog them to the highest bidder.'

'You're talking about *me*? Sorry, General, you'll have to explain – we were talking about Josephine Valentine. The bullet missed her heart, then?'

'Made a bit of a mess of some ribs but the doc says it'll hardly leave a scar. Pity, she's been a pain in the arse for years. Like her to have a nice scar to remind her to stay out of our business, goddam drama queen. Pity we didn't catch her boyfriend alive, he could have given us some useful information.'

'She didn't talk at all?'

'Wouldn't tell us a damn thing, just demanded to see the American consul. But we developed eighteen rolls of her film and we got some good intelligence on enemy hardware – and saw a few familiar faces. She's threatened to sue us, of course.' He smiled.

'Where is she now?'

'In Pretoria; we're getting rid of her next week when she's fit enough to travel. Daddy is coming out to take care of his darling wayward daughter. Anyway . . .' the general plucked a grape off the bunch he had brought

19

Harker, '. . . as I was saying: publishing is ideal cover for an espionage agent.' He looked solemn.

Harker smiled. 'As you were saying. But I'm afraid you're going to have to explain that too.'

Tanner smiled. 'Or there's the import-export business – but it's rather dull. Running a restaurant or a small hotel might be okay but it can be hard work – and putting you in charge of a bar would be like putting a rabbit in charge of a lettuce patch, aha-ha-ha!' The general popped the grape into his mouth. 'Whereas publishing,' he chewed, 'would be fun, particularly in an exciting place like New York. Respectability, lots of long lunches and cocktail parties, plenty of intellectual people to stimulate you.' He shrugged. 'However, if you don't fancy that, I can offer you a whole range of jobs. Running a clothing store in Brussels, for example.'

Harker grinned. 'I'm afraid you'll still have to explain.'

The general picked another grape off the bunch. 'You're finished, Jack. You'll never fight another battle. Half of one lung gone, one thigh-bone fucked. It's HQ for you now, old man, fighting a desk. Or you can work for me in Military Intelligence. So I'm offering you a job as a publisher.'

'You own a publishing house, General? In New York?'

The general smiled. 'The only house I own is in Pretoria where my wife and children live. And that's mortgaged.' He looked at Harker. 'But I *control* businesses all over the world, Jack.' He smiled. 'Ever heard of the CCB? The Civil Cooperation Bureau?'

Harker was mystified. 'No.'

'Good. And if you repeat this conversation to anybody you'll be in breach of the Defence Act, the Official Secrets Act, and Christ knows what else. You'll be court-martialled.' He smiled again. 'Got that, Jack?'

Jesus. 'Yes.'

The general sat back. 'Well, the CCB is the new covert arm of Military Intelligence. The new *civilian* espionage arm of our army. Very new. In short, the top brass has made a study of the CIA, the KGB, Mossad and MI6, and the Civil Cooperation Bureau is the result. Emphasis on the *civil*. Our civilian agents operate all over the world, in particular in those countries where South Africa is not allowed to have embassies or consulates or trade offices because of apartheid. As you know, every embassy of every country has an intelligence officer who works in the guise of "cultural attaché" or something like that. Well, because we have so few embassies, we have created the CCB instead. Our CCB agent is set up in a suitable business to make him look kosher. He recruits suitable local sub-agents, spies, to gather information about our enemies – just like every government does. Our agent sends the information back to me. I then do whatever is necessary to spike our enemies' guns – just like I do when I get information from our attachés in our official embassies.' He paused. 'I must add that our CCB businesses are usually profitable. Our agents make good money.' He smiled. 'Much better than a major's pay.' He paused again. 'I'm offering you a job in the CCB, Jack. I suggest publishing because of your English name, and accent – and you're an intellectual sort of chap. You will draw a good salary – and, of course, you will be pensionable when you eventually retire. You'll have a share of the publishing profits. We'll provide you with an apartment in New York, as well as the actual offices – and a cost-of-living allowance, a car and an entertainment allowance. And we'll pay your membership fees of all the necessary clubs – the yacht club, and so forth.' General Tanner looked at him. 'Sounds pretty good to me, Jack. Bit of a sinecure. Much better than selling life insurance, which is about all an ex-soldier can do.'

It sounded pretty good to Harker, too. 'But what do I know about publishing?'

'You're smart. You're one of the few intellectuals this army's got – apart from me, of course.' He grinned. 'We've got another small publishing house in London. We'll send

21

you there for a few months for some high-density, high-tech literary training. But it really doesn't matter because the editors you hire will know the ropes and you'll learn on the job.'

'But espionage? What do I know about that? And how do I recruit my agents?'

'All will be explained. You'll recruit men yourself when necessary, but your immediate boss, the guy you'll report to, is stationed in Washington and he has already set up the network which you will inherit. He ran the whole show from Washington but it's too much work now, so you'll be responsible for New York and Florida via your publishing house.'

Harker was bemused. 'It's just information you want?'

General Tanner said: 'New York is an important listening post. The United Nations is there – all those black communist countries shouting about us, plotting mayhem, harbouring ANC and SWAPO terrorists. And down in Florida there are all those Cuban exiles with all kinds of information about Castro's army. You'll be responsible for all that intelligence.'

Harker looked at the older man. He really liked him. That was mutual. 'But I'm a soldier, not a spy.'

'Military intelligence is a very important part of soldiering.'

'Of course. But I mean I'm a soldier, not a hit-man. I don't want to have to kill anybody.'

'You won't have to get your hands bloody, Jack.' General Tanner smiled. 'You'll be told all you need to know when you have agreed and signed up. But let me say this much: any actions will be military ones – against the sort of people you've killed plenty of on the battlefield, and who've tried to kill you. That's a soldier's job, to kill as many of the enemy as possible, isn't it? But the responsibility will be entirely mine as head of Military Intelligence.' He ended: 'We are fighting a total onslaught by the communist forces of darkness, Jack. That's why America is helping us.

22

Openly. And Britain, secretly. To fight this total onslaught we need a total strategy. And the CCB is an important part of that total strategy . . .'

3

Harvest House was a nice old brownstone overlooking Gramercy Park on New York's East Side. Harker bought it for the CCB in his first month in town, having found out how expensive conventional office space is. It was easily big enough for the staff he hired: one editor, two personal assistants, a sales director who doubled as publicity director, and a general clerk. He found these people, all experienced in publishing, quickly because he advertised salaries above the average. The building was a big old nineteenth-century house: the numerous bedrooms became offices, the dining room became the conference room – there was space to spare. Harker, as managing director, had the best office: the large living room with its old marble fireplace and bay window overlooking the park.

When the building was remodelled, his staff in place, he hired a few of the catering trade's leggiest waitresses and threw a large cocktail party for all the literary agents in New York to announce his start in business. 'Why have we called ourselves Harvest?' he said in his welcoming speech. 'Because we want to gather up the bountiful talent that lies neglected by the other brainier-than-thou publishing houses . . .' The literary agents responded: in the first year of business Harvest published eleven books, all by first-time authors, and made a respectable profit – partly because the production was done economically by another CCB enterprise, a printing works in Ottawa – enough to pay all salaries and overheads with some left over for reinvestment. Harker had a flair for publishing, a nose for a profitable book. And it was fun: there were boozy lunches with agents and authors, lots of interesting, intelligent people to meet. It seemed an easy living, the authors, agents and editors doing most of the work. It sure beat getting the shit shot out of you on the battlefields of Angola.

And his covert work for the Civil Cooperation Bureau was not difficult either.

'The CCB divides the world into regions,' General Tanner had explained. 'America is Region One, England Region Two, and so on. America itself is divided: Head Office is in Washington, Region One A, where Felix Dupont is the overall Regional Director – he's your boss. New York, where you'll be, is Region One B – your title is Regional *Manager*. You will also be responsible for our CCB business in Miami, Region One C, where a guy called Ricardo Diego is the Regional *Sub*-manager – he's a South African Spaniard. His front-business is a bar in the Cuban exile community, which is very valuable to us. He has agents planted in Cuba itself, who give us a lot of information on military matters. You'll remember a number of occasions in Angola where we suddenly knew exactly about Cuban reinforcements?'

Harker nodded.

'A lot of that was thanks to the CIA, of course, but also to Ricardo's agents in Havana – who have agents in Luanda. Ricardo is very valuable. Trouble is, he's not real management material. You'll have to keep a close eye on him – Felix Dupont is too busy now, monitoring the Capitol scene and the rest of America. So Ricardo will report to you, and you report to Dupont. My orders will come to you through Dupont. As I said before, Dupont has a network of agents in place in New York, so you'll inherit a going concern. Most of them don't know each other, and only the "senior salesmen" will know you; you'll probably never see the "juniors" – most of them don't even know they're working for us. Some think they're working for the CIA, or for a European government, or for a firm of detectives. In fact, one of our senior salesmen is a private investigator, chap called Trengrove. We need all kinds of information about those United Nations nincompoops, not just hard military facts – who's sleeping with who, who's a homosexual, who's got gambling debts, et cetera, so we can squeeze them. Another salesman has a very good whorehouse – one of the best in New York, I'm told. Anyway, as soon as you leave hospital you go to training school to learn all the general principles, then to London to get the hang of the publishing business, then you fly to Washington to stay with Felix Dupont for a few weeks, getting the nitty-gritty – he's got a nice hotel. Did you ever meet Felix in the army?'

'No.'

'Remarkable man in martial arts. Took a bullet through the knee. However, after a few weeks with Felix you'll spend a week in Miami with Ricardo, getting his picture. Nice bar he's got – and *lovely* strippers, those Cuban girls sure are well-nourished. And Ricardo serves the best steaks in town.'

'What about weapons?' Harker said. 'I presume I can't take my own.'

'Certainly not. No, Felix will supply all the hardware. You'll have one or two licensed firearms, but most of the hardware will be unlicensed and untraceable. If you ever have to use a gun, dump it in the river straight afterwards. And if anybody ever shoots *you*, you tell the cops it was just another robbery. But you'll learn all this at training school.'

'Shoot me? I thought I was through with all that strong-arm stuff.'

'You are, you're a Regional Manager, not a salesman.' The general hurried over that one. 'Anyway, after a week with Ricardo you go to New York, move into the apartment Felix's got for you, and set up Harvest House, get yourself a girlfriend, and settle into the role of the shit-hot, wing-ding new publisher in town.' He smiled. 'Easy. Wish I were you.' He added: 'I've never seen so many beautiful girls as in New York. And they outnumber the men six

26

to one.' He grinned. 'You're going to have a good time, Jack . . .'

Yes, the CCB work was easy enough. The reports trickled in from his senior salesmen, by telephone, encoded fax, scrambled e-mail, dead-letter box, undercover meetings: Harker digested it, collated it, gave any instructions, re-encoded it and sent it on to Felix Dupont in Washington. The information was a mish-mash of facts and conjecture, but Dupont made sense of it all in his jigsaw of espionage – and so too, after a while, did Harker: the pieces fell into place, the gaps becoming clear, the necessary instructions to the salesmen becoming self-evident. Once a month, sometimes twice, he went to Washington for a conference with Dupont. He usually combined these trips with an onward journey to Miami to check on Ricardo. This was always fun: whereas Dupont was a self-satisfied, de-tribalized Englishman with a painful body who thoroughly detested his enemies, Ricardo exuberantly enjoyed life and only really hated Fidel Castro. He loved South Africans and Americans who were giving the bastard a hard time in Angola. The clientele of his *bar-ristorante* felt the same way: anybody who took a swipe at Castro, the robber of their plantations and businesses, was okay with Ricardo and his customers at Bar Casa Blanca in Little Havana. None of Ricardo's noisy patrons, nor his silent salesmen, knew who Harker was, but there was never a shortage of the *senoritas* in his hotel bedroom at the end of the day spent debriefing Ricardo, trying to make sure he had understood all his communications in Spanglish.

'Ricardo, do us all a favour – buy a good Spanish-English dictionary, to check your spelling, we'll pay for it. And take some English lessons, because when encoded your information can be misleading if you misspell or get the idiom wrong.'

'So we confuse the enemy too, huh, compadre! But enough of work now –' he waggled his dark eyebrows

27

– 'we go back to Casa Blanca to *las senoritas*? Or maybe I send one up here to you, *jefe*?' He thumped his hand on his chest: 'Clean! *Garantizada* . . .'

Yes, as General Tanner had promised, it was an easy job, and even satisfying once the jigsaw began to make sense. However, Harker's jigsaw was usually incomplete because Dupont received information from the CIA direct and he only told Harker as much as he needed to know. Equally valuable was the detail coming out of the United Nations. Several of the delegations from African countries leaked information copiously to Harker's salesmen, as a result of either blackmail or greed, but it was often only gossip about other delegates' weaknesses or bad behaviour. Nonetheless, from time to time, important intelligence emerged about ANC bases in Angola, Uganda, Kenya, Zambia, about scandals and rivalries within the exiled hierarchy. Dupont and General Tanner – the 'Chairman' – prized these snippets highly. And it was Harker's United Nations salesman who first learned about atrocities committed in the ANC's military camps in Angola, torture of their own soldiers by Mbokodo, the ANC's security police, apparently condoned by the top leadership, which resulted in two full-blown mutinies: Dupont and the Chairman were cock-a-hoop about that intelligence. When the story was broken in the international press it did the ANC considerable harm.

It was interesting, if often frustrating, and it certainly beat working in Military Intelligence headquarters in Pretoria. But Harker did not enjoy his work involving the anti-apartheid movement: keeping track of their plans, compiling dossiers on their activists, looking for ways to discredit them or minimize their impact. During the time Harker spent in Washington learning the ropes, Dupont ordered him to organize a burglary of the Anti-Apartheid League's offices in New York, as a training exercise. The salesmen copied every computer disk, thus getting a mountain of information, then wiped the original disks clean, leaving the League's administration and financial affairs in a shambles. Dupont and the Chairman were delighted with the information they got, but Harker studied it and couldn't see what the excitement was about: sure, the burglary produced thousands of names of members, their addresses and telephone numbers, much correspondence between branches about fund-raising plans, proposed protest marches, lobbying of congressmen, reams of bank statements – but so what? There wasn't mention of one spy, one arms cache, one target, one battle, let alone one revolution. Harker considered the Anti-Apartheid Leaguers a harmless bunch: they made a lot of noise but it was mostly a case of thundering to the converted. Indeed Harker sympathized with them – he didn't approve of apartheid either. However, when he settled down in New York he studied the many dossiers on activists that Felix Dupont had compiled, updated them with new information received from his salesmen and passed it all back to Washington. He considered it a waste of effort, and found it distasteful to be prying into people's private lives looking for peccadilloes with which to haunt them; but Dupont was very strict about keeping the files up to date. Dupont supported apartheid as vehemently as he hated communism and scorned blacks.

'No, I don't hate blacks,' he once said, 'I just have contempt for their politics and government. They cannot govern – look at the mess the rest of Africa is. Why? Three reasons. One, their culture – it's totally different to ours, they see the civil service as an opportunity for power and enriching themselves – an opportunity for corruption. Two, Affirmative Action – they want to put black faces behind every desk to give jobs to their own race, so corporals become colonels overnight, constables become commissioners, clerks become magistrates. Stupid black pride makes them insist that black upstarts can do any job as well as any experienced white man. The result – shambles and corruption. And three: they then fuck up the entire economy by turning the country into a Marxist one-party dictatorship.' Dupont snorted. 'No black is ever going to rule me. And that's what makes the anti-apartheid activists so important to us – they *want* the blacks to rule South Africa, which means that they are supporting the communists who want to ride to power on the backs of the blacks. Over my dead body! So keep those files strictly up to date, please.'

So Harker did. And it was through this diligence that he again encounered Josephine Valentine.

Security is always a problem for the spymaster: where does he keep the secret files so that nobody will find them or even suspect they exist? In his own country his office is in some government building, in foreign lands it is deep in the innards of his country's embassy or consular office; but in the case of the Civil Cooperation Bureau no South African ambassador, consul or clerk even knew of its existence. So Harker's spymaster office was off the base-ment boiler-room of Harvest House in Gramercy Park. On Dupont's instructions Harker had installed a brand-new boiler that would not require attention for years and he hired a different company to install a steel door lead-ing off it to a 'storage room'. From that room another steel door, behind shelves of odds and ends, led to the Civil Cooperation Bureau's New York espionage centre. Here Harker had a desk, a computer, filing cabinets, a telephone and fax line in the name of a fictitious insur-ance broker, and a shredding machine. There was no win-dow: the walls were raw stone, the floor plain concrete. Standing orders required Harker to be in this neon-lit subterranean cell at seven o'clock every morning, before Harvest opened for business, to receive NTKs (Need-to-know Situation reports), to transmit SEEMs (Scrambled Encoded E-Mail reports), and to make any RTCs (Restricted Telephonic Communications) using codes or a litany of ENAVs (encoded nouns, adjectives and verbs) to report what the dark world of espionage had come up with in the last twenty-four hours.

Harker found this regime no hardship: his military training caused him to wake naturally at five a.m. no matter how
late he went to bed; he pulled on a tracksuit and for the
next hour he jogged through the dark concrete canyons of
Manhattan, taking it gently so as not to strain his damaged
leg; six o'clock saw him having breakfast at his favourite
'all-nite dinette' off Union Square, seven saw him showered
and besuited at his desk in his bleak cell ready to put in a
couple of hours' work for the South African Defence Force,
even if it only meant ploughing through reams of boring
and insignificant detail about the private lives of members
of the devilish Anti-Apartheid League.

But Harker did not find the fat dossier that Dupont had
compiled over the years on Josephine Franklin Valentine
boring. On the contrary, he found it fascinating, exotic. He
felt as if he knew her personally. And hadn't he saved her
life? He had survived her furious attempted murder of him,
had seen her thrust the pistol at her beautiful breast, seen
the shocking splotch of blood, seen her blown backwards,
arms outflung as if crucified. He had dragged himself over
to her, blood pumping from his shoulder and thigh, put his
ear to her bloody breast, heard her heart still beating; he
had stuffed his field emergency dressing into her shocking
wound, then plunged his mouth on to hers to force some air
into her lungs – it was he who had yelled for the medics and
ordered them to evacuate her on the first helicopter. Jack
Harker felt he had saved her life even if in truth it was the
medics who had done that. And what South African soldier
would have let a white woman bleed to death on a black
battlefield when medics were swarming around – particularly a beautiful half-naked, English-speaking woman who
could obviously give her captors a lot of military intelligence
about the Cuban enemy?

But Josephine Valentine had not told anybody anything.
Harker had tried to question her while the medics were
loading her on to the stretcher, tried to find out how many
tanks and armoured cars the Cubans had down the road,

to discover the name of the dead Cuban officer she was so upset about, and she had repeatedly told him to 'fuck off' – even when he asked her for the name of her next of kin in case she died. She had even refused to tell him her blood group. *'I don't want you to save my fucking life, asshole, haven't you noticed?'*

Nor did the Military Intelligence boys back at base camp in South West Africa have any success with her when she recovered consciousness after surgery, though her language improved. 'Get lost,' she said, 'I demand to see the American Ambassador,' and when the Intelligence boys had developed her numerous rolls of film and tried to question her about faces and equipment depicted therein she had demanded a lawyer, and told them she and her numerous high-powered publishers were going to sue the South African government to Kingdom Come. In short, Military Intelligence didn't know how to squeeze information from a furious, beautiful American journalist with a wound in her breast – Military Intelligence was accustomed to black terrorist captives who quickly spilt the beans under a bit of robust interrogation and they didn't have the nerve to third-degree information from a well-known American photo-journalist. General Tanner himself had flown out from Pretoria to try to deal with her; he had eventually called in the most senior CIA operative of the Angolan desk all the way from Lusaka, but even their formidable combined expertise failed to extract information and they had finally thankfully delivered her into the custody of the American Ambassador and her father, a big-wheel lawyer from Boston who arrived with a crack of thunder and placed her in a private clinic in Pretoria pending her deportation as an Undesirable Alien. She had refused even to divulge the identity of her dead Cuban lover. Harker had felt almost proud of her when General Tanner had told him what a load of trouble she was. A very desirable Undesirable.

That was over two years ago, and now here she was

32

back in his life as he sat in his dungeon in Harvest House reading her thick file. The beautiful Josephine Franklin Valentine smiled at him ravishingly from the pages of many magazine and newspaper cuttings containing her war photographs and stories – wars in Israel, the Middle East, Afghanistan, Mozambique, Rhodesia, Angola: wherever men made war Ms Josephine Valentine went in with her cameras blazing, her typewriter pounding out the staccato Hemingwayesque prose. Very good, lean, evocative writing – you could almost smell the blood and dust and cordite. She evidently loved the high drama of war, the strange business of going into battle, the extraordinary courage it required; she obviously deeply admired the men who did all this for a living when they could be making lots more money in a nice air-conditioned office. Yet she was very liberal, and a strict political analyst. She bitterly condemned the South African government but she was also condemnatory of the Russians for invading Afghanistan; she sympathized with the Israelis, admired their fighting men; she was dismissive of the Arabs as soldiers while very sympathetic to the Palestinians' cause. She had a high opinion of the Egyptians for making peace with the Jews, and there was a splendid photograph of her sitting in Gaddafi's ceremonial tent drinking camel's milk, earnestly discussing his holy Jihad against the West, but in her story she blasted him as an enemy of mankind, particularly for the Lockerbie Disaster bomb. She had great admiration for the Rhodesians as soldiers, as Davids taking on the Goliaths of Russia and China, but she condemned most of their politicians as constituting a 'cowboy government'. She applauded the Cuban army for fighting the South Africans in Angola – indeed it was she who had deeply embarrassed the President of the United States by revealing to the world that America was waging a secret war on the side of pariah South Africa against the communists, thus causing both countries to pull out of Angola for several years. But now the whole Western world was covertly on the side of the

South Africans to drive the Cubans out of Africa, the war was at full blast again and Josephine Valentine was there, boots and all, sweat-stains on her khaki outfit, dust sticking to her face, blonde hair awry, stealing the show with her photographs and stories – until the Bassinga raid that Harker had led.

Josephine had written a dramatic piece about the battle. She admitted that the South Africans had saved her life, but there was no admission that she had attempted suicide – she attributed the self-inflicted wound to her engagement in the heroic battle in which her Cuban lover had been killed at her side. She did not divulge the dead man's name but the South Africans had eventually identified him from photographs: Brigadier Paulo Rodriguez, forty-four years old, one of Fidel Castro's top military strategists, the man expected to liberate South Africa from the apartheid yoke after his communist forces conquered Angola and Namibia. And for the first time she declared her political colours. She wrote:

'I am not a communist, though I am very liberal – and indeed I am sure communism is going to mellow, as Mr Gorbachev's glasnost and perestroika portend. But for the time being the Cubans are the only knights in shining armour around with the guts to take on the dragon of apartheid, and I'm rooting for them . . .'

There were many other cuttings and photographs from the society pages that Dupont had collected over the years: Josephine Valentine at country club balls, at yacht club regattas, at anti-apartheid functions. There were a dozen large colour photographs taken by Dupont's salesmen with telephoto lenses: and, yes, she was certainly beautiful: that long blonde flowing hair, those big dark-blue eyes that looked both sparkling and short-sighted, a wide smile of full lips and perfect teeth, a slightly dimpled chin – and long legs and a bust to break any man's heart. There were several clippings of her magazine articles condemning America's policy of economic sanctions against Cuba – 'Why beggar thy neighbour if you want him to like you?' Harker read them carefully: she had great admiration for the machismo of Fidel Castro, Che Guevara and the boys of the Sierra Maestro even if she wasn't a Marxist. He turned to the Covering Report compiled by Dupont over the years.

Codename Bigmouth

Valentine, Josephine Franklin, female Caucasian, born 27 February 1962, in Boston, Massachusetts, US citizen. Parents Denys Adam Valentine, American, well-known lawyer in Boston, mother Elaine Franklin, née O'Reilly, Irish, allegedly aristocracy, naturalized American, now deceased . . .

Catholic College, Boston . . . Berkeley University . . . graduated in Political Philosophy and English Literature . . . post-graduate course in journalism, University of New York, before becoming a freelance journalist writing for various political magazines . . . political leanings strongly to left, possibly communist though no actual membership of any party known . . . tends to the Ban-the-Bomb, long-haired movements, often seen at protest rallies of various kinds . . . staunch supporter of Anti-Apartheid League, secretary of Chelsea Branch . . .

Financial situation: evidently wealthy, financed by Valentine Trust in her favour . . .

Sports interests include yacht racing, tennis, skiing, skating, cycling . . .

Cultural interests include opera, art, literature . . .

Lifestyle appears to fluctuate between the extravagant and the quiet . . . likes fast cars . . .

No criminal record . . .

Apparently good health . . . contact lenses . . . front teeth capped . . .

Sex Life . . .

At this point Harker got up, went to his little refrigerator, extracted ice and poured whisky into a glass.

Sex life? This detail he found really distasteful. It was offensive that ordinary people out there should be sleuthed by his salesmen trying to get smutty details of their sex lives. The hypocrisy of it! Sex, the great equalizer, the great common denominator, why the hell can't we all just decriminalize sex? But no, almost the whole English-speaking world felt compelled to adhere to the hypocrisy, marriages were broken, careers ruined, ministers and governments fell. And what irritated Harker as he went back to his desk with his whisky was that he was, pruriently, looking forward to reading about the beautiful Josephine Valentine's sex life . . . He took a sip of whisky and began to read on.

Scandal on campus when subject was having an affair with a married professor, Cedric Mansell, wife Elizabeth threatened to cite her as co-respondent . . . affair with Joshuah Danning, son of Senator Danning of Massachusetts . . . became engaged to football star Stephen Dickason who was subsequently jailed for drug-possession . . . affair with sportswriter Jim Nichols of *New York Post* . . . weekend in Poconos Mountains with Columnist Frederick Jackson of *Washington Post* . . .

Subject leaving US to take up residence in London. Case summary sent to Regional Director of Region Two, Chairman alerted in case she attempts to enter South Africa . . .

Conclusion: subject is dangerous because of her access to the media and because of her influential social connections, particularly in New York and Boston.

CAMs: Her sexual appetite generally can be portrayed as promiscuous – father is high-profile Catholic and subject could possibly be prevailed upon to spare him embarrassment. Best CAM is probably evoking scandal by planting evidence of criminal activity such as drug-dealing, paedophilia, pornography, shoplifting . . .

'Jesus!'

Harker had tossed the report aside. Jesus – 'CAMs', Character Assassination Methods. Christ, did he really have to soil his hands with this sort of thing? Did South Africa's military defence really require spending taxpayers' money on an investigator to search back into the woman's girlhood to find possible sexual peccadilloes? It would be laughable if it wasn't so awful. And her sex life looked pretty average – could he really be expected to plant evidence of criminal activity on her? Ruin her life with a smear campaign because she organized protest rallies against apartheid? No way would he obey such an order.

And there was another reason for his truculence: although he didn't admit it to himself, Harker felt possessive towards Josephine Valentine. Goddammit – he had saved her life!

Harker turned back to the large colour photographs of her taken with a telephoto lens when she was on the tennis court: and, Lord, she was beautiful. There were about a dozen shots of her in a variety of poses, bending, stretching, swiping, jumping, volleying, her blonde hair in a long pony-tail whipping dramatically around her face, her eyes flashing. Look at those long golden legs, look at that glorious ass, look at that bust . . .

He wondered where she was now. What wars were there, apart from the Angolan conflict? Plenty – Somalia, Ethiopia, Sudan, Middle East, not to mention Northern Ireland, Cyprus, Tibet, Pakistan, Burma, Indonesia. He could easily find out her whereabouts by putting some of his salesmen on to making discreet enquiries. He could telephone her magazine publishers and ask. And she was a member of the New York Yacht Club – Harker had joined when he first arrived a year ago, maybe he would meet her there one day . . .

And then, that very week, Felix Dupont telephoned him

on the scrambled line and said: 'I see your girlfriend's back in town soon.'

'Which girlfriend?' Harker really did not like his boss. 'I have so many.'

'The one you gave mouth-to-mouth to, old man. Just got a signal from our man in Angola, spotted her at Luanda airport, or what's left of it, boarding a Russian transport flying to Cuba, onward destination New York via Mexico City. Our man in Havana will let us know her arrival details. I want you to have a salesman at the airport to tail her, then get on to her.'

This was interesting news. 'Get on to her?'

'Figuratively – but if you can do so literally so much the better, of course. Fuck the information out of the bitch.'

Oh, Harker really didn't like his boss – and it sounded clear that the man was drinking, at seven o'clock in the morning. 'What information in particular are you looking for?'

'Any information, old man, you know that, don't you remember anything they taught you at Intelligence School? Any fucking information is important in this dog-eat-dog world of espionage, these veritable valleys of dust and ashes in which there are so few oases of hope – any fucking information even if it's what she has for breakfast or how she likes blow-jobs, because we never know when the info will become useful. But what we really want to know urgently is what Castro's knuckle-dragging, tree-dwelling generals are planning in Angola, and we figure that your girlfriend may have some clues from all the pillow-talk she has out there.'

'Is it known that she's got a new lover in Angola?'

'Of course she's had another lover out there, how else does she get her free ride back to Havana? So get on to her and find out what she knows.'

'Any specific orders about how I achieve that?'

'The Three Bs – don't they teach you anything at spy-school? Burglary, Bonking, Blackmail. Burgle her apartment, of course. Don't do it yourself – send Clements in. She's sure to come back with all kinds of film, notes, computer disks and so on – make microfilm and computer copies of everything. And you should also burgle her Anti-Apartheid League's offices; it's about time we dry-cleaned them to find out what they're up to. You never know what snippets our lady may have sent back to them from sunny Angola.' Harker heard Dupont take a swallow of something. 'And then there's bonking. Pillow-talk. Give her some of her medicine, old man. Swear undying love, tell her you want to publish her innermost memoirs, particularly what the generalissimos told her over the vino and cigars. That shouldn't be too much of a hardship.'

Harker grinned to himself. Jesus, did Dupont really think that what this left-wing adventuress might know was worth all the effort?

'And then,' Dupont continued, 'if all else fails, blackmail her. But that's only as a last resort. And don't you do it personally, get Clements on to it – but consult me first.'

Harker smiled. 'Okay, send me her flight details.'

After Dupont hung up, Harker looked at Josephine Valentine's file again. He turned up a colour photograph of her. Yes, she was beautiful . . . So, she was a member of the famous New York Yacht Club. He should try to meet her there before she started dating somebody seriously.

4

The following day Derek Clements checked out her apartment. The locks were standard; he picked them, made impressions, got keys cut. The next day he was at Kennedy Airport to tail her. That night he met Harker in a bar near Union Square.

'How do you know it was her father who met her?' Harker asked.

'I heard her call him Dad.' Clements was a tough, wiry little man with a ferrety face. He had been a US marine before showing up in the Rhodesian army as a mercenary.

'What is the father like?'

'About sixty. Stony-faced sort of guy. Grey hair. Good-looking. Nice suit, obviously lots of dough.'

'How much baggage did Josephine have?'

'One big holdall, one rucksack, sleeping bag. Camera box, video case, one camera around her neck.'

Harker was making notes. 'And then?'

'They took a taxi into Manhattan. I followed. They went straight to her apartment block on East Eightieth Street. It was now lunchtime, five-past-one. While she entered, the old man went to the delicatessen on the corner and came back with a package. He went inside. I went to the same deli, bought a coffee and sat and observed her apartment block. At two-thirty a taxi arrived, the old man emerged, got in and drove off. I waited another hour – had another coffee – waited to see if subject came out. She didn't. I took a taxi home.' He pulled out a wad of receipts. 'Bureau owes me over a hundred and fifty bucks.'

'Put it on the monthly sheet. Okay, you said you'd give me a plan of her apartment.'

Clements pulled an envelope from his pocket, took out a sheet of paper and unfolded it.

'Small two-bedroom place but a nice view of Central Park. She uses the second bedroom as a study. Here.' He pointed. 'Computer, a rack of disks, lots of stationery. Piles of files with her stories and photos. Lots of framed photos on the wall, mostly military stuff. I microfilmed everything and copied all her disks.' He indicated a small hand-grip on the end of the table.

'When you go back in after she's unpacked, will you be able to identify the new notes and disks?'

'Yeah, all her disks are numbered, and all her notebooks, and all the entries are dated. When do you want me to go in again, sir?'

'Give her a chance to settle down and establish a routine. Maybe she goes to the gym every day, or for a jog. You better set up an OP and find out her movements.'

'Where, in a car?'

'In a car. Read a paper, like they do in the movies. Move the car around, and change the model. Put Spicer on to the job as well, do a rota with him.'

'Does Spicer know about this?'

'No, and there's no need for him to, just tell him I say so.'

'He likes you, Spicer does, wants to know when you're coming to his whorehouse again.'

Harker smiled. 'And give me a call every morning before nine o'clock to report progress.'

A week later Harker had established a pattern of Josephine Valentine's movements: Clements reported that her study light burned until about midnight every night, so she was writing hard. She slept until about mid-morning when she went to the corner delicatessen to buy newspapers, milk and fresh fruit. At one o'clock she emerged again wearing a leotard, wheeling a bicycle and wearing a pink crash helmet: on Mondays, Wednesdays and Fridays she rode across town, belting through the traffic, to attend an aerobics and dance class in a loft studio on the west side of Manhattan. On Tuesdays and Thursdays she rode to the rackets club where she played squash. In both cases she returned to her apartment block at three o'clock; her study light burned until midnight.

'No evidence of a boyfriend yet?'

'Not yet, sir,' Clements said. 'You want me to go in again one lunchtime? She's settled down now, all her new gear must be on that desk.'

Harker sighed. He hated this – the risk, plus the dishonour of it, of unlawfully entering somebody's home. But, war is war.

'Not yet, helluva risk doing it in daylight. We've done well in a week. Let's cool it, I'll see if I can meet her at the yacht club or the rackets club before we do anything dangerous.'

It was much easier to meet her than anticipated. He had imagined that she would be surrounded by friends, that he would have to bide his time and ask somebody to introduce him, or contrive, with his usual uneasiness, to strike up a casual conversation. But she was alone when he first saw her, sitting at a table reading *Time* magazine: she was dressed to play squash, wearing a short white skirt, her racket on the table.

'Miss Valentine?'

He had expected her to have a no-nonsense manner but she looked up with a ready smile. 'Yes?' And she was even more beautiful than her photograph suggested. And, for a flash, Harker glimpsed her again in that room in the heat of battle, naked but for her white panties, her breasts swinging as she turned on him.

'I'm Jack Harker, I'm a member here. I saw your picture in the paper some time back and I've read a number of the war stories you've written. So I decided to be bold and introduce myself, because I admired them.'

'Why, thank you!' Josephine Valentine beamed. Praise is

the quickest way to a writer's heart but she surprised Harker by seeming flustered by it; he had expected a hard-nosed war journo who had seen and heard all the blandishments – instead she was blushing.

'May I sit down a moment?'

'Certainly, but I'm off to play squash in a few minutes.' Harker sat, and she continued hastily, for something to say: 'And what are you doing in New York, Mr Harker? You're not American, with that accent.'

'No, I'm a sort of British–South African mongrel.'

'I see.'

He wondered whether she thought she saw a racist. 'I run a publishing firm here, Harvest House. We're fairly new in town but we're keen. And that's another reason I've introduced myself, apart from the pleasure of meeting you – I wondered whether you've considered writing a book?'

He felt he saw the light in her eyes.

'As a matter of fact,' she said, 'I'm busy writing one right now. About South Africa, in fact.'

'*Well*,' Harker said, 'would you consider having lunch with me one day to discuss it? Or dinner?'

'That would be lovely.'

He felt a shit but he *was* a publisher. And war requires espionage. Personally, he felt as pleased as she was. As he watched her walk away to her squash date he thought: what a lovely girl, what lovely legs . . .

5

'Never conceal,' the Chairman had said, 'that you were in the South African army. People like Clements and Spicer can do that but you'll be too high-profile to get away with a lie like that – you may fool people for a while but sooner or later somebody who knows you will blow into town and people will wonder why you concealed the truth. So tell 'em upfront: you were a professional officer fighting an honourable war against communism. Rub in Sandhurst, the sword of honour, all that good stuff. But disown apartheid, make all the usual noises against it – these people love to hear others singing their song . . .'

But it wasn't that easy when Harker met Josephine Valentine the next Saturday for lunch at the Tavern on the Green. She came striding into the restaurant, ravishingly beautiful, her long blonde hair flowing, wreathed in smiles for her potential publisher, the file containing her typescript under her arm. He had intended telling her that they had met at the Battle of Bassinga only if the conversation and atmosphere between them warranted it: within minutes of the small-talk beginning he saw a look enter her eyes, a glint of challenge when he mentioned his military background, and he decided against it. She listened with close attention as he sketched in his personal history, fiddling with the cutlery. Then she politely took up the cudgel.

An honourable war? Yes, she understood how a career officer had to do his duty to the state, even if he didn't personally approve of all its policies. And she understood how most people might consider the communists to be dangerous people, she could understand that honourable soldiers would feel justified in fighting them to their last breath

– one took up a military career to defend one's country and that would necessarily involve killing as many of the perceived enemy as possible. But in the case of South Africa, the communist 'enemy' – she made quotation marks with her fingers – was also fighting for the liberation of South Africa from the apartheid yoke, helping the ANC in their armed struggle. This surely made the Cubans the honourable soldiers, because apartheid – 'on your own admission, Mr Harker' – is evil, and the intelligent, honourable South African army officer must surely have seen this paradox and been in a quandary, not so? He was indirectly – indeed directly, surely? – fighting for the evil of apartheid? So how this officer could have justified his actions, if only to himself, profoundly puzzled her. A moral dilemma, no?

'Did you come up against this quandary in yourself, Mr Harker? Or in any of your brother officers?'

'Please call me Jack.' Harker could see his potential relationship with this lovely woman going out of the window. He didn't give a damn about the CCB's loss, it was his own. He said, truthfully, 'Oh yes. We didn't talk about it much in the officers' mess but I and a good few others had considerable qualms. But I considered myself to be fighting the greater evil of communism only, the important thing was to defeat the enemy, drive him into the sea, and then let the politicians unscramble the mess of apartheid.'

She smiled sweetly. 'And if the politicians had not unscrambled the mess of apartheid, what would you have done? Would you have quit the army?'

'I quit anyway. The politicians still haven't unscrambled apartheid, but here I am.'

'But you were wounded.'

'But not killed. I could have stayed in the army in a non-combatant role.'

She looked at him calculatingly, smiling. 'Okay, but when you went into battle did you really feel that you were only fighting against communism?'

Harker smiled. 'Yes.' That was more or less true.

45

'But in the heat of battle too?'

He didn't think it would be helpful to explain that in the heat of the battle all you felt was terrified hatred for the bastards trying to kill you. Like the saying 'There are no atheists in a fox-hole', there are few starry-eyed liberals on an African battlefield. But he didn't want an argument with this beautiful woman, he wanted to have a nice lunch while Clements burgled her apartment again and then, if at all possible, he wanted to get laid. If not today then some time. Soon. 'Yes, in battle too. Shall we order?'

She gave him a dazzling smile. 'A bit later perhaps; I'm enjoying this conversation, I'll bring it into my book.'

Harker smiled. The Chairman would love that. 'So tell me about your book. May I?' He indicated the folder containing her typescript.

She placed her hand protectively on it. 'Please, not yet.' She gave him another dazzling smile. 'I've only written about ten chapters so far, anyway. I thought I was ready to show them to you but now I know I'm not. You've given me some new ideas.' She grinned, then hunched forward earnestly. 'So tell me, what's going to happen in South Africa?'

This was the opening he was waiting for, the reason why Clements was burgling her apartment at this moment. He turned the question around: 'What do you think is going to happen?' He particularized: 'In Angola?'

'I asked first.'

He decided to give his honest opinion rather than the propagandist one.

'The war will go on for some time. But communism is on the ropes. Russia is in big economic trouble. Cuba is Russia's cat's-paw and Russia cannot afford to support them much longer. Angola is Russia's Vietnam. However, nor can South Africa afford it much longer, though we're in better shape than Russia and Cuba. So even if we don't achieve a knockout blow now and drive the Cubans back home – which we could do militarily – Russia's poverty will eventually do the job for us. So I think South Africa will finally win the war.' He added, in the hopes of drawing her out, 'I don't think the South Africans will ever quit, no matter what economic hardships they encounter. And I think Castro realizes this and he'll soon start looking for a face-saving way to make a peace deal.' He added, 'Don't you?'

Josephine was not to be drawn. She had her hands clasped under her chin, her eyes attentive. 'And what's going to happen to apartheid?'

Harker took a sip of wine. 'Meanwhile apartheid is on the ropes too. It is a proven failure. Cruel, and economically unjust – and economically wasteful. So there will be reform – already the state president has warned his Volk that they must "adapt or die", and a lot of apartheid's petty laws are not being enforced. So after the communist threat is removed, I expect apartheid will be eroded until there is none of it left. There'll be resistance to the process, of course, diehards threatening civil war, but my guess is that by the turn of the century apartheid will be well and truly dead and we can get on with reforming ourselves our way.'

Josephine took an energetic sip of wine. 'And what is "our" way? One man, one vote?'

'Yes, but we must prepare for that over at least a decade. To instil a democratic culture into the blacks.' He added, 'One of the greatest sins of apartheid is that we *wasted* forty years during which we could have done that, brought them up gradually into political maturity. Instead, apartheid just translocated them back into their tribal homelands, threw independence at them and let them make a mess of it.'

Josephine sat back, on her hobby horse. 'You don't think that their "mess" is perhaps a teeny-weeny bit due to the rape of colonialism?'

Harker sat back also. He frowned reasonably. 'Indeed, some of it. The Germans, for example, were bad colonialists, ruling by the whip. But they were kicked out of

Africa during the First World War. The Portuguese were also bad – but at least the Latins didn't practise segregation. King Leopold raped the Belgian Congo and brutalized the natives with forced labour, and the government did nothing to prepare the natives for the independence they threw at them at the first sign of rebellion, so of course the place erupted in chaos – particularly as the Russians and Chinese were fuelling the flames in their quest for worldwide communist revolution. Yes,' he agreed sagely, 'the communist powers were very bad neo-colonialists.'

Josephine sat back firmly in her chair, one hand clutching her wine glass to her breast.

'And the Dutch were bad colonialists,' Harker continued. 'They subjugated the natives, very much like you Americans did with the Red Indians – you people were also bad colonialists.' He smiled and took a sip of wine, then frowned. 'But the British were pretty good colonialists, Josephine. They tried to teach the Africans democracy, tried to bring them into government gradually. But the Wind of Change forced them to go too fast, grant independence too soon and their colonies became corrupt dictatorships.' He ended mildly: 'Don't you think?'

'So,' Josephine said, 'you think that South Africa should spend the next ten years teaching them a democratic culture, before giving them the vote?'

'It's starting now. The government has created a separate parliament for Coloureds, by that I mean the half-castes, and another one for Indians. Apartheid is in retreat.'

Josephine leant forward. 'Bullshit!' She tapped her breast. 'I've just come from that neck of the woods and I can tell you that apartheid is monstrously alive and hideously well! South Africa is not ruled by parliament any more, it's ruled by the goddam security forces! By so-called securocrats. By the so-called State Security Council which is nothing more than a committee of police and army generals which bypass the whole goddam parliament!' She looked at him.

'Your parliament is irrelevant now, the country is run by the goddam generals, like the Argentine was. Like Chile.' She glared at him. Before Harker could respond she went on, 'And what about the NSMS – the National Security Management System that this State Security Council has set up – hundreds of secret intelligence committees across the country with tentacles into every facet of life, spying on absolutely everybody, committing murders and mayhem. Absolutely above the law.' She glared. 'What your parliament says is irrelevant in these days of the Total Onslaught, Total Strategy.'

Harker was impressed with her general knowledge. He said: 'But that sort of thing happens all over the world when a state of emergency is declared. However, I doubt that parliament is irrelevant. I agree that in matters of security the State Security Council bypasses parliament, but I don't believe that they are above the law.'

Josephine said: 'You don't think that the South African police has a hit-squad or two? Boys in dark sunglasses who knock off the odd enemy of the apartheid state?'

Harker shook his head. 'No.'

'Nor the army? The army hasn't got Special Forces capable of hit-and-run skulduggery?'

Harker dearly wished to change the subject. 'Of course, all armies have. Like the British SAS, the American Green Berets. But hit-squads? No.'

Josephine had her hands clasped beneath her chin, eyes bright. Then: 'Not even with the policy of Total Onslaught, Total Strategy inaugurated by your President P.W. Botha ten years ago – in 1978 to be exact. The ends justify the means – any means?'

Harker shook his head, and took a sip of wine. 'Not "any means".'

Josephine looked at him, very polite. 'But what about the bomb that exploded at the ANC headquarters in London in 1982? Who did that? And who blew up Cosatu House last year in downtown Johannesburg – the headquarters of the Congress of South African Trade Unions? The Boy Scouts? And who blew up Khotso House only last year, the headquarters of the South Africa Council of Churches – also alleged to be the underground headquarters of the ANC?' She smiled at him. 'President Botha blamed it on "the Godless communists".' She snorted. 'What crap. As if the communists would blow up the ANC's headquarters – their ally. And what about Khanya House, the united church's building in Pretoria, a couple of months later? And what about Dulcie September? And what about the beautiful Jeanette Schoon, who worked for the British Volunteer Service in Angola, got blown to bits with her little daughter by a parcel bomb. You remember that case, only last year?'

Harker remembered reading about it. He had attributed it to rogue cops. 'Yes.'

'Who do you think sent the Schoons that nice parcel bomb? Father Christmas? And what about Albie Sachs, the ANC lawyer in Mozambique, somebody rigged a bomb to his car last year which blew his arm off when he opened the door. Who did that, d'you think?' She frowned. 'Albie Sachs was the sixth senior ANC official to be targeted in foreign countries.' She looked at him. 'Doesn't that suggest to you that there is a department in the South African government that specializes in that sort of thing?'

Harker badly wanted to get off this subject. 'That could all be the work of individual rogue cops acting on their own initiatives.'

Josephine smiled and sat back. 'Come on. Taking all the evidence together, the irresistible conclusion seems to be that the Total Strategy means the police and army can do what they goddam like to combat the perceived enemy.' Josephine took a sip of wine. 'Anyway, what's your opinion of the anti-apartheid movement?'

Harker was relieved to change the focus of the subject. 'They do important work, raising public awareness.'

Josephine looked surprised. 'Really? Would you be pre-pared to join us? Work with us?'

Harker could almost hear Dupont and the Chairman whooping in glee. He said, 'Sure, though I don't know how much practical work I could do.'

Her demeanour had changed. 'Oh, your name as a pub-lisher would help us a lot. We've got some famous com-panies and organizations supporting us. And seen being associated with a good organization like ours would surely do Harvest House some good.'

Harker inwardly sighed. 'Quite possibly.'

She hesitated, then said, 'And if a good anti-apartheid book were written, you would consider publishing it?'

Christ, what would the Chairman think about that? 'If I considered it a commercially profitable book, yes. Indeed that –' he indicated the folder containing her typescript – 'is what I hoped this meeting today was about.'

Josephine evidently had decided suddenly that this South African was okay. 'Oh yes, but I wasn't sure it would be your kind of book, you being a heavy-duty battle-scarred war veteran and all that jazz.' She grinned. 'Thought maybe I was barking up the wrong tree.' She leant forward earnestly. 'I hope I didn't offend you?'

'Not at all.' Harker smiled. Very relieved to be off the subject of South African hit-squads. He added, to ease his conscience about raising false hopes, 'However, a bigger publisher may do better for you than Harvest House. But your literary agent will advise you on all that, of course.'

She said earnestly, 'But I'd really like to give you first go at it, I mean, being a South African you know what I'm talking about, you'd be very helpful editorially.'

I'm a bastard, getting this woman's hopes up, Harker thought. But he would be able to pass the buck to his editor. 'Well, let's drink to that prospect.' He raised his glass.

'Right!' Josephine picked up hers and they clinked across the table. 'Oh,' she beamed, 'this is exciting. I'm going to go home and work like hell on my revisions. Can we meet again next week, so I can show the first few chapters to you without dying of embarrassment?'

Harker grinned. 'Same time, same place?'

'Perfect. And I'll be paying!'

'You will not.' The South African taxpayer was paying. Harker was very pleased she had relaxed. She's a volatile one, he thought. He was pleased not because he was fulfilling Dupont's orders so unexpectedly easily, but because he really wanted to meet her again next week. Even if, regrettably, he might never get laid now that their relationship had unfortunately degenerated into a potential one of publisher and author – Ms Josephine Franklin Valentine looked too smart to make the mistake of sleeping with her mentor. Authors like to keep their publishers on pedestals. But had she not screwed plenty of army officers for helicopter rides into battle-zones? He said: 'So, shall we order?'

'I feel like getting drunk first!'

Harker laughed. 'So do I.' He beckoned to their waiter and pointed at the wine bottle for a replacement. He turned to Josephine. 'So,' he said, not for duty's sake, 'tell me why you got deported from South Africa.'

'The cops raided my hotel room, confiscated my writing and escorted me on to an aircraft to London.'

'But what had you done to make them raid your hotel room?'

Josephine smiled. God, she was beautiful.

'When the Soweto riots broke out in South Africa – turmoil. I flew down to Johannesburg to get some action. I had to tag along behind the press corps – not being a full-blooded journalist accredited to any newspaper I was vulnerable. Anyway, there I was, a hanger-on, and the police commander called a press conference to explain to the world why so many blacks had been killed in Soweto that day. And I had the audacity to say: "But Brigadier Swanepoel, couldn't you have used rubber bullets instead of real ones?" And Brigadier Swanepoel looked at me with his Afrikaner beetle-brow' – Josephine furrowed her forehead in imitation – 'and responded: "Rrubber bullets? Madam, I will starrt using rrubber bullets when those kaffirrs starrt thrrowing rrubber rrocks!"'

Harker threw back his head and laughed.

Of course she'd done a hell of a lot more than criticize Brigadier Swanepoel to antagonize the authorities into deporting her: Dupont had said in his covering report that she shouldn't have been let into the country in the first place. She was obviously a communist, the South African Embassy in America should never have granted her a visa, somebody had slipped up as fucking usual. But Josephine didn't want to talk any more about it. 'It'll all be in my book, I don't want to steal my own thunder by telling you twice, so let's just have a jolly lunch . . .'

And it was jolly. The initial suspicions and fencing behind them, the conversation flowed like the wine, copiously. She hardly mentioned her experiences as a photo-journalist again: instead she regaled him with anecdotes about her other adventures around the world, her work for the anti-apartheid movement in London, her investigation into the politics of Hong Kong, into the plight of the Aborigines in Australia, of the Palestinians in Israel, the plight of the whale, the coral reefs – 'The whole goddam environment's in a mess!'

'Did you write about all those subjects?' He had not seen any cuttings about the environment in her CCB file.

'You bet. I'll show you my file of cuttings one day.'

She wanted to set the world on fire. 'But I'm not a communist, Jack. I'm all for enterprise, it's the unacceptable face of capitalism I'm against. The monopolies, the exploitation, the sweated labour.' She waved a hand. 'Of course, when I was a starry-eyed freshman at university I went through the usual phase of communist idealism, but I grew out of that. And I think the world had to go through this period of communist revolution to sweep aside the feudal injustices of centuries, to redress the obscene imbalance of wealth and power that existed at the time. I admire the communists' achievements.'

Like what? Harker was about to say, but changed it in his mouth: 'Which ones?'

'It's undeniable,' she said earnestly, 'that the average Russian and Chinese peasant – the vast majority of those two massive countries – it's undeniable that they're much better off now than before their revolutions.'

Harker didn't want to argue but he had to say, 'But it's 1998 now, and though the average Russian and Chinese probably is better off than his grandparents, he's still very poor compared to his modern Western counterpart.'

'Yeah? What about the poor of South America? The masses of India? They're supposedly "Western" too in the sense that they're in the West's sphere of influence.'

'But the moral wrongs in those countries don't make the economic and moral wrongs in Russia and China right, do they?'

'True.' She grinned. 'So we're coming up with profound truths. And I'm feeling more profound every minute.' She pointed her finger at his nose. 'But only a *revolution* will sweep aside the wrongs of most Third World countries, and the only power capable of making such a revolution is communism. All the other kinds are pussy-footing and piss-weak. So I *applaud* those underground communists who're plotting to overthrow the repressive governments of Argentina and Chile and the like. I *applaud* the likes of Fidel Castro – I support the Cubans in Africa because even if they are driven back into the sea as you want, I betcha –' she jabbed a finger – 'that win or lose the Cubans will have been a big factor in the eventual collapse of apartheid.'

She looked at him an earnest moment, then thrust her warm smooth hand on his. 'But even though you don't like that, Major Jack Harker, sir –' she gave a little salute – 'will you please please please still consider publishing my shit-hot humdinger of a book?'

Harker threw back his head and laughed. It all seemed terribly funny.

'Oh . . .' she laughed, 'I'm having a lovely day . . .'

Yes, it was a lovely day. On their second Irish coffee he just wanted to take her hand and walk with this lovely young woman through this lovely park with its trees in full summer bloom, its lovers and roller-skaters and musicians and horse-drawn carriages – just walk hand in hand, being frightfully learned and amusing, telling each other more about each other, going through that delightfully earnest process of impressing: that's what Jack Harker wanted to do, then hail a taxi to take them back to his nice old apartment off Gramercy Park, then fold her in his arms. But there was going to be none of that delightful business: it was a non-starter because Josephine wanted to rush home to work.

'While my writing blood is up! I'm not going to waste all this booze, I'm going to go'n pound out the prose so I bowl you over next Saturday, Jack Harker of Harvest House fame . . .' She blew him a dazzling kiss as her taxi pulled away from the Tavern on the Green.

Harker watched her go with regret. As her cab disappeared she twiddled her fingers over her shoulder at him. He grinned and waved. Then he pulled out his cellphone and dialled Clements.

'The eagle is on her way back,' he said.

'I'm clear,' Clements replied.

'Anything new?'

'Some.'

'So, drop everything around to me tonight.'

It was a wistful Harker who walked through Central Park, sat in the Sherry-Netherland's bar and drank a row of whiskies. He had spent a lovely day with a lovely young woman and he wanted to savour it – and he was going to report none of it to Felix Dupont.

But when he got back to his apartment there was a

coded message from Dupont on his answering machine, ordering him to proceed to Washington the next day for a conference. The following Saturday Harker could not meet Josephine Valentine as arranged because he was preparing to commit murder.

6

Colonel Felix Dupont, Director of Region One of the Civil Cooperation Bureau, ran a good, small hotel called the Royalton in a side street not far from Pennsylvania Avenue. It had only fifty rooms and the place was rather British: the interior was half-panelled in dark mahogany, the reception area had potted palms. Hunting trophies adorned the walls, antique chandeliers hung from the ornate ceiling. It had a handsome horseshoe bar called Churchill's, also fitted out in mahogany with dark booths. All the bar staff were busty ladies – Felix Dupont didn't hire any other kind. Churchill's did good trade. The Royalton had no restaurant so it was inexpensive by Washington standards and therefore popular with travelling salesmen and husbands cheating on their wives. It was a profitable little hotel because of the low overheads, and its administration was undemanding, which left Dupont plenty of time for his covert Civil Cooperation Bureau duties.

Felix Dupont was a man of about fifty with dark bushy eyebrows over a round, bearded face. He had piercing blue eyes that could be jolly. He was a devout Afrikaner, but an Anglicized one from Cape Town. He had gone to the best private school of British persuasion and had even considered going to Oxford University before he opted for a career in the South African army. He had a very good military reputation. Harker respected his abilities but didn't like him. The man was an unmitigated racist. The antagonism was mutual: Dupont respected Harker's record as a soldier but he resented his Sandhurst background, his British culture and manners. Ninety years ago Dupont's father and grandfather had fought the likes of Harker's

57

in the long and bitter Boer War, his grandmother and most of her children had perished of disease and malnutrition in the British concentration camps along with twenty-six thousand other Boers. If Dupont had had his way Harker would have been transferred to Region Two, London, where he could 'ponce about with those English sonsabitches'. Now Dupont had a nasty job for Harker, codenamed Operation Marigold, and he relished the man's reaction.

'Jesus.' It was the first time in his CCB career that Harker had been ordered to kill anybody.

Dupont waited, amused, his blue eyes hooded.

'How?' Harker demanded.

'Softly-softly. We want to know what exactly these guys are planning before we bump them off – who their accomplices are, where they are, et cetera. And we want all the documents they may have in their possession. So before you hit them you record their party talk with a long-range listening device which the CIA will provide.' He smiled wolfishly. 'Then, when the dear boys are sleepy and go to bed, you burst in there and shoot the shit out of them. You then collect up every document you can find, every scrap of evidence in their wallets and briefcases, then you plant explosive charges and you blow them all to Kingdom Come.' He added, 'In fact you not only blow up the house, you also strap explosives to the bodies and blow them to smithereens too, so there's no possibility of identification afterwards.'

Jesus. 'And supposing I don't hear anything incriminating on the listening device? Supposing they're not planning sabotage?'

Dupont said, 'You just listen until they're getting ready for bed, then you attack. First you lob a few stun grenades through the windows, then burst in the back and front door simultaneously.'

Harker shook his head grimly. 'But how do we know this tip-off is reliable? The identity of the targets, for starters.

Who exactly in the CIA gave you the information? They've been known to be wrong in the past.'

'You have no need to know who. Just take my word for it – and my orders.'

'But how do we know they're plotting sabotage inside South Africa?'

'I repeat, you have no need to know. Suffice it to say the CIA have informers amongst the Cuban military. The ANC guys have just completed a course in urban terrorism in Havana. Brigadier Moreno is the Cuban army's top intelligence officer in Angola.'

'But,' Harker said, 'why the hell are these guys meeting in America? This is very hostile territory for them.'

'Yours not to reason why, Major. Just accept the CIA's information gratefully. Suffice it to say they're here under false identities and they're here for good reason.'

'But does the Chairman know about this?'

'You take your orders from me, Major!' Dupont said sharply. 'But, yes, he knows. And approves.'

Harker did not like this. He had killed plenty of men on the battlefield without compunction but he had never killed in cold blood.

'It's a golden opportunity,' Dupont said.

Harker could see the military desirability of the action: an opportunity to kill two top Cuban officers meeting three senior ANC officials trained in urban terrorism to discuss sabotage strategies within South Africa was not to be missed. He just wished it wasn't he who had to do it, particularly on American soil. 'And where is this ANC safe-house where they're meeting?'

'It's a *Russian* safe-house. It's a farmhouse, in a lonely part of Long Island, New York. No other houses nearby. The CIA have given us a plan of the place.' He tapped a roll of architectural drawings. 'And skeleton keys.'

'Why the hell don't the CIA do the damn job themselves if they're so keen to be helpful?'

Dupont was enjoying Harker's anxiety. 'Because they

want to keep their noses clean. They want us to do their dirty work for them.' He added: 'They'll blame the job on the anti-Castro exile community in Miami.'

'But why me? I'm not an assassin. You've got plenty of other operatives who could do the job, why me?'

'You received training in termination techniques, didn't you? You signed the fucking oath of faithful service?'

'But the Chairman told me I wouldn't have to get my hands bloody!'

'Well the Chairman was wrong, wasn't he? Things have got a bit tougher since he recruited you.' He glared. 'And if there's any insubordination you'll be posted back home. And court-martialled! And you can kiss your high-brow Harvest House goodbye. *Do you hear me?*'

Court-martialled? Harker clenched his teeth: it wasn't an offence under the Defence Force Act to refuse to commit murder on foreign soil. But losing Harvest House? He glanced back at Dupont, then muttered: 'I hear you.'

Dupont sat back. 'Jesus Christ,' he glowered, 'here we have the opportunity to get rid of two top Cuban officers, Sanchez and Moreno, the two top bastards who're killing our boys in the bush, and they're meeting three ANC swines to plot murder of innocent civilians with their bombs and sabotage – and you're squeamish!'

Harker glared at him. 'I fully recognize them as legitimate military targets – I also went to war-school. I would bump them off joyfully if I could get near enough to them in the war zone. But you're damn right if you mean I'm scared of doing it in the civilian environs of America – *sir*. If anything goes wrong I'll be tried for murder. *Sir*.'

Dupont smiled carnivorously. 'When you say "sir" you'd better sound as if you mean it, old boy.'

Harker sighed angrily. Dupont looked at him icily, but decided to let it go. 'Major, if you land in trouble the CIA will see that you get out of it. They're as keen on this job as we are. And they assure me that when you've reconnoitred the killing ground you'll see it's a cinch.'

Harker snorted. Dupont glanced at his wristwatch and said, 'Okay, tell me about Bigmouth.'

Harker groaned angrily. He said, 'I've reviewed everything Clements got from her apartment yesterday, her notebooks, her disks. Here's my report.' He put his hand in his pocket, withdrew an envelope and tossed it in front of his boss.

'And?'

'And,' Harker said, 'she's harmless. There is nothing of significance that we don't know already. Apart from her war photography she's no different from all the other bleeding hearts in the anti-apartheid movement.'

Dupont pushed the report aside and said grimly, 'She's not fucking harmless, she's a troublemaker. All those demonstrations and fund-raising, all the crap she writes. It's not just a movement, it's an *industry* – all these "Free Mandela" T-shirts and crap. Did she tell you about this book she's supposed to be writing?'

'No,' Harker said.

'When are you seeing her again?'

'I can meet her again through the yacht club.'

Dupont jabbed his finger. 'Well, get on to it. And find out about this book – tell her you want to read it, you're a fancy publisher. And if it looks like getting published *you* publish it. And *kill* it. Tell her you're printing thousands of copies but print a few hundred and *bury* the fucking thing . . .'

7

It was touch-and-go whether Harker refused to obey orders concerning the assassination, resigned his commission in the army, kissed goodbye to Harvest House and tried to make a new career for himself at the age of thirty-eight. He had no moral compunction about killing General Sanchez and Brigadier Moreno of the Cuban army – he had been killing their soldiers for years on the battlefield, as they had been trying to kill him. He wasn't even much concerned about his own skin: the CIA with their wheels within wheels would cover his tracks if he left any and if he still got in the shit they would pull the right strings to fish him out – unless it suited them to let him take the rap, but he didn't seriously think they would do that. Nor was it fear of danger; he had penetrated behind enemy lines to reconnoitre targets over terrain much more dangerous than an empty farmhouse in the tranquil American countryside. Nor was it fear of the poverty that might ensue if he resigned in protest: true, he would lose Harvest House, the job of publisher he really enjoyed, but he had a good reputation in New York and he could surely get another position in publishing. Nor was it fear of his own army that worried him: sure, if he resigned in protest they would watch him like hawks, he would be a dead man if he dared spill the beans – but Harker would not spill any beans. No, it was murdering those three ANC officials that worried him.

They were civilians, not soldiers. Okay, they were going to be plotting sabotage within South Africa, and that made them murderers – five years ago ANC agents had planted a car-bomb outside the South African air force headquarters in Pretoria and killed and injured many people, most of them civilian passers-by. That was despicable, but on the other hand wasn't the air force headquarters a legitimate military target for the ANC, hadn't the bomb blown out all the windows and a fucking great hole in the wall? Sure it was despicable to blow up civilians, but hadn't the explosion impressed the shit out of South Africans, delivered the message that apartheid was a dangerous, bloody business? And then had come the murder of Dulcie September; the whole world had had no doubt that South Africa had done the job, and Harker now had no doubt that the CCB was responsible. The thought had sickened him. *Christ* – soldiers were legitimate targets, but unarmed civilians who had committed no wrong other than espouse a political cause opposed to your political masters' credo stuck in his craw. Jesus, he'd hoped such action would never be required of him.

'They're plotting murder,' Dupont had said.

Yes, most probably, Harker admitted to the passing twinkling lights beyond the Amtrak dining saloon carrying him back to New York with the suitcase of explosives the CIA had provided; yes, most probably they would be plotting murder, but how do we know for sure? We have only the CIA's word for it. Perhaps they're discussing something like children's nutritional aid, or the ANC's next tactic around the corridors of the United Nations which Harker would hear all about from his salesmen anyway . . .

'Of course they're saboteurs,' Dupont had shouted. 'Why else are they meeting Sanchez and Moreno?'

Yes, they must be, but he wished he knew their names so he could try to verify the fact, and he wished he had more than the CIA's word for the purpose of the meeting.

It took him a long time to go to sleep that Monday night, staring out of the train window, watching the night lights of America slip by.

The reconnaissance was easy.

Harker did not do it himself because his CCB cover as a

publisher would have been blown if he had been caught. He sent one of his senior salesmen, Derek Clements, the very tough American who had been a US Marine and a mercenary in the Rhodesian army. He was one of the best soldiers Harker had known, the right sort to have on your side in a tight corner: amongst other military accomplishments he was a tracking and survival expert, an instructor in hand-to-hand combat, an expert in demolition work. Clements had been in the CCB longer than Harker, who had inherited him from Dupont. His front-business in America was a car-hire firm much patronized by United Nations officials: his rank and pay scale in Military Intelligence was that of lieutenant. But he was really staff-sergeant material, one of the breed of men who kick ass and make an army function.

Harker drove Clements to Long Island that Tuesday afternoon in a Hertz car rented in a false name. They located the area of the farm, then went to eat at a roadhouse. When darkness fell they synchronized watches and drove back to the area. Clements was dropped off at the roadside. He disappeared into the dark, and Harker drove on.

The farmhouse was surrounded by woods and, as Dupont had promised, it was deserted. There wasn't another dwelling for over a mile. Clements approached carefully. There was no light. He observed the old clapboard house for half an hour, looking for signs of life, then he crept to the back door and let himself in with the keys Dupont had given to Harker.

And, yes, though the place was empty, it was in use: the kitchen was clean, there was water in the taps. Clements went through it slowly, shining a shaded torch. There were a few cans of food in the small pantry and some Cuban rum. The living room was the only suitable place for a meeting: there was a dining table surrounded by eight chairs. The bookshelves were empty, there was no paper anywhere. Upstairs there were three bedrooms holding ten narrow beds, made up with blankets but no sheets. All the cupboards and drawers were bare. There was one used bar of soap in the small bathroom but nothing else. All the floors were made of wood, covered with a scattering of worn mats.

Clements went back downstairs. He began to go through the house again systematically, carefully noting every detail, the position of the furniture, of the mats. Then he let himself out by the kitchen door, and crept back through the woods. At ten o'clock exactly Harker's headlights appeared down the road. Clements emerged from the darkness, and Harker picked him up.

'Well?'

'It'll be a cinch,' Clements said. 'We hit all three entrances as shown on the architect's drawing. And the place is a tinder-box, everything is wood. A couple of bombs will blow the lot sky-high. It's obviously just a safe-house for transients. No armour, no communications, not even a phone. So who are these guys we're hitting?'

'Sorry, you have no need to know. Is there a good place for the listening device?'

'Perfect. One just under the floorboards as a back-up, the main just inside the surrounding forest – plenty of undergrowth, but a clean field of fire if the action starts at the wrong time.'

'Okay, so plant the gear on Thursday night. Rent a car, park it at the hamburger joint and walk to the scene. Rig your listening device in the right place and then make yourself scarce. Take Spicer to cover you. Then we rendezvous on Saturday, with our hardware – the CIA are supplying us with the Russian machine pistols that the Cubans use, and the grenades. The CIA are tailing the targets all day to see what else they get up to. When they arrive here the CIA will radio me. We move into the forest and listen. At the right time we hit 'em, front door, kitchen door and french window. Then we get their documents and blow the place up.'

'How many of us?'

'Four. You, me, Spicer and Trengrove.'

Clements said, 'Wish we could hit them as they arrive, as they're getting out of the car.'

'Wish we could too. But the boss wants to hear what they're talking about.'

'Well,' Clements said with a smile, 'sounds like fun, sir. About time we did something exciting.'

Exciting? Harker felt ill in his guts. He was sick of war. He sighed grimly. 'Okay, we'll go back to Harvest and I'll give you the listening gear Dupont gave me.'

8

Yes, Harker was sick of war, sick of soldiering: he didn't feel like a soldier any more, he felt like a publisher. He didn't even feel much like an African: he felt more of an Anglo-American now. But a professional soldier he was. He owed his position as a publisher to his military superiors, and he was at war. And the purpose of warfare, every military scientist agrees, is to kill as many of the enemy as possible as fast as possible in the pursuit of victory: you only stop killing the enemy when he is defeated or makes peace. It is the characteristic of the professional military man that once he has made up his mind on a course of action he carries it out: he only departs from his objective if he has to make a tactical retreat.

Harker's character and talents fitted him perfectly for a successful military career. Yes, he was sick of war but he regarded it as a just battle against the communist forces of darkness. By the time the train had carried him back to New York from Washington he had made up his mind that the persons meeting at the safe-house in Long Island were legitimate military targets: the CIA said so, the Chairman said so, Dupont said so. The qualms he had about the ANC officials being civilians were groundless – they were plotting sabotage within South Africa which would surely involve innocent civilian casualties. Harker wished he knew more but he had no need to know before accepting his superiors' word for this. True, his action would be highly illegal under the laws of America, first degree murder, but that did not diminish the moral legitimacy of it under the laws of war.

Nonetheless Harker felt sick in his guts. He did not waver,

but the fact that those ANC officials were civilians kept nagging at him. He grimly told himself that his qualms were illogical, attributable to his war-weariness, to being softened. He pushed the point out of his mind but it kept stalking him. It was a very tense week. He did not sleep well.

Before midnight on Thursday Clements telephoned him at home. 'All systems go,' he said. 'The story is written exactly as outlined. It'll be publishable on schedule.'

'Good.'

Harker poured himself another drink. Yes it was good, for Christ's sake, good that five bastards plotting murder were going to be taken out, that innocent civilian lives in South Africa were going to be spared . . . But he had been secretly hoping that Clements might report that the mission had proved impossible – then the CIA would have had to do their own dirty work.

That wouldn't bother you one bit, so why the hell are you bothered now? The result would be the same!

The next morning he was about to call Josephine Valentine to postpone their Saturday lunch date when she telephoned him.

'Well, Major,' she said cheerfully, 'it's all systems go. I've polished up those first ten chapters and they're fit to be read. This is to confirm tomorrow's date.'

Harker closed his eyes. *All systems go.* That she had used the same words as Clements made him flinch. 'I'm terribly sorry, Josie, but I was about to phone you to ask if we can postpone, something very important has come up.'

'Oh.' She sounded very disappointed. 'Of course. Till when?'

He wanted to give himself a week to lie low, to settle down, to get the debriefing over, reports sent, to get over the whole incident. He could almost feel her disappointment – authors want their praise immediately. 'How about the following Saturday?'

'Fine!' Her relief that the postponement was not longer

was palpable. 'I know – let me take *you* to lunch at the yacht club. It's my favourite day there – a superb buffet.'

'Yacht club it is,' Harker said. 'We'll fight about the bill.'

'I'm paying,' she said. 'You're giving up part of your weekend for me!'

Saturday was tense. Harvest House was deserted, echoing. His instructions were to stay in his command post in the basement to be in secure contact with both the faceless CIA and the ugly face of Dupont in Washington until H-hour, the time for action. It was a long day. He tried to do some publishing work but could not concentrate. He turned to some CCB preparation, reviewing his salesmen's latest information in readiness for his routine monthly report to Dupont, but he could not settle to it. He tried to catch up on the wads of South African newspapers that arrived twice a week, a task he usually enjoyed, but he could not even keep his mind on the reports about the Angolan war. Most of the news was bullshit anyway – the journalists usually only knew what the army chose to tell them to boost morale, to keep the public supportive. In reality the war was going to be South Africa's Vietnam if a deal wasn't made soon – he just wished to God the politicians could learn from America's mistakes, pull out all the stops, hit the Cubans with everything the army had, drive them into the sea once and for all, get the war over, then settle South Africa's internal problems – dismantle goddam apartheid and bring moderate blacks into government. But South Africa dared not do that because there would be an international outcry – the West also wanted Russia and Cuba out of the continent but South Africa, which was capable of achieving that, was its own worst enemy with its goddam apartheid, a pariah. So the battles raged on, people dying, taxpayers' money haemorrhaging into the hot sands of Angola along with the blood.

Harker shoved the newspapers aside in frustration. He

held his face. *And what he was doing today was part of that process. Another nail in the coffin of communism.*

He had to get up and start pacing up and down the basement to ease his nerves.

It was always like this before an action, he reminded himself. Once you knew you were going in at H-hour you were a bundle of tension. You try to rest, to eat, to read, to pray, you know you can't change anything, the plan is laid, the orders given so all you can do is hope – hope that you come out alive. That's for an overt action, where it's more or less each man for himself when the bullets start flying – it was much worse for a covert action where you were sent behind enemy lines and the main hope you had was that they didn't capture you alive and torture you to death. So what's new about this fucking tension?

What's new is that you've gone soft in two years in New York – your heart's not in soldiering any more . . .

God, he wanted a drink. To ease his nerves, to help his hangover – that was certainly part of his problem, he'd been drinking too much. But he dared not.

To kill the time he pulled out Josephine's file, and he sat down behind his desk and tried to read again the stories she had written. But he could not concentrate on that either; he flipped through the file, looking for photographs of her.

Oh, she was beautiful. Just then the telephone rang. He snatched up the receiver. 'Hullo?'

'Is that Buttons and Bows Night Club?' Dupont said.

Harker closed his eyes, his heart knocking. 'Sorry, wrong number.' He hung up.

Harker slumped, then picked up his cellphone, his hand shaking. He dialled.

'Buttons and Bows,' Clements said.

'I want to speak to Mr Buttons, please.'

'He'll call you back in about twenty minutes, sir.'

It was a long twenty minutes waiting for Clements' next call. 'Awaiting your pleasure, sir,' he said.

Harker picked up his holdall and clambered up the narrow staircase into his upper office. He opened the big front door of Harvest House and stepped out into the spring night. The car was parked fifty yards down the road: the driver flashed his headlights once. Harker climbed into the front passenger seat. A man called Parker, one of Clements' salesmen, was at the wheel. 'Good evening, sir,' they all said.

'Good evening,' Harker said tensely. 'Let's go.'

At nine o'clock that Saturday night they were creeping through the forest, approaching the farmhouse. Now they were all in black tracksuits, wearing balaclavas, carrying the machine-pistols Harker had distributed.

The clapboard house was about fifty years old, the paint peeling off the wood, the yard around it sprinkled with weeds and shrubs. The house was in darkness. The listening gear was in position. Harker gave his instructions and Clements moved to take cover facing the front door, Spicer went off to cover the kitchen door, Trengrove disappeared around the other side of the house to the living room window. Harker remained with the listening device, covering the dining-room French window. They settled down to wait.

It was a very long hour before the headlights came flicking through the forest. The car came up the winding track into the yard, its headlights now blinding. Harker lay beside the listening gear, his heart pounding; the vehicle's doors opened and one by one five dark figures clambered out. They were hardly talking, only a mutter here and there as they stretched and reached for luggage. Then, while the headlights illuminated the kitchen door, they trooped towards it, carrying their briefcases and baggage. For the first time Harker could distinguish the blacks from the Cubans, but he could not identify anybody. They clustered around while one of the Cubans selected and inserted a key.

Harker snorted to himself. It would have been an ideal

moment to hit the whole damn lot of them: no fuss, no risk. But no – goddam Dupont wanted to record what they talked about first. The Cuban unlocked the door and they filed inside. Lights went on. Harker glimpsed them filing through the kitchen into the dining room. They clustered around the table, and one of the Cubans produced a bottle from his briefcase.

Harker put on the headphones of the listening device. He could hear mumbled speech. He turned the tuning knob and the volume. Suddenly he heard a Cuban say, 'Close the curtains. Sit down, please . . .' He heard the scraping of chair legs on the floor. More mumbles. The tinkle of liquor being poured. Then the meeting began.

Harker listened intently, his tape-recorder turning; then he closed his eyes in relief. Thank God . . . Thank God this murder was not unjust. The bastards were certainly plotting murder. Mass murder. Planning to detonate three car-bombs at twenty-four-hour intervals: the first at the Voortrekker Monument on a Sunday, the second at the Houses of Parliament on Monday, Johannesburg's international airport on Tuesday. Harker smiled despite himself – the chain of events would be effective: the Voortrekker Monument job would infuriate, the Houses of Parliament job would vastly impress, the Johannesburg airport job would downright terrify. The psychological impact upon the South African public, coming one after the other, boom boom boom, would be enormous. In fact, listening to the muffled indistinct speech, Harker was surprised they settled for only three bombs – why not half a dozen, throw in the Union Buildings in Pretoria where all the top government departments hang out, the Reserve Bank down the road and, say, the City Hall. Harker had always wondered why the ANC hadn't done all that years ago – they really were, militarily speaking, a milk-and-water bunch. MK, the Spear of the Nation, the ANC's army, had never waged a battle. The only thing that gave them clout was the moral turpitude of apartheid.

For an hour Harker tried to listen to the plotting going on in the house, over the coughs and mumbles and mutters and occasional laughter, the glug of liquor and the click of cigarette lighters; he could only make out snatches of detail and he hoped the tape-recorder was picking up more. Then suddenly the meeting sounded as if it was over: he heard a burst of song in Spanish, followed by guffaws.

Harker took a deep breath – it was time to hit. He took off his headphones and whispered into his radio transmitter.

'H-hour coming up. Do you read me? Come in one at a time.'

'One, copy,' Clements said.

'Two, copy,' Ferdi Spicer said.

'Three, copy,' Trengrove said.

'Okay,' Harker said, 'we hit on zero . . . Five . . . Four . . . Three . . . Two . . . One . . . Zero!'

Out of the forest sprang the four dark forms. They ran through the darkness at the house. Harker raced up to the curtained dining-room French window, a stun grenade in his hand: he yanked out the pin with his teeth and hurled it through the window. There was a shattering of glass, then a detonation that seemed to shake the earth. Then there was a crack as Spicer kicked the kitchen door in, another as Clements did the same to the front door. Harker burst through the window and opened fire. And there was nothing in the world but the popping of his machine pistol, then the noise of Spicer's and Clements' as they covered the two principal escape routes.

In the cacophony Harker did not hear the shattering of the living room window as a black South African called Looksmart Kumalo dived through it, through Trengrove's hail of bullets, scrambled up and fled off into the black forest. Trengrove went bounding frantically after him, gun blazing, but in an instant the darkness had swallowed him up. Trengrove went crashing through the black undergrowth, wildly looking for the runaway man, but Looksmart Kumalo, badly wounded, was hiding under some bushes.

Trengrove crashed about for several hundred yards, then he turned and went racing back to the farmhouse.

Harker was frantically collecting up all the documents, baggage and briefcases while Clements and Spicer were fixing explosives to the dead bodies. 'Where's the other body?' Clements demanded.

'Sir!' Trengrove shouted. 'He escaped into the forest!'

'Christ!' Harker stared. 'Christ, Christ, Christ!'

'Go after him, sir?' Clements rasped.

'Yes!' Harker shouted. 'Spicer stays and finishes the explosives! Rest of you go. Go!'

For twenty minutes Harker, Clements and Trengrove thrashed through the black undergrowth of the forest, trying to flush out the runaway, hoping to stumble across the dead body. It was hopeless – nobody can track in the dark. After twenty minutes Harker barked a halt. If the bastard survived he was unlikely to tell the American police that he was attacked during a murderous conspiracy meeting in an illegal Cuban safe-house.

'Back!' Harker rasped. 'Get the hell out of here!'

Spicer was desperately waiting for them, the explosives emplaced, the listening gear and the seized documents ready to go. Harker spoke into his radio to the getaway car: 'Venus is rising!'

The men went racing up the dark track towards the tarred road. They were several miles away, speeding towards Manhattan, when the house disintegrated in a massive explosion, the bodies blown to tiny pieces.

9

It was always the same after an action. Before going into battle he was very tense but afterwards, when the dust had settled and the bodies had been counted, he slept as if he had been pole-axed even if he knew the action was to resume at dawn – he felt no remorse about the enemy, only grim satisfaction and relief to have survived. It was only the conscripts, the civilians in uniform, who sometimes felt remorse, but usually that didn't last long either because few experiences are more antagonizing than having some bastard trying to shoot the living shit out of you.

Harker woke up that Sunday afternoon rested for the first time in a week, permitting himself no feeling of guilt. The die was cast, nothing could change it. It had been a legitimate military operation and had saved civilian lives. It was front-page news in most of the papers: there were photographs of the area where the safe-house had stood, the earth and shrubbery blackened and blasted. There was one survivor in critical condition: an 'adult male of African origin now in hospital, with multiple injuries, including loss of one eye and an arm so badly mutilated by gunfire that it had to be amputated below the elbow'. The FBI were investigating: they had no comment yet but the local sheriff, who was first on the scene, was moved to hint that this was 'probably a gangland slaying, probably to do with drugs'. Investigations were continuing.

Harker felt a stab of guilt through a chink in his armour when he read about the mutilated survivor, as yet unidentified, but he thrust it aside – he had seen plenty of his soldiers mutilated over the years: if you play with fire you must expect to get your fingers burnt – the bastard had been plotting far worse, he was lucky to be alive and if he'd been caught in South Africa he would have been hanged after the police had wrung the truth out of him. Harker had no fear that the man could be dangerous: no ANC official would be so dumb as to tell the FBI he was meeting with Fidel Castro's henchmen on holy American soil. Without much difficulty Harker parried the thrust of guilt as he encoded his report to Dupont that Sunday afternoon, and when his computer began to print out the information from Washington that the survivor was now positively identified by the CIA as Alexander Looksmart Kumalo, his remorse evaporated further. Looksmart Kumalo was well known to Military Intelligence as one of the ANC's sabotage strategists.

That afternoon Harker took the shuttle flight to Washington to deliver to Dupont all the documents seized at the farmhouse. He had not read them; he had tried, he could read Spanish with difficulty but he could not concentrate; indeed he did not want to know any more than he had to about the misery of war and murderous skulduggeries in its name, and he wanted to forget his work of last night. But when he walked into the soundproof office behind the reception desk of the Royalton Hotel a happily drunk Dupont not only thrust a large whisky at him after pumping his hand in congratulation – 'Jolly good show, *fucking* good show! Sanchez *and* Moreno!' – but also insisted Harker give him a blow by blow account. And sitting in the corner was the CIA man whom Harker knew only by the codename 'Fred', the guy who was Dupont's handler or contact with the United States' 'Dirty Tricks Bureau' as he called it, and Fred wanted every detail on tape.

'*Fucking* good show . . .' Dupont interjected frequently.

Neither Dupont nor Fred was unduly concerned about the survivor, Looksmart Kumalo. It was a pity, of course, that he had not perished with the rest of the blackguards but there was no danger of the bastard spilling the beans: he would be debriefed by the CIA and advised, 'in the nicest possible way', that not only was his liberty at stake because of the cocaine the FBI had planted on him, but his health was also because – if he didn't have a mysterious fatal heart attack in hospital – he would be deported to South Africa where he belonged and where he would receive a warm welcome from the authorities if he opened his big mouth. And if he broke the bargain he was being so generously offered, the British MI5, France's Sûreté and most of the civilized world's secret services would have him prominently on their shit-list.

'He won't talk publicly,' Froggy Fred croaked, 'and if he does they'll be the last words he utters.'

'You planted cocaine on him?' Harker frowned. 'I thought the FBI were going to blame the whole thing on the Cuban exile community in Miami. Now you're going to claim it was a drug-war assassination?'

'Both,' Fred rumbled. 'We blame it on both, as alternative possibilities, to raise confusion.'

Dupont leered happily, stroking the pile of documents. 'He'll keep his mouth shut, don't worry . . .'

It was after midnight when the debriefing was declared over and a taxi was summoned to take Harker back to the airport. Dupont offered him a room in the hotel – 'The presidential suite indeed' – and Fred volunteered to throw in a good hooker 'on Uncle Sam' – 'Or two!' Dupont cried – but Harker just wanted to get the hell away from yesterday, from these awful guys, from this hotel where they festered.

As he climbed into the taxi, Dupont breathed alcoholically through the window. '*Fucking* good show! Now you relax, disappear to the beach for a few days, then get on to the Bigmouth case . . .'

He did disappear to the coast, but not to enjoy himself – it was to brood. Ah yes, his *soldier's* conscience was clear, more or less, but even soldiers sometimes want to be alone after they have done battle, spilt voluminous blood, mourn not for the enemy but the whole dreadful business of taking so much life. And he did not want to 'get on to the Bigmouth case' – he felt a fraud. He *was* a fraud. Jack Harker dearly wished he was not bound to take the beautiful Josephine Valentine to lunch next Saturday, he wanted to be alone, he dearly wished he did not have to pose fraudulently as her potential publisher in order to further the ends of apartheid. Josephine Valentine's book was hardly a legitimate military target.

And he would not do so.

No, he would not do so. Jack Harker refused to defraud Josephine Valentine any further by pretending that he was interested in publishing her book. He would have to pay her the courtesy of reading her ten chapters, and he would give her his honest opinion, but he would tell her immediately thereafter that Harvest would not publish it. He was *not* going to give her false hope, and he certainly was not going to obey orders and *bury* her book, kill it by publishing it badly. *Fuck you, Felix Dupont.*

Having made that decision he felt better. On Saturday, when he drove back to Manhattan, he was again looking forward to having lunch with one of the best-looking women in New York.

When Josephine Valentine came sweeping into the yacht club dining room, clutching her file, beaming, hand extended, she was even lovelier than he remembered.

'Hi!' She pumped his hand energetically: hers was warm and both soft and strong. She was a little breathless, as if she had been hurrying. 'Am I late?'

'Indeed you're two minutes early,' Harker smiled. 'You look beautiful.'

'Thank you. Well . . .' She plonked the file down on the table. 'Here it is.' But she put her hand on it. 'Please, don't look at it now. I want you to give it your undivided attention at home. And,' she grinned, 'I'm nervous as hell.' She sat.

Oh dear. 'Don't be, I know you write well.' Harker sat

down. And he decided that right now was the moment to start extricating himself. 'And I'm not the only publisher in town. Indeed you'll probably do better with a bigger house.'

Consternation crossed her lovely face. 'But you will consider it? Are you saying you're not interested any more?'

Oh Christ. 'I'm just being realistic, for your sake.' He smiled. 'On the contrary, I'm the one who should be nervous that you'll take it to somebody else.'

Josephine sat back and blew out her cheeks. 'For a moment I thought you were trying to tell me something.' Then she said anxiously, 'You will be brutally honest with me, won't you?'

'Of course.'

'Okay.' She sat back, with a brilliant smile. 'And now let's stop talking about it – I've been burning the midnight oil all week.'

'So what'll you have to drink?'

'A double martini for starters. Followed by a bucket of wine. And remember I'm paying.'

'You are not.' The fucking CCB was paying.

They had a good time again that day. They laughed a great deal, drank a lot, became very witty and wise. Harker got into a mood to celebrate too, but he was not sure what: he still felt a fraud. And, God, he just wanted to get this masquerade of being her potential publisher over so he could do what publishers should not do – make a pass at an author. Oh, to take her hand across the table, look into her blue eyes, tell her how beautiful she was, to feel her body against his, to go through the delightful process of courtship: but as long as he was defrauding her his conscience would not permit it, his head had to rule his loins. So the sooner he went through the motions of reading her typescript, grasped the nettle and told her that Harvest could not publish it, the better.

'So tell me, Major Jack Harker,' she said over the rim of

her first glass of Irish coffee, 'whatever happened to Mrs Harker?'

'There hasn't been one. There very nearly was, but she changed her mind. One of the casualties of war. She's now Mrs Somebody Else.'

'Oh. Well, all I can say is that she was either very, very stupid or Mr Somebody Else must be very, very nice. So tell me . . .' she raised her glass to her wide full lips and looked at him, 'is some lucky American gal filling her stilettos?'

'Nobody special.' He felt himself blushing. 'And how about you?'

She grinned. 'Nobody special. I've only just hit town after a long time away.'

Oh, Harker badly wanted to know about her past, how many of the legends about her were true. In particular he wanted to know about that dead Cuban lying on the floor of the building at Bassinga when she had tried to kill herself – but the time was not right for a confession that he had killed her lover, and doubtless never would be.

'I'm sure you've been close to marrying?' he said.

'Several times. But, at the last minute, there was always something amiss.' She flashed him a smile from underneath her dark eyebrows. 'Like, not enough soulmateship.' She added: 'I've got the feeling you know what I'm talking about.'

'Soulmates? Sure. Lovers who think and feel alike. Share the same interests.'

'And *passions*. Interests and passions. Like . . . Justice. And Democracy. Freedom. A fair wage for a fair day's labour. And poetry, and music. And . . . *God*.' She looked at him seriously, then flashed him a smile. 'All that good stuff.'

'And have you ever found it?'

Josephine nodded sagely at her glass. 'I thought so, several times. But each time it turned out to be a false alarm. Or something like that. Until the last time, I think. Maybe. But he was killed.'

Oh Christ. Harker waited, then said, 'How?'

80

She said to her glass, 'He was a soldier, like you.' She smirked. 'And he lost his life fighting you guys.' She looked up. 'The Battle of Bassinga? Mean anything to you?'

Harker feigned a sigh. What do you say? 'It was a big do, I believe. I was in hospital at the time, wounded in an earlier action, the one that pensioned me out.' He glanced at her. 'So, what happened exactly?'

Josephine took a sip of Irish coffee. 'I'd been living with him in his base camp for about a month. First met him up north in Luanda, then flew down with him to cover the southern front. We were asleep in his quarters when your guys struck, just before dawn. Helluva mess. Anyway, Paulo got shot at the beginning. So did I, but that was later on.'

So she wasn't admitting attempted suicide. 'You were shot in the cross-fire?'

'When Paulo was shot I went berserk, I grabbed his AK47 and started firing out the window. There was a box of loaded magazines and I just kept firing, slapping in one magazine after another. Stupid, because journos aren't supposed to become combatants if they don't want to be treated as an enemy, but I was frantic about Paulo. Anyway, finally a bullet got me. Here.' She tapped her left breast. 'Missed my heart, fortunately. Next thing I knew I was being loaded into one of your helicopters and flown off to one of your bases, where they patched me up – which was nice of them, seeing as I'd been trying to shoot the hell out of them an hour earlier. Then they deported me.'

'Oh, yes, I heard about this. So you're the blonde bomb-shell who threatened to sue us. Wasn't there a row about your photographs?'

She smiled. 'Your guys developed my film to see what they could find out about the enemy's hardware. I kicked up a fuss and they gave me my negatives back.'

'Did they interrogate you?'

'Sure, but I told them to go to hell.' She added, 'I must

admit, grudgingly, that they were perfectly gentlemanly about it.'

Harker wondered what she would feel and say if he told her he knew the truth. 'And this man Paulo – you were in love with him?'

She nodded. 'Wildly. Or I thought so. I'd only known him for a little more than a month. Now with the wisdom of hindsight I realize that I was only infatuated, and confused by my admiration for him. He was a very admirable man. And swashbuckling.' She smiled.

'And handsome, no doubt.'

'But that doesn't cut much ice with me. It is what's in here that counts.' She tapped her heart. 'And here.' She tapped her head. 'He was an entirely honest, dedicated social scientist, if that's the word, dedicated to the well-being and betterment of his people – a true Christian, but for the fact that he was an atheist, of course, being a communist. Dedicated. His men loved him. Several medals for bravery. And a great sense of humour. And a great reader, a very good conversationalist in both Spanish and English.'

Harker couldn't stand the man. No doubt a fantastic Latin lover too. 'Sounds good. But?'

'But,' Josie smiled, 'I now realize it wouldn't have worked. For one thing I'm not a communist. For another I espouse God. English is my mother tongue, and freedom of speech and of the press is my credo. And I'm a fully liberated Americano who regards herself as every inch her man's equal, not as a Latino wife. Oh, he was macho, Paulo. *Machissimo*.' She smiled wanly. 'And there was something else wrong. I knew it at the time but wouldn't admit it to myself – there was lots of lust, and lots of fun, but I knew deep down that it was just a rip-roaring affair, not love with a capital L.'

Harker was pleased to hear that: Señor Paulo sounded quite a tough act to follow. Before he could muster something appropriate Josephine asked with a smile, 'And what

82

about that extremely silly lady who nearly became Mrs Harker, then lost her marbles?'

Harker smiled. 'Well . . .' He was tempted to exaggerate, to match her description of Paulo, then he decided to do it straight. 'Well, rather like your Paulo, who had something missing, my Pauline – and that was truly her name, would you believe the coincidence? Pauline was also dedicated to liberal politics, uplifting the Africans. Trade unionism, defeating apartheid, et cetera. She was a teacher, and she was going to set the world on fire. Anyway, I was off in the bush most of the time, dealing with her pals the enemy, and she met this crash-hot stockbroker who took her away from it all.'

'And the first you knew about it was when you came back from the bush?' She shook her head. 'Well, he must have been one hell of a sexy stockbroker.' She smiled at him.

The compliment made Harker's heart turn over. And he longed to reach out across the table for her hand.

Then she confused him by changing the subject abruptly. 'And tell me, do you believe in God?'

For the next half hour, through another round of Irish coffees, religion was the animated if solemn topic. Yes, Harker did believe in a Creator but he had arrived at this conclusion by logic rather than by what had been instilled into him at Sunday School: the upshot was an inability, on the evidence, to conclude whether He was the Christian, Islamic, Buddhist, African or some other kind of god. Josephine on the other hand described herself as 'eighteen-carat Catholic': 'Alas, I believe in Heaven and Hell, the whole nine yards.'

'But why the "alas"?'

Josephine tossed back her head and grinned at the ceiling: '"Oh Lord, make me good, but not yet".'

Harker smiled. 'Saint Augustine.'

Josephine pointed a red fingernail at his nose. 'So you're not such an infidel after all. Inside that rugged exterior there's a Christian trying to get out . . .'

And then she said, halfway through the third Irish coffee, 'And they tell me, Major, you're a shit-hot sailor.'

Harker was surprised. 'Who told you that?'

'I've made a few enquiries around this club, and the feedback is you're probably a gentleman, maybe even a scholar, but certainly a very good sailor. But you don't come here often enough, they say.'

Harker was pleased with his credentials. And more pleased that she had enquired. 'Unfortunately I can't afford the time to come here often. But, yes, I've put my name down as crew for a few regattas and some kind skippers have taken me on. I've had a lot of fun.'

She leant forward: 'Oh, isn't sailing *fun*?' Her eyes sparkled. 'The wind, harnessing it, squeezing the most out of the sails? Even the skipper bawling you out. And getting drenched, and all the bullshit back in the clubhouse, the hot toddies and the post-mortems – I love it!' She looked at him happily. 'I'm a very competitive soul, Jack Harker. And I think you are too, huh?'

Harker ached to take her hand. Yes, of course he was fucking competitive, you have to be in the military. But a lot of the steam, the fight, seemed to have gone out of him since he had become a civilian in New York. 'Not as much as I used to be. Something to do with age.'

'Bull*shit*. You're not even forty. And you emerge from God-knows-how-many years of mortal combat and decide to become a publisher! That's a very competitive business.' Oh, he felt a fraud. She continued. 'It takes *balls*. In New York, of all places. Why did you choose America?'

'The American dream?' He smiled.

'See? Anyway, before I tell you my American dream, have you ever sailed across an ocean?'

'I've been crew in the Cape Town to Rio de Janeiro yacht race several times.'

'*Oh*, I'd love to do that! Was it scary? Those huge waves?'

'Well, you knew you had a good strong boat and a good strong crew.'

'*Love* to do it. And one day I will.' She hunched forward. 'Okay, my American dream: I'm going to make a pile of money out of writing, then buy a good strong boat and sail around the world.' She grinned. 'What do you think of that?'

Oh yes, Harker would love to do that. 'Marvellous.'

She said with a twinkle in her eyes, 'Okay, so what else are we compatible about, Major? We've canvassed books, booze and boating very successfully.'

'How about ballooning?'

'It's wonderful!' Josephine cried. 'Did it in Kenya, over the Serengeti game reserve. Oh, what a sensation! Tell you what, a friend of mine has started a ballooning business upstate, we'll do it one weekend!'

'Sounds good.'

She took a gulp of her Irish coffee. 'And, of course, you must be a parachutist?'

'Had to be.'

'And *I'm* a parachutist. Though only one jump, in England. But I've got my certificate. And *boy* – what a thrill. I'm dying to do it again.'

Harker was impressed. 'Weren't you scared?'

'Terrified shitless! Standing at that door? But, boy, when that 'chute bursts open you feel king of the world. And what a ride! I've got to do it again. Were you scared, the first time you jumped?'

'Hell, yes.'

'But then you liked it?'

'No. I wasn't worried about the jump any more, it was who was waiting for me on the ground that bothered me.'

'Hell, yes . . .' She looked at him solemnly. Then she sat up straight. 'What else are we both mad about? I suppose it's too much to expect, coming from darkest Africa, that you ski as well?'

'As a matter of fact,' Harker smiled, 'I'm a very good skier. I learned here in America. Almost every weekend during the winter I go upstate.'

Josephine slumped back and smiled at him broadly. 'You know, Major Harker, sir, if I weren't looking at you through rose-coloured spectacles as my future publisher I think I could develop a terrible case of the hots for you!'

Harker laughed. And his heart seemed to turn over. She burst into laughter with him, her eyes shining. It all seemed terribly funny. Oh, she would be very easy to fall in love with. 'You keep wearing your rose-coloured spectacles and I'll keep wearing mine.'

Her laughter subsided. She lowered her head slightly and peered at him from under her extravagant eyelashes. 'Does that mean you *are* actually, *seriously* looking at me as your potential author?'

Oh dear. He heard himself say, 'That's how we've come to be meeting today, isn't it?'

She looked at him. 'Wouldn't it be taboo?'

All Harker's good intentions had gone out the window. But he didn't care any more. He said, 'Out there in the market-place all kinds of doctors, lawyers, accountants are getting involved with their clients, their patients.'

Josephine looked at him solemnly. 'And do I understand correctly that despite that jazz about rose-coloured spectacles you find me attractive?'

Harker wanted to burst into laughter, but he put on a serious face.

'*Very* attractive.'

She said earnestly, with a touch of impatience: 'I mean as a *person*.'

Harker suppressed his grin into a smile. 'Your body is superlatively attractive. But, yes, I mean as a person. An intellect. A soul.' He meant every word.

'Not as a one-night stand?'

Harker had to restrain himself from laughing. He said solemnly, 'Correct.'

She regarded him closely. 'Because if it is just a one-night stand, fine. Provided that in the morning we look each other in the eye and say to each other, honestly, "Thanks, pal, that was fun." Hopefully, we'll be able to say that much at least – "that was fun but let's forget it happened".' She looked at him. 'Promise me you'll be honest?'

Harker couldn't conceal his wide smile. 'I promise.'

The corners of her lovely mouth twitched. 'And whatever happens in the morning, it won't affect your decision as to whether you publish my book or not?'

The remnants of Harker's conscience spluttered out. 'Absolutely not.'

'It's a deal?'

'It's a deal.'

She regarded him for a long moment; then her mouth went into a wide grin. 'Okay,' she said. 'So. As they say in the classics, my place or yours?'

The CCB paid for the lunch, despite her protests. 'I'd like to feel I'm retaining some measure of control over my virtue, Major – if I kick you out in the morning at least I won't feel in your debt!' It all seemed terribly funny – and very erotic: here was an unconditional agreement about carnal experimentation between two adults with no illusions, no promises, no complaints entertained afterwards. 'No prisoners taken, Major?' They were both smiling broadly as they walked down the steps of the New York Yacht Club and hailed a cab. And when the driver said 'Where to?' Josephine spluttered, 'What the hell, let's go to *your* place, driver!' It seemed uproariously funny.

But when they reached Harker's apartment block down on East 22nd Street, and opened the ornate wrought-iron gate into the archway, then crossed the courtyard towards the rear block, a solemnity seemed to descend on her. They walked in silence down the corridor to his door. While he unlocked his apartment, she stared at the floor. He opened the door and let her enter first. She took a few paces inside, then turned, and leant back against the wall.

She looked at him. 'Sure this is wise? Mixing business with pleasure?'

With the last vestige of his conscience Harker replied, 'I never said it was wise. I just said it wasn't unusual.' He added, 'And we're not in business yet.'

'But I'm hoping we will be,' Josephine said softly. She looked at him a long moment, then said solemnly: 'You won't feel compromised?'

Oh Jesus. 'Not if you won't.'

'How can I be compromised? You're the one who has to decide about my book.' She looked at him. 'If you want to pull out of our little deal, fine.' She was clutching her folder to her breasts.

This was his out. He could kiss her on the cheek and offer to call her a taxi with a clear conscience. But he didn't want to do that, he didn't care about his conscience. He asked, 'Do you want to pull out?'

She stood at the wall, looking at him from under her dark eyebrows. She shook her head slightly. 'Uh-uh.'

Harker grinned. Then Josephine smiled widely, and he took her in his arms.

He crushed her against him, her folder between them. Then her arm went around his neck, and she kissed him ravenously. Their teeth clashed and her tongue flashed into his mouth and she moaned. His hand slid down her back over her buttocks and thighs. Oh, the wonderful soft smooth feel of her. She thrust her pelvis against his loins and kissed him hard: then she broke the kiss, and leant back in his arms, eyes smouldering.

'Just please don't bullshit me about my book,' she breathed.

'It's a deal.'

Harker turned, took her hand, and led her down the short corridor, into his bedroom.

It was tidy, the double bed made because he had been away for most of the week. Josephine solemnly put her folder on to a table. Harker put his arms around her and kissed her again. Then he clutched her breast, and the full firm soft beauty of it made him groan. He plucked at the buttons of her blouse, and she peeled his jacket off his shoulders. Then her fingers went to his tie. They feverishly fumbled and pulled the garments off each other, their mouths crushed together, their hands groping and sliding. Then she turned out of his clasp, her hair awry. She opened the door to his bathroom.

She slid back the glass door of the shower and turned on the tap. Hot water began to gush. Steam billowed. She held out her hand to him. Harker struggled out of his trousers. Then he stepped under the teeming water and took her nakedness in his arms. And, oh, the glorious naked feel of her, her back and hips and belly and breasts and thighs against him as they kissed feverishly.

10

Harker woke up about midnight. Josephine was sprawled on the bed beside him, one long leg bent, her blonde tresses spreadeagled across the pillow. The bedside lamp was on, the night lights of Manhattan glowed in the big window.

He looked at her lying there: he could see the small scar on her left breast where she had shot herself, the exit scar near her armpit. Oh, she was beautiful, the swell of her hip, the line of her legs seemed the loveliest he had ever seen. And their lovemaking had been the most glorious he had ever known. The evening seemed a dream, a haze of breathtaking sensuality. And, oh, it felt like love.

What was he going to do about this?

He lay on his back, staring at the ceiling.

He had lived long enough to know it couldn't be love yet, of course. But it was certainly the start of that delicious phenomenon, and what was absolutely certain was that he did not want to let this woman go – he simply had to pursue it. But what was equally clear was that no way could he betray her.

So there was only one honourable thing to do: get this publisher-author masquerade right out of the way, tell her that Harvest House could not publish her book, tell Felix Dupont that Josephine did not want him to do so because she had a better publisher in mind – and tell Dupont that he would learn absolutely nothing new about her anti-apartheid activities because she wasn't interested in seeing him again.

Harker sighed grimly at the ceiling.

Yes, but when Dupont found out that he was still seeing her – as he would, sooner rather than later – the bastard would rub his hands in glee and put the screws on him to deliver information about her. He could not be party to a deception like that, so he would either have to deceive Dupont, or deliver insignificant information the bastard knew already.

Or refuse.

Yes, and if he refused he would be fired. Being fired from the CCB didn't worry him – but fired from Harvest House? His American work-permit revoked? Sent back to Pretoria?

Harker sighed again. The only alternative was to take up her offer of walking out: drop her right now. Tell her that last night was all a big mistake. And that Harvest House didn't think it wise to publish a political book . . .

Harker lay there beside her on the double bed in the glow of Manhattan's lights. Yes, undoubtedly, that is what he should do. Get out of this potential briar patch of multiple deceit while he could still do so with reasonable grace and a reasonably clear conscience. It would wound her feelings, but only her pride and that would be good, she'd keep well away from him, from the clutches of the CC fucking B. In fact *he* would be the only one to be hurt.

He lay there, thinking it through. At least he had to go through the motions of reading her book and rejecting it.

He hated this. With all his lustful heart he just wanted to roll over and take her beautiful body in his arms again. But he had best get up and start reading that book so he could tell her when she woke up that Harvest would not publish it.

He got up off the bed carefully so as not to waken her, and pulled on trousers. He picked up her folder and walked barefoot across the room. He stopped at the door and looked back at her. *What a crying-out pity . . .*

It was one o'clock on a Sunday morning in June. He was wide-awake now. He went into his kitchen, opened the refrigerator and got a beer. He snapped the cap off and upended it to his mouth. He sighed grimly and returned to the living room, picked up the folder, and sat down on the sofa.

And within ten minutes he knew that his decision, this whole thing, was an even bigger crying tragedy. Because this book was going to be brilliant.

Harker went to the kitchen and got himself another beer. *Christ, it was good.* He had only speed-read thirty pages in ten minutes but if the next two hundred were as good it was going to be a bestseller. Oh, it needed editing, she was a slash-and-burn writer who wrote wrote wrote, letting it all hang out, repeating herself shamelessly, flying off on descriptive tangents that left the reader both breathless and impatient. But it was brilliant. Harker returned to the sofa with his bottle of beer. He stared out of the bay window at the pretty little courtyard.

What was he going to say to her about this? How could he tell her that her book didn't have promise?

He took a tasteless swig of his beer.

You tell her it's got loads of promise but you don't consider it's suitable for Harvest House because Harvest doesn't publish political works, you solemnly advise her to take her brilliant book to Random House when it's finished, or Doubleday or one of the other big guns who throw money around like confetti hyping up books.

He sighed. Just the book Harvest needed to really put itself fair and square at the upper part of the publishing totem pole. But worse than that, much, much worse, was that not only did he have to tell her it wasn't worth Harvest's while publishing, he also had to watch this beautiful, talented woman walk off into the morning, freeze her out, tell his secretary to make excuses that he wasn't in, not return her calls. Whereas all he wanted to do was walk back into that bedroom and take her glorious body in his arms.

Harker took a deep breath, and reverted to her typescript.

It was called *Outrage*. It showed an astonishing grasp of the causes of the great South African historical drama: in the first forty pages Josephine Valentine transported the reader through the Frontier Wars of the eastern Cape, through the Great Trek that followed, the turbulent opening up of the Cape Colony's northern frontier by the Dutch wagoneers rebelliously moving away from the recent British occupation of the Cape of Good Hope and their Abolition of Slavery Act. Then came the horrors of the Mfecane, Shaka's crushing, the battles with Mzilikazi's Matabeles and Dingaan's Zulus, the establishment of the independent Voortrekker republics, the discovery of gold and the bitter Boer War that brought them back into the British Empire, through the horrors of two World Wars where the defeated Boers fought for their British victors against their German soulmates. It was a gripping piece of storytelling. Somehow, through these opening rampant pages, Josephine Valentine had managed to weave in her principal characters, American clipper-ship captains who traded, lived and loved amongst these rough tough Boers until the reader leapt a hundred years to 1948 when the Boers triumphed in the elections, won their beloved South Africa back from the British and immediately instituted their policy of apartheid to contain the Black Peril.

Harker stared through the window at the dark courtyard. The book showed a professorial understanding of the background to the modern curse of apartheid, its roots in the battles of not so long ago. All this Josephine had squeezed digestibly into forty bounding pages, making it high adventure: it showed remarkable narrative talent. How could he tell the author differently? Harvest House should jump for joy and shout Hallelujah for stumbling upon this book which should make any publisher a lot of money.

He gave a sigh, took a swig of his beer and read on.

The next thirty pages encapsulated the oppressive doctrine of apartheid in a speech in parliament by the descendant of the American traders which tore the doomed policy to tatters, heaping shame upon its creators, proving its folly, its cruelty, its repressiveness, evoking pity for its black victims. It was a brilliant speech made poignant by the vivid character who articulated it – everything anybody would want to allege against apartheid, logical argument unfolding irresistibly, yet all in narrative form.

Christ, this woman can write.

Harker got up off the sofa and walked back to the kitchen. He reached for a bottle of whisky and poured a big dash. He stood at the sink, staring out of the back window.

It squeezed his heart to turn down a book like this. And it broke his heart to walk away from this woman.

But he had to do both. If he did not, Dupont would get his hooks into her, Harker would either have to betray her or lie to Dupont – either way led to a treacherous, duplicitous life. No – he had to be cruel to be honourable, cruellest of all to himself – because all he wanted to do right now was walk back into that bedroom and enfold that beautiful, talented, captivating woman, and then wake up beside her at midday and take her to brunch and drink wine while he looked into her big earnest eyes and told her how great she was, how Harvest House was behind her all the way, what a talented person she was, how captivating, how she was stealing his heart . . . He walked back towards the living room and abruptly halted in the doorway.

The most beautiful, most talented, most captivating woman in the world stood before him, fully dressed, her book clasped to her breast, her hair awry.

'I'm going home now,' she announced. 'I'm afraid this has all been a mistake. Forgive me.' She stared at him from under her eyebrows.

Harker was astonished. 'What's a mistake?'

She waved a hand. 'Mixing business and pleasure. You're supposed to be my goddam publisher – I mean, that's what I *hoped* you are. And here I am falling into bed with you like a goddam Hollywood starlet flinging herself on the casting couch.'

Harker closed his eyes. Oh, this was being made easy for him. He heard himself say, 'Don't be ridiculous.'

'I've already been ridiculous!' she hissed softly. 'Not you – no man's got any sense when it comes to willing womanflesh!' She glared at him from under her dark eyebrows, then said, 'Believe me, Jack, that as a totally liberated woman I consider myself fully entitled to as much sexual freedom as you guys. And I've been around, in plenty of tighter corners than this. But this book –' she thumped it against her bosom – 'is the most important thing in my life right now and I was a fool to give you – my potential publisher – the impression that I'll whore for it, that I'm a brainless fuck-the-boss bimbo. So I'm going home, to spare you the embarrassment of dropping a panting wannabe author and to spare me the embarrassment of being dropped.' She pointed at him across the sofa: 'But I want you to know, Jack Harker, that I did *not* jump into bed with you in the hopes that thereby you would be persuaded to publish my pathetic book – I did so because, in my inflamed, intoxicated state I *wanted* to do so. And before I disappear out that door, never to darken it again, I want you to know that I do not, repeat *not*, expect you to publish my book. Goodnight and sorry I was such a pest.' She flashed him a brittle smile and turned for the door.

'Josie? It's not a pathetic book. It's brilliant.'

She stopped. She turned slowly and looked back at him. 'You're just saying that to protect my feelings.' She turned for the door again.

'Josie,' he said, 'it's brilliant. If the rest is as good as the pages I've read it deserves to be a bestseller.'

She had stopped again, her hand on the doorknob. He thought, Why am I saying this? He continued, to assuage his guilt, 'And please don't feel bad about last night. These things happen.'

'You mean your female authors are always hopping into bed with you?'

'I mean,' Harker said with a bleak smile, 'that I don't

misinterpret your motive. Indeed,' he added, trying to make a joke of it, 'I rather hoped it was because of my big blue eyes.'

She looked at him, unamused. 'So, I should come back to bed now, huh?'

Oh, he would love her to come back to bed now. 'No. And no hard feelings, that's the deal we made yesterday.'

She looked at him, then demanded, 'Do you want me to stay?'

Oh Christ. 'Only if *you* don't want to go.'

She snorted sulkily. Then: 'It's just that I feel such an ass. Christ, I'm twenty-six years old, I've been in half the battles of the world, and here I am giving a vivid impersonation of a silly little tart.'

Harker snorted. 'Please don't feel that, it's not true.'

Her hand was still on the doorknob. 'Do you really like my book so far?'

Harker had to dash back to his guns. 'Yes, it's good –'

'You said "brilliant" before!'

Harker had to steel himself. 'Yes, when it's edited.'

Josephine groaned. 'But I spent the whole of last fucking week re-editing for you!'

'Well, authors don't always make the best editors of their own work.' *Stick to your guns.* 'Josephine, it's good but I don't think Harvest House should publish it. I think that you'll do much better with a bigger house, like Random or Doubleday.' He added for good measure: 'I'm afraid it's too political for Harvest.'

He could see the cloud cross her soul. She stared at him a moment; then said, 'Of course. Thank you for the advice.'

'Josephine, your agent will advise you – you must get an agent – but I'm sure he'll tell you the same. Harvest is too small.'

She smiled thinly, still holding the door-handle. 'Thank you for that selfless advice.'

'Josephine, believe me –'

'The trouble is I *don't* believe you, Jack. If another publishing house can make it a bestseller I don't understand why Harvest is passing up the opportunity to do the same and make money!'

'Josie, we simply haven't got the budget to do all the publicity razzmatazz your book will need – will deserve.'

'Of course,' she said quietly. 'I understand. Perfectly. And, as you say, it's rather too political.' She forced a bright smile. 'And there's one thing I want *you* to understand perfectly, Jack: I went to bed with you only because I was inflamed by strong drink and lust – *not* because I hoped thereby to persuade you to publish my pathetic book!' She flipped the lock and opened the door.

Oh Jesus. 'Josephine – let me call you a taxi.'

'I've already called one, from your bedroom telephone. Bye-eee . . .' She flashed him a dazzling smile from the corridor.

'I'll come outside and wait with you till it comes.'

'Bye-ee.' She twiddled her fingers at him and closed the door.

Harker strode back to the bedroom. He cast about for his shirt, snatched it up off the floor, pulled it on as he hurried back to the front door. He dashed barefoot across the courtyard into the archway of the front block. He burst out on to East 22nd Street.

It was deserted. Josephine's taxi was disappearing round the corner. Harker retraced his steps grimly. He locked the door behind him and walked back to the bedroom. And there, on his bedside table, were her earrings. He looked at them regretfully. Then he collapsed on to the bed and stared up at the ceiling.

Oh, what a crying pity. He closed his eyes and breathed deeply, heart-sore.

Well, he had done the right thing, if that was any consolation. He had saved her from Dupont's clutches, sent her packing on her way to the success she deserved. At least he didn't have it on his conscience that he was deceiving her. But, God, what a crying-out-loud shame that Harvest House wasn't going to zoom to the top of the bestseller list for the first time in its life and make a fortune.

And even more sad was the fact that he was not going to possess that glorious body again. Not going to fall in love with her after all, the most captivating woman he had ever met – oh, those long legs, those perfect breasts – and her ravishing smile as she tumbled joyfully into bed and took him in her arms, her pelvis thrusting to meet him. He would love to be meeting her for lunch again today, love to go walking through the park with her, hand in hand, finding out about her, going through that delightful insanity of falling in love, feeling on top of the world, laughing and being frightfully witty and wise. Oh yes, he was infatuated, and it was a tragedy that it wasn't going to happen.

He swung up off the bed and looked at her earrings lying on the bedside table. A sad memento of a lovely day. He would take them to the office and post them to her. He walked to the kitchen and poured more whisky into his glass.

But it was for the best. She was a very sensitive person – you'd have to be on guard all the time lest you upset her. Volatile. Doubtless moody – most creative people are. A delicate bloom, yet with robust convictions. She would have been a difficult soul to be in love with, it would have been no bed of roses with her – perhaps indeed a bed of neuroses. Goddam writers are a load of trouble, all steamed up then flat as a pancake, locked in a love-hate relationship with their work.

Yes, it was all for the best. But, oh, what a crying-out pity.

11

He was woken late Sunday morning, with a hangover, by
the buzzing of his entry-phone. He draped a towel round
his waist and went to his front door. 'Yes?' he said into the
apparatus.

'Sorry, did I wake you?'

Harker's heart seemed to miss a beat. 'I was just getting up.'

'I've got a letter for you,' Josephine said. 'I was just
going to slip it into your mailbox, then I remembered my
earrings.'

'A letter?'

'Of apology, for flouncing out like that last night. I was
very boring and girlie and rude and unfair and I apologize,
you'd done nothing to deserve that. Okay?'

'Okay,' Harker smiled. 'And you weren't any of those
things.'

'May I come in, just to get my earrings?'

'Of course.' Harker pressed the button and hurried back
to his bedroom. He pulled on a bathrobe and ran his fingers
through his hair. He dashed into his bathroom and took
a swig of mouthwash. As he re-entered the living room
Josephine was crossing the courtyard. He opened his front
door wide. 'Good morning.'

'Hi.' Josephine entered, her brow a little lowered, half-
smiling. She seemed even more beautiful. 'Sorry again.'

'Nonsense. Sit down, I'll fetch your earrings.'

'I won't stay. Here's your letter.' She held out an envelope. 'Please don't read it until I've gone in case the earth
really does swallow me up.'

Harker smiled and put the letter on the dining table. Oh,

he didn't want her to stay, he didn't want to destabilize his resolution, but he had to be polite. 'Would you like some coffee?'

She hesitated. 'If you're having some.'

'Actually I'm going to have a beer. I was up until dawn.'

'So was I, must have drunk a gallon of wine. Re-editing my bloody book, I feel like death. It's far too intense and flowery. But . . .' She looked at him almost pleadingly. 'It's not a heap of crap, is it?'

Here we go again. Harker wanted to take her in his arms and tell her Harvest would be the luckiest house in town if it could publish it – but he had to stick to his guns. He turned for the kitchen. 'No.' He opened the refrigerator, took out two bottles of beer and reached for glasses. 'And don't, repeat *don't,*' he said as he re-entered the living room, 'edit out the flamboyance and the floweriness.' He handed her a bottle and glass. 'Leave those decisions to your editor. Just cut out some of the repetition.'

She was looking at him from under her eyebrows, hanging on his words. It was hard to imagine this was the hard-bitten photo-journo who screwed her way to the front lines. In fact he didn't believe that that was how she got there. 'You really think so?' She put the glass on the table, upended the bottle to her mouth and glugged down three big swallows, looking at him round the neck. She lowered it and breathed deeply. 'Thank God . . . I believe you now, you weren't bullshitting me last night. I know because that's exactly the decision I reached at dawn – "Leave it to the editor".' She flashed him a grateful smile and stretched up her arms. 'I'm so *happy!*'

Harker wanted to get off this painful subject. 'Won't you sit down?'

'No.' She held up her hand. 'I must fly.' She turned and began to pace across the room, head down, holding her beer bottle. She waved a hand. 'Neat,' she said.

Harker stood by the sofa. He did not sit down because then she probably would do the same. 'What is?'

She waved her beer bottle and paced back towards him. 'Your apartment. Tidy. Suppose that's because you were a soldier, soldiers have to be tidy, right?'

'The army drums that into you, yes.'

Josephine paced back towards the window. 'Like your mind,' she mused. 'You see things clearly. Put your finger on the essence straight away.' She smirked. 'You should see my apartment. Untidy as hell. Like my mind. A psychiatrist would make heavy weather of that, I guess.'

He would love to see her apartment. And into her untidy mind. She turned at the window, and pointed absently at the door behind him. 'What's through there?'

'Madam Velvet's.'

Josephine stopped. 'Did you say "Madam"?'

Harker smiled. 'Velvet. That door leads down to the basement. This apartment used to be Madam Velvet's upmarket whorehouse. Speciality, domination and sado-masochism. One of my authors, Clive Jones, he works part-time for *Screw* magazine. Know it?'

'Every New Yorker knows *Screw* magazine. Though nice folk like *me* don't read it.'

Harker smiled. 'Well, the first night Clive came around here he immediately identified this place as formerly Madam Velvet's den for the kinky – he had come here some years earlier to write it up for *Screw*. There're still some of her fixtures down there – the cage, a few ringbolts on the walls, the Roman bath. But she took the rack and whips and chains with her when she left. I just use it as my gym.'

'How exotic. Can we go down and have a look?'

'Sure.' He turned for the door.

A staircase led down into darkness. He switched on a light and led the way. They descended a dozen stone steps, into a stone-lined basement the size of the apartment above. A neon light illuminated the scene.

A bare cement floor had a few scattered rugs on it: there was a cycling machine. In one corner was a tiled whirlpool bath, empty. In another was a pinewood cubicle, a sauna.

Between them stood Harker's washing machine. In the third corner was a brick-built bar with a curved wooden counter, a few wooden shelves behind it: the other wall was lined by a row of rusty iron bars, a prison-cage, the door open.

'Wow,' Josephine said.

'And note the ringbolts on the walls, where the silver-haired sado-masochists liked to be chained up while Madam Velvet and her girls did their thing.'

'What an extraordinary place . . . Do the whirlpool and the sauna work?'

'Sure.'

'You should replace that neon light with flickering candles. And have a water-bed on the floor. Wow . . .' She turned and paced off across the dungeon, head down. 'Look,' she said, 'I fully understand that Harvest doesn't want to take the risk of publishing a political book like mine – and I'm not asking you to change your mind. *But* . . .' She turned and faced him across the dungeon. 'But I would be terribly grateful if you read the rest of my book and gave me your opinion on it. Your advice.' She explained wanly: 'It's all in my humble letter. I mean I'm terribly fortunate to have you here in New York, not only a literary man with artistic judgement but somebody who knows Africa well and can correct me on historical detail.' She appealed: 'Is that a terrible cheek, after the way I flounced out last night?'

Harker smiled. He knew he should make an excuse and get rid of this problem once and for all – but he did not have the heart. Nor did he want to. He heard himself say, 'Certainly, Josie.' He added, to salve his conscience. 'But you shouldn't rely on my judgement alone – you must get a good agent, and take his advice above mine.'

'Oh, *great*!' Josephine strode across the dungeon, wreathed in smiles, and planted a kiss on his cheek. She laced her hands behind his neck and leant back. 'Oh, I'm so lucky to have my own African guru!' Then she stepped backwards and waved a finger: 'But there'll be no more girlish nonsense like last night – our friendship is going to be purely platonic. That's the only thing I was right about yesterday, that's why I was so angry with myself.' Then she smacked her forehead: 'Oh, I am an ass! I don't mean I find you unattractive. On the contrary I find you *very* attractive. I simply mean –' she waved a hand – 'that it won't be a problem again.'

Harker grinned. 'A problem?'

'*You* know, getting all uptight about a simple thing like an injudicious one-night stand.' She looked at him. 'And,' she said, 'I insist on paying you a fee.'

'A *fee?*'

Josephine slapped her forehead again. 'Oh God, that sounds terrible.' She laughed. 'No, not a stud-fee – an *editorial* fee! Your face! *No* – you're going to be devoting many precious hours to my book and I insist I pay for your time. And thereby keep our relationship on a businesslike, platonic keel.'

Yes, he could be smitten by this woman. And, yes, as he wasn't going to publish her book, couldn't he pull this trick off, have his cake and eat it? He heard himself say, 'And what if I don't want your fee? What if it isn't a businesslike, platonic relationship?'

She looked at him from under her eyebrows. 'You mean if we become lovers?'

Harker grinned. 'Well, you haven't exactly got to commit yourself for life. It wouldn't be hard to just sort of carry on from where we left off last night.' Christ, what was he saying this for?

She looked at him solemnly. 'You mean we should go back to bed now?' Before he could deny it she made up her mind. 'No.' She held up a hand, 'No, just friends. So I insist on paying you a fee. You're going to help edit my book, I'm extremely grateful, I'm not going to endanger all that with emotional, messy, untidy sex stuff.'

Fine, so that was understood again, his conscience was clear – more or less.

'I'll help you with your book on two conditions,' he said. 'One, no fee. Two, you must tell absolutely nobody that I'm helping you. Not your friends, not your agent, not your publisher when you've got one – not even your father.' Harker did not want Dupont learning that he had any access to her book or her.

Josephine said earnestly: 'Do you mind telling me why not?'

'Personal reasons – and professional. And there's another thing I feel I must tell you.'

Then he changed his mind. As he was sticking to his decision about theirs being a platonic relationship he had been moved to confess to her that he had been less than honest about the Battle of Bassinga, that it was probably he who had shot her lover, that it was he who shot the fourteen-year-old boy with the wooden gun, that it was he, Harker, whom she had tried to kill and wounded so badly that he had been disabled out of the military, that he knew she had tried to commit suicide, that it was he who had plugged her wounds. But he stopped himself – why embarrass her by refuting the romantic version which she had given him, why mortify the woman by confronting her with her attempted suicide?

'What?' Josephine asked. 'What's the other thing?'

'Nothing,' Harker smiled.

'*What?*'

'No, it's unimportant.'

'*Please.*'

'It doesn't matter. Well, as that's decided why don't we go upstairs and have a decent bottle of champagne to kill the germs in that beer?'

Josephine took both his hands and squeezed. 'Thank you for helping me!' she said. 'I'm so excited. But I think I'd better fly now, I've got so much work to do if I'm going to take full advantage of your help, you've got me all fired up. And I can tell by the twinkle in your eye that if I stay for a bottle of celebratory champagne we'll end up in bed.' She pointed her finger to his nose: 'Platonic friendship only!'

He grinned. 'Absolutely. So let us seal the deal with that bottle of champagne.'

PART II

12

They had a lovely time that long hot summer of 1988.

Mostly she slept at his place. Before dawn she crept out of bed so as not to wake him, pulled on her tracksuit, shouldered her small backpack, donned her crash-helmet, tiptoed out, unlocked her bicycle and set off up the quiet canyons of Manhattan. She rode the sixty blocks to her apartment as fast as she could to get the maximum benefit from the exercise while the air was comparatively unpolluted. Soon after sunrise she was at her desk, chomping through an apple and two bananas as she peered anxiously at her computer screen, marshalling her thoughts, picking up the threads from last night. By lunchtime she had done about a thousand words: she changed into a leotard, pulled a tracksuit over it, stuffed some fresh underwear into her backpack and rode her bike flat out across town to her dance class at the Studio: for the next forty minutes she pranced around with thirty other women of various shapes and sizes in a mirrored loft, working up a sweat under the tutelage of Fellini, a muscle-bound bald gay who volubly despaired of ever making a dancer out of any of them. For the next half hour she had her first conversation of the day while she showered before adjourning to the health bar for a salad and colourful dialogue about boyfriends, husbands, bosses, work, fashions, waistlines. By two-thirty she was cycling back across town to knock out another five hundred words. At four-thirty she permitted herself the first beer of the day to try to squeeze out another two hundred words. At about five-thirty she hit the buttons to print and telephoned Harker at his office. 'The workers are knocking off, how about the fat-cats?'

'Okay, want me to pick up something?'

'I'll pick up a couple of steaks.'

'I'll get 'em, just you ride carefully, please.'

By six-thirty she was pedalling downtown to Gramercy Park, zipping in and out of traffic. She let herself into the apartment complex, locked up her bicycle in the archway and strode across the courtyard to the rear building. She let herself into his ground-floor apartment. 'I'm home . . .'

It worried Harker, her riding that bicycle in rush-hour traffic: he didn't mind her cycling in the early morning, but New York traffic in the evening gave him the willies – and she rode so fast. Once she did have an accident, skidded into the back of a braking car, took a bad fall, sprained her wrist and was nearly run over, but she was only concerned about her goddam bike. He offered to fetch her every evening in his car, he even offered to have a cycle-rack fitted so she could take the machine with her and cycle back to her apartment in the morning – but no, she insisted she needed the exercise both ways, 'after all we drink.'

'You're in magnificent condition; go to a gym if you need more exercise.'

'Gyms are so *boring*. Aerobic classes are *boring*. But riding a bike is a little adventure each time, you see people and things. That's why I like dancing, *expressing* yourself in motion, letting it all hang out . . .'

She was in very good condition but, yes, they did drink a good deal. Like most soldiers, Harker was accustomed to heavy drinking to unwind, and now that there was no combat he could unwind as much as he liked. Similarly, like most writers, Josephine drank to unwind.

'I spend my entire working day alone, without colleagues, without anybody to talk to except myself, nobody to seek advice from, and by the end of the day I'm pretty damn sick of myself and I want a bit of fun.'

Josephine redecorated Madam Velvet's dungeon, installed subdued lighting, put plants around the Roman-style whirlpool bath, scattered imitation bearskin rugs on the cement floor, stocked the ornate bar, filled the prisoners' cage with colourful imitation flowers; she even hung some kinky whips, chains and leather boots from the ringbolts in the wall. She brought in two armchairs, a television set with a video-player – and, in the corner, some more up-to-date gymnasium equipment. In one piece of daunting machinery the manufacturers had managed to squeeze every artefact for the torturous development of the muscular system.

'Everything you can get in a well-run gym, but in the privacy of your own home, to quote the advertisement.'

Harker looked at the gleaming contraption. 'Is it safe?'

'Don't you like it?'

'Shouldn't it be fenced off to protect visitors? Shouldn't we be wearing hard hats like those politicians on television? What's this costing me?'

'It's your birthday present!'

Every day he worked out before going to Harvest House; and he found it a turn-on to watch her sweating on the machine. He bought himself a mountain bike like Josephine's and on weekends they rode in Central Park and around Manhattan Island, sometimes across the Hudson River into New Jersey. In the fall they took a week off work and rode into upstate New York to see the riotously beautiful autumn colours. They rode almost five hundred miles in seven days and when they returned to Manhattan they were so glowing with health they did not want to stop.

'Then let's not. Let's say to hell with work and just keep going all the way to Florida . . .'

That night, lying in the hot whirlpool bath in Madam Velvet's dungeon, sipping cold wine, she said, 'Know what I want to do one day? Have a farm. Maybe only twenty acres, but in beautiful country like where we've just been, with a tumbling stream and some forest and pastures for grazing a few horses and a cow or two, and a big pond for ducks and geese who'll all have names, and a few chickens to give us eggs. And the horses will be mares so we can breed good foals, and we'll have a tractor so we can grow alfalfa for them. And we'll exhibit our animals at the livestock fairs and win prizes.' She smiled. 'I love New York, it's so stimulating, but really I'm a country girl.' She added, 'Our house won't be very big, more like a cottage really, because I don't like housekeeping, but it'll be *very* pretty. And my study will be upstairs, so I have a view of the pastures and the pond while I write.'

It was a pretty thought. 'Well,' Harker said, 'we can achieve all that, but what about my work?'

'Well,' Josephine said reasonably, 'you'll be able to do a great deal of your publishing work at home, of course, but our country place will be close enough to Manhattan for you to be able to drive down once or twice a week so you can keep your finger on Harvest's pulse – that'll be no sweat, particularly if you have a chauffeur. Daddy's got two, neither of them have enough to do and he's promised me the use of one of them if I move closer to him upstate.'

In the late autumn Josephine decided it was time to take Harker up to Massachusetts to meet her father. The country was beautiful. The gates to the Valentine property loomed up majestically against green pastures, a winding avenue of old oaks led up to an imposing mansion, the walls covered in ivy. Harker switched off the engine outside the ornate front door.

Josephine said, 'Just be your ever-charming self. You've been in tighter corners than this.'

Harker expected the big front door to burst open, the old man to come beaming out. But no: the door was locked. It was a butler who opened it.

The library was the size of a badminton court, the walls lined with laden bookshelves, the big room divided by more bookcases; a mezzanine floor was above, equally lined and laden. Denys Valentine, about sixty years old, tallish, thick-set, grey-haired, handsome, stood in front of his big marble fireplace, before the crescent of leather arm-chairs, whisky glass in hand, and said with a self-conscious smile, 'Josephine's told me a bit about you, of course, on the telephone. It's a pleasure to meet you.' He gave a thin smile. 'A great pleasure.'

Harker had been invited to sit down but he preferred to remain standing because his host was doing that. He knew he was being assessed and he felt on his mettle. 'Equally, Denys,' he said with a smile, and waited.

Denys Valentine cleared his throat, then said resolutely, 'Josephine has indicated to me that you and she are . . . more or less living together.' He cleared his throat again.

Harker resented this: he and Josie were mature people, for Chrissakes.

'That's true. But she continues to maintain her own apartment, where she works every day. We only see each other in the evenings.'

Denys Valentine said, with another thin smile, 'And in the mornings.'

Harker looked at him, also with a thin smile. 'That's true, yes.' He added: 'And I'm confident I speak for Josephine when I say we are very happy.'

Valentine turned a steely eye on Harker. 'But I am not happy. If you'll forgive me for saying so.' He paused. Then: 'I don't think any father likes his daughter living in sin.'

Harker had to conceal his smile. 'Sin?' He shook his head politely. 'I don't believe that's how it is, Denys. To be happy, to be in love, can hardly be a sin.'

Denys Valentine looked at him. 'Out of wedlock it is a mortal sin, I'm afraid, the scriptures are clear. "Cursed are the fornicators." Quote, unquote.'

Harker had to stop himself smiling. What do you say to that? So he nodded politely.

'Well, Jack?'

'Well what, Denys?'

'What are you going to do about it?' Valentine paused, then went on, 'To me it is clear. You must either desist or you must marry. Immediately.'

Harker looked at him with a twinkle in his eye. 'And

113

which of those two options would you prefer to see happen?'

Valentine shifted, then turned to the liquor cabinet. 'How's your glass?'

'Fine at the moment.'

'Please help yourself when you're ready.' He poured whisky for himself and said: 'I want what's best for Josephine. Clearly it is not good for her – for her immortal soul – to be living in sin. But alas that doesn't mean that getting married is necessarily good for her either.' He turned back to Harker. 'I must be frank and tell you that I have great difficulty in reconciling myself to your previous career, Jack.'

Harker frowned. 'You mean you don't like the fact that I was in the South African military?'

'But more that that,' Valentine said, 'I am a pacifist. When I was drafted into the army during the Korean War I was a conscientious objector at heart. I don't believe in taking human life – that's my Catholic belief, my family's belief. The only reason I didn't appeal against being drafted was because my law degree and a few of my father's friends in politics guaranteed me a non-combatant role in the Judge Advocate's department, doing court-martials.'

Harker smiled politely. 'Josephine has never indicated that she's a pacifist.'

Valentine said resolutely, 'The only circumstance that justifies the taking of human life is to protect the lives of those whom one has a legal and moral duty to defend – like your children. However . . .' He smiled thinly. 'You're completely finished with the army now, thank the Lord – Josie tells me you don't miss it at all. However,' Valentine said, 'there remains the matter of whose army you were in – namely the South African.' He glanced at Harker. 'I have great difficulty with this. Josephine has tried to explain that you were fighting communism, and evidently she has accepted your . . . she has adjusted to the anomalous situation. But so far I regret I am unable to do so.' He cleared his throat. 'All my family are dedicated to democracy. To me

114

it is incomprehensible that an honourable soldier can fight on the side of South Africa's apartheid regime.' He looked at Harker and spread his hands. 'I'm sorry if I offend.'

Harker said quietly: 'Would you rather your honourable soldier fought on the side of Godless communism which does not permit any form of democracy?'

Denys Valentine gave him a wisp of a smile. 'Two tyrants fighting each other makes neither right. But since you ask, I am sure that the life of the average worker, the man-on-the-street in Russia, is more just and congenial by far than that of the average black man in South Africa.'

Harker said grimly, 'I do not defend South Africa's apartheid, Denys. However, I assure you that it is much better by far than the destructive, chaotic poverty and bloody tyranny that communism and the Cold War have forced on the rest of Africa. And I assure you that the only political power capable – or willing – to take on communism in Africa these days is South Africa, I assure you that it is highly advisable to allow South Africa to defeat the communist tyrant before apartheid itself is defeated – as it will be soon, by its own people. Because without South Africa communism will overrun what's left of Africa and the poor bloody continent will never recover.' He raised his finger. 'In other words, the only hope for Africa is *South* Africa – the only hope is that it will defeat the communist onslaught, and thereafter become the economic engine that will slowly revive the rest of Africa.' He ended, 'Without South Africa's survival, the rest of Africa is a basket case, for ever.'

Denys Valentine looked at him. 'You think that South Africa is going to rejoin the human race soon? When will this miracle come to pass?'

Harker resented the tone, not the disbelief. 'When the war in Angola ends – and that's going to happen soon. There are overtures by Cuba already. Russia cannot afford the Angolan war much longer – it's an economic basket case and this new president – Gorbachev – is pulling Russia's horns in. Soon he'll sue for peace. South Africa will readily accept because the Angolan war is our Vietnam too and these international sanctions are starting to bite hard.' He took a sip of whisky. 'When the communist threat is removed, the new South Africa will start.'

Valentine looked dubious. 'And then what? How do you feel about being governed by blacks?'

Harker was tired of being subjected to tests. He said, 'I'm cautiously optimistic.'

Valentine frowned. 'Why "cautiously"?'

Harker sighed. 'Well,' Harker said, 'the rest of Africa has been chaotically misgoverned. But there's a chance it will be different in our case because the failures of Africa are in part attributable to Africa being a Cold War battle-ground – both Russia and China threw money at the black tyrants to get them on side and so the West did the same, so mis-government was allowed to flourish. Tyranny, corruption, genocide, inefficiency were rewarded with more and more money which the tyrants put into their Swiss bank accounts while poverty and disease descended on their unfortunate people. So a culture of shameless corruption developed which was tolerated by the rest of the world. But when the Cold War ends, that tolerance will change – if black politicians do not behave they'll have their aid cut off. So I think South Africa's black leaders will not have the freedom to abuse the country as happened in the rest of Africa. They'll have to behave themselves.'

Valentine's judicial countenance turned irritated. '*Behave* themselves? Isn't that rather arrogant? Have you shared your views with Josephine?'

Harker was irritated too: he resisted the temptation to say, They're hardly views, they're fucking facts. 'Of course I have. And she agrees with some of it. On other points we agree to differ.'

'And what do you think of this book she's writing?'

Harker hoped he was changing the focus. 'Well, I don't know much about it,' he said.

116

'But she says you're her *guru*.'

Harker was annoyed that Josephine had told him. 'She discusses parts of it with me sometimes, but she only allows me to read small bits now and again. But what I've read is very good.' He added, 'I'm not acting as her editor.'

'Nor, I believe, do you intend to publish it?' Valentine added, 'I must say I agree, never mix business with pleasure.'

'It's more a matter of finance, Denys. Harvest is a small house. We published twelve books last year – two of them lost money, the other ten made a respectable profit, but not enough to enable us to put the effort into Josie's book that it will deserve – advertising, publicity tours, et cetera.' He looked at the older man.

'And what do you think of her agent, Priscilla Fischer.'

'She's a tough cookie, Priscilla. She'll make sure Josie gets the best deal in town.'

Denys Valentine took a sip of whisky, then said: 'Reverting to the matter of you two living together. Have you any plans about marriage?'

Harker smiled uncomfortably. 'It's a bit early to say – we've only known each other a few months. But we have talked about it. I think Josie feels she'd like to retain her freedom for a while yet, to experience more of the world. That's not unusual in writers.' He looked at the older man, and waited.

'And how do you feel about that?'

'If and when we get married I want her to feel she's seen life and has plenty to write about.'

'"If and when"? I'm pleased to hear that you're so realistic about this.' He took a self-conscious sip of whisky. 'Because I also don't think Josie's ready for marriage yet. She's an exceedingly intelligent and talented person and she shouldn't be burdened with the responsibilities of marriage for a long time yet – children and so forth.'

Harker understood loud and clear that he was being

warned off. 'Well, Josephine will know her own mind in the fullness of time.'

'But will she?' Valentine said. 'Artistic people often don't know their own minds about anything although they think they do. Heads in the clouds most of the time.'

Harker resented the innuendo. 'She's always seemed pretty sensible to me, Denys.'

'Oh, extremely intelligent – all her life she's been an A-grade student capable of figuring things out for herself. But, for all that, she is a dreamer who is really motivated by . . . unrealistic, unwise impulses.'

Unwise impulses like me? 'Well, Denys, you seem to be in a most unsatisfactory situation. You don't want Josephine to live in sin with me, and yet you don't want her to marry me.' He restrained himself from saying, 'So what the hell are you going to do about it?'

Valentine cleared his throat, fiddled with his glass, then said, 'I'd like to ask you for your cooperation – yours and Josephine's.' He paused. 'Don't see each other for six months.'

Harker was taken aback. 'And after six months?'

'If after six months you still want to be together, so be it. I'll accept it, but you'll only have my blessing if you marry.'

Jesus. Harker wanted to smile. It was the sort of thing a father might say to the suitor of his teenage daughter. Before he could muster a response, Valentine continued.

'I'm prepared to make it as easy as possible for the pair of you to cooperate – I'll pay for Josie to go abroad for those six months. Anywhere she likes.'

Jesus. You are *prepared* . . . The arrogance of it. 'And if we do not cooperate with you?'

'I regret having to say this, but if you do not, I will not give either of you the time of day ever again.'

Harker looked at the man. *Jesus*. And Jesus again! He could not conceal his smile. 'Have you discussed this with Josephine?'

'Not yet. But she has an inkling of my disquiet.'

Your disquiet? Harker took a breath. 'Well,' he said, 'I cannot speak for Josephine, of course, but I can assure you right now that you will *not* have my cooperation, Denys. And I'll be astonished if you get Josephine's. I point out that not only are we both adults but we are both rather worldly ones who have seen rather a lot of life – and death. I'll be astonished if you can tempt Josephine into cooperation by offering her an air-ticket to anywhere.' He resisted the temptation to add that he very much doubted she would be intimidated by the man's refusal to speak to her.

Valentine said grimly, 'You are doubtless aware that Josephine inherits a great deal of money on her marriage or on her thirty-fifth birthday, whichever happens soonest. From a trust set up for her by her grandfather.'

Doubtless? Harker looked him in the eye. 'Josie has mentioned it. But I don't know the details.' That was a lie.

'No? Well, she will inherit at least two million dollars. Meanwhile, until her marriage or thirty-fifth birthday I, as trustee, have a discretion as to whether or not to pay her an annual allowance of fifty thousand dollars. Since Josephine's come back to America and begun writing this book I've been paying her that amount.'

Harker knew this too. 'Lucky Josephine.'

'You didn't know?'

Harker lied. 'As I said, I didn't know the details.'

Valentine smiled thinly. 'Strange. Josephine told me on the phone last night that she had told you all about it.'

Harker looked the man in the eye. 'Really? So it appears I have forgotten. But what is definite is that I resent your insinuations that I am after Josephine's money.' He smiled. 'Denys,' he added.

Denys Valentine looked at him grimly. 'Be that as it may, as the sole trustee, I have the authority to withhold Josephine's annual income and let it accumulate if for any reason I feel it is in her best interest. For example, if Josephine were wasting the money.'

Harker smiled. 'On unworthy lovers who are only after her loot. Quite right too, Denys – Josie's grandfather was a wise man to protect his granddaughter from rogues. But I am hurt, and angered, that you evidently thus categorize me. And I am taken aback, to say the least, that a supposedly responsible lawyer like you will use your trustee's powers to penalize your own daughter on so little evidence that I am a rogue.'

Denys Valentine's grey eyes were steady. 'I have said no such thing, Jack,' he said smoothly. 'I have only confided in you, been upfront, as the saying goes. And my mention of my powers of trusteeship was intended to elucidate, not intimidate.' He smiled. 'And so I'll pass over your unfounded anxieties and proceed to the next question any conscientious father would ask. Namely, if you do marry my daughter are you able to support her in the manner to which she is accustomed?'

Harker wanted to retort, 'Please remember that Josephine is over twenty-one, Denys, and it is not within your legal power to prohibit her doing a fucking thing.' But he said quietly: 'Unfortunately, I am not, Denys. Few men my age would be unless they had wealthy parents.' He added, 'Or grandparents.'

'Then do you mind indicating what your financial situation is?'

Harker looked at him. 'Yes, I do mind. However, I will tell you.' He took an extravagant breath. 'I have a military pension of about three thousand pounds a year which, at today's rate of exchange, is only about five thousand dollars. Still it pays for my booze. As managing director of Harvest, I give myself a salary of twenty-four thousand dollars a year – that's not a great sum but Harvest is a new house.' He paused, then proceeded to gild the lily: 'In addition I own fifty-one per cent of the shares in Harvest House. And my small apartment in Gramercy Park.' That was only technically true: although he was the registered shareholder of fifty-one per cent of Harvest's shares, they were held by him on behalf of Westminster NV, the CCB's parent company in the Netherlands Antilles. The apartment was leased. He smiled at Denys Valentine. 'That about puts you in the picture. Except for that middle-aged Mercedes parked out there.'

'And do you mind telling me who owns the other forty-nine per cent of Harvest House?'

Yes, Harker certainly did mind – no way did he want to discuss who was behind Westminster NV. He said, 'It's all recorded at the Registrar of Companies, or whatever he's called.'

'I know, I've seen those records. The other forty-nine per cent is owned by a company called Westminster NV. I mean, who owns the shares of Westminster?'

Harker's pulse tripped. Christ, he'd searched the records.

'I don't know. Westminster is a trust company set up by another trust company in England called Westminster International. All to do with tax laws which I don't try to understand. And Westminster International owns, in whole or part, the publishing house in London called Five Seasons, which one way or another set up Harvest House in New York.' He added, 'Harvest House existed only on paper when I was sent here to take it over.'

'How did you land that job?'

Jesus, did the man suspect the CCB existed? Or something like it?

'When I was invalided out of the army, friends got me a job as a trainee executive in Five Seasons in London. After six months they offered me the Harvest job in New York – and the shares.'

Valentine smiled thinly. 'You must have impressed them. You must be good.'

Harker looked at him. What the hell did that mean? Before he could muster a response Valentine said: 'I must confess that when Josie first mentioned you to me, I had you investigated.'

Harker's pulse tripped again. *Investigated?* He controlled the fluster in his breast. 'Indeed? Where?'

'I engaged a reputable firm of private investigators in New York to look into your background.'

Harker stared at him, trying to look unperturbed. *Oh Jesus.* 'Well?'

Valentine continued: 'And through lawyers I have contact with in South Africa, I arranged for private investigators to look into your history there.'

Harker felt himself go white. 'In South Africa, indeed? And?'

Denys Valentine smiled thinly. He said, 'And in fairness I must tell you that I have heard nothing adverse. Neither from the publishing industry nor from the military.'

Harker wanted to close his eyes in relief. Instead he glared.

'I'm *so* glad. So?'

'So the ball's in your court. You know my views – and my wishes. And now I think we should go and get ready for dinner, don't you?'

Harker put his glass down on the mantelpiece. 'No,' he said. He was going to say 'Like hell'. 'No, I'll go and find Josephine and send her in here so you can put your ultimatum to her – your draconian ultimatum, if you don't mind my saying so. And the ball is no longer in my court, Denys, because I've made my decision. I'm sure you'll understand when I say I won't be staying for dinner, whatever Josie decides, much less for the night.' He smiled coldly. 'So it only remains for me to say goodbye, Denys. And to add that I very much hope you change your mind and accept your daughter's decision if it is the same as mine.'

Harker was going to say if she tells you to stick your ultimatum up your ass, but restrained himself. He turned and walked down the rows of bookshelves, out of the library.

He found Josephine alone in the living room. 'What's the matter?' she asked.

'Your father wants to see you in the library,' he said. 'Immediately.'

She frowned. 'You've got a face like thunder. What's the matter?'

'I'll be waiting for you in the car.' He turned and walked out of the living room.

He went upstairs to his bedroom, retrieved his overnight bag. He descended the sweeping staircase, went outside and got into his car.

Ten minutes later Josephine emerged through the big front door. She was carrying her overnight bag too. She strode to the car, flung open the door, slung her bag on the back seat and got in. Her eyes were red, she had been crying. She looked at Harker.

'He says you don't love me. That you're a soldier of fortune. He says you're only after my money.'

Harker snorted. 'So?'

'I told him to go to hell.'

Harker sighed and shook his head. 'So he's going to cut off your allowance under the trust? Fifty thousand dollars a year.' He looked at her. 'Are you sure our relationship is worth that?'

She looked at him angrily. 'Don't you start! Those were exactly his words. Yes, I am quite sure, goddammit! But that's only half the point. The other half is I goddam refuse to be bought, to prostitute myself. I'll love and live with who I goddam choose, not who he or anybody else dictates!' She jerked her head. 'Let's go!'

'Lot of money, Josie.'

Josephine glared at him. 'Exactly what he said – word for fucking word!' She snorted and looked away. 'Yes, a lot of money. But in terms of my grandfather's will any undistributed income gets ploughed back into the trust so I get it all in the end anyway. Besides, I think Dad will come round, change his mind. I think he's just waving a big stick now. He so detests apartheid. And he's such a strict Catholic – when I was a kid I wanted to be a nun, thanks to him and my poor mother.' She turned and glared through the windscreen. 'You're not a soldier of fortune, are you?'

Harker closed his eyes.

'No, Josie.'

Josephine turned and clutched his knee. 'Oh, I'm sorry that Daddy upset you, I really do believe you, I know he's talking nonsense but that's what happens when one has family rows and your heavy-duty father says something momentous like your lover doesn't love you.'

'Poisons the mind.'

She gripped his knee. 'My mind's not poisoned. And Dad didn't mean it to be *poisoned* – he really means everything he said for the best, in my best interests as he perceives it – it's just that he's so . . .' She waved her hand. 'So *powerful*. He's such a big wheel in Boston, the earth trembles when he arrives, he's so accustomed to getting his own way. He fully expected both me and you to knuckle under in there today, to accept his terms of six months apart.' She looked at him and squeezed his knee again. 'You do love me, don't you?'

Harker closed his eyes. 'Jesus. This is what happens when parents interfere.' He turned to her: 'Yes, I love you, Josephine. More to the point, are you sure you love me?'

She looked at him. Then she jerked her thumb at the big house. 'I've just knocked back fifty thousand bucks a year. That says I love you, doesn't it?'

Harker smiled. 'So why don't we just get married? Tomorrow. And silence our goddam critics.'

Josephine looked at him. 'Tomorrow? You can't get married that fast in this state, can you?' She shook her head. 'This isn't Nevada.'

'Then let's go to Las Vegas.'

Josephine frowned. 'But I'm Catholic, Jack. A Las Vegas

marriage would not be recognized by the Church.' She added: 'Or by my father.'

'So we can have another religious ceremony six weeks later or however long it takes to satisfy the requirements of the Catholic Church. But we'll have satisfied the terms of your grandfather's trust.'

Josephine said slowly: 'I'll have satisfied the terms of the Valentine Trust. And I can collect the two million plus dollars.'

'Exactly. It's your goddam money, you're an adult – how could your father deprive you of it?'

'He's not depriving me of it – he's only postponing my receipt of it.'

'But meanwhile he's putting you to hardship until you come up to his exquisite expectations of marrying a nice Catholic stockbroker who's a fund-raiser for the Democratic Party – meanwhile you're desperately trying to finish your book, scrimping and wishing you'd never disobeyed Big Daddy. Until finally you'll go limping back, say you're very sorry and that you've cut me out of your life. That's his strategy.'

Josephine looked through the windscreen. 'He said you would now ask me to marry you. So that we could access the trust money.'

Harker glared. Then: 'Jesus.' He reached and twisted the ignition angrily. The engine started. 'Well, consider my offer of matrimony withdrawn.'

'Darling!' Josephine leant out and switched off the engine. She looked at him pleadingly. *'Please* – I'm only telling you what he said in there, not what I think. I do *not* think you're after the money.'

Harker glared through the windscreen. 'Okay, so let's get married.'

Josephine sighed, and put her hand back on his knee. 'Yes, I do want to marry you. One day. I know I do. But not yet. Not because I'm worried we don't know each other well enough, and not because I'm not sure whether

I love you enough. But because of *me*. I feel there's still things I want to do, I *need* to do, places I've got to see, and research and . . . feelings I've got to feel, for my soul, for my worldliness – for my wisdom. Before I nail myself down to the responsibilities of marriage.'

'You can still do those things when you're married. I won't stop you going off and researching subjects. You're a writer, for Christ's sake, I don't expect to change that.'

'I'm not afraid of that,' she said. 'It's *me*. I just don't feel ready for being responsible for your *happiness*. I just don't feel . . . *mature* enough. For a while I want to just coast along and enjoy our affair, I don't want it spoilt by any deadlines, I want it to be an entirely voluntary association of two lovers without legal constraints.' She looked at him and squeezed his hand. 'If I have to go away to research something or photograph some dramatic event I will be faithful to you because I *want* to be, not because the laws of marriage require it of me. Am I making sense?'

Harker sighed grimly, still angry with her father. Yes, what she was saying made some kind of sense, emotionally. In fact, he felt the same way. It was a relief, emotionally, that she was putting his proposal on hold for the time being. Emotionally, but not financially. 'No,' he said, and twisted the ignition. The car started again.

'*Jack* . . .' Josephine clutched his arm. 'Please believe that I love you. The rest will come!'

He grinned at her humourlessly. 'What's the rest? And please don't echo your father and say "the money"!' He released the handbrake and let out the clutch with a crunch of gravel.

Josephine slumped back in her seat. 'Oh boy.'

'Yes,' Harker said as he drove down the avenue of oaks. 'Oh boy.'

'This is what happens when parents interfere.' Josephine turned to him. 'Jack, when I said the rest will follow I was not, repeat *not*, referring to the fucking money!'

'Good.'

'Then why are you angry?'

Harker swung the old Mercedes out of the big gates and rammed the gears.

'Oh Christ . . .' Josephine groaned. She slumped back.

13

Although he was supposed to be her guru, Josephine seldom let Harker read her book: she was possessive about it, nervous about his judgement. 'No, I want to put my best foot forward . . .' That was fine with Harker – the less he knew of her book, the less he could be somehow forced to tell Dupont, the less she could hope he might publish it. But, for the purposes of her book, she often discussed South African politics, and that situation was bad.

The vast industrial areas and sprawling black townships around Johannesburg and Pretoria were in chaos as the ANC's youth strove to make the country ungovernable with strikes and boycotts and running battles with the police, as the ANC fought for political turf with the Inkatha Party's Zulus. Down in the lush lowlands of KwaZulu Natal open warfare raged between ANC Zulus and Inkatha Zulus, the rolling green hills resounding with the clatter of AK47 gunfire and the clash of spears and axes. Thousands were killed; sixty thousand people rendered homeless, fleeing into the white towns, gangs of starving children roaming the forests robbing travellers, raiding farms.

'The South African government is promoting this black-on-black violence,' Josephine insisted, 'in order to create the impression that blacks are incapable of behaving democratically. And in order to divide and rule – that has always been the Afrikaners' strategy: let the Inkatha Party smash the ANC, let Inkatha do our dirty work for us.'

Harker didn't agree: he insisted the warfare was simply typical African politics at work. 'Josie, Africans don't really understand our Western democracy – they can't accept the principle of a loyal opposition who wants to try to take over

128

the government at the next election. In their culture such opposition is a threat that must be crushed. Might is right in African politics, whoever gains power clings to it by the sword – opposition is not tolerated. That's why so many of these African countries are one-party states.'

'Then why isn't the South African government sending in the army and police to stamp out the violence?'

'When they stamp it out in one place it breaks out in another.'

'Bull*shit*, Jack, the government has been sitting on the lid of the boiling apartheid pot for decades by brute force, they could saturate the countryside with troops and police if they wanted to. But they don't want to, they want the ANC and Inkatha to exsanguinate each other so they can divide and rule . . .'

And there were angry allegations in the South African press of a 'Third Force' which was instigating and orchestrating the violence, the ANC furiously declaring that this was government-sponsored in order to make the black political parties destroy each other. The government loudly denied it but many believed it, including the Anti-Apartheid League and Josephine Valentine. Harker denied it although he thought it quite possible: there was the CCB, so why shouldn't there be a Third Force? If the army had operatives like him all over the world getting rid of the odd enemy of the state, why shouldn't the government organize a Third Force to knock the shit out of the state's enemies inside South Africa? Indeed perhaps the Third Force *was* the CCB, or part of it. And oh *God* the thought sickened him. Was he part of an organization that instigated such violence as was raging in Zululand, civil war? Or was it some other branch of government, like the police? Please God it was the police, not the army. Or was this Third Force just the work of a rogue cabal of right-wing officers? That was a distinct possibility.

'But, my dear fellow, there is no such thing as a Third Force,' Dupont said. 'That's an invention of the ANC. They're

129

terribly embarrassed that their blacks are so patently incapable of democratic behaviour so they try to put the blame on the government . . .'

And then there were new rumours in the press that the government was training a secret battalion of Zulus on the Caprivi Strip as a massive hit-squad to be let loose on the ANC. The government again denied it, but one day truckloads of heavily armed Zulus in war regalia came up from the lowlands on to the highveldt around Johannesburg without the police making any effort to stop them. All hell broke loose in Soweto and the other black townships as pitched battles raged between the Zulus and the ANC battalions, machine guns rattling, flames leaping, smoke barrelling, roadblocks thrown up, houses burned down, thousands killed and injured.

'This proves there's a Third Force,' Josephine cried. 'Why didn't the police and army stop those truckloads of Zulu warriors? Because they were the hit-squads that the government has been training on the Caprivi Strip . . .'

And, oh God, Harker wanted out, wanted to wash his hands of the CCB, of the whole goddam South African army. He was a soldier, a professional, not a spy, not a cloak-and-dagger man, certainly not a Third Force man who associated with instigators of civil war. And, dear God, he wished he could fax off his resignation to Pretoria, tell them he wanted to retire right now . . .

But, alas, he could not do that – for one very compelling reason: Harvest. If he resigned he would lose Harvest House, and he loved the place. Jack Harker wished he'd chosen publishing as a career a hundred years ago when he graduated from high school – wished he'd studied English Literature instead of goddam military science. He had studied battles instead of books, enemies instead of authors, politics instead of poetry. In short Jack Harker had discovered he was a square peg in a round hole. In a *treacherous* hole, a black hole of unofficial and deniable murder and mayhem, if Josephine and the left-wing press were to be believed. And now secretly he believed them. And, God, he wanted out. But he could not, for three reasons: money, money and money.

Firstly he needed the salary Harvest House – or Military Intelligence – paid him. Secondly, he needed the apartment that Military Intelligence provided for him. Thirdly, he needed the expense account that the military allowed him in order to run a publishing house in New York: he had never abused this, but he had grown accustomed to the good life it permitted. But more important than all that: when the CCB was disbanded, as it surely one day would be when apartheid collapsed, Harvest House would be sold: in terms of his deal with the CCB he would have first option to buy it at a fair price, and there was no way he was going to forgo that golden opportunity by quitting the army prematurely – he had built Harvest House into a prosperous publishing company, for Chrissakes, and he loved every stick and stone of the place, every dollar it had in the bank.

But these days Josephine never allowed Harker to read any of her book. 'I want it to be as perfect as possible before you advise me on it . . .' That was just fine with Harker – the less he knew about that book the better, and with a bit of luck he might not have to have anything to do with it because Josephine's new literary agent, Priscilla Fischer, was a flashy, fleshy, hard-boiled Jewish lady who specialized in books by hard-boiled authors of feminist persuasion. She represented one of Harker's authors and what he knew of Priscilla Fischer he didn't much like. 'Piranha Fisch' she was called in the publishing business, and particularly in Harvest House. Harker considered her the wrong agent for Josephine, though he didn't say so. But Piranha Fisch also didn't much like Jack Harker and so she probably would not suggest he publish Josephine's book. And certainly Piranha would get Josephine the best deal in town, beyond Harvest's budget – which was what

Harker wanted. It was almost the truth when he answered Dupont:

'Look, you can forget about that bloody book, her agent hates my guts and if it's publishable at all she won't give it to Harvest. And I haven't a clue what it's about except it's anti-apartheid. So what? With all the anti-South African literature around what difference does one more half-assed book make?'

'She's a goddam troublemaker.'

'She's just another starry-eyed liberal.'

'*She*,' Dupont said, 'is a thorn in the flesh and I want you to get some dirt on her! How much do you see of her?'

It really surprised Harker that Dupont didn't know about his relationship with her yet. But then he, Harker, was supposed to be in charge of espionage in New York, not Dupont. 'I see her,' he said, 'at the yacht club. We meet for drinks and dinner occasionally, we're on friendly terms but she doesn't confide in me.'

'Well, get on confidential terms,' Dupont commanded, 'even if you've got to fuck the bitch – that shouldn't be much of a hardship. And what about her Anti-Apartheid League's activities?'

'I've sent you everything I know. They're an open book, they shout it from the rooftops, it's in the press. They're fund-raising for the ANC, stuffing leaflets though letter-boxes, picketing the South African consulate and preaching to the converted – so what's new?'

'They're lobbying congressmen across America to pressurize Ronald Reagan into pulling out of Angola, that's what. And to impose sanctions.'

'Sure, that's in the press too.'

'Pretoria wants it,' Dupont said, 'from the horse's mouth *before* her friends swing into action across America, so that our diplomatic boys can try to do something about it *before* it gets to Congress. *That*, Major, is what Intelligence is all about! So get on to this woman with whatever blandishments are necessary – offer to publish her fucking book right now, if necessary – but find *out*! Join the fucking League yourself, attend their meetings, get elected to the local committee . . .'

Harker did join the Anti-Apartheid League, but it was Josephine who persuaded him to do so, not Dupont. Lying in the whirlpool bath one night that autumn, she said, 'That first time I slept with you and woke up in the middle of the night so angry with myself? Well, one of the reasons – apart from feeling I'd made a tart of myself – was that I suspected you were a racist. The next morning, I realized I'd probably been unfair. Now, of course, I know you're not a racist.'

He wondered where this conversation was heading. 'Thanks, pal. So?'

'Well, would you consider addressing one of our meetings? Just a short speech, say twenty minutes, about the realities of apartheid. You coming from South Africa, and being a publisher to boot, would make it most interesting to our members.'

Harker reached for his wine glass. No way did he want to get involved with her anti-apartheid activities, what he didn't know he couldn't be expected to report to Dupont. 'From what I've heard, your members know all about apartheid, there's nothing new I can tell them.'

'But you've got *inside* experience. You're articulate, and witty. Knowledgeable. And,' she grinned, 'good-looking.'

'Flattery will get you nowhere.'

'And,' she trailed her finger up his thigh, 'all the ladies will double their donations.'

'This is a fund-raising meeting?'

'All our meetings are fund-raisers in that we pass the hat around. But where I'm actually asking you to make a speech is at our big annual fund-raising dinner in December.' She looked at him hopefully: 'Black tie and all.'

No way. 'Josie, there're plenty of better speakers than me for a big do like that. I'm not a public speaker, I'm just used to shouting at troopers.'

'And a publisher. With years of experience in Africa.'

'If I relate some of my experiences in Africa they *will* think I'm a racist, like you first did.'

'Not,' Josephine said, 'if you join the League. Look, all I'm asking is that you consider it, it's a long way ahead yet. But I'd be so pleased if you'd come along to our meeting next month and meet some of our members. It's even fun – we have a bit of a cocktail party afterwards, everybody brings a bottle or two. Will you do that?'

He did it for Josephine, not for Dupont. And it was exactly as he had expected: from a Military Intelligence point of view it was worthless and so transparent that the proceedings were reported almost verbatim in the *Village Voice*.

The church hall in Greenwich Village was full. Harker signed up as a member at the door, and sat with Josephine in the front row. There were about three hundred people present, about fifty of whom, he learnt from the outgoing chairperson's speech, were newcomers. 'Let's make 1988 a bumper year for new members!' Applause. Then the minutes from the last meeting were read – the usual stuff about funds raised . . . special thanks to . . . a resounding resolution to redouble their efforts (Applause) in particular by mobilizing League branches to pressure congressmen to widen sanctions against South Africa, redouble efforts to induce the American government to withdraw from Angola – *'We're going to sock it to 'em!'* Applause. Then the committee formally resigned and elections were held for a new one. Every member was re-elected except the chairperson who declined to stand again due to pressure of his professional work: the person unanimously elected in his place was Josephine Valentine.

The applause was prolonged. Harker knew she was popular, but *this* popular? He felt proud of her as she made her way up to the platform, beaming and beautiful and businesslike. She made a brief but ringing acceptance speech in which she promised her members a vigorous leadership and pledged her committee to fulfilment of all the worthy resolutions passed: and, being also New York State's delegate to the League's National Executive Committee, she promised to 'kick ass in Washington *and* Pretoria!' Thunderous applause. And, thought Harker, the meeting was about to break up and adjourn to the trestle tables for cheese and wine when Josephine, with her most dazzling smile, announced that there was a special new member present tonight, somebody from South Africa itself, whom she would like to call upon to say a few words: 'Ladies and gentlemen, please welcome Jack Harker . . .'

Harker was taken aback by her treachery. He glared up at her through the applause, but she was grinning at him mischievously. Blushing, he rose to the occasion – *Dupont was going to love this* . . . He mounted the platform, desperately trying to marshal some thoughts. He took the microphone from a grinning Josephine and faced the audience.

'Ladies and gentlemen, it ill behoves me, as a new member, to tell you how to go about your worthy work, and I don't intend to do so. And I want to say at the outset that I agree with you entirely that apartheid is an unjust, cruel political system, and every effort must be made to end it – we are all in absolute agreement on that. But, that said, there are two things we heard tonight that worry me. The first concerns the tightening of economic sanctions against South Africa.' He paused. The audience was entirely silent. 'Like Margaret Thatcher, the British Prime Minister, I worry that sanctions are counter-productive because when the economy falters the first to suffer are the workers. I mean blacks. They are poor people who cannot afford to lose their jobs, and more and more will do so if the sanctions are tightened. I respectfully suggest you reflect upon those black jobs.'

Harker paused again. The hall was silent. He glanced at Josephine, who was staring at the table with a small smile.

He continued: 'The second point that worried me tonight was about America's involvement on the side of South

135

Africa in the Angolan war against the communist government and Cuban–ANC alliance . . .' He held up his palms: 'I understand the sentiment – you good people want the ANC to overthrow apartheid. But I ask you to remember that Cuba is *Russia*'s cat's-paw in this war, communist Russia's surrogate, and no matter how much we sympathize with Nelson Mandela and his ANC there are precious few of us here tonight who are *communists*. So although we all want apartheid to fall we do *not* want South Africa, that last bastion of civilization on the continent, to become another communist basket case.' He paused again, looking over the little sea of faces. 'As sensible Americans you surely don't want *that*. But that is what Russia and Cuba intend. *Ah* – but there is good news here, as everybody who reads the newspapers will know: Russia is in economic trouble and cannot afford this war in Angola much longer, and their new president, Gorbachev, knows it. My bet is that he will soon pull out, to save money, and the Angolan war will splutter out, and then South Africa will withdraw from the territory because she can't afford the war either. Indeed, there are unconfirmed rumours already of secret peace talks . . .'

A man jumped up in the audience. 'So you're saying that we should not campaign against America's involvement in her pro-apartheid war?'

'America is not fighting *for* apartheid, sir, she is fighting *against* communism. Yes, I'm saying that you should not campaign against America's involvement, nor for more sanctions. But perhaps,' he smiled widely, 'if you are going to campaign against America's involvement you should also campaign against Russia's. And Cuba's.' He ended: 'Thank you.'

He nodded to the committee, to Josephine, turned and walked off the platform.

There was some polite, hesitant applause.

Well, Dupont would be pleased with that, the prick couldn't complain that he was doing nothing. Even though it amounted to fuck-all.

* * *

Josephine wasn't pleased, though she did not say so. 'Sorry if I said the wrong thing,' Harker said going home in the taxi.

'You're a League member,' Josephine said to the passing scene. 'You're entitled to your opinion even if it does mean throwing cold water on some plans and policies.'

'It happens to be my honest opinion.'

Josephine stared out of the window. 'And the League happens to disagree. I think America's involvement on the side of South Africa is shameful and I intend that the League will say so, loud and clear. Like I think America's treatment of Cuba is shameful – we apply all those sanctions to sabotage her economy and starve her into submission yet we trade with China, and Russia. Listen, Jack . . .' She turned to him. 'As far as I'm concerned – and the League – my enemy's enemy is my friend. South Africa is our enemy because it oppresses the underdog, therefore Russia and Cuba are my allies in this matter. And I hope that your closing remark, that we should campaign against Russia and Cuba as well, was a joke.'

'I didn't seriously expect the League to start picketing the Russian embassy and throwing eggs.'

'So if you speak again at meetings, please be serious, Jack. Because I assure you we are *very* serious people.'

Christ. A storm in a teacup. 'Can we forget it now?'

But when the taxi reached Gramercy Mews she said: 'I won't come in, there's League work I want to do while my memory's fresh.'

'But what about some dinner?'

'I'll fix something at home, I'll call you tomorrow.' And she told the cab-driver her address and drove off into the Manhattan night.

Harker considered the meeting completely unimportant from the CCB viewpoint, but Dupont was very pleased with the information he sent – the minutes of the last meeting with its resolutions, details of the office-bearers, the local newspaper's account of the whole evening which included a verbatim report of his little speech. 'Now you're getting somewhere,' Dupont said on the e-mail, 'keep it up!'

Harker was amused: God, were they so paranoid – or so thick? – in Pretoria that they so prized information they could get from the *Village Voice* and the League's monthly newsletter? And he had no intention of keeping it up: his frosty parting from Josephine had confirmed his resolve to have as little as possible to do with her anti-apartheid activities. He had been worried the following day when she had not telephoned and it had taken considerable self-restraint not to call her – for God's sake, he had to be able to speak his mind! Finally, at five o'clock, he had telephoned, but there was no reply. It had been with intense relief that he had seen her striding across the courtyard of Gramercy Mews, swinging her pink crash-helmet: she came into the front door, wreathed in her usual breathless smiles as if she had been racing.

'Hi! Been the whole day in the Bronx organizing our sub-branch.'

Harker hugged her – it seemed a long time since he had seen her. Intense relief. And there was more: she made no further mention of his speaking at the annual fund-raising dinner in December. Thank God.

To keep Dupont quiet Harker sent him the details of the League's planned marches, the routes, the dates, the times, the transport arrangements; this pleased the man but it was information that was to be published across the land the following week in the League's monthly broadsheet, the *Clarion*.

Later that summer the marches took place in Washington and Manhattan. Josephine led the march in Washington: Harker, following Dupont's orders, positioned himself just behind the front rank of the National Committee, carrying a life-size poster of Nelson Mandela while Dupont's salesmen

video-filmed the entire event. In New York, Harker's salesmen videoed a similar march to enable the CCB to identify
new enemies of South Africa, new targets for possible
character assassination. (Harker shook his head in amazement.) The marches were impressive and Josephine was
very pleased: but they were a waste of effort and expense
because, as Harker had foreseen, the following month
the news broke across the world that Mikhail Gorbachev
had announced Russia was withdrawing from Africa, that
South Africa had ordered all her armed forces to withdraw
from Angola, that her troops and tanks and armoured vehi-
cles were streaming back through the hot bush towards the
border. The war in Angola was over.

A month later, a few days before Christmas, on an island
in New York harbour, a peace agreement was signed,
amidst fanfare, between South Africa, Cuba and Angola.
Cuba undertook to withdraw its forces from Angola permanently, Angola to remove all the ANC military bases from
its territory permanently. South Africa agreed to withdraw
her troops and to grant independence to Namibia, the con-
tiguous former German colonial territory she had governed
on a United Nations mandate since the end of the Second
World War.

The war in Angola was over. It was the beginning of the
end of white rule in South Africa. Harker was sure it was
also the beginning of the end of the CCB.

14

Harker's Christmas present to Josephine was to be a fort-night's sailing holiday in the Caribbean. Hers to him was a fortnight's skiing holiday in Vermont.

There was the usual hectic round of Christmas celebrations, publishers' parties, literary agents', Harvest's, the Yacht Club's, the Racket Club's and Ike's, Mike's and Spike's – even Ferdi Spicer threw a black-tie binge at Cleopatra's Retreat for favoured United Nations clients, which, of course, Harker dared not attend though he would have liked to do so. The Anti-Apartheid League held a bring-a-bottle bash down in Greenwich Village. At all these parties the end of the Angolan war, the peace treaty so dramatized in New York's harbour, was a much-mentioned topic. At the Anti-Apartheid League's party the war's end was joyfully toasted as a South African collapse largely attributable to League efforts. Josephine made a ringing speech urging her troops ever onwards. 'Once more into the breach, dear friends – victory is in sight at last!'

On Christmas Eve, and again on Christmas Day, Josephine telephoned her father to try to make peace but she only reached his answering machine. She left messages 'from Jack and me' but there was no response. They left for the snow the day after Christmas. The forested mountains were breathtakingly beautiful. Dusk was falling as they drove up to their skiing lodge, its lights twinkling cosily amongst the snowy trees, jolly music coming from the rustic bar, red-nosed skiers crunching home for the day, a roaring log fire in the reception hall. Their room had a magnificent view of the valley, with a balcony and a heart-shaped Jacuzzi.

Josephine grinned. 'In the summertime this area has a reputation for dirty weekenders.'

They didn't make it to a single breakfast that week. Only when the sun was about halfway down the mountain across the valley did they think about getting up. It was lovely to lie deep in the big double bed together in the hours after morning love, drifting in and out of sleep, revelling in the fact that she was not going to leap out of bed on to her bicycle with her passion-pink crash-helmet and go hurtling uptown. It was lovely to take a long time waking up before ringing room service for croissants, orange juice and champagne and then slopping into the Jacuzzi to consume it, letting the hot jets and bubbles ease the stiffness and aches of yesterday's skiing while the Buck's Fizz did its gentle work. It was not before noon that they were togged up in boots and ski-gear, feeling no pain. Five or six hours later, after numerous eggnogs and Glühweins and a long lunch in one of the many little bars on the beautiful slopes, they came skidding to a stop back at their lodge in the sunset, unclipped their skis, put them in their locker and went tramping into the bar for an hour's jolly socializing before trudging back upstairs to their heart-shaped Jacuzzi. It was bliss lying in the whirling hot water, letting the jets massage them, the air bubbles titillate them whilst they sipped wine, feeling their stiffness and aches seeping out into the hot water. Each night they intended to get their act together and go downstairs to dinner but each night it was too much effort, much more fun to ring room service. It was not until New Year's Eve that they finally made it downstairs to dinner.

'Do you have a reservation, sir?' the head waiter asked.

'We're residents,' Harker said. 'Room three-oh-seven.'

'Three-oh-*seven*!' the head waiter beamed. 'Room service is going to be *very* disappointed . . .'

Their table was in a corner near the big log fire; they were alone in a crowd which was how they wanted to be. When midnight came they joined hands with adjoining tables and sang 'Auld Lang Syne' at the top of their voices, but when the whistle-blowing and kissing of strangers began they ducked out and headed back upstairs. While Harker opened a bottle of champagne Josephine threw herself on the bed, and stared up at the ceiling, arms outflung.

'You know, this time last year I danced until dawn. This year all I want to do is go to bed with you. Could this be love?'

'See how you feel this time next year.'

'I know exactly how I'll feel this time next year.'

Harker put a glass of champagne in her hand, then took a sip of his own. 'So why don't you want to get married?' He sat down beside her.

'Oh I do. Don't you?'

'So?' He waited, took another sip.

Josephine smiled, staring up at the ceiling. 'Oh I *do*,' she repeated. 'But not just yet.' Then she sat up and kissed him hard. 'You know I adore you.' She collapsed back on the pillows again. 'But I'm not ready yet. And that's got nothing to do with loving you. It's just that . . . I just need to be technically free for a while yet. It's just . . . until my book is finished and published – *if* it's ever published – I want to be free to complete my education, as it were.' She looked at him. 'Free to be a bit selfish, I suppose. Is that very terrible of me?'

Harker sighed. 'Yes,' he said. 'But I suppose people are like that until they know their own mind.'

'What do you mean by that?'

'For Christ's sake, Josie, we've been together six months. And you're twenty-seven next birthday, not seventeen. Isn't it time you knew your own mind?'

'But I *do* know my own mind – that I want to marry you! But not until I'm older and wiser. Okay? In fact . . .' She frowned at him, then stretched her arm around his neck and squeezed him. 'In fact, my New Year's wish is that I finish my book before this summer and that it's so brilliant you *insist* on publishing it and you make us both such a pile of money that we keep on as a team for the rest of our lives. So that we're *both* free, free for the rest of our lives to roam the world seeing wonderful sights and plumbing the depths of mysteries, talking and listening and reading and writing and publishing. And trying to teach the world – about its folly, about the political mess it is in and the terrible environmental wreck we're making with our pollution and acid rain and global warming, and the oceans that we're stripping and killing.' She looked at him, eyes bright. 'That's what I want to be free to do – with you. But as of now we cannot do it together because you're a publisher with a load of responsibilities. You simply cannot turn your back on them and come away with me to the rainforests of the Amazon, you simply cannot jump on a plane with me to the Kalahari to research the Bushmen. Can you?'

Harker shrugged.

'But I'm a writer, Jack,' Josephine said. 'I *can* do those things and it's a crying shame if I don't.' She looked at him earnestly. 'It would be irresponsible of me to get married and then disappear on these junkets. It would be a recipe for divorce.'

'But most of the time I could probably disappear on those junkets with you.'

'But how could you afford to leave your work?'

Harker shrugged again. 'Harvest is up and running now. Sure, we've got bank overdrafts but every publisher has those. I could leave the office to the editor and our account-ant for a while and fly out to join you for a few weeks in Timbuktu or Rio, wherever you are.'

Josephine smiled. 'It's a pretty thought. But I don't think it'll work out as simply as that when the chips are down, I think you'll be too busy. Or something.'

'Where there's a will there's a way.' He added, '*Without* relying on your inheritance.'

Josephine said earnestly, 'When we're married you're welcome to rely on me for anything, as I will rely on you for anything and everything, I didn't imagine otherwise.

143

But darling?' She smiled at him ravishingly: 'Not just yet, please?' She skated over that one and raised her glass high. 'This is my New Year's wish. I wish that I write such a good book that you'll be *desperate* to publish it and be my editor *and* my guru. So we can plan future books and projects together, wonderful trips to faraway places with strange-sounding names, researching important subjects of international moral significance, publishing wonderful books which are going to make the world sit up and do something constructive. Can we drink to that?'

Harker smiled. 'But when am I going to be allowed to read this fabulous book?'

'It won't be ready before next summer. I want to put absolutely my best foot forward. So . . .' She raised her glass high again: 'To 1989. It's going to be a wonderful year, I know . . .'

15

At the end of that fortnight they drove back down to New York – their skiing skills honed, their stiffness and aches replaced with muscle-toning, their faces glowing with snow-tanned health, and they went back to work. But every weekend for that January and February they returned to the mountains to ski, and a couple of nights a week they went skating. Sometimes they went up to the Rockefeller Plaza to waltz around the rink to music with all the beautiful people but more often they took a cab down to Greenwich Village and whizzed around with the fun people for a couple of hours before adjourning to Ye Olde Shakespeare, where they met up with Josie's League comrades. And then, in the spring, they went south to the Virgin Islands, to enjoy Harker's Christmas present.

That was a lovely time. They took delivery of their forty-five foot chartered ketch from The Moorings jetty in Tortola, British Virgin Islands, and sailed off into the best cruising grounds in the world where the trade winds blow gently all year over the long chain of palm-slung islands stretching from the eastern bulge of South America across to Cuba. On their first day Harker set their course due south for Venezuela and they went creaming out into the clear blue Caribbean under a riotously sunny sky, the sails taut, the deck gently heeled, the bow-wave *sh-sh-ing* down the hull; Harker and Josephine lounged behind the wheel, the wind in their hair, champagne glasses in hand. 'This even beats skiing,' Josie said. They creamed southwards for a hundred miles, then, in the moonlight, they swung east-north-east towards Barbados to begin their meander through the most beautiful string of islands in the world.

They had a lovely time. Cruising through the islands on an even keel, the trade winds astern, the sails gently full, the water turquoise, the palmy beaches white. For a fortnight they wore hardly any clothes. Lying at anchor in peaceful bays, the water crystal clear, the coral reefs just below them. Snorkelling along the reefs in the underwater wonderworld amongst the myriads of many-coloured fish, Josephine's long legs smoothly working, her long blonde hair streaming silkily behind her: she was the most naked woman in the world. And wallowing together in the little waves lapping on the white beaches, and lying flat out naked in the sun – it was all beautiful, and very erotic. Sometimes there were one or two other yachts in the bay, but usually they had their beach to themselves. If anybody was watching them through binoculars they did not care.

'Let 'em have a good time,' Josephine said. 'I am, the best time of my life.'

Thus they meandered westwards on through the turquoise waters, through islands called Guadeloupe and Montserrat and Antigua and St Kitts and St Bart's and Anguilla. On the second-last day of their holiday they were back where they started from, lying at anchor in a beautiful bay in the British Virgin Islands. The sun was going down in a glorious blaze of red, shimmering on the water, tinting the tropical verdure of the encircling islands with mauvey gold. Harker and Josephine sat in the cockpit drinking rum punches, picking on cashew nuts, tanned golden brown, glowing, fresh from their snorkelling and wallowing, fresh from their showers: they felt good and healthy and rested, and sad that tomorrow it was all over, that they were handing this yacht back to the charter company before taking a taxi out to the little airfield and boarding a plane to Puerto Rico and New York.

Josephine said, as if in answer to his question: 'Oh, I don't want to go home tomorrow. Sure I love New York, I love my work, my friends, I love all the hurly-burly and bullshit, but it will all get along perfectly well without me.' She sighed.

146

'D'you know what I think we must do, pardner? What we must work towards?'

'Tell me. Pardner.'

Josephine said, 'When my book is published let's buy a boat like this. A bit fancier of course but about this size, and let's live on her. I can write aboard – one of the joys of being a writer is that you can work anywhere, so why don't we work aboard a yacht while we sail her slowly around the world? First we'll keep her right here in the Caribbean, exploring all these magnificent islands again, and Mexico and Costa Rica and Nicaragua, and Brazil and Argentina. And then we sail her through the Panama Canal into the Pacific, over to the Galapagos Islands. Then right over to Tahiti and Micronesia. And all the time I'm writing my books, you see. And from New Zealand we sail across to Australia, and then up the Great Barrier Reef. Then up into Indonesia and Malaysia, then across to India . . .' She looked at him. 'Wouldn't you love to spend a few years doing that?'

Yes, he would love it. 'And what about Harvest House?'

Josephine lifted her finger. 'I've been thinking about this – I've been thinking about little else for the last two weeks. Well, in a few years we'll know whether I am making it as a writer or not. But surely to God by then Harvest is going to be very prosperous – Priscilla Fischer tells me so. So with a bit of luck in a few years you'll be able to hire some wizard to take over as managing director so you can rest on your laurels and sail around the world. Right?'

Harker smiled. 'It's a pretty thought.'

'And not impossible.'

'Okay, let's work at it.'

'It's a deal. I'll work my sweet ass off!'

Harker knew that the end of the Angolan war was also the beginning of the end of the CCB, but Dupont didn't. Dupont was cock-a-hoop that the Russian empire was collapsing, the Cubans were withdrawing in disarray without a paymaster, that Fidel Castro had the king-size headache of what to do with fifty thousand troops returning to his impoverished island. Dupont was delighted that the peace treaty required that the ANC remove their military bases from Angola – 'Now we can really knock the living shit out of them! But that's Pretoria's job, our job is to concentrate on these anti-apartheid activists now that there's not much military intelligence for us to worry about . . .'

Harker was amazed that Dupont couldn't see the writing on the wall. Sure, South Africa had the military resources to pursue the ANC from their old bases in Angola all the way to Cairo if she wanted to – but the world would not allow her to do so. America would no longer support her now that the Cuban threat was gone, the world would be outraged if she invaded across her borders again, increased sanctions would rain down on her, her economy would be truly broken. The likes of Dupont – and, evidently, the Chairman – just could not see that although South Africa had the military ability to conquer the whole of fucking Africa she did not have the *money*, the *economy*, to keep it up, and another blast of sanctions would flatten her. Meanwhile the situation inside the country was chaotic, the black townships aflame with rebellion.

And it amazed Harker that Josephine did not see the writing on the wall either: she was aghast at Gorbachev abandoning the Cubans in their valiant war against apartheid, dismayed that the ANC now had to move their military bases and that the undivided resources of the South African army could now be dedicated to knocking the living shit out of them. She was entirely convinced, like Dupont, that apartheid had the strength to continue crushing opposition indefinitely: she was determined that the League's efforts had to be redoubled to increase economic sanctions on South Africa.

'Bullshit,' Harker sighed. 'Apartheid is on its last legs – segregation is hardly enforced any more, South Africa is burning –'

'Bull*shit*, South Africa's going to go for the kill now! And what about *Grand* apartheid, all those millions of blacks forcibly translocated to their impoverished home-lands because their labour is surplus to the white man's requirements – Big Crocodile P.W. Botha will never change that –'

'Josie,' Harker sighed, 'believe me, President Botha is on his way out too. Rebellion is brewing in his party.'

And then, at the beginning of that fateful summer of 1989, a murder took place that made Harker think that Josephine might be right. Dr David Webster, a lecturer in sociology at the famous University of Witwatersrand and a leading anti-apartheid activist, had just returned from his Saturday morning jog when he was gunned down by white men driving past in a car, his chest blown to bits by a shotgun blast outside his suburban front gate. Harker was astounded at the gangland style of the slaying, Josephine was outraged.

'*Christ, David Webster* – one of the nicest guys you could meet! Such a tower of strength for the League! All that guy did was stand up for justice, and decent, Christian social principles – and so apartheid murders him!'

'We don't know yet who shot him.'

'Christ,' Josephine cried. 'It wasn't a robbery, it was a cold-blooded drive-by murder. So – who do you think these white men were? Christián revivalists? Or a government hit-squad?'

'They may be ordinary AWB, ordinary right-wing Afrikaner thugs.'

Josephine snorted, 'Ordinary Afrikaner thugs wouldn't *dare* be so brazen as to shoot down a leading figure in broad daylight! Those gunmen knew that if they were caught they would get off, that the police would make sure there wasn't a conviction.' She held her face. 'Oh Christ – David Webster. I wonder who's next?'

And much as he wanted to believe otherwise, Harker also thought it was a hit-squad job – he only had to remember the Long Island farm, the smashing of windows, the clatter of the machine pistols. But the Long Island job had stopped a terrorist campaign, saved innocent lives – what had the murder of David Webster achieved? Christ, was this what the mentality of the South African securocrats had sunk to? Was this the system he was part of? Please God the army wasn't involved, please God it was the security police who did it.

'Doctor *who*?' Dupont chuckled when Harker called him demanding reassurance. 'Never heard of the man, dear fellow. But I dare say the civilized world is better off without him.' He chuckled again.

'If it was us I want out right now!'

'Have you taken leave of your senses? Of course it wasn't us. Goodness gracious me!'

Oh Jesus, Jesus. All that summer the riots and strikes and boycotts racked South Africa. Josephine was convinced that all the black-on-black violence was the work of the mysterious Third Force. Harker could not believe it, did not want to believe it – and then another shocking murder occurred. On the eve of the democratic elections that would finally bring Namibia independence from South Africa, Advocate Anton Lubowski, a well-known anti-apartheid white man certain to become the first Minister of Justice in the forthcoming black government, was gunned down gangland-style outside his suburban home, just as David Webster had been, nine shots from an AK47 fired from a passing car, his blood and guts blasted across the garden. The murder provoked furious international headlines, furious fingers pointed at the South African government. Josephine was outraged all over again – she had met Anton Lubowski through the Anti-Apartheid League.

'*Anton of all people* . . .' she wept. 'Now do you believe there's a Third Force assassinating apartheid's opponents?'

Harker did not know what to believe. 'But the South African government has just granted independence to Namibia, so why should they murder one of the candidates – especially a white man who's likely to have a stabilizing influence on the new black government?'

'*Because*,' Josephine hissed furiously, 'the apartheid government does not *want* the new black Namibian government to be stable! They want it to be a failure so that they can say to the world, "We told you blacks can't govern themselves!"'

Oh God, Harker could not quite believe his government would be guilty of such treachery.

'Never heard of Anton Lubowski,' Dupont chortled, 'but whoever bumped him off deserves a medal, aha-ha-ha!'

'What the hell does that mean? Just tell me – was it us, because if it was I want to retire forthwith and exercise my contractual right to buy Harvest! I'm not an assassin – the war is over, we're irrelevant now and I want to be demobilized!'

'You,' Dupont snarled, 'will remain at your post. The most important war is just beginning and we're going to win it now we've got the albatross of Angola off our backs!'

'Can't you see that apartheid is fucking finished?' Harker cried. 'South Africa is burning!'

Yes, Harker could see the writing on the wall for apartheid, for P.W. Botha and his securocrats, for the CCB, for General Tanner, for Colonel Felix Dupont, for Major Jack Harker. He was intensely relieved that the war he had waged was finished, that there were no more real battles except possibly rearguard actions while the forthcoming new South Africa sorted itself out. *Thank God*, is what Harker felt on those scores. But what was going to happen to Harvest House? The government would sell it when it disbanded the CCB. But could Harker afford to buy it?

He instructed Harvest's accountant to calculate the value of the company; an effective shareholding was way beyond his reach without a crippling bank loan. The building alone was worth a lot: the goodwill and author list alone would be beyond him. And would the Defence Force even release him from his military service? They could refuse to accept his resignation and if he declined to return to South Africa his pension would be forfeited and he would be court-martialled for desertion if they ever got their hands on him.

But much worse than all that, much much worse: What would happen to his relationship with Josephine if he was recalled to South Africa?

It would mean revealing to her that he had deceived her all along, that Harvest House was a front for the apartheid regime she detested – she would loathe him, she would never believe that all the anti-apartheid sentiments he had expressed were true, he would never see her again.

He had to stay in America, he had to find a way of buying Harvest House, by hook or by crook.

16

Harker's next move was to write an official memorandum. He summarized the military situation, the political situation and its likely developments. He posed a number of alternative scenarios as to what could happen to the CCB in the near future, then asked what would happen to CCB operatives, their front businesses, files, assets, bank accounts in the different circumstances envisaged. After proposing answers to the questions he concluded:

With the threat of communism removed, South Africa is going to enter a new era: apartheid is now a proven failure. It is almost common knowledge that President Botha's own party want him to step down now and be replaced with a younger leader who will throw off the apartheid ball-and-chain. Clearly, a rapidly diminishing role for the CCB lies ahead, until it disappears completely.

To avoid a disorderly liquidation of CCB assets, I respectfully suggest that those operatives who wish to do so be allowed to purchase their business under a payment system linked into their salary schemes to mitigate financial hardship. This would have the double merit of immediately reducing Defence Force expenditure and relieving operatives' anxieties about their future. Operatives should be allowed to resign their commissions or terminate their contracts . . .

Contrary to departmental regulations, Harker sent this memorandum direct to the Chairman, General Tanner, in Pretoria, bypassing Dupont in Washington. But it was Dupont who responded, by telephone.

'What the fuck are you doing writing to the boss direct? You know everything has to go through me as your senior officer! And what the fuck are you talking about, saying the CCB is going into liquidation? Bull*shit*, man – the CCB is more important than ever now that we've won the war in Angola and the ANC are on the run! Now we can concentrate all our efforts on busting sanctions and kicking ANC ass! Things have never looked better! And it's absolute crap to suggest that P.W. Botha is on his way out!' Dupont paused, breathing heavily. 'And as for buying Harvest House, forget it! Produce some results or you'll have your cushy number kicked out from under your ass and you'll be posted back to Pretoria! And if you write another letter to the Chairman without sending it through me you'll be disciplined!'

Jesus. *Now we've won the war?* But Dupont knew things Harker didn't; the left hand doesn't know what the right is doing in the espionage game. Perhaps apartheid was going to be reinforced, maybe the CCB was going to function for years . . . But, Jesus, Harker did not believe it – did not *want* to believe it.

The summer went this way. In South Africa it was winter: the fires of outrage mounted, the black townships resounding with the clatter of AK47s as ANC impis fought it out with Inkatha impis, as ANC youths barricaded roads with burning tyres and pelted the buses bringing the black people home from work and beat them with sticks and made them eat the soap powder and foodstuffs they had bought in the white man's shops. And all the time the running battles with the police and army. South Africa was in a hell of a mess, the ANC's policy of 'Liberation before Education' and rendering the country ungovernable was certainly paying off. The Anti-Apartheid League in South Africa e-mailed daily digests of the situation to Josephine and it made very scary reading indeed. Josephine was cock-a-hoop that apartheid was collapsing; Harker would have been too, had he not been so worried about what was going to happen to his beloved Harvest House. To keep within his orders he sometimes sent Dupont information about these League communications but it was nothing the man wouldn't know two days later from reading the *Clarion*. There was little other CCB work now that there was no significant military intelligence to gather on this side of the Atlantic. And then, towards the end of that year the news broke across the world that P.W. Botha, President of the Republic of South Africa, had been bullied by his cabinet into resigning from office. The headline of the *New York Herald* shouted gleefully: THE OLD BIG CROCODILE BITES THE DUST AT LAST.

Mr F.W. de Klerk was elected by his party caucus to replace him, and he announced to an astonished and sceptical world that when parliament resumed after the Christmas recess he would introduce legislation that would dismantle the edifice of apartheid, and institute a Great Indaba between all races which would bring about a totally new South Africa.

Harker would have rejoiced at the news had it not been for his worry about Harvest.

'Bull*shit*!' Josephine snorted. 'Dismantle apartheid, my poor achin' ass! All this guy de Klerk will do is abolish some of the most offensive aspects but he won't touch *Grand* apartheid, no *sir*, not the so-called homelands. He won't repeal the Group Areas Act and let blacks live next door to whites, he won't let black kids go to the same schools as his precious white Afrikaners, he won't give blacks the vote – I tell you the League still has years of work!'

Harker didn't believe it, but Dupont did. Harker wrote him another memorandum reiterating his urgent recommendations for the purchase by operatives of CCB businesses in preparation for the day the organization was disbanded, but Dupont barked on the phone: 'You really believe that F.W. de Klerk is going to commit political suicide? For Christ's sake, it's only window-dressing to get the world off our back. All he's promised is that there's going to be a Great Indaba.'

'For a completely new South Africa wherein no race oppresses another, quote unquote.'

'Christ,' Dupont rasped impatiently, 'we've heard that all before, even from Botha himself. Relax, man, the CCB has lots of work ahead.'

Harker even began to wonder whether the writing he saw on the wall was illusory – Dupont must have some good reason for such conviction – and he was ashamed to admit that he wanted to think he was.

And then the Berlin Wall came crashing down.

Harker stared at the dramatic scene on his television screen. People were joyously getting stuck into the dreaded wall with picks and sledgehammers, hijacked mobile cranes were taking great bites out of it. Harker was almost unable to believe that the communist ogre he had spent his life fighting was dying so ignominiously before his eyes: and he was convinced that the walls of apartheid would collapse now too.

'I'll believe it when I see it,' Josephine retorted.

Dupont thought so too. 'Like hell this proves that the CCB are finished,' he responded to Harker; 'we can really knock the living shit out of the ANC now that they've lost their paymaster – I just wish this had happened before we gave up Namibia!'

Then something totally unexpected happened that cracked the ramparts of apartheid's securocrats. One Thursday night in Pretoria Central Prison a condemned black man who was due to be hanged in the morning for a murder committed in the course of a burglary broke down when he was told that a last-minute reprieve was not forthcoming, and he screamed for a lawyer.

His name was Daniel Sipholo and he frantically told the lawyer who came to his condemned cell that he was a

156

member of an undercover government hit-squad, based on a police farm called Platplaas, which murdered the state's enemies. He named his commanding officers, the chain of command. Daniel Sipholo had expected his police superiors to arrange for his reprieve at the last moment in exchange for his silence about hit-squads: a hysterical Daniel instructed the lawyer to tell the Minister of Justice that unless he issued a reprieve the scandal would be released to the press. The lawyer did better than that: he telephoned the newspapers, then got the Minister of Justice out of bed and told him that unless he signed a stay of execution to enable the shocking claims to be investigated the government would be forever condemned for hanging a man to prevent him from revealing state atrocities.

The Minister of Justice, while protesting at such scurrilous allegations by a man trying to save his worthless neck, had no choice: a stay of execution was ordered. The next morning the story was front-page news around the world.

17

Josephine was absolutely delighted. 'At last the truth is out! My God – *police* death-squads?! The people who're supposed to be upholding law and order are going around *murdering* people who oppose apartheid! Oh boy, what's Ronald Reagan going to do about *this* one? Oh *boy* – is the League going to go to town on *this* story!'

Harker was a very worried man. Once this investigation began the existence of the CCB could emerge. The military would hotly deny it, the Minister of Defence would vow in parliament that it was a pack of nonsense, but the press would pick it up, there would be a public outcry. 'Did *you* know that there were police hit-squads?' Josephine demanded.

'Of course not.' That was the truth.

'But didn't you *suspect*?'

'I only knew that the security police had a bad reputation, that a number of people have died in police custody over the years, that's common knowledge. But I attributed that to rogue elements, not to organized hit-squads, for Christ's sake.'

Josephine snorted. 'Really, you surprise me, darling. Well, now we all know who blew up those guys in Long Island last year.'

Harker flinched inwardly. 'That was the Cuban exile community – the FBI said so. What would the South African police be doing in America, for Christ's sake?'

'The same as the ones who burgled the League's offices three years ago!'

Oh Jesus. Harker telephoned Dupont. 'I'm coming to Washington to discuss the fall-out from this death-squad affair.'

'Stay where you are!' Dupont ordered. 'There's not going to be any fall-out . . .'

Harker took the shuttle flight to Washington the next morning without telling Josephine.

'I ordered you to stay where you were!' Dupont barked as Harker walked into his panelled office at the Royalton Hotel. 'We have nothing to do with the police, they don't even know of the CCB's existence!'

Oh, this was such crap. 'How can that be? Military Intelligence set up the CCB, therefore the Minister of Defence knows about us. He sits on the State Security Council along with the Minister of Police, therefore the top brass in the police must know about us. So how far down the ranks does this knowledge extend? And how much is going to come out when this investigation into these death-squads starts and Daniel Sipholo spills all the beans? And when the other cops *he* fingers start passing the buck – how long before one of them tries to blame the CCB for one of their murders – then they'll start investigating *us*.'

Dupont looked at him sagely, his round, hard face solemn, his eyes wide. 'Really?'

'Yes, really! Am I the only guy with any foresight in this goddam department?!'

Dupont laced his knuckles under his chin and leant across the desk.

'Really,' he said, 'you surprise me . . . You believe that there is going to be a *real* investigation? You're so full of all that Sandhurst crap about officers and gentlemen that you're not really cut out for this military intelligence game, are you?' He shook his head. 'Do you imagine that the Minister of Defence, let alone our new President with all his new South Africa mumbo-jumbo, is going to let a condemned man bring down the government?' His fat face crinkled in disparagement. 'Do you really think that an investigative tribunal is going to *believe* this condemned man desperately trying to save his neck from the hangman by making these *scurrilous* allegations?'

Harker stared. 'But surely there's going to be an open investigation by a *judge*, proceedings open to the press?'

'The proceedings will be conducted by the Attorney General.' Dupont leered, then waved a fat hand. 'Oh, all the relevant police officers will be called as witnesses, all will be very impressive when they deny Daniel's allegations.' He smiled. 'Who is going to believe a desperate man?' He smiled again. 'Don't worry.'

Harker stared at his boss, and was ashamed that he wanted to believe him. 'So after the Attorney General's bullshit investigation Daniel will go through the hangman's trapdoor disbelieved. And the whole scandal will die with him?'

Dupont spread his hands. 'What scandal, old boy?' He glared, his blue eyes suddenly piercing. 'Do I make myself clear, Major?'

Harker said quietly, 'Was it the CCB who murdered Dulcie September in Paris? And blew the arm off Albie Sachs? And blew up Mrs Schoon and her daughter in Angola – and Ruth First?' He looked at Dupont grimly. 'Or was it the police?'

Felix Dupont sat back with a twinkle in his eyes. 'I don't know what you're talking about, old boy. Dulcie who? Albie? Don't remember them, old chap. But if those people are now deceased, it's nothing to do with us, and I'm quite sure their demise is nothing to do with our police either. As I'm sure the forthcoming investigation will confirm.' Then he frowned, puzzled. 'But what worries me, Jack, as your boss, is that you even *ask* the question. Surely you know that even if I knew the answer I would not tell you? Because *you* have no *need to know*!' Dupont looked at him sharply, then rasped, 'Now get your ass back to your post and stop worrying!'

*   *   *

But there was plenty to worry about.

That month the Attorney General's investigation into Daniel Sipholo's allegations began. It seemed that Dupont's assessment was correct. One by one the senior police officers named by Daniel entered the witness box and denied that Platplaas was anything more than a counter-insurgency base, denied having ordered the murder of anyone: if anybody had ever been murdered it must have been done on the orders of Daniel's immediate commanding officer, Captain Erik Badenhorst, acting on his own unlawful initiative. And Captain Erik Badenhorst was a very worried man: his testimony was being kept till last and it was clear to Harker, reading the reports five thousand miles away, that he was going to be made the scapegoat.

Then one day Erik Badenhorst walked into the Pretoria offices of Lawyers for Human Rights, and asked for their help. He told them that everything Daniel said was true, that he, Badenhorst, wanted to blow the whole story to the international press, that he wanted to escape from the country and join the ANC, the only people with an organization big enough to protect him from the might of the South African Police. Lawyers for Human Rights immediately put him in the hands of a lawyer named Luke Mahoney who was also an established writer. A week later his bloodcurdling story of police mayhem and murder was front-page news around the world.

There was international outrage. Harker, reading the League's faxed reports that Josephine brought every evening when she came hurtling downtown on her bicycle, was aghast at the depravity of the security forces he was serving. And then his anger turned to fear as he read the final paragraphs of the article written by Luke Mahoney.

I asked Erik Badenhorst if he knew who had gunned down Dulcie September in Paris, Anton Lubowski, Dr David Webster, blown up Jeanette Schoon and her daughter with a parcel bomb, who had assassinated the Cuban and ANC officers in Long Island New York – to name a few. He replied:

'Those weren't police jobs, too far afield for us cops. But I've got a bladdy good idea who did it – the CCB.'

'The CCB,' said I; 'who are they?''

Badenhorst replied: 'The Civil Cooperation Bureau. I don't know much about them but they're part of Military Intelligence. They operate worldwide. They pretend to be businessmen but really they're spies and hit-men for South Africa . . .'

Harker slapped down the report and stared, his heart pounding. *Oh Jesus, Jesus!*

Across the world there were headlines and editorials about the comeuppance of apartheid; in the United Nations there was outrage, in South Africa there was an outcry for a public judicial inquiry. In parliament the new president, F.W. de Klerk, wrung his hands, told the world that he was assured by his Minister of Defence that this so-called Civil Cooperation Bureau did not exist, that it was the wild invention of this rogue Erik Badenhorst. A judicial inquiry, he said, would distract the nation from all the reforms he intended to make, open a Pandora's Box of recriminations . . .

The outcry redoubled. And then, that same week, two white men, former policemen, were arrested in connection with the murders of Anton Lubowski and Dr David Webster.

Both men claimed to work for Military Intelligence, for an outfit called the Civil Cooperation Bureau, the CCB.

18

Harker's heart lurched when he read that news. Sick in his guts, he left Harvest House immediately, without telling his secretary where he was going, and flagged a taxi to take him to the airport. He caught the shuttle flight to Washington. He walked into Dupont's office without knocking.

'So it *was* us who hit those two left-wingers, Webster and Lubowski!'

Dupont had bloodshot eyes, smudges beneath them. 'What the *fuck* you doing here?'

Harker glared at him. 'Two guys have just been arrested for those murders in Pretoria and they said they were working for Military Intelligence! For the CCB, in fact!'

'Calm down!' Dupont rasped. 'They haven't *admitted* to murder – they've only been *arrested*, protesting their innocence saying they worked for Military Intelligence. And anyway, why the holier-than-thou? I seem to remember you doing something similar a while ago.'

Jesus. Harker said slowly: 'My targets were military personnel plotting sabotage and murder. Not civilians whose only crime was that they opposed apartheid!'

'Want to resign?' Dupont sneered. 'Give up Harvest House? And I repeat, what the fuck you doing here?'

Harker cursed. Damn right he'd love to resign, wash his hands of the whole stinking fucking business! 'There'll have to be a judicial commission of enquiry now and the whole CCB will be blown sky-high. *That's* why I'm here – to discuss what the hell we're going to do about that little problem.'

Dupont's face creased in exasperation. 'My dear fellow, there will be *no* commission of enquiry. If our illustrious new president exposed us, the whole security establishment would turn against him, he knows that. All the top brass in the police and army would turn on him. And so would most of Afrikanerdom, there'd be a *coup d'état*, if not civil war.' Dupont shook his face. 'So stop worrying and get back to work. When parliament resumes in February the president is going to make his oh-so-dramatic announcement about the so-called new South Africa and the press will forget all about police hit-squads and Military Intelligence.'

Harker wanted to believe it. 'What do you mean the *so-called* new South Africa?'

'I'm suggesting, dear fellow, that our wonderful new reformist president is not going to commit political suicide – *national* suicide. Whatever reforms the dear man's got in mind, I'm quite sure there's going to be a healthy remnant of apartheid in such titchy little matters as overall political power remaining firmly in white hands for the foreseeable future – including the security forces. What *will* go by the board is *petty* apartheid. *You* know, kaffirs will be allowed to sit next to you in a pub, or on the bus, probably even swim in the same bit of sea as you, maybe even shit in the same public lavatories – though perish *that* thought. But political power? No, that will remain firmly in white hands.' He smiled unpleasantly. 'I don't think you need worry about commissions of enquiry into the CCB, dear fellow. Your beloved Harvest House is safe for a long while yet.' He leered: 'Unless, of course, you blot your copybook and don't produce results . . .'

But both Dupont and Josephine were wrong. On 2 February 1990 parliament reconvened with all its pomp and ceremony, and President F.W. de Klerk introduced the new South Africa. An astonished world was told that his government was unbanning the ANC, that he would call a Great Indaba of all political parties to negotiate a new constitution on the principle of one man, one vote. And he announced that Nelson Mandela and other political prisoners would be released.

Harker had gone to the office early to watch the opening of parliament on television: it was five a.m. in New York as the dramatic scenes unfolded in faraway Cape Town, the opposition Conservative Party storming out of the legislative chamber in protest at this 'capitulation' whilst outside there was dancing in the streets, jubilation. Harker stared at the scenes, joy flooding over him, joy that apartheid was finally over, that the wars were over – and profound relief that surely there would be no commission of enquiry into the CCB now! Surely to God in this new South Africa goodwill would abound and all the battles of not so long ago would have to be forgiven and forgotten as the parties forgathered round the Great Indaba table to work out a new constitution. All the acts of sabotage and murder committed by all sides would surely have to be relegated to history as acts of war, surely there would have to be amnesty for all as the returning soldiers beat their swords into ploughshares, the CCB would be quietly disbanded, surely Military Intelligence would quietly sell off its foreign companies . . .

So now was the time to make sure Harvest House was sold to him and not to anybody else. He snatched up the telephone and dialled Felix Dupont.

'For Christ's sake,' Dupont rasped, 'it's six o'clock in the morning!'

'You haven't heard the news?'

'Of course I've heard the fucking news, I've been up all night talking to the Chairman, my e-mail is running hot, I want to go to bed!' He sounded drunk. 'So what do you want – apart from buying Harvest at a knock-down fucking price?'

'*Right*,' Harker said. 'Apartheid is over, so the CCB is going to be disbanded. Now the battle is going to be between the ANC and the Zulus for supremacy; they'll leave us whites alone because we're irrelevant now. So let's fold our tents smartly and get out of the crossfire.'

Dupont said angrily: 'The whites are *not* irrelevant now and the CCB is *not* going to be disbanded.'

'Christ,' Harker cried, 'sure, the Conservative Party are going to threaten war and start blowing up buildings but that'll have nothing to do with us in America!'

'You're missing the fucking point!' Dupont shouted. 'Do you imagine that the ANC is going to disband *its* army, *its* military intelligence? No *way*! And anyway, when the ANC and Zulus go to war against each other, whose side do you think we're going to be on?'

Harker stared across the basement. He said slowly, 'I presume the South African Defence Force is going to be on the side of law and order. I presume we're going to do our duty and *stop* them fighting each other!'

Dupont snorted. 'Oh, you make me sick. Don't be so pukkah, for Christ's sake! We're going to let the Zulus do our work for us, knock the living daylights out of the ANC.'

Jesus Christ. 'Is that what the Chairman's told you?'

'You have no need to know what the fucking Chairman's told me! All you need to know is that the CCB ain't going to be disbanded and that you're to stay at your fucking post and await orders! And now I'm going to bed!' He slammed down the telephone.

Harker jumped up and strode to his computer. He punched the keys and on the screen appeared his last memorandum concerning the disposal of CCB assets, addressed to the Chairman. He rewrote the opening paragraph to read: *In view of today's parliamentary developments I respectfully submit that the initiatives outlined below are now most urgent.*

He scrambled it and hit the transmission button.

He got up, went to his refrigerator and took out a beer. *Fuck 'em.* He had not joined the fucking army to fight civil wars!

Just then his telephone rang. He snatched it up. 'Yes?'

'Hullo, darling,' Josephine said. 'What're you doing at the office so early? Have you seen the television?'

'I came here to watch it so I wouldn't wake you. Where are you?'

'Back at my apartment. Isn't it wonderful news? They're dancing in the streets! But d'you realize what this is going to do for my book – it's going to make it a bestseller!'

'It's going to be a bestseller anyway.'

'Thank you, so that means you want to publish it, huh?'

And why not? Harker thought. If it was going to be a bestseller and if he was going to buy Harvest, why shouldn't he have the benefit of it? Apartheid was finished, so the CCB was finished; there was no reason why Harvest should not become the best publisher for Josephine Valentine.

'Well, I'm looking forward to seeing it when it's finished. Tell Priscilla Fischer to talk to me about it.'

'Is this for *real*?' she cried.

Harker hedged his conscience: 'But a bigger publishing house may still be better for you. However, Piranha Fisch will advise you well, she didn't get that nickname for nothing.'

'Oh, darling, I love you! *So*,' she said happily, 'what's going to happen now in South Africa?'

Harker wanted to say, The shit's going to hit the fan. 'What do you think?'

'I think everything's going to be wonderful! I think I can end the book right there, with Nelson Mandela walking out of prison to roars of applause. The new South Africa . . .'

19

But it didn't happen like that.

Thousands of people lined the road outside the Victor Verster Prison in Cape Town, newsmen from around the world were there to report on the release of Nelson Mandela, the world's most famous prisoner upon whose shoulders most of the hopes of South Africa now rested.

'Indeed the hopes of all Africa,' the CNN television anchorman said, 'because the leadership of the new South Africa will be vital for the regeneration of the whole desperate continent. The atmosphere here this glorious summer's day is charged with excitement and emotion . . .'

Harker felt emotional too. Josephine, sitting beside him in Madam Velvet's dungeon at four o'clock that New York morning – ten o'clock in South Africa – had tears in her eyes.

Suddenly roars of applause went up as the prison gates opened, mad cheering and waving and clapping, fists thrust aloft. And there was the grand old man, his hair white, hand in hand with his wife Winnie, smiling, waving, reaching out to shake eager hands, answering greetings. He walked down that avenue of adulation, smiles all over his handsome face, and Harker's eyes were moist: he could almost feel the joy in that old man's breast, at being free at last, his triumph of having won the long, bloody battle against apartheid. The tears were streaming down Josephine's face. At the end of the long walk to freedom Nelson Mandela climbed into his waiting limousine to drive into Cape Town centre to make the speech the world was waiting to hear.

And when it was made, from the grand mayoral balcony of City Hall against the backdrop of Table Mountain, the world watching and listening agog, Harker's heart sank. Josephine was rapt, tears dropping on to her notebook as she scribbled, but Harker felt the cold hand of despair, for himself and for South Africa: it seemed that everything Felix Dupont had prophesied was going to come true, that the battles were a long way from over. For Nelson Mandela, the grand old man of African politics, proclaimed to the world that until the democratic process was complete the ANC's war against South Africa would continue, that South Africa would become a socialist state, the land would be redistributed amongst the proletariat, 'the commanding heights of commerce nationalized', and that until a demo-cratic government was installed the world must continue to apply economic sanctions.

Harker groaned. But Josephine sobbed: 'Isn't it wonder-ful? This is how I'm going to end the book!'

For the next three days he did not see Josephine as she toiled over the final chapters of her book in her uptown apartment; they only spoke by telephone when she was having something to eat. 'Jack, I'm looking after myself just fine, eating lots of high-energy food, trust me. But when I finally pack it in for the night I'm just too tired to think about getting a taxi.'

Late on the fourth night she came striding across the mews courtyard carrying a big plastic shopping bag in one hand and a bottle of champagne in the other. She burst into the apartment, wreathed in smiles and smelling of wine. She threw the shopping bag on the dining table.

'There it is!'

Harker clutched her tight. *'Congratulations . . .'* It seemed she had been away on a long journey. And, oh, the sweet feel of her in his arms.

'Save your felicitations until you've read it. So who's a gal gotta fuck around here to get a drink?'

Harker tapped his breast. 'Me . . .'

It was after midnight. Josephine sprawled magnificently

naked, fast asleep, her long blonde hair flaming across the pillows, when Harker pulled on a dressing-gown and tip-toed out of the bedroom down to Madam Velvet's dungeon to read.

It was dawn when he crept back into bed beside her and took her in his arms.

'It's brilliant,' he whispered to her warm sleeping form.

At ten o'clock that morning he left the apartment with her typescript, leaving her still fast asleep. At Harvest House he sent for his editor-in-chief. He handed him the first half of the book and said, 'Start reading this. Drop everything else. I want your opinion fast.'

Harker continued reading the latter half. At one o'clock Josephine telephoned. 'Well?' she said. 'No, don't tell me.'

'It's very good. Congratulations.'

She sighed. 'Oh darling, I love you! So can I tell Priscilla to call you?'

'If you're sure that's what you want.'

'Oh darling, I'm so excited!'

On his way out of the building to meet Priscilla Fischer he put his head in the editor's doorway. 'Well, Alan?'

'It's brilliant,' Alan said.

'How high should I go?'

Alan sighed. 'A couple of hundred thousand? Once Piranha Fisch starts hyping this around town the sky's the limit.'

Harker met Priscilla Fischer in the restaurant of the Algonquin Hotel. She was a tough, glamorous redhead with big, dancing, green eyes, perfect capped teeth and a cleavage she displayed to full advantage. The rumour was she had screwed most of the publishers in New York. 'Christ,' Harker said, almost snorting into his martini. 'Half a *million* dollars?'

'I'll get it easily if I hold an auction,' Priscilla said. 'And I must tell you I am offering it first to you against my better judgement. Sure I respect Harvest but I feel this book deserves the biggest and best. However, the author insists I offer it to you.'

'Half a million,' Harker said, 'is too much for Harvest.'

He even felt relieved. This spared him the responsibility for Josie's professional advancement.

'But you do agree the book is worth half a million upfront?'

Harker smiled inwardly. Oh, he would love to take the CCB's half a million and give it to Josephine – what poetic justice that would be. Trouble was, it was taxpayers' money. 'Yes. And I think Josephine may make twice that when the book's in the shops. But half a million is too much for me.' He added, 'I think you should warn her about the ending. It's a great piece of writing describing Mandela's release, but it's too optimistic about the future. I think further violence is going to break out as the different black political parties battle for supremacy.'

'Sounds a rather racist statement.'

'Just a realistic one. That's the African way. All I'm suggesting is that Josephine writes in a paragraph or two somewhere which allows for the possibility of undemocratic violence ahead.'

Priscilla Fischer sniffed. 'Doubt that's necessary, I think we've got a perfect ending. Well,' she said, 'my instructions are not to rush you. So you have until six o'clock this afternoon to decide. After that the book goes on auction.' She folded her knuckles under her chin and looked at him. 'So tell me about my client who's about to take the literary world by storm. You *very* serious about each other?'

Harker smiled. 'What does Josephine say?'

'Hasn't confided in me. Strikes me as a very serious sort. So?'

'Yes,' Harker said, 'we're serious.'

'Marriage-type serious?'

'One day.'

'But not yet. Author wants to spread her literary wings? Warm both hands before the fires of life? Meanwhile, back at the ranch, you ain't in no hurry either.'

'No.'

'Why not? Promiscuous?'

Harker smiled. 'Not any more.'

'Faithful type? Or because AIDS has dealt a numbing blow to the one-night stand?'

'Faithful type.'

Priscilla nodded at him speculatively. 'Good. Look after my client, or I'll kick your ass all the way to my apartment.' She smiled carnivorously, then snapped her fingers at the waiter. 'More martinis here. Feel like getting sloshed. Not every day I've got a bestseller on my hands.'

It was after five o'clock when the taxi dropped Harker back at Harvest House. He was feeling just fine with three martinis and a bottle of wine sloshing around inside him. On the way to his office he encountered his editor-in-chief.

'Well?' Alan said.

'Half a million advance,' Harker said.

'*Lord*. We can't afford that, can we?'

'We just have,' Harker said. 'Have you finished reading it?'

'Yes. As I said, brilliant.'

'Exactly. So even if Harvest has to hock itself to the eyeballs we'll get our money back. In fact we'll do that when we auction the paperback rights.' He thought, as he proceeded on to his office, *and even if we don't it's the CCB's problem, not mine* . . .

As he got to his desk his private phone rang. He picked it up. 'Hullo?'

'Oh darling,' Josephine cried, 'Priscilla's just phoned with the news! Oh, I'm so thrilled, I can't thank you enough! But darling, are you sure you want to do it?'

'Harvest House,' Harker said, 'is proud to be Josephine Valentine's publisher.'

'But half a million dollars is an awful lot of money.' She sounded tipsy.

'Worth every penny,' Harker said grandly. 'Harvest will earn it back several times over. And you're going to be rich as well as beautiful, with the best-looking publisher in town. How's the hangover?'

'Oh darling, I'm so excited.'

'How's the hangover, I said.'

172

'My hangover's fine, I'm in Madam Velvet's about to start my second bottle of champagne.'

'Keep at it, babe, I'll be home in half an hour, then I'm taking you for the best damn dinner in town.'

He hung up and headed out of his office, down to the basement. He unlocked the steel doors, locked them behind him, went to his desk. He stabbed out the numbers for Dupont's secure telephone. 'Yes?' Dupont barked.

'Well, you'll be happy to hear that I've managed – with great difficulty – to buy the book you were worried about.'

There was a pause, then Dupont said grudgingly, 'Well done. And? What do you think? How damaging is it?'

'It's crap,' Harker said. 'But it's crap that will sell like hot cakes if we're not careful.'

'It's your job,' Dupont said, 'to make sure it doesn't sell! Like don't reprint if she gets good reviews. Have breakdowns in the system. So, what did you have to pay for this pile of shit?'

Harker said, 'Not too bad at all – only half a million.' He added, 'Dollars, not pounds.'

There was a stunned silence. Then: 'Jesus Christ.'

'Yeah,' Harker said reasonably, 'a bit pricey, but believe me we got it cheap. The agent was about to hold an auction and I'm quite sure it would have sold for a million or more. And whatever publisher bought it at that price would put so much sales effort into it that it was *bound* to be a bestseller.' He added, 'Internationally.'

Another stunned silence. Then: 'Okay, suppose half a million bucks to stifle bad publicity may be reasonable.'

'Call that a million,' Harker said, 'by the time we actually print the book.'

'You're gonna print the *minimum!*'

'Sure, but I'm going to have an agent called Piranha Fisch breathing down my neck to see I print an acceptable number, and that I advertise and do the right promotions, like cocktail parties to launch the book, television chat-shows, radio, press, all that.'

'None of that publicity crap!' Then: 'Half a million upfront! That puts you over your credit facility with the bank, huh?'

'Yes.' Harker tried not to sound cheerful.

'So, what're you going to do?'

Harker had to work on it to keep his delight out of his voice. 'You,' he said, 'will have to ask the Chairman for more money.'

Dupont said angrily: 'The Chairman will go through the fucking roof. Half a *million* dollars for one fucking book?' He added, 'But I suppose it'll save us millions of dollars' worth of bad publicity.' He sighed. 'Will the bank extend your revolving credit?'

'Yes. But we'll be in deep.'

'How the fuck did you get Harvest into this financial position?'

Harker kept the grin out of his voice. 'Your orders,' he said, trying to sound injured.

'I didn't order you to get into terrible debt! Do you realize that this makes Harvest House almost worthless as a business? Military Intelligence can almost write it off!'

Wonderful, so I'll buy it cheap. 'Well, I followed your orders,' Harker said. He added, 'Sir.'

'Jesus, half a million bucks . . . Well, get that bank overdraft extended. And, if necessary, I suppose I'll have to give Harvest some support from the Slush Fund. So, what's the publishing schedule?'

'The agent wants me to bring it out in about six months, in September, to catch the Christmas trade.'

'No way!' Dupont rasped. 'Stall her. For twelve months. Let the hoohah about Mandela's release die down, schedule it for this time next year, then put it off for another six months. Got that?'

'Sure.' Harker tried not to grin. 'So what's going to happen back home now that Nelson's out?'

Dupont snorted. 'The shit's going to hit the fan. What does Miz Valentine say?'

'Hearts and flowers,' Harker said. 'It's crap.'

174

'Half a million bucks worth of crap?' Dupont groaned, and Harker wanted to drum his heels in delight.

And then, that very night, the violence erupted in South Africa.

It was mindless, an orgy of anarchy in celebration of Nelson Mandela's release. Josephine watched the scenes on television aghast; never had she anticipated this, the swarming mobs burning schools, attacking factories and shops, petrol-bombing post offices and police stations, burning farms, throwing up blazing roadblocks, running battles with the police. For five days the nihilism reigned, the smoke barrelling, the flames leaping, as the world watched in horror, demanding, *Why . . . ?*

'I'll tell you why!' Josephine said. 'Their hatred of apartheid is so great they have to attack its symbols – the police stations, the post offices, the farms of the oppressors, the schools where they were given inferior apartheid education – it's a spontaneous outbreak of democratic joy!'

Harker snorted. 'But what about the factories? Maybe it wasn't much of a job but at least they got paid at the end of every week.'

'The factories are the creation of the oppressor too.'

'No, the factories were the creation of businessmen. And the people are not going to get paid next Friday, are they? So who do they expect to pay them – Nelson Mandela?' He held up a finger to stop her interrupting. 'I'm trying to help you with your book – which I am committed to publishing.' He pointed at the television set. 'What we've just seen shows that there was no thought for tomorrow because those people believe that tomorrow the skies will start raining banknotes and bicycles because Nelson Mandela is released. Of course I'm delighted that apartheid is over, but I'm a realist. The fact is that Mandela has just said that the commanding heights of commerce will be nationalized, and the bulk of the population are peasants who think that means it will all be given to them.'

'A realist or a racist?'

And then the violence in Natal redoubled as the power struggle between the ANC and Zulus took on a new fury as ANC exiles started returning. While the Great Indaba opened with much fanfare in Johannesburg before the media of the world, while the ANC and government sat down with delegates from all political parties to thrash out a constitution for the new democratic South Africa, the rolling green hills of Natal resounded with the clatter of gunfire, the smash and crash of axes and assegais and sticks as Inkatha impis attacked ANC strongholds, as ANC impis attacked Inkatha strongholds, petrol bombs flying, kraals burnt, buses machine-gunned, refugees swarming into the white towns. South Africa was in chaos.

Then came an event that changed the course of Harker's life: a police squad panicked and opened fire on a hostile mob. The world was shocked – this was almost as bad as the Sharpeville massacre. An outraged Nelson Mandela announced that the ANC was breaking off talks at the Great Indaba.

The world stared, aghast: if the Great Indaba stopped the armed struggle would intensify, the reform process would be rent asunder, South Africa would be consumed in a furious conflagration of civil war. For days the world waited with bated breath as the violence swept the land and President de Klerk decided what to do.

Then came his dramatic announcement that in order to get the ANC back to the negotiating table he was appointing a judicial enquiry into the massacre, into police death-squads, and into the Civil Cooperation Bureau.

'We will cut these allegations to the bone,' he said.

Harker stared at his television screen, his sick heart knocking. The Civil Cooperation Bureau . . .

20

It was before dawn in New York when that announcement was made. Harker stared at his television screen, then he snatched up the telephone and dialled Dupont. 'Now what the hell's going to happen?'

Dupont said slowly, 'We keep our heads down, that's what.' It was the first time Harker had heard the man sound worried. 'We suspend all activities. Tell the salesmen to cool it and lie low . . . However, de Klerk has said that the judicial investigation can only enquire into activities by police hit-squads and the CCB which have taken place *inside* South Africa. That excludes us – the judge cannot listen to evidence about us.'

Harker felt sick in his guts. 'That'll fool nobody. Everybody will know that CCB offices exist *outside* the borders.'

'But there'll be no *evidence*, nobody will be able to testify about Harvest House or the Royalton Hotel.'

'Names could slip out – even if the judge has to ignore it, the press won't. Nor will the ANC. And then, will the Chairman be forced to give evidence? This judicial commission of enquiry won't be like Daniel's last one, where the Attorney General was both judge and prosecutor. And all interested parties, like the ANC, the army, the police, will have their own lawyers and witnesses.'

'The Chairman will deny everything,' Dupont said grimly. 'The ones to worry about are these two CCB guys who've been arrested for the murders of Anton Lubowski and David Webster.'

'Exactly,' Harker said. 'They'll deny the murders but they'll have to tell the court about the CCB, about their regional manager and regional director, and so on. Then

177

the regional director will have to be called as witness and he'll have to tell the court about the Chairman being his boss. Then the Chairman will have to give evidence, and what's he going to say – everybody's telling a pack of lies?' He shook his head. 'And what about all his files? If they're found we're in the shit.'

'The files won't be found. The Chairman will have hidden them by now, standard procedure.'

'So what about our files, here in America? Surely we should get rid of all evidence right now?'

'*No.* Await orders from Head Office, for Christ's sake.'

Harker seethed. 'I respectfully suggest you seek instructions from Head Office *now*! Look, the CCB is likely to be disbanded in a panic – so let's minimize the panic by asking permission to get rid of the evidence now.'

There was a steely silence. Then Dupont said, 'Will you kindly stop telling me my job?' There was a pause, then he barked, 'Now follow orders and keep your head down! I assure you the CCB is not going to be disbanded! There is no "panic". And *you*, Major, will shut up and await orders!'

Jesus! Harker was about to shout, 'And you, Colonel, can go to hell!' – but Dupont slammed down the telephone.

Harker slumped back in his chair. Then the other telephone rang, the extension from his office upstairs. It was seven-thirty a.m. 'Harvest House,' he said tensely.

'Hullo, darling,' Josephine said happily, 'have you seen the news? About the commission of enquiry?'

Harker closed his eyes. 'Yes.'

'Isn't this wonderful? We're going to get Nuremberg-style trials, hopefully, the bastards are going to get their comeuppance! Darling, are you there?'

'Yes.'

'Look, how do I find out more about this CCB?'

Harker closed his eyes. 'Not a clue.'

'Know any old soldiers who might be able to fill me in?'

Harker smiled bitterly despite himself. 'Not in this country.'

178

'Well,' Josephine said, 'this commission of enquiry will come up with some humdinger truths. *Oh*, this is going to be fun, watching those apartheid goons run for cover! And that's what my next book's going to be about! What do you think of that?'

Harker took a deep breath. He said: 'You've already written the big Africa novel – another Africa book will be an anti-climax.'

'Oh, I disagree!' Josephine said. 'Hit-squads, taking the lid off apartheid's secrets is the natural sequel . . .'

It was a very tense time, waiting for the judicial enquiry to begin.

There was a blackout on information from Military Intelligence Headquarters. In the South African newspapers there was a welter of speculation that was often contradictory. Indeed the most reliable material came from Josephine's friends in the Anti-Apartheid League in Johannesburg. Their reports gave a picture of the police and Military Intelligence in disarray, the ANC's lawyers bullishly vowing to leave no stone unturned in exposing the whole truth, Lawyers for Human Rights vowing to get the enquiry extended to uncover skulduggery worldwide, lawyers for Daniel Sipholo and Badenhorst likewise. Josephine delighted in contemplating the fear in the apartheid-mongers' breasts, she gleefully buried herself in her second book. It was provisionally titled *Wages of Sin*. Harker felt feverish.

At stake in this enquiry was not only Harvest House, but his freedom and his relationship with Josephine: if the truth came out – he had no confidence in the territorial restrictions placed upon the enquiry – Josephine would loathe him, abandon him to his fate. And his fate would be horrendous: he would be prosecuted in America for the Long Island murders; he would spend the rest of his life in prison.

'For Christ's sake, what about our files?' he demanded of Dupont.

'I don't know anything more than you do. Just keep your head down!'

'But haven't you had *any* contact at all from Head Office?'

'If the Chairman doesn't see fit to give us any orders he isn't worried about our files being an embarrassment.'

Harker didn't believe that Dupont had had no contact with Head Office – it just wasn't credible. What worried him was the possibility that he was being kept in the dark by Dupont so that he could be made a scapegoat. If only a glimmer of the truth emerged at the judicial enquiry to the effect that the CCB had an operative in New York, the press would be on to the story in a flash and there were several of his salesmen out there who might be tempted to talk to an investigative journalist in exchange for money. And there were those two impecunious bastards in the United Nations, Deep Throat and Falsetto, who didn't know his identity but who sure knew they were selling information to Derek Clements and Ferdi Spicer for the benefit of the South African government. And there was Froggy Fred, the CIA man: Harker knew nothing about Fred beyond his codename and his passwords but Fred sure looked like a nasty piece of work who would not hesitate to abandon a sinking ship. And then there was Ricardo down in Miami. Ricardo was a dedicated Castrophobe, but if he was about to lose his well-paid CCB job how tempted would he be to spill the beans?

Oh Jesus, Jesus . . . And then there was Felix Dupont himself. Harker had never trusted that man. Oh, sure, he had an admirable military record, decorations for valour, but he was unquestionably a bully, and bullies are usually snakes-in-the-grass. The more Harker thought about it the more he worried that Felix Dupont might be setting him up. Felix Dupont knew everything about Harker's CCB activities, but what did Harker know about Dupont's? Fuck all. Nowhere in his files was there a word that incriminated Dupont, or even mentioned his name . . .

21

Five days before the commission of enquiry began Josephine left for South Africa to research her new book, *Wages of Sin*.

In the weeks leading up to her departure, she was full of enthusiasm for her new project, full of anticipation of the lurid incriminating detail that was going to emerge, full of malicious satisfaction that some of apartheid's villains were going to get their comeuppance at last. Harker was dogged by foreboding. He tried to rationalize it, to convince himself that nobody was going to give away a damn thing, that in the dark world of espionage nobody admitted anything, that the enquiry was going to be a shambles, a white-wash, the judge was going to come up against a blank wall of denial. The Chairman, the whole of Military Intelligence, would deny the CCB was anything other than an intelligence-gathering department, they would denounce their two operatives arrested for the murder of Lubowski and Webster as liars. And if all those bastards with all their experience in mendacity were going to stonewall the judge successfully, how the hell was Josephine Valentine going to do a Watergate, find a Deep Throat to get to the truth? No way. Forget it . . .

But he could not forget it: he was dogged by the dread that his darling Josephine, the prize-winning war photographer with the reputation of being hard as nails, would somehow get to the bottom of the Civil Cooperation Bureau and find Jack Harker in the midst of it. That would mean losing not only her, but also Harvest and his liberty, because most assuredly he would be prosecuted in America and sent to jail for the rest of his life. He tried his best to dissuade Josephine from going to South Africa but it was to no avail.

'Darling, this represents the culmination of all my years of photo-journalism in Africa. I'm going to come back covered in glory and write a wonderful book which is going to make us both rich . . .'

In her last few days he wanted to follow her around, to be in her presence all the time as if afraid she would never come back to him. The night before she left he took her to a bistro in their neighbourhood and, looking at her healthy loveliness sitting opposite him in the candlelight, he had suddenly had enough of all the tension and demons. All he wanted to do was get out of this lie he was living, get out of this treacherous CCB, out of the grasp of Felix Dupont, even out of Harvest House, right clean out of America.

'Josie? Don't go to South Africa. Let's get married instead. Tomorrow.'

She stared at him, her fork poised.

He continued earnestly, 'You're chasing a story that won't come to anything because this whole enquiry is going to be a sham. So don't waste your time – let's just get married, say to hell with everything else.'

Josephine was still staring at him. 'And do what?'

'Live happily ever after, like they do in the movies. And –' he took her hand across the table – 'when your book's published in September, after you've finished your publicity razzmatazz, let's just disappear for a while. Buy a couple of round-the-world air-tickets and take off.'

'But what about Harvest House?'

'The place can run without me – I'm due lots of vacation anyway. Or let's just swan around the Caribbean for a while – buy that boat we've been talking about.'

'But,' Josephine said, 'why can't we do all that after I come back from Africa?'

'*No,*' Harker said, 'I love you, goddammit, and I don't want you to go away! Especially on a wild-goose chase in dangerous South Africa.'

She squeezed his hand. 'South Africa's not that dangerous.'

'It's never been so fucking dangerous. The Zulus and the ANC are kicking the shit out of each other, there's complete lawlessness in Johannesburg, Natal is burning. For Christ's sake, South Africa's one of the most dangerous places on earth right now.'

'But how can we get married tomorrow? New York State requires us to publish banns, doesn't it?'

'Then we'll fly to Las Vegas tonight.'

'To*night*?'

'Why not – the wedding chapels are open twenty-four hours a day.'

'For the romantic gamblers, huh?'

'There's no gamble in our romance, baby.'

'Oh yes there is.'

'Oh no there isn't. So let's get our asses out to the airport! Before I change my mind.'

'Before *you* change your mind, huh?'

'Or you.'

'Me? I haven't yet made up my mind!'

'Yes you have. You love me.'

'No – I *adore* you. But what about my dress?'

'Fuck your dress. I'll buy you one in sunny Las Vegas but you won't be wearing it long!'

It was fun all the way: they cracked a bottle of champagne in the taxi on the way to the airport and as soon as they boarded the first-class cabin of the shuttle to Las Vegas the flight attendant cracked another. The excellent dinner was served with fine wine and when they were requested to fasten their seatbelts for landing they were feeling no pain whatsoever. Harker carried their unfinished bottle of Dom Pérignon into the terminal.

'Where to, sir?' the taxi driver said.

'The best damn wedding chapel in town!'

It was called Famous Blessed Unions Inc, and the charges

were very reasonable: $249.99 for the minimum service, $9.99 for the music, $4.99 for the ring cushion, $4.99 for a framed copy of the Holy Vows, $3.99 for the candles, $2.99 for a framed copy of the Marriage Certificate, while a full colour video of the whole shooting-match was thrown in for FREE FREE FREE. Outside the lights of Las Vegas pulsated like a galactic orgasm. The Gothic archway of Famous Blessed Unions Inc glowed like a portal to heaven, celestial music wafting out, the altar awash with cherubs flitting in subdued lights against a background of placid clouds tinged in glorious sunrise, the whole ensemble dominated by an iridescent crucifix. And standing before this altar, hands clasped in eager piety, was Pastor Oswald C. McDougal III, proprietor. 'Good evening,' went his sepulchral voice, 'or should I say good morning?'

'Good morning,' Harker said. 'We would like to get married, please.'

'How *wonderful*!' Pastor Oswald C. McDougal III sang. 'How absolutely *won*derful, and may the Lord bless your joyful union. And it will be the full marriage service you'll be requiring, will it?'

'No,' Josephine said.

'Oh, I understand,' the Pastor cooed. 'The quicker the better, eh, and the extra fifty dollars might be better spent on the wedding breakfast or on the down-payment for the baby-carriage, aha-ha-ha. And how about the ring, have you got one or would you like to see our lovely selection?'

'No,' Josephine said. 'Excuse me.' She turned, took Harker's hand and walked rapidly down the aisle. She stepped out into the neon lights, slumped back against the chapel wall and hung her head. 'I'm sorry,' she said.

'What?' Harker said. He put his hand on her shoulder.

Josephine tossed back her head and looked at him. 'I'm sorry. Not like this.'

Harker squeezed her shoulder. 'Okay, we can go to a regular Catholic church right here in town tomorrow.'

She shook her head. 'It's not this chapel – though God knows it's ghastly. Jack?' She looked at him. 'I can't go through with it. Sorry. Can't.'

Harker stared at her. 'Meaning?'

'Yes. Sorry. No – I mean *no*, I do love you, but I don't want to get married. Not now. And not like this. Oh God, it's got nothing to do with religion or anything like that, I mean –' her eyes were bleak – 'I've simply got too much to do, too much work ahead of me to get married. Too many places to see, and to photograph and you know – *experience*.' She looked at him. 'I'm sorry, Jack, but I've got to go to South Africa tomorrow and do my work.'

Harker stepped back. 'Jesus Christ,' he said.

'What?'

Harker turned and walked away. 'I said Jesus Christ.'

'Where are you going?'

'To get drunk.'

'Wait for me . . .'

The day after she left for South Africa, Derek Clements demanded a meeting. They rendezvoused in Union Square in the evening rush hour.

Clements said: 'I went to see the Director in Washington yesterday.'

Harker was taken aback. 'You know you're not allowed to do that. If you've got any problems you come to me first!'

Clements' hard face was grim. 'I've known Dupont longer than you, he's the guy who recruited me before you arrived on the scene, sir. And as you can't tell me what's happening at Head Office I went to see him. 'Cause I'm getting worried about this enquiry that's starting in Pretoria.' *You and me both.*

'So what happened with Dupont?'

Clements said grimly: 'He was furious with me for walking in, but I expected that. What I didn't expect was what

185

he said when I told him I was worried about the Long Island job.'

'What did he say?'

Clements stopped walking and turned to Harker, his blue eyes piercing. 'Said he didn't know what I was talking about, sir. Said he'd never even heard of the incident. Then denied he knew anything about the Anti-Apartheid League burglary.'

Harker stared at him. A coldness in his gut. People hurried past in both directions.

'Jesus. What else?'

Clements said slowly: 'He said that my job was intelligence-gathering, pure and simple, that anything I had done beyond that was my lookout. He asked me if you had ordered the Long Island job, sir.'

Harker stared. *Oh God.*

Clements continued, 'I told him yes you had. He was furious – or pretended to be. Said you must be a madman, acting on your own initiative, beyond the scope of your orders.'

Jesus. Harker looked the man in his icy eye. '*Bastard.* What else?'

'That's it. Ordered me out of the hotel. Told me to get my ass back to Manhattan, do nothing until I received orders from him.'

'From *him*? Not from me?'

'No,' Clements said carefully. 'Direct from him.' His eyes were unwavering. 'You weren't acting on your own initiative, were you, sir? About the Long Island job?'

For a perverse moment Harker almost wanted to laugh – *This is what happens when thieves fall out?* 'Of course not!'

Clements nodded slowly. 'You were acting on orders from the Director?'

'Of course.'

Clements seemed to relax somewhat. A thin smile appeared. 'Fine, sir. So I'll keep my head down. Until I receive orders.' He frowned. 'But from you or the Director?'

'From me!' Harker snapped. 'Standard procedures. And if the Director speaks to you direct, I expect you to tell me.' Then he realized that was a hopeless order: Felix fucking Dupont could go right over his head and order Clements to keep his mouth shut about anything. 'Look, Derek, tough times could be ahead. And it's quite clear from your visit to Washington that you and I need to stick together. So you report all developments to me.' He tried to make it sound like an order, not a conspiracy.

Clements smiled. 'Right, sir. We're a team.'

'Right.'

'Right. So now business is over can I buy you a drink, sir?'

Harker shook his head. 'Thank you, but I'm expecting a phone call from my girlfriend.'

'Of course,' Clements said. 'Is that still Miss Valentine, sir? The anti-apartheid lady?' Harker was taken aback. He knew all about Clements' girlfriends because it was all on file, but he had never mentioned his own love-life to Clements. Coming from a junior officer the question was almost an impertinence. 'Yes,' he said.

Clements held out his hand. 'Okay, goodnight, sir.' Then he added, as if an afterthought, 'By the way, are you wired? Have you been tape-recording this conversation, sir?'

Harker glared. 'I know what "wired" means, for Christ's sake. The answer is no. Why?'

Clements smirked. 'Well, I have. After my little experience with the Director I thought it wise – wish I'd been wired when I saw him.' He smiled. 'Nothing to worry about, sir. I won't drop you in the shit if you don't drop me. Goodnight, sir.'

He turned and walked away into the rush-hour crowds.

22

Ferdi Spicer's CCB front company, Cleopatra's Retreat, an upmarket whorehouse on West 57th Street near the river, was a converted warehouse. It had three floors, each bigger than a tennis court. The ground floor was mostly a reception area where the girls lounged around while the client took his pick: there was a king-size Jacuzzi beside a big mahogany bar, and a small fast-food restaurant. There was a small dance floor for people who wanted to smooch with or without their clothes on: if you wanted to copulate right there, or in the Jacuzzi, or up at the bar, it was okay at Cleopatra's Retreat. Beyond the bar was the Swing Room, all sides mirrored, with wall-to-wall mattresses: here anything went, group sex abounded. Beyond were smaller rooms, also for swingers but for those who preferred more privacy, fewer participants. At weekends, Cleopatra's swing rooms were jumping, but during the week most of the fornication was done upstairs in the twenty well-appointed suites which had all the whorehouse accoutrements: pornographic videos, mirrored ceilings, sadomasochism equipment, vibrators, dildoes, perfumes, unctions.

Harker rang the front door bell. The spy glass darkened and Stella, Ferdi's girlfriend, opened the door. 'Hi, Mr Hogan, long time no see.'

'Is the boss in, Stella?'

'He's having his bath. Would you like to wait at the bar?'

'No, I'll wait in your private sitting room, please.'

Stella led him down a corridor, past the Jacuzzi, the bar, the swing rooms, to their apartment at the rear of the warehouse. It overlooked a sanitary lane and fire escapes. Stella disappeared through to the bathroom. Harker walked to the booze cabinet and poured himself a whisky. There were numerous photographs of Ferdi in military garb, leaping out of a helicopter, landing by parachute, singing drinking songs in a bush bar – Harker was in that one, with Derek Clements. Stella reappeared, her diaphanous see-through pyjama suit leaving nothing to the imagination. 'He's coming now, Mr Hogan.'

'Thank you.'

Stella left the room and a moment later Ferdi came bursting through, dripping, clutching a towelling dressing gown about his big frame. 'Sir, long time no see!'

'You've never seen me before, Ferdi, remember that.'

'Sure, sir, never. But what a pleasure, it would be nice if you've come to be sociable, know what I mean, lots of pretty ladies and they're on the house.'

'Thanks, Ferdi, another time.' He took a breath. 'Meanwhile you've heard about this commission of enquiry into hit-squads, the police and the CCB?'

'Yes sir, been in the papers, and the Director got hold of me about it. And Clements too.'

Harker stared. '*Dupont* did? And what did he say?'

'Told me to keep my mouth zipped. About everything, but especially about Long Island. And Mr Beauregard said the same.'

'Beauregard did?' Beauregard was the codename for the CIA man who was Froggy Fred's superior officer. What the fuck was he doing talking direct to salesmen? 'And what did he have to say?'

'That the CIA would be merciless if I dropped them in the shit over the Long Island job – or if any of us did. And he pointed a gun in my guts.'

'Jesus. Where were you?'

'Right here where you're standing.'

'Christ. And what happened with Clements?'

Ferdi said, 'Clements was just worried about you spilling the beans. Because you'd been to Sandhurst and all that jazz. Said I must report anything fishy directly to him.'

Harker stared. *Jesus* ... 'Why should Sandhurst make any difference? Now listen, Ferdi – you report directly to me, not to Clements. If anybody approaches you, no matter who, I want to know about it immediately. Got that?'

Ferdi Spicer nodded earnestly. 'Got it, sir. Except under standing orders I'm not supposed to know who you are, sir, I'm only supposed to know Clements.'

'Well, you *do* fucking know me and I'm your boss! And I'm the guy you report to, okay?'

'Okay, sir,' Ferdi said. 'And if Clements asks me?'

'Tell him to ask *me*. Got that? And tell me – how much does Stella know about us?'

'Nothing, sir,' Spicer assured him. 'She knows I was in the US Marines, of course, and that I was a mercenary in the Rhodesian army, but that's all.'

'And what does she know about me?'

'Nothing, sir, honest! She only knows you're my friend from way back in the Rhodesian army.'

'Now look here, Ferdi, I must make something abundantly plain to you ...' He paused, then pointed. 'Next week, when this commission of enquiry starts in Pretoria, if any journalist comes snooping around asking questions – or anybody else – you know nothing, you don't know what he's talking about. And that particularly applies to Deep Throat and Falsetto and any other of that United Nations gang – they may get nervous when they hear about this commission. And if Clements or Dupont or Fred or Beauregard speak to you about anything, or try to give you instructions, you report to me *immediately*, even if it's the middle of the night. Got that?'

'Yes, sir.'

'Because if it is suspected that the CCB has a base in New York, guys like you and me with an African background will be suspect. And if the cops find out we were involved in the Long Island job we'll go to jail for the rest of our lives.' Harker glared. 'Got that, Ferdi?'

23

The week after Josephine left was a bad time for Harker, waiting for the judicial enquiry to begin, waiting for Josephine to call to give him her address, her cellphone number, her news. He was worried sick. Josephine could ask questions the judge could not, she could listen to hearsay and rumours. On the third day he could bear the suspense no longer and he telephoned Annie, her friend in the anti-apartheid movement in Johannesburg, but he had to leave a message on her answering machine. And then, on Sunday, the day before the commission of enquiry opened, she telephoned.

'I'm sorry, darling,' she said.

Thank God. 'For what, exactly?'

'For not calling earlier.'

'Why didn't you?'

She sighed. 'Because I didn't know what to say. I needed my own space. Because . . . Oh hell, I felt bad about letting you down in Las Vegas.'

Harker snorted. 'What does that mean? That you wish we had got married?'

Josephine sighed again. 'I don't know what it means, except I'm sorry I hurt you. We should not have got as far as Las Vegas, I should have said no in New York.'

'That's great. Don't bother saying it again now.'

'Oh, I'm sorry.'

'So don't let's talk about it any more. Tell me what's happening out there.'

She sighed. 'Christ, Jack, the violence is appalling. Every day there are pitched battles round Johannesburg between the ANC warriors and Inkatha Zulus. The power-struggle has moved up here in a big way.'

'But that's been going on for a year.'

'But it's the government's strategy of divide and rule, getting the Zulus to do their dirty work for them so that the ANC will be intimidated at the Great Indaba. These Zulus are hit-squads – they're part of this Third Force.'

'I don't believe that,' Harker said grimly.

'Then why didn't the police stop those truckloads of Zulu warriors coming up from Natal? For decades the police have been able to enforce apartheid but now they can't put up a few roadblocks to stop a civil war? Why? Because the government *wants* the Zulus to do their dirty work. So even when the commission of enquiry into hit-squads is about to start the government is using hit-squads on a massive scale!'

'Josie, you're on a wild-goose chase; come home.'

'No way, I'm going to get to the bottom of this even if the commission of enquiry fails . . .'

Those words filled Harker with dread.

At four a.m. Monday morning Harker sat in Madam Velvet's dungeon watching the television footage of the crowds outside the commission of enquiry in Pretoria: in South Africa it was ten a.m. The CNN reporter stood in front of her camera.

'This is a very important event. Today evidence about the apartheid government's alleged death-squads is about to emerge which, if true, is going to shock the nation, and the world. The consequences will be enormous, for the government, for the police, for the army – and for the individual officers who carried out the dirty tricks alleged. If the allegations prove to be true the government could fall, heads will roll, many could be prosecuted – and the guilt could stretch right the way to the very top of the chain of command. This is what the lawyers representing the ANC and other black political parties are going to try to prove. Many people say that this enquiry is going to be a cover-up because the government has ordered that only crimes committed *inside* South Africa may be investigated. The ANC will protest loudly about this, claiming that many of its representatives were murdered abroad, and it will try to widen the enquiry.'

The reporter glanced at her wristwatch and continued: 'There is high feeling in the crowd you see behind me – derision, glee, indignation, animosity, depending on which side of the political fence individuals are. Alas, I cannot take the camera inside but the numerous lawyers for all parties are lined up at their long tables with their piles of files awaiting the entrance of the Honourable Mr Justice le Roux to commence the enquiry . . .'

At dawn Harker was at his desk at Harvest House, trying to work, but he could not concentrate. At noon he bought the midday newspapers, but there was still no news beyond what CNN had told him. Nor was there any fresh news in the evening papers. That night he telephoned Dupont. 'What's happening?' he demanded.

Dupont sounded drunk. 'What's happening about fucking what? You've got the wrong fuckin' number, buddie!' He banged down the telephone.

Harker dialled again furiously. 'What the hell're you playing at, Colonel?!'

'Please,' Dupont said wearily, 'consult directory enquiries. You've got the wrong number.' He hung up.

Jesus! The rats deserting the sinking ship! He was on the point of punching out Dupont's number again when the other telephone rang. 'Hullo?'

'Hullo, darling,' Josephine shouted from Pretoria.

Harker closed his eyes. 'Are you all right?'

'Fine. But what *isn't* fine is this goddam enquiry! We're *never* going to get to the truth!'

Harker closed his eyes in relief.

'An absolute farce!' she said. 'Everybody's furious. There're these guys from Military Intelligence sitting in the gallery with false beards and dark glasses glaring at their colleagues in the witness box – who're also wearing disguises! And these witnesses are simply refusing to answer questions on the grounds that they may incriminate themselves! The lawyers for the ANC and Human Rights are hopping mad. Jack, it's a circus! When the lawyers – or even the judge – demand to see their files these guys simply shrug and say they've disappeared, that they don't know where they are!'

Thank God. 'And?'

'And the judge is powerless – he hasn't got the practical power to do the job F.W. de Klerk gave him! It's all a massive cover-up!'

Thank God. 'So the judge isn't finding out anything about the CCB?'

Josephine snorted in disgust. 'We're just glimpsing the tip of the iceberg. We've learnt that there's a total of *sixty-four* CCB offices across the globe, pretending to be businesses. But really they're spies – *and* hit-men no doubt, though nobody's admitting to that little detail. *Sixty-four.* Did you know that, when you were in the army?'

Harker had his eyes closed again. 'No.'

'And these so-called CCB businesses employ *hundreds* of spies. And hitmen. Christ, they've doubtless got an "office" right under our noses in New York.'

'Amazing.'

She said, 'Remember that assassination in Long Island, killing those Cubans and Africans in 1988? That was probably the work of those CCB bastards.'

Panic lurched through the sickness in his guts. He managed to say, 'No, surely that was a Cuban exile job?'

Josephine snorted. 'Yeah? Anyway, all that these heavily disguised army officers are giving us is snippets while the ANC lawyers and the judge get more and more furious, while outside in the street the right-wing Afrikaner mobs are staging rallies in protest at the nation's heroes being persecuted for their "services to South Africa". God, what a circus!'

194

'So as it's a farce why don't you come home now? If the judge can't get to the bottom of this, how can you?'

'By talking to the right people. Like Lawyers for Human Rights, the ANC's lawyers, the press. Paying information money to the right people in the military, the police – my hands aren't tied like the judge's.'

Oh Jesus Jesus. '*Don't,*' he said, 'go anywhere *near* the military.'

'Where else am I going to get the information for my book?'

The next day the story was covered by all the New York newspapers: all the reports damned the enquiry as a whitewashing of the security forces. There was television footage of the right-wing demonstrations in the streets.

The CNN reporter said, '. . . while evidence of police and military skulduggery must come to a dead stop the moment the story crosses South Africa's borders, lawyers for the police have been allowed to lead evidence attributing five thousand political murders to the ANC – without specifying where they took place, whether they're attributable to actual hit-squads or the random tribal violence which is racking the country . . .'

That night Josephine telephoned him, seething with righteous indignation, giving him the same report.

'The ANC lawyers are up in arms. They've told the press they're going to retaliate by demanding permission to lead evidence about all the high-profile murders of anti-apartheid people that've happened overseas – by hook or by crook they're going to squeeze in those hideous crimes to put the record straight!'

Harker felt his guts contract. 'Which crimes?'

'*You* know.' He heard the rustle of her notebook. She read, 'Anton Lubowski in Namibia, Albie Sachs getting his arm blown off by a car bomb in Mozambique, Dulcie September gunned down in Paris, David Webster, and that godalmighty assassination on Long Island where those

Cubans and ANC people were killed. It was officially blamed on the Cuban exiles, right? Well, it now turns out the job was done by Military Intelligence, by this CCB we've just learned about!'

Harker heard ringing in his ears. 'Nonsense – who said that?'

'The ANC! One of their men survived the blast, remember? His name's Looksmart Kumalo. I've spoken to him, he's a very bright guy. He lost a hand in the shooting. Anyway, he says he can prove that it was the CCB who did it, *not* the Cuban exiles.'

Harker felt himself whiten. 'How can he prove it?'

'Oh, it's common knowledge now that the CIA were hand-in-glove with the South African military over the Angolan war – the CIA told the FBI to blame it on the Cubans. He's got informers in the Cuban exile community who say it definitely *wasn't* their work, they had no idea those two Cuban officers were in America or they would have kidnapped them to squeeze information from them.'

'Of course the Cuban exiles would deny it.'

'Well, Looksmart Kumalo is hiring private detectives and he's going to sue the South African government – and see that the perpetrators are prosecuted for murder.'

Oh Jesus, Jesus . . .

Harker could not report this conversation to Dupont because he didn't want the bastard to know that Josephine was in South Africa. He telephoned his CCB man, Ricardo, in Miami.

'You may have a double-agent amongst the exiled top brass,' Harker told him. 'Somebody who's talked to the ANC about Operation Marigold. Make some enquiries.'

Josephine did not telephone the next day but she faxed some newspaper cuttings. There were also reports in most of New York's papers. One newspaper editorialized: '. . . *The South African government's underground network is said to be in panic. We have learned that there have been over ten murders of potential witnesses since the enquiry began. Today evidence*

196

emerged that even the Johannesburg City Council has its own spy-network, a fully fledged department spying on left-wing ratepayers and carrying out skulduggery against them. South Africa is rotten with apartheid's paranoia, the nation has developed a whole covert culture under her "Total Onslaught" mentality . . .'

Ten witnesses murdered? Jesus, Harker had had no idea of the depth of the depravity he was involved in.

The next night Josephine telephoned: 'Did you read about the witnesses who've been murdered?'

'Yes.'

She sighed angrily. 'God, I'm so glad you're out of all that – imagine if you were still in the army, you'd be so *tainted*!' Then: 'Jack? When you were in the army you didn't know about any of this, did you?'

Harker closed his eyes. 'Of course not.'

'Okay. So, what's happening in sunny New York?'

He said shakily: 'I'm missing you, that's what's happening.'

'Oh, I miss you too – but I'm going to write a very good book.'

A very good book. Oh God.

Those were long days waiting for Josephine to telephone, waiting for the news on the radio, waiting for the newspapers. And then, a week after the enquiry started, Josephine telephoned at dawn.

'Have you heard the news? President de Klerk has just announced in parliament that he has officially disbanded this so-called CCB!'

Harker stared across the room. Incredulous. Then relief flooded through him. Then joy. *Oh thank God.* He groped for words. 'About time . . .'

'Do you believe it?' Josephine cried indignantly. 'I certainly don't! Nor do any of the journalists or lawyers I've spoken to! It's all part of the great big cover-up! First de Klerk denied the CCB existed, like he denied he knew anything about police hit-squads, now he piously announces that the *CCB* exists – though *not* the police hit-squads. And, says he, with a wave of his hand, he's now disbanded them!' She snorted. 'Christ, you can't believe it, can you?'

Harker's eyes were closed. 'He wouldn't dare make such a public statement if it wasn't true.'

'I believe you but thousands wouldn't!' Josie cried. 'Look, South Africa was a police state – still is – and her army were her shock-troops – and nothing's changed. And I don't believe for a moment that the CCB is disbanded – de Klerk's holding the organization together for the final battles so that he's got all his big battalions intact in case the Great Indaba doesn't go the way he wants it.'

Oh, Harker desperately wanted to be disbanded. He heard himself say, 'Well, the ANC hasn't disbanded its army either.'

'Of course not! Every army keeps its powder dry during peace negotiations. So why should we believe de Klerk has disbanded the CCB? He's keeping them in reserve, the whole CCB organization is untamed worldwide. *Disbanded?* All those thousands of CCB agents have suddenly vaporized, all their files, all their secret bank accounts? Bull*shit*! It'll leap into action as soon as the government doesn't get its own way – and it'll remain a terrible right-wing threat for years, with masses of money at its disposal to overthrow democracy and restore apartheid!' Josephine snorted, then went on: 'This proves the ANC are right when they say that there's a Third Force provoking the political warfare in South Africa – it's the bloody army who's stirring up the bloodshed to give the world the impression that blacks are incapable of democracy!' She added: 'And I bet it was those CCB bastards who raided the Anti-Apartheid League's premises.'

Harker's heard himself say: 'I can't imagine the army going to all that trouble over a minor –'

'*Minor?*' Josephine echoed dangerously.

'I mean over a civilian, *peaceable* organization like the Anti-Apartheid League when they were fighting a major war.'

'Who else would it be – the Ku Klux Klan?'

Harker sighed. 'When are you coming home?' he said quietly. 'I'm missing you like hell.'

'Oh, I miss you too,' she said. 'But this is too big a story, I've got to see it through.'

'But that could take months . . .'

Immediately afterwards, Harker telephoned Dupont. His heart was tingling with tentative joy that the bastard would soon no longer be his boss. 'So what's the procedure for disbandment and demobilization, sir?' he said.

There was a pause during which Dupont breathed drunkenly. Then the man rasped: 'Until it's official you'll remain at your fucking post.'

Harker had half expected the sonofabitch to deny he knew him. 'Look, De Klerk's announced our disbanding in parliament – what could be more official than that?'

More drunken breathing. 'We take our orders,' Dupont said, 'from the Chairman, not from President de Klerk. The Chairman takes his orders from the Minister of Defence. That's the fucking truth of the matter whether you like it or not – it doesn't matter a damn what De Klerk may or may not say in fucking parliament.'

'*That*,' Harker smiled, 'may be the de facto position, but it is certainly not the *law*. The law is that parliament is supreme and De Klerk has announced in parliament, as president and commander-in-chief, that the CCB is disbanded – and that's good enough for me. *Sir*.'

Harker heard his Regional Director take a slurp of something. 'Well, it is *not* good enough for the fucking army! Until we see it in black and white from the Chairman you will remain at your fucking post or face fucking court-martial. Not to mention your fucking pension. I do not believe for one *second* that we are disbanded. The fucking trouble is only about to *begin*.'

'Meaning?'

'Jesus. Do I have to spoon-feed it to you?' Pause. Slurp.

'Now the Zulus are really going to get stuck into the ANC – and we want the Zulus to win, don't we? Maybe they're going to need a little helping hand now'n again.'

Harker stared across the basement. He said slowly, 'It's the army's job to quell violence, sir, not to promote it. The army's job is to fight the nation's *enemies*, not to murder its legitimate citizens.'

Dupont snorted. 'The ANC are legitimate citizens?'

'They've been unbanned, they've got the same rights now as everybody else.'

'They're still the fucking enemy. What about Operation Vula, smuggling all their fucking armaments into Natal the moment they were unbanned – call that fucking legitimate?'

'But that's over now – it's *us* who aren't legitimate – what about these police death-squads, what about the illegitimate things we've done? So dry your eyes about Operation Vula!'

Dupont was silent for a moment, as if digesting this. Then he sounded very puzzled: 'What illegitimate things have "we" done, dear fellow?' Harker could almost see his round face shaking in bemusement. 'I always considered the gathering of military intelligence a perfectly *legitimate* thing for an army to do. All the textbooks say so.'

'Cut the crap!' Harker rasped. 'I'm referring to the Long Island job. And Operation Heartbeat, when we burgled the Anti-Apartheid League's offices.'

Dupont breathed. 'The Long Island job?' He sounded very puzzled. 'Never heard of it, old boy.'

Harker took a furious breath. 'So you're denying you gave me the orders?'

Dupont slurred airily, 'You must be dreaming, old man. Never heard of any Long Island job. Or Operation Heartbeat. Good heavens, what would Military Intelligence care about a bunch of anti-apartheid bleeding hearts? Got any document with my signal on it to refresh my memory, old man?' He shook his head. 'Goodness gracious, all MI is interested in is *military* intelligence. If you acted on your own initiative, don't try to pass the buck to me.' He paused: 'Do I make myself clear?'

Harker's blood was up. *Jesus he hated the bastard.* He said softly, 'Perfectly. That you're passing the buck to me, just like the police are trying to do to Badenhorst.' He paused, full of controlled fury. 'And I understand perfectly that you're the full-time shit I've always thought you were. And now I'm going to make *myself* perfectly clear.' He paused, breathing angrily. 'And the first point is this: if you ever try to drop me in the shit over the Long Island job – or any other operation – I will blow the whistle on you. I will not only tell the South African press, I'll shout it from the rooftops of Manhattan. I'm a publisher, remember.' He paused again. 'And the second point is that, because I'm not a shit like you, I *will* keep my mouth shut, as standing orders and the Defence Force Act require – *provided* you keep *your* fucking mouth shut. Got that, Felix? However, I have two conditions for my silence. The first is that I quit, that my resignation from the CCB is accepted at once. In fact I regard myself as disbanded as of now, demobilized by President de Klerk's statement in parliament, and I shall conduct myself accordingly. I shall destroy all files in accordance with Standing Instruction 127. And my second condition is that my pension entitlements and my contractual rights to buy the shares of Harvest House be fulfilled immediately.'

There was a long pause. Then: 'Your resignation,' Dupont slurred, 'is hereby rejected. You are subject to my orders, or you're a deserter.'

Harker said maliciously: 'Your orders are no longer valid because the CCB has been disbanded by President de Klerk, our commander-in-chief!' He slammed down the telephone.

He slumped back in his chair and held his face. His fingers were trembling, but an elation was simmering through him.

He was free! Thank God President de Klerk had freed him!

201

He dragged his hands down his face, and took a deep breath. So what was the next step?

It was no good trying to contact the Chairman to tell him what he was doing – if he managed to contact the bastard at all he would disown him . . .

That only left standing instructions.

Standing Instruction 127: In the event of emergency destroy all files.

Harker looked at the shredding machine standing in the corner of his basement office. Then he decided to give the Chairman a call before he burnt his boats. He sat down at his computer.

> Dear Sir, In view of President De Klerk's announcement in Parliament this morning I regard myself as disbanded and it is my intention, within the next three hours . . .

He scrambled the text and transmitted it.

He held his face. Was this too good to be true?

Now what?

No way could he concentrate on any work whilst he waited for a response. He jumped up, mounted the staircase up to his office, and left Harvest House to walk the streets of New York for the next hour.

When he returned to the basement his computer screen announced incoming e-mail. He hastily typed in his unscrambling code.

It was a terse message from Dupont.

> Instructions from Head Office: your branch is to be shut down with immediate effect, all documentation treated in terms of 127. You may exercise your right to buy all shares at prices yet to be determined based on goodwill, fixed assets and other details. You will retain your pension entitlements on condition you observe strictest, repeat, strictest confidentiality, in default of

which there will be extreme prejudice. Acknowledge.
Message ends.

Harker stared at the screen, a joyful smile spreading all over his gaunt face, a song rising in his heart. Then he threw back his head. '*Yahoo!*'

He jumped up and thrust his fist aloft. Then he threw himself down at the computer, drummed his heels and acknowledged receipt of the instructions.

Then he telephoned his bank manager and made an immediate appointment.

He set out again into the New York morning with a spring in his step and a song in his heart, to borrow big money. He did not yet know how much but he knew it was going to be a lot.

As a soldier, fear had been part of Jack Harker's stock-in-trade, an occupational hazard. But now he was terrified, as he emerged from the portals of the First National City Bank – actually terrified. Because he had just arranged a loan facility of up to three million dollars.

Absolutely terrifying – but it also felt marvellous! Jack Harker was his own boss at last! Jack Harker was a real publisher at last! And an honest lover at last! The daily deceptions were over!

And, oh he loved his girl . . .

It was noon when he got back to Harvest House, six p.m. in Pretoria. He wanted to tell Josephine what he had done but he could not because she believed he had always been the majority shareholder, always thought he was a real publisher. He dialled her cellphone number.

'I just called . . .' he crooned, 'to say . . . I love you . . . And to ask . . . when the hell . . . you're coming home . . .'

PART III

24

Harker got an excellent deal when he bought Harvest House from the CCB: because of the panic in Pretoria following President de Klerk's announcement of the disbandment, and because he had placed Harvest into substantial debt buying the publishing rights to Josephine's book, Harker managed to buy both the shares he held as nominee for the Defence Force plus Westminster's residual shareholding for much less than their real value: it was a bargain, a case of luck and right timing. True, it was nonetheless a lot of money and for months while *Outrage* was in production both Harker and Harvest were technically bankrupt – but when *Outrage* was finally released it went straight on to the *New York Times* bestseller list and made Harker more than enough to pay off his personal debt to the bank plus Harvest's revolving overdraft. It was hailed as 'the definitive African novel', 'the *Gone With the Wind* of South Africa', 'a rampantly successful dramatization of heartbreaking history'. Both *Time* and *Newsweek* reviewed it enthusiastically. Josephine was bursting with pride and excitement. Harker had arranged saturation publicity, the effort and expense paid off handsomely and Josephine handled the exhausting schedule with charm and panache: for several weeks she jetted around America appearing on television chat-shows, at book-launch parties; immediately she became a household name and face, and her background as an intrepid war photo-journalist added a swashbuckling, derring-do mystique to her talent – and being beautiful helped. Harker was immensely proud of her.

And he was very relieved that her intended sequel, *Wages of Sin*, was never written because the commission of enquiry into police hit-squads and the CCB was, as both she and Felix Dupont had anticipated, a whitewash which totally exonerated the police: Judge le Roux declared Daniel Sipholo and Erik Badenhorst craven liars trying to save their necks from the hangman, while finding that the CCB did commit certain minor acts of sabotage inside South Africa. Josephine was furious and declared she was going to write the book nonetheless, but Harker took Priscilla Fischer to lunch and persuaded her to talk Josephine out of it.

Priscilla looked at him with her big green cat's eyes. 'And that's the only point of this expensive lunch? Okay, I must say I agree, so I'll advise her to cool it.' Then she stroked her long red fingernail down the back of his wrist. 'So where, I ask myself, is this meeting of minds likely to end?'

Harker poured more wine. Before he could respond Priscilla went on with a mock sigh. 'Well, one can always hope. So, reverting to business, what would you like to see Josephine write next?'

'A love story. Preferably set here in America.'

'But she's all steamed up about Africa, you know how politically minded she is.'

'Okay, let her set her story against Africa's political background but you should tell her to steer away from skulduggery, hit-squads and so forth.'

'Very well, but assuming I can persuade Josephine, what contract will you offer her on the type of book you want?'

Harker sighed. He had known it was coming sooner or later – he had hoped it would be later. 'Well,' he said, 'what do you suggest?'

Priscilla Fischer twiddled her wine glass, her eyes alight. 'A three-book contract,' she said. 'Five million dollars. One million on signature of contract, one million on delivery of the first book, one million on delivery of the second book, one million on delivery of the third book, one million on publication of that third book.' She sat back.

'Jesus Christ . . .' Harker said.

'I can take her to any of the big guns. Random, Doubleday, Little Brown, Knopf, they'll give me six million, easy. Seven. She's probably the most popular writer in America right now and the most popular face. And beautiful. Half of America is jerking off over her. In fact . . .' Priscilla opened her file and pulled out a document. '*Playboy* want to do a piece on her.'

Harker ran his eye over it. *Playboy* offered 'half a million dollars for an exclusive frank interview with Josephine Valentine in her home, together with her publisher Mr Jonathan Harker; we will also need a minimum of a dozen published photographs of her in a state of "modest semi-nudity"'.

'No way,' Harker said. 'Josie would never agree.'

Priscilla smiled and took a sip of wine. 'With all due respect, dwarling, it's not up to you to say yea or nay – it's up to Josephine, and me, as her advisor. And I will point out to her – and you – that *Playboy* has a circulation of many millions which represents a wonderful amount of free publicity *plus* the half-million bucks they're offering on top.'

'Less your ten per cent.'

'Less my ten per cent – a mere fifty thousand.'

Harker smiled. 'No way.'

'*Playboy* will settle for her in a bikini. And perhaps a bit of bum as she descends into the swimming pool. No pubic hair necessary.'

'We haven't got a swimming pool.'

'You've got Madam Velvet's Jacuzzi. Very sexy. Put in a few more artificial flowers. Ferns, that sort of thing.'

Harker grinned. 'How do you know about Madam Velvet's?'

'Josie told me. And I remembered the story in *Screw* magazine.' She added, with a twinkle in her eye, 'I read *Screw* occasionally, you see. I enjoy a bit of hard-core sometimes. When I'm feeling lonely.' She added, 'Know what I mean?'

Harker grinned, then said, 'I've only just got Harvest out of debt with *Outrage*. No way can I afford five million for Josie's next three books.'

Priscilla smiled. 'I can do simple arithmetic, buddy. You're more than out of debt, Harvest is about two million in the black thanks to *Outrage*.'

'So, isn't a publisher entitled to a little profit? We took the risk.'

'What risk? A blind man could see that book was a winner. And you call two million a "little profit"? Come on. Any dumb-ass publisher can see that if you invest five million spread over the next three books you'll turn the investment into ten big ones. Ten million for five? Nice work if you can get it.'

Harker shook his head. 'Five million is too rich for Harvest's blood.'

'Shall I try elsewhere?' Piranha leered. 'I bet Doubleday won't object to *Playboy*'s little offer. That's got to be worth – oh? – a million or two of free publicity by itself.'

'Josie will refuse to do it, unless she is fully clothed in all photographs. Maybe a few shots in a bikini, on a beach.'

'So what's your best offer on a three-book contract?'

Harker sighed. 'I'll have to discuss it with my editorial board,' he said. 'But my feeling is –'

'Don't bullshit me, Jack – you've already discussed it with your editorial board.'

'And my feeling is,' Harker said, 'that we'll settle for two million payable over the four stages you've mentioned, provided –'

'Don't make me laugh.'

'– *provided* none of the books is about South African hit-squads . . .'

25

Jack Harker ended up signing a contract for four million dollars for Josephine Valentine's next three unwritten books.

'This contract is lopsided,' Alan Moore, editor-in-chief, warned Harker. 'We're paying too much, and without even the guarantees about subject-matter. Okay, she's a bravura talent but I'm very worried about all this.'

Harker was worried too. He had only just got out of debt and now he had plunged straight back into it. It was for this reason that he took out two policies of 'key-man' insurance on Josephine's life, totalling four million dollars. Both were term insurance policies, the first of three million, payable to Harvest House, the premiums paid by Harvest; the second policy of one million was payable to himself, the premiums paid by him. The reasons for the first policy were sound enough: Harvest had to make a massive investment in Josephine Valentine and her premature death would cause a huge financial loss. He did not have to explain the second policy as nobody knew about it. And years later, he denied ever insuring her. 'But,' his police interrogator said disbelievingly, 'a man has a legitimate insurable interest in the woman he intends to marry, especially if that woman is also the source of his income.'

'Harvest House was the source of my income!'

'Indeed, and Josephine was a large source of income for Harvest. But then something happened. Her second book didn't sell very well, did it – it was an anticlimax after the success of *Outrage* – Harvest only just broke even. And her third book didn't sell well either, did it? In fact Harvest didn't even break even. And now she was writing her fourth book – the third in terms of her contract . . . So tell me what happened during those intervening years, from the time Josephine's first book was published till the time you eventually married her . . .'

Only the broad details of what happened during those intervening years matter.

While the delegates thrashed it out at the Great Indaba there erupted violence such as the turbulent land had never known as black political parties slugged it out for domination in the new South Africa, as the Boers of the Afrikaner Resistance Movement fought the government, as the government battled with everybody, sometimes more to divide and rule than to keep the peace. While the delegates at the Great Indaba argued and harangued, the land resounded with the clatter of machine guns and rifles and bomb explosions, flames crackling, smoke barrelling, blood flowing, as Zulu impis sallied forth with assegais and iron clubs and AK47s to butcher ANC impis and vice versa, as the ANC marched on the independent homelands to liberate them from their upstart dictators. Drive-by black gunmen opened up with machine guns on black bus queues in downtown Johannesburg, as black butchers wielding machetes burst on to trains carrying black commuters back to the townships, slashing, chopping, slaughtering indiscriminately.

'Now do you believe in this Third Force?' Josephine cried. 'What sense is there in this madness otherwise . . . ?'

What matters is that President F.W. de Klerk was forced by international opinion to appoint the Goldstone Commission of Enquiry regarding the Prevention of Public Violence and Intimidation. And what is really important is that in the midst of this mayhem, at the end of 1992, a year after Josephine's first book was published to great acclaim, Judge Richard Goldstone and his commission raided a building called Momentum Mews in suburban Pretoria and found it to be the secret headquarters of the

Department of Covert Collection, the secret successor to the Civil Cooperation Bureau.

Josephine was cock-a-hoop when the news broke. Harker was amazed that the CCB was still functioning under another name – had President de Klerk lost control of his security forces? He was aghast at what the files seized might reveal about him, about Harvest House, about the Long Island assassination . . .

There was public outcry but at first nothing much seemed to happen, except that President de Klerk fired twenty-three senior security force officers. The violence continued unabated, but amidst it all, the Great Indaba announced that the various parties had cobbled together agreement on an interim constitution, an election date was announced – the political violence redoubled, and the Afrikaner Resistance Movement smashed down the huge glass windows of the Great Indaba building with a vehicle and seized control of the premises. All this was shocking but it seemed to Harker in faraway New York that the importance of the Goldstone Commission had receded. But then, three weeks before the first democratic elections in South Africa's history, Judge Goldstone made his dramatic findings public.

It became known as his 'Third Force Report'. Judge Goldstone shocked the country by announcing that there was a 'horrible network of criminal activity' – gun-running, death squads, smear campaigns, exploitation and orchestration of public violence – operating within the military and police, aimed at destabilizing South Africa's democratization in general and the ANC in particular.

Harker was astonished, shocked that the military he had served had degenerated to this level – and he was very relieved that he was well clear of all that. And, once he'd thought about it, he was even relieved that the truth was out: now surely to God with the present government's guilt undeniable and the first democratic elections coming up, the ANC assured of victory, surely all these recriminations must be relegated to the garbage can of history as the ANC got on with the business of rehabilitating South Africa?

But Harker was very wrong. Soon after the Goldstone Commission's bombshell South Africa's first democratic elections were held; to the world's euphoria they were peaceable, as the ANC swept to power on a wave of international goodwill. But one of the first pieces of legislation the new government introduced was the Promotion of National Unity and Reconciliation Act which created a commission of enquiry to uncover the wounds of apartheid.

It was called the Truth and Reconciliation Commission.

PART IV

26

The noble purpose of the Truth and Reconciliation Commission – the TRC – was to heal the deep wounds of apartheid by providing a forum for victims wherein they could testify about their suffering, 'Speak out their pain', so that anger could be appeased by sympathy, so that mothers could find out what happened to husbands and children who had disappeared, so that everybody could tell of their humiliation, economic degradation from translocation and every other kind of racial discrimination. The Truth Commission was empowered to grant financial compensation to these victims of apartheid – and to grant amnesty to those perpetrators who fully and truthfully owned up to politically motivated crimes.

There was great opposition to the creation of the Truth Commission. There was consternation among security force members, past and present, great fear that the Commission would turn into a witch-hunt, great distrust, fear that amnesty would be refused despite confession, fear that even assuming amnesty was granted there would be terrible vengeance by the victims or from colleagues whom the applicant had to inculpate in order to secure amnesty. And then there was *esprit de corps*, the reluctance to drop friends in the shit.

Jack Harker was desperately worried, Josephine Valentine was angry.

'My God – how can bastards like that be granted amnesty? Murderers! *Multiple* murderers! Torturers! They should be sent to the gallows! Sent to prison for life!' She snorted. 'But maybe this commission will give us the truth at last about this Civil Cooperation Bureau we've heard about.'

'Judge Goldstone hasn't got any proof of what they did.'

'Well,' Josephine said with satisfaction, 'maybe now we're going to get some proof! And this TRC, my darling, reopens the subject of that book you persuaded me to drop, *Wages of Sin*. I'm going to blow the dust off it.'

'Josie, you must concentrate on some other subject.'

'Oh no, lover, you talked me out of this one before – this Truth Commission is going to be a big story, all the apartheid skeletons crashing out of the cupboards. Except, of course, we should be having Nuremberg-type trials, not reconciliation!'

Harker would have loved to make a clean breast to the Truth Commission and secure amnesty – but he dared not. It would explode his relationship with Josephine, ruin Harvest House; he would be prosecuted for murder in America even though he had received amnesty in South Africa.

'Forget it, Josie,' he said. 'I doubt many transgressors will come forward. They won't trust the Commission.'

She appeared not to hear him. 'Oh boy,' she said maliciously, 'there must be a lot of worried bastards in South Africa right now. Can you imagine the frantic deals being struck? The threats? The bribes?'

Yes, Harker could imagine it because that was exactly how he felt. Fear that he could be inculpated by Derek Clements over the Long Island job, by Ferdi Spicer, by Felix Dupont. Even by the Chairman.

Josephine took both his hands across the table. 'Darling,' she smiled, 'I'm afraid this means I'll have to make another trip to South Africa.'

Harker's heart was sinking.

He said grimly, 'Josie, Harvest has a lot of money invested in you. You have a responsibility to us. Both morally and contractually. And you have an even greater responsibility to me, as your partner.'

Josephine nodded solemnly. 'Agreed.'

'And,' Harker said, 'I am telling you now, as my author,

that I made no money on your last two books and I can't afford that on your next one. I therefore beg you not to even think about writing *Wages of Sin*. And I must warn you that if you do so I will probably be unable to publish it, no matter what our contract says.'

Josephine nodded solemnly, still holding his hands. 'I assure you I have no intention of asking you to publish a book you may lose money on. All I ask is that you consider the book. If you don't have confidence, we'll forget about it, stuff it under the bed, and I'll write you another one, a humdinger.' She squeezed his hands. 'But, darling, I've just got to go when this Truth Commission starts, and see the action.'

Harker's heart was sinking. 'I beg you,' he said, '*beg* you to get your beautiful ass to an anchor right here in New York and start writing something else.'

Josephine held his hands. 'Darling,' she said, 'please understand that I've just got to witness this drama . . .'

Loud opposition to the creation of the Truth Commission came from Afrikaner politicians, from the security forces, from many Zulus, all of whom had much to hide; but there was also much opposition from many members of the ANC and other black political groups who wanted to see apartheid's crimes against humanity punished in Nuremberg-style trials. There was loud opposition from some high-profile victims of apartheid who wanted to sue the perpetrators for civil damages: they argued that the legislation creating the Truth Commission was unconstitutional because amnesty gave the villains immunity from civil action as well as from prosecution. Feelings ran high. F.W. de Klerk proclaimed in parliament that a Truth Commission would rip the stitches from the healing wounds of apartheid; Chief Buthelezi of the Zulus pronounced the Truth Commission 'the stuff of Disneyland', which would make right-wingers take the law into their own hands; General Constand Viljoen of the Freedom Front warned parliament that the Commission would produce neither truth nor reconciliation; the Commissioner of Police, General van der Merwe, darkly warned that the truth about atrocities committed by the ANC would prove a grave embarrassment.

But the ANC government proclaimed that the Truth and Reconciliation Commission would begin in April the following year, 1996, that the villains had better start preparing their confessions.

And then, to hurry them along, the Attorney General launched a massive prosecution against the last officer commanding the police death-squad base on the farm called Platplaas, Colonel Eugene de Kock, a man whom his own hit-men called Prime Evil.

27

The Truth and Reconciliation Commission was a quasi-judicial body; its seventeen members, all with impeccable credentials, were presided over by Archbishop Desmond Tutu. The Commission had three standing committees, all independent of each other.

The first was the Committee on Human Rights Violations: its purpose was to hear evidence of gross injustices, to identify those responsible, to ascertain whether such abuses were the 'result of deliberate planning' with a political objective.

The function of the second committee, the Committee on Amnesty, chaired by a judge, was to decide on applications for amnesty for violations of human rights: to grant amnesty the committee had to be satisfied that the violation had a 'political objective' and that the applicant had made a full disclosure of all relevant facts.

The function of the third committee, on Reparation and Rehabilitation, was to compensate the victims. In addition the Truth Commission had a high-powered investigation unit: top-ranking detectives were provided by Denmark, Norway, Sweden, Ireland and the Netherlands, while the governments of Ireland, Norway and Sweden provided the giant computer database. The Truth Commission had power to subpoena witnesses, seize documents and other exhibits, exhume bodies. The Violation of Human Rights Committee, therefore, could subpoena an alleged perpetrator to appear and answer allegations. If that perpetrator made a full confession and his crime was proportionate to the political objective, the Amnesty Committee would grant him indemnity from both prosecution and civil damages. If the Committee were not so satisfied the matter would be handed over to the police for prosecution.

Alternatively, a perpetrator could, of his own accord, apply to the Amnesty Committee for indemnity before 15 December 1996. If the Amnesty Committee concluded that he had told the whole truth he was safe from prosecution and civil damages; if the Committee was not satisfied, they could throw the book at him, although the confession made to the Commission could not be used against him at his trial.

The Truth Commission headquarters were in Cape Town, but its various sub-committees toured the country like a circuit court to hear complaints, different tribunals sitting in different places at the same time.

The day after Josephine Valentine arrived in South Africa the Truth and Reconciliation Commission officially opened with solemn fanfare in the City Hall of East London in the Eastern Cape, with ringing speeches about the noble purpose, prayers for guidance, truth and justice. 'The Truth Shall Make Us Free' proclaimed the massive banner above the commissioners' bench. 'Even-handedness will be our watchword,' announced the chairman, Archbishop Desmond Tutu, for the 'TRC does not allow its members to say this kind of violence is better than that kind of violence . . .'

The Eastern Cape was an appropriate setting for this historic event, for the area had been the first battleground between black and white in South Africa – ten so-called Kaffir Wars had been fought there over the centuries. Those wars had been the cause of the Great Trek which led to the opening-up of the subcontinent by the Boers and all the heartbreak that brought about, including the political science of apartheid. The City Hall of East London was crammed with dignitaries, international observers and the international media, their cameras and sound equipment. The proceedings were broadcast live worldwide.

In New York's pre-dawn Harker sat grimly in Madam

Velvet's dungeon, notebook and pen in hand. He looked for Josephine in the sea of faces though he knew, because she had telephoned him, that the media were mostly holed up in an adjoining room with simultaneous translation facilities. He listened intently as the official leader of evidence slowly led the witnesses through their bitter stories of suffering. Harker watched grimly as witness after witness began to flesh out the horrors of the apartheid system, as black widows and bereaved mothers tearfully, bitterly told what had happened to them, to their loved ones, their husbands, sons, daughters who were anti-apartheid activists.

It was a terrible litany of state oppression, of cruelty, callous murder to ensure the supremacy of the white man over the black. Harker had had little idea of the extent of the brutality, of the ruthless lengths the government had gone to in order to suppress dissent, he'd had little notion of the dehumanization that this apartheid mentality had engendered. Sure, he had always thought that apartheid was wrong, but he had never dreamed that its officials committed such torture and murder. In the army his job had been to fight the enemy's soldiers, not the enemy's civilians. *Oh Jesus, this awful story unfolding now was what he had been associated with?*

At the lunch adjournment, Josephine telephoned him. It was only breakfast time in New York. 'Please tell me you didn't know about this sort of thing, Jack.'

Harker shook his head grimly. 'I promise you I did not . . .'

Hour after hour on that first day the Truth Commission heard about blacks' personal horrors; and then they listened to some of the other side, from victims of ANC atrocities, from white men and women who had suffered from ANC bombs and gunmen, from innocents who had had arms and legs blown off by bombs planted in bars, from farmers' wives whose husbands had been gunned down.

'Yes,' Josephine said when she telephoned him during the lunch adjournment, 'but no white man was really

223

"innocent", was he? He supported the government *indirectly* by not protesting, by enjoying his privileged position as a white man.'

And then, at the end of that first harrowing day, a black man called Alexander Looksmart Kumalo was called to give evidence.

His face was scarred, he had a patch over one eye. He walked across the hushed chamber to the witness table with a limp, and his right arm was amputated below the elbow.

'*Looksmart* . . .' Josephine whispered in the media room. She snatched up her cellphone and dialled Harker in New York. 'Have you got the television on?'

'No, I've just come home for lunch.'

'Switch it on, it's Looksmart Kumalo testifying, the guy I told you about – I met him during the hit-squad commission, remember? He survived that assassination attack on Long Island . . .'

Harker's heart lurched. He snapped on the set. He stared at the man, feeling sick. Staring at his stump of arm, at his scarred face. *Oh God* . . .

Looksmart Kumalo took the oath to tell the truth. Then the counsel for the Commission rose to lead his evidence.

'Mr Kumalo, were you an official in the African National Congress, a liaison officer in MK, the armed wing of the ANC?'

'Yes, sir.'

'Please tell us briefly your history, starting with when you joined the ANC.'

Looksmart Kumalo faced the commission grimly, his scarred, hawkish face sullen: he held his stump of forearm across his chest like a sash for the television cameras. In measured tones resonant with bitterness, he described how he had joined MK after the outbreak of the Soweto riots in 1976, when black students had rebelled against the government's decree that they must receive their schooling in Afrikaans. For several years the riots had continued with running battles between the security forces and the students; an extraordinary detail of all this mayhem was that it was the rebellious youth who effectively governed the townships, it was the so-called Students' Representative Council who issued the orders to the black schoolmasters and shopkeepers and shebeen-owners and all the millions of workers. The students' council called the strikes and boycotts, ruthlessly enforced them and brought about this beginning of the end of apartheid. It was not their browbeaten parents, not the ANC leadership, which had fled into exile many years earlier.

'I was one of the student leaders. I was on the Soweto Students' Representative Council from 1976 until 1978 when I decided like many others to leave the country and join the ANC in exile. We got to the Swaziland border with great difficulty, then crossed at night. We found the ANC office. After some months they smuggled us across Rhodesia into Zambia. This was very dangerous because Rhodesia was under white control and they were at war with the freedom fighters of Robert Mugabe and Joshua Nkomo. Finally we crossed the Zambezi river into Zambia, and we were put in an ANC camp. After some months we were sent overseas for military training.'

'Where were you sent?'

'Russia. And Cuba.'

'For how long?'

'Two years. Then I was sent to the ANC's headquarters in Angola, as a military intelligence officer. It was now 1981. The Cubans were helping the Angolans fight their UNITA rebels and the South Africans, so I worked closely with Cuban military intelligence. Then, in 1987 I was posted to New York.'

'Why?'

'I was posted to the United Nations, attached to the Angolan delegation. My duties were the gathering of military intelligence about South Africa's war effort in Angola.

225

The UN was one of the few places where intelligence could be collected – it was almost impossible in Pretoria, or anywhere else in South Africa. The UN was good because everybody has an office there and you hear lots of information.'

Harker snorted to himself: he had not known that a Mr Looksmart Kumalo was in the UN – Clements, Deep Throat and Falsetto had slipped up.

The lawyer was saying, 'Now, tell us how you came by those injuries we see.'

Harker massaged his eyelids with thumb and forefinger. And Looksmart Kumalo told his story.

On 12 June 1988 he received information as a result of which he proceeded to a private airfield in Florida where he met a light aircraft that was arriving from the Dominican Republic. Aboard were two passengers, General Alfonso Sanchez and Brigadier Juan Moreno, both of the Cuban army, both of whom Looksmart Kumalo had last seen in Angola where they were based. They were now returning from Cuba to Angola via America because – amongst other reasons – they wished to consult with Kumalo and two other members of the ANC based in America; one was Clarence Ndlovu, in Washington, the other Steve Ncube, in New York, both undercover intelligence officers. The purpose of the meeting was to discuss military strategies against South Africa. No, Looksmart Kumalo told the Truth Commission, he could not elaborate because he was bound by secrecy.

Harker muttered to himself, 'Blowing up women and children . . .'

The lawyer was asking, 'Now where was this meeting to be held?'

'In a safe-house on Long Island belonging to the Russian authorities.'

'Why was the meeting held there and not in one of your private offices in the United Nations building?'

'Because the Cubans were sure that the CIA would

have bugged all the offices in the UN. The Cubans were in America illegally, and they had other secret business which I knew nothing about.'

'So tell us what happened after you met them at the airfield in Florida.'

Looksmart Kumalo explained that following the directions of the Cuban officers he drove them via circuitous country roads to New York State, then across to Long Island. At a filling-station outside West Hampton they rendezvoused with another car occupied by the other two ANC officials. In one car they drove down a number of dirt roads through patches of forest and farmlands; finally they arrived at the house.

'Describe it, please.'

Harker closed his eyes: he could visualize it vividly, the peeling tinderbox of a place.

'I did not feel very safe,' Kumalo said, 'because there was no security at all. I was very surprised. But the Cubans told me they had used the house before, the Russians assured them it was okay.'

It was dark when they arrived. The Cubans were tired and wanted to eat before starting work. The ANC men had brought three barbecued chickens and some rum. Looksmart Kumalo did not say so at the Truth Commission but the black men resented the Cubans' manner, resented being treated as underlings, almost as servants. The Cubans swigged rum while they devoured two of the three chickens, ripping them apart with their bare hands, while the Africans picked on the third in silence. The meal over, the Cubans told the black men to clear the table while they unpacked their briefcases, spread their maps and notes. The three black men returned from their chores in the kitchen and the Cubans, wreathed in the smoke of Havana cigars, immediately launched into their plan. Looksmart Kumalo did not mention any of this to the Truth Commission, but Harker knew what happened because he had tape-recorded the meeting, heard the plans being hatched to blow up the Voortrekker Monument, the Houses of Parliament and Johannesburg's airport. Looksmart Kumalo told the Truth Commission only that the five of them had discussed 'military matters' until about midnight.

At that juncture, Looksmart said, he had left the dining room and gone to his bag in the living room to fetch more cigarettes. Suddenly he had heard gunfire, the front and back doors bursting open, shouts, cries. He had flung himself out of the living room window on to the verandah. He landed on floorboards, lacerated, one eye gashed. He saw a form burst out of the darkness. He scrambled up and threw himself into the darkness under a hail of bullets. He felt his right arm and hand shot to pieces, another bullet ripped through his cheek, he ran into the black undergrowth and sprawled. He lost consciousness. He came to some time later with the sound of an explosion, the earth shaking, the world seeming to erupt around him. Stunned, he saw the house disintegrate in flying debris. He managed to scramble up and stagger on for a short distance before collapsing and passing out.

When he regained consciousness there were flashing lights and policemen and he was being loaded into an ambulance; he remembered looking for the house – it had disappeared, only smoking debris marked where it had stood. His next memory was of coming round in a hospital bed, to find he had only one complete arm, only one eye, his face swathed in bandages, his right leg in plaster. And the pain. The agony.

But he knew who had attacked him.

'I'm afraid you can't give us hearsay,' the lawyer said.

Kumalo looked at the lawyer with his one withering eye. 'Sir,' he said, 'I know who attacked that house and I shall tell the world whether your laws permit it or not. It was the CCB, the Civil Cooperation Bureau. They were the Military Intelligence hit-squads. They are the same bastards who shot Dulcie September in Paris and Anton Lubowski in

Namibia and blew up the ANC offices in London. And it was the CIA who helped the CCB!'

'Mr Kumalo, this is hearsay and that's not allowed.'

'Sir,' Looksmart Kumalo said with clenched teeth, his one-eyed scarred face murderous, 'I am here to tell you that the CIA were hand-in-glove all those years with the South African army in Angola, and they were the same in this massacre. To protect the South African assassins the CIA told the FBI that the massacre was committed by drug-barons, or by the anti-Castro Cubans from Miami. But the ANC has many informers in the Cuban-exile community in Miami, and it is clear that nobody knew about the meeting – if they had known they would have *kidnapped* the Cuban officers to get information out of them, they would *not* have killed them.'

'And what is your feeling now towards the people, who-ever they are, who did this to you?' the lawyer ended.

Six thousand miles away, Harker could see the glint in the man's eye as Kumalo quietly hissed, 'I oppose this so-called Truth and Reconciliation Commission because I do not want the people who killed my comrades and mutilated my body to be forgiven. I do not want them to be given amnesty. No, I want them to be prosecuted, and I want them to pay damages for my pain and suffering, and for the handicaps I now have. I feel great bitterness and if I could do so I would personally be their hangman, I would personally put the rope around their apartheid necks and watch them fall . . . But first I want them to pay me damages for my suffering. *That* is how I feel.' He shook his head. 'I will never forgive. Nobody must get amnesty, sir.'

Harker wanted to shout, *And what about the women and children you were plotting to blow up?* But he had his eyes closed, sick in his guts.

'Oh, Je-*zuz* . . .' he whispered.

28

The next afternoon, as he walked back grimly to Harvest House from another lonely lunch watching the Truth Commission proceedings on television, he was astonished to find Felix Dupont suddenly beside him.

'Keep walking,' Dupont said. 'And get into that green car over there.'

Harker's heart was racing. He glanced at the green car: a man sat in the back seat, looking at him. He stopped.

'Go to hell, Felix, you're not my boss any more, I don't want to get into any green cars. If you want to talk we can do so in my office across the park. If you want to take me for a ride so you can dump my body in the Hudson, forget it.'

Dupont smirked. 'Always the wise guy, huh? Okay, go to that park bench.' He pointed.

The other man was getting out of the car. Harker walked to the bench just inside little Gramercy Park. He sat. 'Well?' he demanded.

Dupont sat down beside him. The other man appeared and sat down beside Dupont. 'Who's our friend?' Harker said.

'"Mike" will do. CIA,' the man said.

CIA, huh? Harker gave a smile. 'I can't wait to hear what you heavyweights want.'

Dupont said: 'Two points.' He held up a finger: 'First: a matter of fraud. Fraud committed against the South African Defence Force, because your girlfriend's book *Outrage* was not buried by Harvest, it was a bestseller.' Before Harker could respond Dupont continued, eyes narrow: 'Don't argue; you cheated Military Intelligence and that is always a dangerous thing to do. *Very* dangerous.'

Harker glared at him. 'Don't tell me you still work for Military Intelligence now that Nelson Mandela has taken over?' Dupont started to speak but Harker continued, 'Didn't the Chairman let you buy the Royalton Hotel?'

Dupont ignored the interruption and held up two fingers. 'Secondly, the so-called Truth and Reconciliation Commission started this week.'

Harker felt sick. 'No kidding?'

'And a kaffir called Looksmart Kumalo gave evidence.'

Harker tried to look mystified. 'You don't say. Who's he?'

'I do say. And you know very well who he is, because you tried to murder him. So I'm told. And I'm told you succeeded in murdering his four companions.'

Harker had been expecting this but it was nonetheless like a blow to the guts. 'You're *told*, huh?'

Dupont's blue eyes were narrow, his round face looked waxen. 'And I'm here to tell you – *advise* you – that under no circumstances should you consider applying to this Truth Commission for amnesty.' He paused. 'Don't even *dream* about confessing in order to ease your exquisite conscience.'

Harker looked at Dupont. 'You don't say?'

Dupont looked back at him. 'I do say. And what does that mean?'

Harker managed to glare. 'It means,' he said, '*why*? Why do *you* think I should keep my mouth shut?'

'Because – not to put too fine a point on it – if you open it you'll be treated with extreme prejudice.'

Harker had known it was coming. 'Who says? The Chairman?'

'I says,' Dupont said. 'And furthermore I want you to know a few things. Three things, actually. First, a confession by you to the Truth Commission is no guarantee of amnesty – they can refuse if they feel your crime was disproportionate to your political objective, or if they suspect you're not telling the whole truth. Secondly, even if you get amnesty in South Africa that won't protect you anywhere else – you will be prosecuted for murder right here in America where you committed the crime, and the District Attorney will have your full confession as evidence. Thirdly, you expose yourself to revenge – this bastard Looksmart Kumalo will get you.' He smiled wolfishly. 'Not to mention your former colleagues. Jack, if you so much as *think* about putting your name down with the Truth Commission to give evidence you will . . . shall we say, come to an untimely end?'

Harker had hate in his heart. 'And what's your nice CIA friend here got to do with all this? Is he the guy who gave you the tip-off about the meeting in the Russian safe-house, who wanted you to do the CIA's dirty work for them?'

Dupont smiled. 'He's here as a witness to the fact that this conversation never took place.'

Harker snorted. 'Like the Long Island job you just haven't mentioned?' He got to his feet. His blood was up but his legs felt weak. 'Well, gentlemen, rest assured that I don't know what the fuck you're talking about either.' He smiled shakily. 'Truth and Reconciliation Commission? I certainly have no intention of fronting up to them because, like you, I have nothing to confess. So you needn't bother killing me.' He held out a trembling finger. 'However, just in case you try, I am now advising you two shit-heads that I have written a full affidavit and I have lodged it, sealed, with three different attorneys in three different parts of the world. My affidavit happens to mention everybody involved, by name. Including you, Felix. And our CIA friends. The attorneys have instructions that the affidavit be handed to the police in the event of my untimely death. And now, if you'll excuse me, I have work to do.'

He turned and walked away across the little park. His face was grim, his gait firm, but his heart was pounding.

*   *   *

He had not written any such affidavit. But, God, should he not do so?

It took Harker several days to make his decision to consult an attorney. It is an unnerving business, confessing to murder.

The attorney's name was Ian Redfern and his offices were near the World Trade Center. He was the man Harker had consulted to check the contract when he bought the shareholdings in Harvest House – though the lawyer had not been told the true background, he had overseen the legalities. He was a cocky, slick Irishman of indeterminate age with dyed-black hair and a wide rapacious smile. He said in answer to Harker's question, 'Of course anything you tell me is absolutely confidential, Jack.'

Harker opened his briefcase and took out a copy of the legislation creating the Truth and Reconciliation Commission: he had ordered a copy to be air-mailed from South Africa. 'Have you heard of this?'

Redfern looked at it. 'Read a thing or two about it. There was a bit in *Time* or *Newsweek*.'

Harker took a tense breath. 'You may remember, about seven years ago, two Cubans and two Africans were murdered on Long Island. The FBI blamed it on the Cuban exile community.'

Redfern nodded. 'Yes. Vaguely.'

Harker sighed grimly: 'Well, I did it.'

The lawyer stared. 'Jesus, Joseph and Mary . . .'

Redfern listened to Harker's story with amazement. Then he picked up the legislation. For almost fifteen minutes he read it, then he tossed it aside, got up and began to pace.

'Jesus, Joseph and Mary . . . You'd be crazy to confess to this Truth Commission. Our District Attorney would throw the book at you, even assuming you are granted amnesty in South Africa. He's a real zealot, a heavy left-winger.'

Harker said, 'Could he extradite me to face trial in

America? Even though I've been granted amnesty in South Africa?'

'He sure could.'

'And this guy Looksmart Kumalo who's given evidence – could he sue me in an American court for his pain and suffering?'

'He sure could! For millions.'

Harker got up and began to pace also. He said, 'The law says that the confession made by the applicant cannot be used against him in any subsequent prosecution. And amnesty, if it is granted, wipes out any civil liability for damages. But could the DA here use my confession in an American court?'

'The DA here isn't bound by any funny legislation in South Africa, Jack,' Redfern said. 'If your confession satisfies our American rules of evidence it could be used in an American court, absolutely. And remember' – he tapped the Act – 'the Truth Commission has the power to seize documents, including secret military documents. Our DA here would have access to those documents once they were seized and became matters of public record. Or he could lead any witnesses who gave evidence to the Truth Commission.'

Oh Jesus. 'The Truth Commission has already raided several military bases in South Africa, looking for records. But all the files have gone missing. Obviously destroyed.'

The lawyer snorted. 'Don't bank on that. I imagine that spymasters have a habit of hiding files that may be useful as leverage one day – or worth money.'

Harker said worriedly, 'The Act gives the Truth Commission the power to subpoena witnesses who can give information about any crime. Well, this guy Looksmart Kumalo has testified, and blamed Military Intelligence – the CCB. So presumably the Truth Commission can now subpoena the head of Military Intelligence, General Tanner, and ask him questions?'

'Absolutely,' the lawyer said.

'General Tanner would doubtless deny that the CCB was responsible but he can't deny the CCB *existed* because President de Klerk has admitted its existence and announced he's disbanded it. So if Tanner is asked whether the CCB had an office in New York he may well say yes and tell them that I was the guy in charge here. Then the Truth Commission may subpoena me?'

'Yes,' the lawyer said.

'So what should I do if that happens?'

Redfern snorted. 'Lie,' he said flatly. He added, 'I'll deny I ever said that.'

Harker was ashen. He nodded. 'I understand.'

Redfern looked at him. 'Do you? Do you understand that, contrary to public misconception, lawyers do not, or should not, concoct evidence or tell their clients to lie? If lawyers do that, and they're found out, they're struck off.'

'I understand,' Harker said.

'Okay,' the lawyer said. 'So if the Truth Commission subpoenas you, tell the truth about everything else but *don't* admit to any crime.' He looked at Harker accusingly. 'Have you committed any other crimes?'

Harker snorted grimly. 'One can't be a spymaster and not commit a few crimes.'

'Like what?' Redfern demanded.

Harker sighed. 'Bribery. Extortion. A spot of burglary.'

'Who have you bribed? And blackmailed?'

Harker shook his head wearily. 'African officials at the United Nations. And my flunkies have burgled a few offices to get information.'

The lawyer sighed. 'Well, admit none of it. You tell them you were just an honest gatherer of military information from sources within the United Nations.'

'But if they don't believe me? They cross-examine me and the whole story may start to unravel. Then I'm a proven liar, a non-credible witness.'

'But they can't prove you were involved in the Long

Island assassination unless you confess. Or unless Clements or this guy Ferdi Spicer or Felix Dupont applies for amnesty and drops you in the shit. But I doubt they'll do that.'

Harker massaged his eyelids. 'They certainly *might*. Something may happen to make a guy like Dupont decide to rush for amnesty – perhaps because somebody else has dropped him in the shit when they applied for amnesty, implicated him in another crime I know nothing about. For all I know Dupont is in all kinds of other trouble.' He frowned at the lawyer feverishly. 'If that happens, and I've already lied to the Truth Commission, I'll be refused amnesty when I rush back to them applying. Because I've lied.'

The lawyer nodded as he paced. 'Well, that's a risk you'll just have to take.' He added thoughtfully: 'Unless you do a disappearing trick, so that no subpoena can be served upon you.' He turned and paced back, thinking. 'Disappear over the horizon until this whole Truth Commission has blown over. A few years should do it. And hope that nobody like Dupont puts his finger on you if he applies for amnesty.'

'You serious? Just disappear? I've got a publishing house to run. Business loans to pay off to the bank.'

The lawyer rubbed his chin. 'You said Josephine doesn't know anything about this. But would she be supportive if you told her about the assassination?'

'*Christ no*. She'd be devastated. Possibly even denounce me to the police.'

'But she knows your military background?'

'Not that I was in Military Intelligence. She thinks I was invalided out of the army after being wounded.'

'But she must be well-off?'

'She's made a lot of money.' He added: 'And, of course, Harvest House has made quite a good profit out of her.'

'But you say Harvest is still in debt to the bank?'

'Publishers are always in debt to their bank. And Harvest signed a contract with Josephine that commits us to a great deal of money. But all up, Harvest is in fair shape. It's me personally who is still in trouble with the bank because I borrowed money to buy those shares in Harvest.'

The lawyer stroked his chin. 'And when is the cut-off date for amnesty applications?'

'Fifteenth of December 1996. This year.'

'Seven months,' Redfern said. He thought a moment. 'But Harvest would continue making money if you weren't there?'

Harker shrugged. 'I've got a good staff.'

'The point is, after the deadline nobody is going to confess to the Truth Commission, are they? Because they won't get amnesty. So you should be safe from anybody fingering you *after* that date.' The lawyer looked at him pensively. 'Would Josephine be disposed to the pair of you taking off for the next six or seven months – to Tahiti, say, or Turkey – on a holiday. Would she go along with that?'

Harker sighed grimly. 'We've often talked about buying a boat and seeing the world. But I can't afford that now.'

The lawyer looked at him. 'Well,' he said, 'you should think about it fast. Once somebody stands up at this Truth Commission and points a finger at you it will be too late to disappear. So . . .' He sat down, swivelled in his chair and looked out of the window at the Hudson. 'What we must do is this.' He raised a finger. 'You must keep several irons in the fire. You should admit *nothing* to the Truth Commission now – you *don't* apply for amnesty – but we should record a detailed affidavit from you now, confessing to everything, as if you were applying for amnesty. I will keep this affidavit here in New York in case something happens to make us change our mind and decide to grab for amnesty before the deadline. For example, if this ex-boss of yours – what's his name?'

'Dupont.'

'If Dupont decides to make a last-minute dive for amnesty – perhaps because one of his accomplices in some other crime decides to drop him in the shit, as you say – well, if that happens we're prepared, we can bash your amnesty application in at a moment's notice, perhaps even blaming me as your attorney for the delay.'

'I don't want your secretary to know about this affidavit,' Harker said feverishly. 'Or anybody else but you.'

'Sure,' Redfern said. 'So we'll record it right now, on to my computer, you sign it, I'll place it in my safe, to which only I have access. Okay?'

Harker sighed worriedly. 'And then?'

'Well,' Redfern said, 'I think I should get a second opinion from a lawyer in South Africa. Without mentioning your name, of course. And instruct him to keep a watching brief for us reporting any developments so we can take appropriate action.'

Harker hated all these people knowing. 'And what'll those guys cost?'

'Depends. I'll find out before I commit you, of course, but it won't be much by American standards. Or do you have anybody in South Africa, somebody reliable who will keep track of events and warn us immediately if something worrisome is developing?'

'I've got a relative in South Africa who's a lawyer. I've never met him but he's my second or third cousin. His name is Luke Mahoney, he's a QC, used to be a big wheel lawyer in Hong Kong, now he's in Johannesburg. I would prefer him to give us our second opinion rather than anyone else.'

'And who do you know who will give you reliable updates on developments in the Truth Commission?'

Harker snorted. 'Josephine's out there right now, she's phoning me every second day. And her friends in the old anti-apartheid movement will fax through any information if I ask for it, newspaper cuttings and so on. Josephine and her buddies will happily keep us up to date.'

'When is she coming home?'

'God knows, she's only recently got there. This Truth Commission is going to go on for months.'

'Can't you persuade her to come home?'

'I tried to stop her going, believe me.'

'And these former subordinates of yours, Clements and – Spicer, is it? When did you last have any contact with them?'

Harker briefly told the lawyer about seeing Spicer at Cleopatra's Retreat, his recent visit from Dupont and his CIA companion, his meeting with Clements several years ago in Union Square.

'Well,' Redfern said, 'obviously these guys are as keen as you are on keeping quiet. That's good. But we must be careful about this guy Dupont passing the buck to you, he sounds like trouble.'

'He is. A snake-in-the-grass.'

'And you've had no recent contact with this CIA guy you call Froggy Fred? Or Beauregard?'

'No.'

'Well,' Redfern said, 'don't contact any of them but if they contact you just act dumb, deny everything, you don't know what they're talking about. And if possible tape-record the meeting. And report everything to me.'

'Okay.' Harker sighed tensely.

'Well,' Redfern said thoughtfully, 'let's prepare this confession. But think seriously about disappearing, about going on a long cruise.'

'It's a pretty thought, believe me.'

29

It was over three years since Harker had seen Ferdi Spicer. Spicer had only been a 'salesman' in the old CCB whereas Clements was a 'senior salesman': therefore Spicer reported to Clements who reported to Harker. Spicer was a 'conscious salesman' in that he was aware he worked for the CCB but he was not supposed to know the identity of his 'Regional Manager', Harker, nor his 'Regional Director', Dupont; however, Spicer knew both identities because somewhere along the line somebody had slipped up. Technically Spicer should therefore have been redeployed on pain of death if he blew anybody's cover but a compromise was found because he was so successful in running that little whorehouse in Manhattan where so many United Nations delegates liked to relax.

It was popular for many reasons: its convenient location, its decor, and its very reasonable prices. Indeed, for delegates of African extraction and those from former communist countries there was often no charge at all because they were either the guests of other clients in the United Nations who were in the CCB's pay or Ferdi Spicer said, 'What the hell, just do me a favour one day.' Despite all this haphazard generosity and the enormous monthly booze bill, Spicer's whorehouse made a good deal of money and produced many other dividends of espionage value. In short, Cleopatra's Retreat was a roaring success, both financially and in espionage terms, and General Tanner had refused to tinker with a winning combination just because Ferdi had discovered Harker's identity. Ferdi Spicer might not be the brightest of soldiers in the Intelligence business but his loyalty was not questioned.

'Good evening, sir!' Spicer exclaimed when he opened his door and recognized Harker under the false moustache and spectacles. His pleasure was genuine.

'How's business, Ferdi?'

'Good, sir! Monday is a quiet night, of course, our lunchtime trade has left, you're our only visitor at the moment but generally, yeah, it's good, sir. And how're things with you, sir?' Harker walked into the scent of women.

The ornate mahogany bar had been extended. Chandeliers now twinkled from the ceiling, there was a lounge area festooned in fragrant flowers. Steam rose silkily from the large Roman-style whirlpool bath and two pretty girls languished in it. Half a dozen others lounged on stools around the bar: they were all dressed in satin corsets of different colours, stockings and stiletto heels.

'What'll you have to drink, sir?' Spicer asked.

'Nothing, thanks. Why did you enlarge the bar? It was plenty big enough.'

'Clements suggested it, you get more talk around a bigger bar. Sit down, sir.'

'Can we go through to your apartment?'

'Sure.' Spicer led the way down the corridor to the rear. On the way they passed a good-looking woman on her way to the reception area in her underwear, Spicer's girlfriend Stella.

'Good evening, Mr Hogan!' she beamed at Harker.

'Good evening, Stella, nice to see you again.'

They entered the rear apartment. Harker glanced into Spicer's office: he saw the bank of small television screens, showing every bedroom. 'Are you still recording people on video?'

'Yes, sir, the important ones Clements tells me to.'

Jesus. Harker thought about how to put the next question. 'So you see a lot of Clements?'

Spicer started to answer, then hesitated. 'Only when he brings customers, sir.'

'You hesitated, Ferdi. Why?'

Spicer looked uncomfortable. 'Did I, sir? Didn't notice.'

'You hesitated because you realized you'd slipped up by admitting to me that you see still take orders from Clements.'

Spicer shifted. 'I don't take no orders from him, sir.'

'You said he tells you which important customers to video – and he told you to enlarge the bar. Look at me, Ferdi.' Ferdi looked at him unhappily. 'What do you do with those videos? Give 'em to Clements, don't you? And what does he do with them?'

'Dunno, sir.'

'Like hell you don't know, Ferdi!' Harker said. 'Clements blackmails the customers with them, doesn't he? Either for money or for information. Or he intends to do so when the time is ripe. Which is it, Ferdi – money or information?'

Ferdi shifted again. 'Dunno, sir.'

'Like hell! Well, let me point a few things out to you, Ferdi – if it's money, you're playing with fire. Your victim may run to the police, or to the Mafia, or he may have to steal to pay you – either way you run a huge risk of going to jail for a long, long time! And all your CCB activities will be exposed and you'll drop us all in the shit.' He glared at Spicer, who was staring at the floor. 'Or is it political information you guys are after – political leverage? And if so, for what purpose?'

Spicer looked down. 'Dunno, sir.'

'Of course you fucking know, Spicer!'

Spicer shuffled. 'Not permitted to say, sir.' He added, 'You know how this business works, sir.'

Harker glared furiously. He whispered: 'What business, Ferdi? The CCB is fucking disbanded, remember?'

Spicer looked at his former commander, and suddenly his eyes had the steel Harker remembered.

'You know I'm a dead man if I tell you, sir. And so will you be if they find out. Sorry I slipped up, sir. So, please, no more questions. Let's just have a nice drink for old time's sake.'

Harker glared at him. 'Ferdi, if you and Clements are working for a right-wing political organization like the Afrikaner Resistance Movement – forget it. None of those outfits have a hope in hell of getting an independent homeland, let alone recapturing South Africa. Do you hear me, Ferdi?'

Spicer shifted his feet. 'Yes, sir. Shall we go back to the bar, sir?'

Oh Jesus, the implications of this were enormous. Who was he working for – the Department of Covert Collection or whatever they had renamed it now? Or was he only working for Clements' blackmail ring? But Spicer was on his guard now and Harker would find out nothing more tonight. Maybe he should try to talk to Stella. He said: 'What I really wanted to see you about was this Truth Commission that began in South Africa recently. You know about it?'

'Yes, sir. Clements told me.'

'And?'

'He told me to deny everything, keep my mouth shut. If any cops come around just say I don't know what they're talking about.'

'Don't know anything about what, exactly?'

'About the CCB, sir, that job we did on Long Island, the Anti-Apartheid League office, that sort of thing. Just act dumb.'

Harker took a tense breath. At least they were all in agreement on this. 'You understand that even if you were granted amnesty in South Africa you would be prosecuted here?'

'But,' Spicer said, 'supposing somebody splits on us to this Truth Commission, sir? Supposing somebody in the CIA talks or tries to blackmail us?'

'Nobody in the CIA could do that without dropping himself in big trouble.'

'But somebody *else* in the CIA,' Spicer insisted, 'who never actually worked with us may find out about us.'

'I doubt that will ever happen.'

Spicer cracked his knuckles. Then he said unhappily, 'It's already happened, sir.'

Harker's mind seemed to lurch. 'What are you talking about?'

Spicer said miserably: 'Swear to God you won't tell Clements I told you?'

'Of course! Spit it out, Ferdi!'

Spicer gave a troubled sigh. 'I'm only telling you because I trust you, sir, and I want to ask what I should do, sir. Well, last week, Clements tells me somebody in the CIA is trying to blackmail us. He didn't say who, except it wasn't either of the two guys I know. Clements says I must go with him to Central Park to meet this guy and we're going to jump on him and find out how much he knows, then bump him off. So we go to Central Park last Monday night, and I hide in the bushes. This guy arrives – he's only known to Clements as Jeff.'

Harker's ears felt blocked. 'Go on.'

'He got away, sir. When Clements pretended to hand over the money I jumped out and tried to give him a karate chop but he was well-trained, and the next thing I knew I was on my back and he was running away through the park, and Clements couldn't use his gun because of the noise.'

Harker felt sick. *Blackmail.* 'How much was he demanding?'

'Jesus Christ, it was a million dollars, sir,' Spicer said worriedly. 'We were supposed to be making the first payment of a hundred thousand.'

A million dollars! And that was only the start of it – pay the blackmailer once and you'll be paying for the rest of your life. God, he had to think about this fast. It was terrifying that Clements and probably Dupont too were somehow still in business as the successor to the CCB. Or were they part of a right-wing plot? The implications made the blood run cold. And how long before this CIA guy, Jeff, tried to blackmail *him*? Harker desperately wanted to dig deeper but he had to think about it first – *think*, not rush in where angels fear to tread. Spicer was his ally at the moment, as long as he played his cards right.

'Maybe I will have that drink, Ferdi. A Scotch, please. Touch of water.'

'Coming up, sir.' Spicer was pleased to both change the subject and be of service. 'Shall we join the ladies, sir?'

'Very well.'

They walked down the passage back to the reception area. Spicer lumbered to the bar, scattering girls. They looked wildly erotic in their high heels and suspenders but Harker was too distracted to appreciate. He sat on a stool in the corner. Spicer poured a big dash of Chivas Regal whisky into a glass, and opened a beer for himself. Harker tried to weigh his words as he contemplated his drink.

Ferdi whispered earnestly, 'So what should I do, sir? Do we bump off this CIA bloke, or what?'

Harker massaged his eyelids. Oh God, how could he tell Ferdi that, yes, the safest thing was to commit murder?

'Keep well clear, Ferdi. Let Clements do his own thing. Refuse to participate. If Jeff comes to you tell him he's crazy, you know nothing, tell him to fuck off before you call the police. But before I can advise you properly, you must tell me absolutely everything that's happened since the CCB was officially disbanded.'

Ferdi stared at his beer for a long moment, then raised his eyes. 'Sorry sir, I can't. You'll understand, having been in the business.'

Harker understood perfectly. It was time to get out of this town. He decided to try a more sympathetic tack. 'But tell me, Ferdi, what are your plans? How do you see your future? Continue working for Clements and company? Or what?'

'I'd like to go back to South Africa, sir. Africa gets in your blood.'

'And do what? There's no future in Military Intelligence.'

'Clements says we're going to take back the country from the blacks.'

Harker snorted. So now it's treason, is it? 'So what would you do in South Africa?'

'Farm,' Spicer said. 'Always wanted to farm.' He added, 'Land's cheap these days with so many whites leaving the country. Sell this place, take my dollars to South Africa, buy a good farm cheap.'

'Not another whorehouse?'

'No, hell, only if they insist, I'm sick of being surrounded by pussy.'

'Only if who insists?'

Spicer glanced around. 'Clements says I've done such a good job here that maybe Military Intelligence will want me to do the same job in Johannesburg or Pretoria, so we can compromise the black politicians with women and so forth. But I'm sick of all that now, sir. What I'd really like to do is go to this Truth Commission and get amnesty, then just raise cattle.'

'*Don't*,' Harker said, 'even dream of talking to the Truth Commission. The Truth Commission will grant you amnesty but the District Attorney here won't. He'll charge you with murder.'

'But I don't think he'd bother, do you, sir? Why should he go to all that trouble for me?' He added, '*And*, they'd have to catch me first.'

'But what about the rest of us?' Harker hissed. 'The DA will charge me and Clements and Trengrove as well!'

'Yeah,' Spicer said. 'I won't go to the Truth Commission, sir, don't worry.'

Harker dragged his hands down his face. *Don't worry?*

Just then the doorbell chimed. Stella got up and sauntered over to the big door, her high heels clicking, her magnificent breasts wobbling. She applied her eye to the spy-hole, her pantied bottom jutting. 'Time for work, ladies . . .'

Harker got to his feet. 'Don't tell Clements or anybody that you've spoken to me about this. Got that?'

'Yes, sir.'

'If Clements finds out that I've been here tell him I just came to knock off one of the girls. We discussed nothing else.'

'Yes, sir.'

'And Ferdi? You've got to tell me everything that's going on between you and Clements. I'll come back in a few days.'

Ferdi said resolutely: 'Sir, you're welcome here anytime, you know that. But I can't tell you any more, sir.'

As Stella opened the door, Harker put on his hat. Four men of Latin extraction were standing on the threshold. 'Buenos tardes!' Stella exclaimed.

Harker nodded goodbye to Spicer, stood aside to let the newcomers file in, then stepped out.

One of Clements' limousines was parked across the street; a black chauffeur was behind the wheel but did not pay any attention. Harker walked away. At the intersection he flagged a taxi.

When he entered his apartment the telephone was ringing.

'Hullo, darling!' Josie cried. 'Where've you been?'

Harker closed his eyes.

'When are you coming home?' he said.

30

'Oh, I'm missing you too.' she said. 'But this is one hell of a big story that's unfolding. The *drama*. It's in*tense*. The outpourings of bitterness, the heartbreak, as mothers and wives and lovers queue up to tell their stories about loved ones who just disappeared at the hands of the police, abducted in the middle of the night, never seen again. And then there're the victims who survived . . . Darling, are you there?'

'Josie, please come home now.'

'Darling, this is too big a story to walk away from – can you imagine the panic, the terror that's reigning in the breasts of the apartheid villains now? And not only the bastards who actually carried out these atrocities, I'm talking about the bigwigs, the politicians and generals who gave the orders. From ex-president P.W. Botha downwards. Big heads are going to roll, and I have to chronicle it all.'

'Josie, there'll be many chroniclers.'

'But I'm going to be the best! God, Jack, at last apartheid has collapsed like Nazi Germany and the bad bastards are about to be brought to book. Some of the biggest nastiest mysteries are about to be solved, like Steve Biko's death – and you tell me to come home? The apartheid villains are quaking in their boots – the bullies and shock-troops of apartheid are cowering under their rocks, desperately hatching excuses and perjury – darling, it's a *wonderful* comeuppance! Any day now one of their stalwarts is going to lose his nerve and run to the Commission – on his knees – and name all his accomplices and the bigwigs and the dam's going to burst!'

Oh God, God, once that dam burst he would be swept away . . .

*   *   *

That summer was bad for Harker. Every day he got a summary of the proceedings from the South African broadcasting service, almost every day Josephine telephoned with her gleeful assessments or she faxed newspaper extracts. Day by day, week by week, the horror of the apartheid years came tumbling out to the Commission, day after day the evidence came piling up against the police and army. But the dam did not burst. Constantly, the Commission appealed to perpetrators to take the golden opportunity to make a clean breast. The newspaper editorials urged the same, but nobody was coming forward. And then one day Josephine telephoned him excitedly at Harvest House: 'Darling, have you heard the dramatic news?!'

'What news?'

She said gleefully, 'Today the Attorney General has announced that he's launching a high-powered prosecution against your old boss, the former Minister of Defence – General Magnus Malan himself! And nineteen other officers, for a massacre of thirteen ANC people eight years ago.' She paused. 'Darling, are you there?'

Harker's ears were ringing. 'What massacre?'

'The allegation is that the army – General Malan and his henchmen – sent an impi of Zulu hit-squadders to wipe out a bunch of ANC sympathizers. Anyway, this is the ANC government shaking the big stick, warning all villains that if you don't want to go to jail for the rest of your life you'd better confess and get amnesty.'

Harker felt sick. Oh God, he would love to be able to do that.

'Josie,' Harker said, 'I need you.'

'Oh darling, I love you too but I'm really on to something very dramatic here.'

'Josie,' Harker said, eyes closed, 'let's just say to hell with everything and sail off around the world in our yacht.'

Josephine laughed. 'Oh, I'm with you, heart and soul, but first I've got to finish this thing.'

The next day General Malan's impending prosecution was front-page news in the New York papers. The day following, Josephine's fax arrived.

> . . . Thousands of guilty securocrats in the police and army are taking the lead from their ex-Minister of Defence, arguing it is better to take your chances in court where the requirements for conviction are proof beyond reasonable doubt, than confess to the Truth Commission cap in hand. And confess to how much? Should they do what the law requires, make a full confession to every apartheid wrong of their entire careers, crimes they have not yet been accused of – or only to those crimes that the complainants had attributed to them, thus taking the risk that their amnesty will be refused if other facts emerge later? And then there is the other factor: honour amongst thieves. 'Is it fair for me to confess if I thus put my accomplices in prison? And what about the revenge they may take? Or my victims may seek revenge.'
> Meanwhile, too, the mammoth trial of Colonel Eugene de Kock, the last commander of Platplaas, the notorious rural base for police hit-squads, charged with 120 counts of murder and human rights violations, continues . . .'

Harker crushed the fax and threw it across the room. *Oh God God God . . .*

Those months went that way. Every day he expected Jeff to contact him – or Clements or Dupont; every day his nerves stretched tighter. And then, in the middle of that long hot summer as the cut-off date for amnesty relentlessly ticked closer, the first crack appeared in apartheid's ramparts of denial. Josephine telephoned gleefully: 'Have you heard about Craig Williamson?'

Harker's heart was sinking. 'Who's Craig Williamson?'

'He's one of the police spymasters – big English type,

frightfully officer-and-gentleman and all that jazz, shows up on television from time to time? Well, evidence has emerged that he masterminded the letter-bomb sent to Angola which killed Jeanette Schoon and her daughter. So Marius Schoon, Jeanette's husband, has now served a summons on him demanding a million rands in damages! Williamson went running to police headquarters for help and they disowned him, so he called a press conference and announced he is going to apply to the Truth Commission for amnesty – and thereby escape this action for a million rands – and he's going to tell them all the crimes he's committed on the orders of his political masters, from P.W. Botha downwards! He was on television last night, fuming. Isn't that wonderful?!'

Oh, absolutely fucking wonderful. Sick-in-his-guts wonderful. Slash-his-wrists sort of wonderful. 'Josie, when are you coming home?'

'Darling, can't you take a few weeks off and come out here?'

Oh sure . . . 'Josie, let's sell up everything and buy a boat and just take off around the world.'

She laughed. 'Darling, you couldn't sell Harvest.'

'Damn wrong I couldn't sell Harvest, I'd sell it tomorrow if I could take off for the wide blue yonder with you!'

And then, in the middle of that long hot New York summer, the Truth Commission announced that it was going to get tough. Archbishop Desmond Tutu announced to the press: 'We are going to take off the velvet gloves and replace them with the knuckledusters that the legislation gives us – start issuing subpoenas against the people who have been named by the victims, we have a long list of names we are going to summons to answer searching questions . . .'

Then the news broke that the former Commissioner of Police, General van der Merwe, had approached the Truth Commission, through his lawyer, seeking amnesty.

It was six o'clock in the morning – noon in South Africa –

when Harker, only half awake, heard that information at the tail end of the South African news broadcast. He was astounded. And aghast. If the Commissioner of Police was breaking down, and the Minister of Defence was on trial, how long before General Tanner of Military Intelligence broke cover? Harker frantically called Josephine on her cellphone but he only got the operator. He left a message for her to call him urgently.

He pulled on a tracksuit and set off into the pre-dawn of Manhattan, his cellphone in his hand. He ran westwards in the lamplit darkness, trying to rasp out his nervous tension. He reached Riverside Drive and turned left. He was half a mile down when Josephine telephoned.

'Hullo, darling, got your message but have you heard about the breakthrough? The Commissioner of Police and two other top generals and nineteen other senior police-men have now run to the Commission and made a joint confession to *twenty* crimes, offering to accept responsibility for the police force as a whole in exchange for amnesty for themselves and for the entire force!'

Harker stared across the Hudson, panting.

'Only *twenty*? What crimes are they confessing to?'

'Exactly – only twenty crimes is laughable! We don't know which crimes yet, but of course the Commission won't accept a collective application like that, but it's a big breaking of the ranks! Oh boy, now the panic starts. There's going to be a flood of confessions now!'

Oh, Jesus . . .

From the secure basement of Harvest House he telephoned his cousin Luke Mahoney, the lawyer in Johannesburg whom Redfern had retained.

'Yes,' Luke said, 'it certainly *is* a breakthrough. The cat is loose amongst the apartheid pigeons now. And it's going to get worse. The Truth Commission has just told these top policemen that their collective application and so-called confession to only twenty crimes is totally unacceptable. These cops represent the jackboot of the apartheid era.'

'What actual crimes did these generals list in their application?'

Luke said: 'Remember the Khotso House bombing in 1988 – it was the headquarters of the South African Council of Churches? Destroyed the whole building. P.W. Botha was state president and he blamed "the Godless Communists". Well, it was the work of the police. Because the building was the underground headquarters of the ANC. That was one of the crimes confessed to.'

Harker was astounded. 'Good God.'

'And remember that huge car bomb that exploded outside army headquarters injuring something like seventy people? That's another crime they confessed to. They did it so the ANC would be blamed, to generate hatred against the ANC because left-wing politicians were recommending dialogue with them.'

Harker was amazed. It was almost impossible to believe that the police force was so depraved as to blow up innocent citizens in order to generate hatred of the enemy. *Jesus. Mindblowing.* 'So what are these bastards going to do now that their collective confession has been rejected?'

'Well,' Luke said, 'they will only get amnesty for specific crimes they personally own up to so they'll have to go back to the Truth Commission with full confessions, telling who all their accomplices were, and that will trigger a flood of other villains desperate to claim amnesty. For example, the Defence Force has been keeping quiet, but now General Meiring has announced that all officers will fully cooperate with the Truth Commission.'

Harker felt his stomach lurch. *Oh Jesus.* 'So what do you advise me to do?'

'Keep lying low,' Luke said. 'Even if there's a flood of confessions, nobody is going to be in a hurry to admit to crimes committed abroad. And, as I've said, I don't think you should have any moral guilt: you took military action against legitimate targets who were plotting murder.'

'But General Meiring has said that the army will cooperate fully. Does that mean he's going to say, yes, the CCB's functions included assassinations; yes, the CCB's man in New York was Major Jack Harker; yes, I've heard the allegations made by Looksmart Kumalo that he was blown up by the CCB – et cetera. Is that going to happen?'

Luke sighed. 'I think it's unlikely – I think the army generals are going to *appear* to cooperate in broad terms, but plead ignorance about details. And they'll probably get away with it because espionage is so complicated that the Truth Commission simply hasn't the time and manpower to try to unravel it all.'

'But if General Tanner, my ex-boss, does decide to make a clean breast and fingers me as their man in New York, what should I do?'

'Admit it,' Luke said. 'But strenuously deny any criminal action. Say your job was *only* legitimate intelligence-gathering.'

'But what about Looksmart Kumalo's accusations?'

'Deny you know anything. He has no proof. And you are clearly a respectable member of the publishing profession. That's the way to play it. Unless the Truth Commission comes up with some specific evidence against you. Then we think again.'

Oh God. 'My attorney over here, Redfern, he's suggested I disappear. Literally. On a yacht. Both Josephine and I are well-known as keen sailors and if we took off for a year or two to sail the world it would be entirely in character. What do you think?'

Luke Mahoney considered. 'While you're sailing will you be able to keep in touch with Redfern? And me?'

'Yes. By these new satellite-telephones.'

Luke thought about this. 'So if the Truth Commission issues a subpoena for you, you can't be found and the whole allegation against you may blow over, perhaps become buried in the welter of paperwork the Commission's got. On the other hand nobody can hold it against you because you were on the high seas. So, provided I can reach you by satellite-telephone I think it's a good idea. If the allegations against you are serious we devise a strategy. Of course, once the cut-off date for amnesty of fifteenth of December is passed you'll have no choice but to deny everything.' He added: 'And I suggest you consider selling Harvest House if you really want to do a disappearing trick.'

Selling Harvest House . . . ?

The summer went this way. And all the time he was praying for Josephine to come home before she found out anything about him. Sometimes as the litany of sufferings and accusations became a fragmented drone in the overseas press Harker was almost able to convince himself that the chances of being singled out were very slim: but then in the small hours of those long hot nights the fear would come creeping back – suddenly he would be wide awake with the cold hand of fear on his heart that today somebody in Military Intelligence would panic, run to the Truth Commission and start an investigation that finally led to Harvest House . . . And, oh God, Harker could hear that amnesty clock ticking.

Then the news broke that five senior policemen from Platplaas had gone to the Truth Commission with full confessions to over forty political murders. Josephine telephoned Harker gleefully.

'Oh boy, now the rats are really going to start leaping out of the woodwork. These five are the hit-squad from Platplaas. They've not only confirmed that Daniel Sipholo and Badenhorst were speaking the truth but they've named all their superior officers who ordered them to commit these forty murders – including the Commissioner of Police himself! The guy who last month confessed – on behalf of the entire police force – to only *twenty* crimes. And – get this – they have subpoenaed him as a witness!' She laughed. 'Did you hear that, Jack? Isn't this exciting?'

Harker had his eyes closed, sick in his guts. Oh, dreadfully exciting. 'Yes.'

Josephine chuckled. 'The shock-waves have reverberated across the country. And the Truth Commission has immediately "invited" seven other generals to show up and tell what they know!' She continued brightly, 'And you remember Looksmart Kumalo, who survived that assassination attack on Long Island, you saw him on television?'

Harker felt a ringing in his ears. 'What about him?'

'I had dinner with him yesterday.'

Harker's heart lurched. 'You had dinner?'

'I invited him to dinner because yesterday he announced to the press that he is issuing a writ in America for ten million dollars against the South African government – against the Defence Force – for the injuries he suffered when he was attacked on Long Island.'

Harker's ears were ringing. 'And?'

'And,' Josephine said, 'he's an interesting man. Highly embittered. *Absolutely* determined to prove that the CCB gave him his injuries, and to sue the bastards to Kingdom Come.'

'He's barking up the wrong tree, the Cuban exile community did it.'

'Anyway, he's going over to New York to hire private detectives to investigate.'

Harker's throat felt constricted. 'You must tell him he's wasting his time. And money.'

'He's being financed by some Danish charity so he's got plenty of that. And he has a number of contacts in the United Nations who're going to help him, and in the Cuban community in Miami.'

Oh Christ, Christ, Christ . . . Harker wanted to bellow it but he controlled it down to a rasp. 'Josephine, I've got some major decisions to discuss with you. If you don't come home immediately I will make the decisions by myself and present you with a *fait accompli*.'

There was a surprised silence. Then: 'What decisions, Jack?'

'I am sick and tired of work,' Harker said shakily. 'I want

256

to say to hell with everything, buy that yacht and set off around the world immediately. In fact, I am going down to Fort Lauderdale this weekend to look at secondhand boats. I want you to come with me.'

'But what about Harvest House?'

'That,' Harker said, 'is one of the decisions I want to discuss with you.'

'Don't tell me you want to sell it.'

'I'm thinking of it,' Harker warned.

There was a pause. Then: 'Jack, you're under strain, I can hear it in your voice. Darling, you need a break. Yes, go down to Fort Lauderdale, have a nice time looking at boats. I promise I'll come back soon but *please* don't make any decisions about Harvest House until you've talked it through exhaustively with me – remember you're my publisher, not just my lover!'

Harker telephoned Luke Mahoney in Johannesburg. He told the lawyer about Looksmart Kumalo's intention to sue the South African Defence Force in the American courts.

'Oh,' Luke said soberly. 'Yes, worrying. But remember he's suing the present South African Defence Force for the sins of the apartheid government, and for that to affect you personally he would have to prove that you are responsible for the attack. That would be very hard.' He added as an afterthought, 'Unless, of course, one of your old CCB accomplices stepped forward and gave evidence against you.'

Harker snorted. 'Exactly.'

'But,' Luke said, 'nobody is likely to do that because they'll expose themselves to a criminal prosecution for murder in America.' He added: 'Unless of course he manages to strike a deal with the District Attorney whereby he gets immunity from prosecution in exchange for giving evidence against you.'

'Exactly. In both the civil *and* criminal action,' Harker said feverishly. 'I could be sued for millions in damages *and* sent to jail for life for murder.'

'But who is likely to do that?' Luke said pensively. 'Surely none of your CCB people in America would take that step? That *risk* – drawing attention to themselves?'

Harker massaged his eyelids. 'Unless they were offered a share of Looksmart's millions? Plus immunity from prosecution for turning prosecution witness . . .'

Then he gave Luke a brief account of his last meeting with Spicer, and the story of the attempted blackmail by the CIA man called Jeff.

'Christ,' Luke said, 'I hope you reported this to Redfern?'

'Of course. He told me to stay away from Spicer entirely in case I get accused of being involved in their conspiracies, whatever they are.'

'Absolutely right,' Luke said.

Harker took a deep breath. 'Luke,' he said, 'I want to hit the high seas. Buy that yacht and disappear.'

Luke sighed. 'Sounds like a wise move. But I thought you said you couldn't afford it yet?'

'I suppose I can borrow some more from the bank. Or Harvest can. Or something.'

'Can't Josephine help out? Anyway, let me know what you're doing. But don't panic . . .'

Don't panic? When cracks are appearing all over, when top brass in the police and army are being hauled before the Truth Commission? Don't panic when everybody else is panicking?

And then, the very next evening, as Harker was leaving Harvest House, locking the big front door, a voice said on the pavement below: 'Mr Jack Harker?'

Harker peered down at the black man standing in the lamplight. His heart was suddenly racing. 'Yes?'

The man took off his hat. He was tall and well-dressed: he had a patch over one eye and a welt of scar below it. His teeth were very white as he smiled.

'Good evening. My name is Alexander Kumalo. My nickname is Looksmart . . .'

31

Harker stared at the man. He heard himself say: 'Do I know you?'

Looksmart Kumalo extended his left hand and held up his right: it was a two-pronged steel claw that glinted in the lamplight. 'Please excuse my right hand.'

Harker took the proffered left hand shakily. 'I don't think I know you.'

Looksmart smiled, 'But I met your lovely lady friend Josephine in Pretoria and she suggested I look you up when I was in New York.'

Harker hastily feigned surprise. 'Oh, yes – she mentioned you, Mr Kumalo.'

'Alexander, please – or Looksmart. So, can we go somewhere nearby for a drink? Or coffee?'

Harker's mind was fumbling. He badly wanted to get rid of the man but he also desperately needed to know what he was up to. He said: 'I have a meeting uptown in half an hour. But there's a bar just across the square, we can go there for a quick drink.'

'Fine.'

As they crossed the park Harker said, 'So how long are you going to be in America, Mr Kumalo?'

Looksmart Kumalo said slowly, 'For as long as it takes to find out who did this to me.' He held up his claw. 'And this.' He indicated his face.

Harker pushed open the bar door shakily. 'How did it happen?'

Looksmart Kumalo entered the bar. 'Do you remember an explosion that occurred eight years ago on Long Island, killing a number of people?'

Harker walked to the counter, pretending to think. 'No. What'll you have?'

'Beer, please.'

'What kind?'

'Any kind of beer is okay.'

'Two Budweisers please, Lenny,' Harker said to the barman. 'No,' he turned back to Kumalo, 'I don't remember.'

Looksmart frowned, then smiled. 'I think you do. Josephine said she had discussed the case with you quite often – she was convinced it was the work of this CCB we've heard about.' He added, 'And so am I.'

Harker felt sick. *He knows* . . . 'Oh, *that* case? So you're the guy who survived? But the FBI proved it was the work of the Cuban exile community in Miami.'

'That was a cover-up.'

Harker feigned further return of memory. 'Oh yes, Josie mentioned something about you hiring a firm of private detectives. Which ones?'

Looksmart smiled wider. 'I've got friends in the United Nations who advise me, they put me on to a firm. In fact I believe you know some of my friends, Mr Harker. For example, Alfonso Santos, from the Angolan delegation?'

Harker's heart was racing. Alfonso Santos' codename in CCB files was Deep Throat, he had been one of their major informers in the old days, a big black man with a penchant for white womanflesh which Clements and Spicer had satisfied in exchange for information. Harker shook his head. 'I don't think I know anybody in the United Nations.'

Looksmart smiled widely. 'How about Joshua Malungu, in the Zambia delegation?'

Harker took a gulp of his beer to conceal the lurch in his guts. Okay, now he knew the bastard knew. Joshua Malungu's codename had been Falsetto. He also had a large appetite for good booze and white women and he too had given Clements and Spicer a host of information over the years about the ANC's plans, military movements, who was back-stabbing who in the hierarchy, who was screwing whose wife or mistress.

'Never heard of him,' Harker said. *Okay, you bastard, what other surprises have you got for me?*

'Really?' Looksmart said conversationally. 'But you must know the guy who both Alfonso and Joshua speak of, an American called . . .' Looksmart frowned, as if trying to remember the name. 'Called Ferdi Spicer, I think – yes, that's it, Ferdi. He runs a very popular brothel – the Best Little Whorehouse in Manhattan, they call it.'

Harker's face felt drained. He took a slug of tasteless beer.

'No, I don't know any Ferdi Spicer.' He added, 'I don't frequent whorehouses.'

Looksmart Kumalo smiled. 'No?' he said softly. 'Now that's strange. Because these two UN guys, Joshua and Alfonso, directed my private detective to Cleopatra's Retreat last night to meet Ferdi Spicer, who they said might be able to assist me in my enquiries, as the saying is. When my detective got there Ferdi refused to talk, and he immediately disappeared. But his girlfriend, the madam, Stella, she finally agreed to talk to my detective. Because he made her an offer that was hard to refuse.' Looksmart paused, smiling. 'And Stella directed me and my detective to you, except she called you Jack Hogan. She gave me your telephone number and I noticed it was the same number that Josephine had given me for you.'

Harker's heart was pounding. He tried to sound astonished. 'Why did she direct you to me?'

Looksmart smiled. 'And we would like to make you the same offer we made to Stella, Mr Harker.'

Harker tried to look puzzled. 'I'm afraid I don't know what you're talking about.'

Looksmart smiled again. 'I'm talking about murder,' he said. 'And money.'

Harker stared at him, and suddenly, through his fear, his adrenaline saved him as it had many a time in battle:

there was still the fear but now there was the courage of a cornered soldier. 'I haven't the foggiest idea of what you're talking about, Looksmart.' He waved a hand. 'Murder? *Money?*'

Looksmart said: 'I'm suing the South African Defence Force for ten million dollars for these injuries. My detectives' enquiries led them to believe that Ferdi Spicer was involved, or knew who was involved. But when we approached Ferdi he promptly disappeared. So we figured his girlfriend, Stella, might know and we made her an offer of ten per cent of my claim if I am successful. One million dollars is a lot of money, and Stella said that Ferdi had hinted that you and he were involved, with others.'

Harker was ashen but his fighting blood was up.

'Whoever this Stella is, she's a liar. She's a whore, she'll say anything for a million dollars.'

Looksmart said: 'I would like to offer you the same deal as Stella – ten per cent, a million dollars, if my claim is successful, for telling the court how and why you did it – who with, on whose orders and so on. Because I am sure you didn't commit the murders on your own initiative.'

Harker was grinning but his heart was pounding. 'I'd love a million dollars, Mr Kumalo, but unfortunately I don't know what you're talking about. And now, excuse me!'

He banged down his glass and turned, but Looksmart laid his claw on his wrist.

'You're a lucky man, Jack. If Ferdi Spicer hadn't taken fright and disappeared he would be getting the million dollars and you would be paying not only with money but with your life in prison.'

Harker glared. 'Is that so?' He wrenched his wrist free.

'But this way you *earn* a million dollars *and* your life. Because my attorney has approached the DA here, who has agreed that if you give evidence in my case you will be granted immunity from prosecution provided you give evidence for the state in the trial of your accomplices who were with you when the murders were committed.'

Harker stared. 'Are you telling me that you have discussed me with the District Attorney?'

'My attorney has, yes.'

'On the word of a fucking whore you accuse me of murder! I'll sue you for defamation of character!'

'I don't think so,' Looksmart smiled. 'I'm making you an offer you shouldn't refuse, Jack.'

Harker's mind was in disarray. Then he rasped furiously, 'I repeat, I don't know what you're talking about. So stay out of my life, Mr Kumalo!'

Harker turned and strode towards the door. As he approached it he was astonished to lock eyes with Derek Clements: the man was sitting in a booth in the corner, watching him, eyes steady, ice-blue. Harker felt his step falter. *This is no coincidence, the bastard's following Looksmart Kumalo and seeing us together doesn't look healthy.* Harker made a snap decision and gave a small jerk of his head to tell Clements to meet him outside. He pushed the bar door and strode out into the lamplit street.

Over the road was the corner of little Gramercy Park. Harker crossed to the entrance. Ten paces within was a bench. He looked back and confirmed he could see the doorway to the bar: then he slumped down on the bench, leant his elbows on his knees and held his face.

Oh Jesus Jesus . . .

He sat there collecting his wits; then he lifted his head and looked for Clements. It was important that he reassure Clements – and Dupont – that he had no intention of accepting Looksmart's deal. But Clements had not emerged. Harker looked at his watch. Must be three minutes since he had walked out. Okay, so Clements was following Mr Looksmart Kumalo. Harker got to his feet and strode away into the darkness of the little park, trying to think.

Think . . .

He had to report this to Redfern. Harker stopped in the park, pulled out his cellphone, dialled Redfern's home number. No reply. He dialled his office and left a message on his answering machine asking him to phone urgently.

He had to speak to Stella, find out how much she knew, how much she had said, he had to find out what had happened to Ferdi . . . Jesus, if what Looksmart had said was true Stella had the power to get Ferdi convicted of mass murder, and Ferdi had the power to turn prosecution witness and throw Harker, Dupont and General Tanner into an American jail and toss away the key – and that was only because New York State had done away with the death penalty, otherwise it would be the electric chair! He feverishly dialled the number of Cleopatra's Retreat.

'Stella's gone out, sir, any message?'

'When's she coming back?'

'Don't know, sir, she only went out for a walk, maybe a drink. Want to leave a message or make an appointment?'

He didn't like leaving his name and number – and was it safe to trust the telephone? 'When can I have an appointment?'

'Say in an hour, sir, eight o'clock.'

Could he bear to wait? 'All right.'

'What name, sir?'

'Hogan.'

Harker went to his apartment. He had a large whisky to steady his nerves, then another. An hour later he telephoned for a taxi.

'Uptown, please, West 57th Street.'

Harker collapsed back on the seat, desperately trying to think what he was going to say to Stella, how he was going to make her tell him everything she knew about Ferdi and the CCB and Jack Harker and Felix Dupont and all the other secret operatives Ferdi had bragged to her about. *And where the hell had Ferdi fucking disappeared to?*

'What number in West 57th Street?' the taxi-driver said.

Harker was peering ahead. 'Slow down . . .' A hundred yards down the road, outside Cleopatra's Retreat, stood a big knot of people, two police cars and an ambulance, lights flashing. 'Keep going,' Harker said, 'slowly.'

The taxi cruised past the people. Harker peered. He recognized nobody.

'Drop me off at the next block.'

As he got out, Harker pulled out his cellphone and dialled Cleopatra's Retreat. It rang a long time before a woman answered. 'Cleopatra's.' She sounded strained.

'Let me speak to Stella, please.'

The woman's voice caught. 'Stella's dead.'

Harker's guts lurched. '*Dead*? How?'

'Murdered,' the girl said. She sniffed. 'Strangled. In her apartment.'

Harker was staring, mind trying to function. 'Who did it?'

'Nobody saw anybody come or go.' The girl sobbed.

'What time did it happen?'

'About half an hour ago the police say. Who's speaking?'

'My name's Peter. What's your name?'

'Irene.'

'Is Ferdi there, Irene?'

'No, Ferdi's gone to South Africa.'

'South Africa? How do you know that?'

'Stella told me.'

Oh Jesus, there was only one reason why Ferdi would run to South Africa. 'Did she say why he went there?'

'Trouble.'

'What kind of trouble?'

'She didn't say.'

'When did he leave?'

'Yesterday, Stella said.'

Harker took a deep anguished breath. 'Okay, thank you. I'm very sorry. Goodbye.'

He hung up, turned and hurried away down the street, frantically looking for another taxi.

Who would murder Stella? Looksmart Kumalo? No,

he would want Stella as a witness to what Ferdi had said. Would Ferdi do it? Possibly, if Stella had threatened to give evidence against him concerning the Long Island massacre – maybe they had had a row, maybe Ferdi had killed her in hot blood. Irene had said Ferdi had left for South Africa yesterday, but perhaps Ferdi had not left for South Africa, maybe he was lurking around town right now with blood on his hands. Would the CCB have murdered Stella? Somebody like Clements, or Dupont? Why would they? Because they had heard that Looksmart Kumalo had hit town breathing fire, had found the UN's favourite whorehouse where Stella had opened her big mouth causing Ferdi to flee in terror back to South Africa to claim amnesty so Looksmart Kumalo could not sue him for ten million dollars or send him to Sing-Sing for the rest of his life? But Ferdi knew that amnesty would not protect him against Looksmart Kumalo in an American court – Harker had explained it to him in words of one syllable. If Ferdi had gone running to the Truth Commission it was to claim amnesty for some other CCB murders committed in Africa, about which Harker knew nothing. Or had Ferdi made a deal with the DA whereby he would get both amnesty from the Truth Commission and indemnity from prosecution in America in exchange for testifying about the Long Island murders?

A yellow taxi appeared in the lamplight around the corner; Harker flagged it down, scrambled in and gave the driver his address.

One thing was for sure – it was time to get out of this town. High time to go down to Fort Lauderdale, buy that yacht and disappear on the high seas before Mr Looksmart fucking Kumalo slapped a writ on him for ten million dollars before throwing him to the DA. And doing that disappearing trick effectively meant selling up Harvest House fast so that it could not be seized by the court to satisfy Looksmart's writ. And marrying Josephine fast too. Because apart from the fact that he had to get her right out of earshot of all this drama before she found out about his past, he was going to need her money until he had sold Harvest.

In fact he would telephone her right now and goddam *tell* her they were getting married! He looked at his watch: nine p.m. in New York, three a.m. tomorrow morning in Johannesburg. He pulled out his cellphone and punched in her numbers. It rang twice before the operator's recorded voice advised him that the subscriber he had dialled was not available.

The taxi pulled up outside Gramercy Mews. He paid and scrambled out. He hurried up to the big iron grille, unlocked it, strode through the archway and across the courtyard. He unlocked his door and snapped on the living room light, went to the corner telephone table, snatched up the directory and leafed through it; then he dialled the after-hours number for Amtrak.

'Do you have a train leaving tonight for Fort Lauderdale, Florida, please?'

Harker listened to the clerk's response, thanked him and slammed down the telephone. Okay, so he would have to drive down through the night – maybe that was better, he would not be able to sleep anyway, and he would need a car in Fort Lauderdale while looking at boats. He turned to the bedroom to pack a few clothes. Then:

'Why are you going to Fort Lauderdale, sir?'

32

A figure stood in the dark entrance of the stairs leading down to Madam Velvet's. Harker's hand flashed to his hip for the pistol he no longer carried.

'What the hell are you doing here, Clements?'

Clements leant against the doorframe. 'Come to pay you a social visit, sir.'

Harker was shaking. 'How the hell did you get in?'

Clements smiled. 'Same way I got into Josephine's apartment the first time you sent me in, sir. Picked the locks.'

Harker pointed at his telephone. 'I'll call the police and have you arrested for housebreaking!'

Clements shook his head and sauntered into the living room. 'Don't think you will, sir. Not when you remember what I can tell the police about you.'

'And remember I can tell them a lot about you!'

Clements elaborately poured himself a whisky. 'Indeed, sir? I doubt it, if you don't mind my saying so. On account of your health, sir.' He shook his head, took a sip of whisky. 'Wouldn't be healthy, sir. Not at all.'

Harker closed his eyes. 'Derek, what the hell do you want here? Kindly spit it out and fuck off.'

Clements smiled. 'Such language is unlike you, sir. This Truth and Reconciliation business getting on your nerves too, is it? It's certainly getting on ours.'

'Who is "ours"?'

'The old gang here in the US. What were you talking to Looksmart Kumalo about?'

Harker had managed to prepare himself for the question. 'Looksmart Kumalo is here to find the CCB operatives responsible for the Long Island job. He's hired private detectives to help him. And a lawyer.' Harker glared. 'Let me put the old gang's collective mind at rest. Kindly tell Dupont that Looksmart Kumalo looked me up today *not* because he suspects me but simply because Josephine, who is in South Africa following the Truth Commission, met him after he'd testified, and told him to look me up when he went to America. Socially. That's it.'

Clements said grimly: 'Didn't he offer to make a deal with you to testify on his behalf, to blow the whistle on the rest of us?'

Harker looked Clements in the eye. 'He certainly did not. Why would he? He has no idea I was involved.'

Clements raised his eyebrows. 'Well, sir, he suspected that Ferdi Spicer may know something because either Deep Throat or Falsetto directed him to Cleopatra's Retreat, to talk to Ferdi. And I know he went there because I was hired to drive him there. So, Looksmart didn't tell you he had been to see Ferdi?'

Jesus, he had to be careful. 'No.'

'Or that he'd seen Stella? He didn't say anything about Cleopatra's?'

Harker forced a frown. 'Stella? No.'

'So your meeting with him was perfectly friendly was it?'

Harker was ready for this one. 'Except at the end. He suggested I was a racist because I fought in the Rhodesian and South African armies. I walked out on him.' He added, 'Damn cheek of the man.'

Clements was watching him closely. 'When you walked out you looked more shaken than indignant, sir. Frightened, not angry.'

Harker glared at him, then walked to the booze cabinet and poured a whisky, trying not to let the bottle shake. 'Is that so?' He added a dash of water. 'Anything else, before you go?'

Clements smiled. 'Yes, Major. What did you do after you left the bar?'

Harker forced another frown. His mind fumbling for a credible answer. He said quietly: 'I resent your tone, Clements. You sound like a bad imitation of a DA. Cut it out.'

Clements smiled. 'Where did you go, sir?'

'I went uptown to the Algonquin Hotel on West 44th Street to meet a literary agent to discuss a possible book deal. Okay?'

'Not okay, sir. Because one of our boys distinctly recognized you as you drove past Cleopatra's Retreat in a yellow cab about half an hour ago. He called my cellphone to report.'

Harker was shaken by this. 'Tell "your boys" they need spectacles. It was some other good-looking guy. And who are "your boys"? I thought the CCB was disbanded.'

'Oh, we are, sir, don't you worry, we are.' Clements smiled wolfishly. 'And when did you last speak to Ferdi, sir?'

'About three months ago. Look, I've had enough of your inquisitorial tone. Please tell me what's on your mind and then piss off!'

'Where did you see Ferdi Spicer three months ago?'

'At Cleopatra's Retreat.'

'Why did you go there?'

'I felt the need for a little female company. But I ended up talking to Ferdi instead and the mood passed.'

'What did you talk about?'

'This and that. About the Truth Commission, naturally. He didn't seem to know much about it. So I impressed upon him that it would be folly for him to think of seeking amnesty for the Long Island job because he could still be prosecuted here.'

'So Ferdi wanted to apply for amnesty?'

'*No,*' Harker said emphatically, 'we were just talking about developments generally. In fact it was I who brought up the subject of amnesty, to make sure he didn't do anything foolish. But he clearly understood the situation even before I brought it up.'

270

'Ferdi was involved in a few high-profile jobs in South Africa, wasn't he?'

Harker was surprised. 'Was he? Which ones?'

Clements smiled. 'Come on. You know, as his overall commanding officer.'

Harker said flatly, 'I assure you I do not. In our game the left hand didn't know what the right was doing, you know that. Do you know which jobs he did?'

'Yes, he told me,' Clements said grimly.

'The fool. Well, which ones?'

'The asshole couldn't keep his mouth shut. I don't know how he ever got into Military Intelligence.'

'Nor do I. Which ones?'

'Look, Ferdi's done a runner. Disappeared. Where to?'

Harker frowned. 'I've no idea. Doesn't Stella know?'

Clements looked at him. 'If she does, she ain't talking. She's dead. Murdered. In her apartment.'

Harker tried to look shocked. '*Christ*. Who did it? And why?'

'Hoped you might have an idea, sir.' Before Harker could answer Clements said: 'You know there's been a big breakthrough in South Africa? Five Platplaas cops have confessed to forty murders, and they've subpoenaed the Commissioner of Police himself.'

'Yes, I heard.'

'Just goes to show how vulnerable we are, doesn't it, sir? All this guy Looksmart Kumalo has got to do is subpoena a guy like Ferdi – or you – or even some big shot like General Tanner if he ever found out about him, and that person would be required by law to appear at the Truth Commission and spill the beans. And drop us all in the shit.' He frowned. 'Worrying, isn't it?'

'Very. So who murdered Stella? Ferdi? Maybe because he had bragged to her over the years about his CCB exploits and now he was nervous because Looksmart Kumalo had shown up? Or was it one of the ex-CCB guys did it, for the same reason?'

'Like you, sir?' Clements smiled.

Harker snorted grimly. 'Well, sergeant, I know I didn't do it. So that leaves one or other of you guys.'

'And I know that neither I nor any of my guys did it,' Clements said glibly. 'So that leaves you, Ferdi, or the CIA. I think you're probably innocent, sir – not like you to strangle a lady. Personally, I think it's Ferdi. That bastard was always unreliable. Just like him to brag around the whorehouse. So? Now he's gone into hiding because Looksmart's in town with his private detectives and all, and suspects him because why else would he come to Cleopatra's? Then he panics because Looksmart may squeeze information out of Stella so he sneaks back to Cleopatra's via the back door and bumps her off.'

'Then where did he go after that?'

'That,' Clements said, 'is what we have to find out before Looksmart does.' He paused. 'I think he's done a runner to South Africa. To the Truth Commission, sir.'

Harker flinched. That was unthinkable. If Ferdi did that he would destroy them all. But Harker did not believe he had gone there.

'Why d'you think that?'

'To get amnesty for the other jobs he did inside South Africa. Ferdi's running scared since he's seen these Platplaas cops break ranks.'

'I don't think he'd be so stupid,' Harker said. 'But if he has, what can you do about it?'

'He hasn't arrived in South Africa yet. We'll know when he does: we've got friends in the Immigration Department who will inform us.' He smiled wolfishly. 'And in the secretariat of the Truth Commission, sir. We'll know the moment anybody we are worried about sneaks along and starts talking about amnesty.' He added: 'Remember that.'

Harker said grimly, 'Do me the courtesy of not threatening me, sergeant.'

'Not threatening, sir, just putting you in the picture. But

if Ferdi Spicer comes to talk to you – as he might because he had great respect for you – please inform me immediately, sir. Keep him talking, get to a telephone and call me. And the same applies to our friend Looksmart Kumalo. He is very likely to contact you again, either just socially or for advice. Get his address, keep him talking and telephone me. Will you do that?'

Oh Jesus, Jesus, he was being told to be an accomplice to more murder. 'And you will do what?'

Clements looked at him grimly. 'Whatever is necessary, sir. Believe me, we don't want to attract police attention *un*necessarily, sir. It may be that Ferdi is harmless, that he's just taken fright and run into hiding. However, I think that's unlikely, considering what's happened to Stella – I think Ferdi did that.'

'If Ferdi murdered Stella to stop her blabbing about the Long Island job, he certainly isn't going to confess to the Truth Commission.'

'But once he gets in front of the Truth Commission to confess to other jobs he might break down under cross-examination by Looksmart's lawyer. And that's a certainty if the DA has promised him immunity against prosecution here in America. So I *don't* think Ferdi is harmless, sir. And as regards Looksmart, we know he's fucking lethal.' Clements looked at him. 'I'm sure you agree that it's in everybody's interests that the necessary action be taken against Looksmart, sir.' He paused. 'So do you undertake to cooperate and call me immediately Ferdi or Looksmart contact you?'

Oh God. *Cooperate in murder? More murder* . . . And if he refused he would sign his own death warrant, because Clements and Dupont and the CIA boys were running scared now. He was about to say 'And if I refuse?' when Clements said softly, 'Please don't talk about Law and Order, sir. Morality. Because if you do I'm going to have to conclude that you're a weak link in the chain, sir. Like Ferdi.' He looked at Harker apologetically. 'And I like you too much for that, sir. Surely to Christ,' he appealed softly, 'as an honest soldier who only did his duty you can see that Looksmart Kumalo deserved to die at the time, sir. It was a perfectly *legitimate* operation, sir. And so surely you can see that in the circumstances it is absolutely advisable – *necessary* – for Looksmart to disappear permanently, and probably Ferdi as well?' He paused, then added, 'You'll notice I'm not asking you to do the necessary yourself, sir. That's because, firstly, I respect your feelings, and secondly –' he smiled – 'we don't believe you'll be very good at it. All we ask is your cooperation.'

Harker took an angry breath. 'Or else I'll have a nasty accident.'

Clements frowned. '*Please*, sir. Nobody wants that.'

Oh God, of course it was in everybody's interests that Looksmart Kumalo and Ferdi Spicer disappeared: it was even almost *just* that they do so, but no way did he want to be party to that rough justice, all he wanted to do was get his ass down to Fort Lauderdale and buy that boat and disappear. But saying he agreed did not mean he did.

'Yes.' He glared at Clements.

'You undertake to do that?'

Christ, it infuriated him to be intimidated by a subordinate: he wanted to grab Clements by the collar and throw him out of the apartment. Except Clements was younger, fitter and a karate expert who would throw him across the room. 'Yes! And now will you kindly fuck off!'

Clements smiled thinly. 'Thank you, sir. And finally, about this book Josephine's writing about the Truth Commission.'

'What about it? I assure you it's not my idea.'

'Oh we *want* you to publish it – because if you don't somebody else will. And we want you to edit it very carefully. Cut out everything the slightest bit compromising about the Long Island job, anything about her pal Looksmart Kumalo blaming South Africa.' He smiled. 'We don't want millions of Americans knowing about us, do we sir? We don't want investigative journalists picking up the story, do we? So you will edit her book very, very carefully, won't you, sir? Because if it embarrasses us, we are going to be very, very angry.'

Harker had to clench his teeth to control his anger. 'And who are "we"? Are you telling me in your roundabout irritating way that the CC fucking B is still alive and well? But with new initials perhaps?'

Clements smiled, then tossed back his whisky. 'Okay, I'll be on my way, sir. Nice seeing you again.' He paused, then: 'Oh, by the way, why are you going to Fort Lauderdale?'

'Mind your own business.'

'But it is my business, sir. Now that Looksmart Kumalo has hit town, on the warpath, and Ferdi Spicer has disappeared, not to mention poor Stella experiencing such breathlessness, all your movements are very much my business.' He smiled. 'So, why Fort Lauderdale?'

'To buy,' Harker replied angrily, 'a boat. Why? Because I like boats. Where am I going to sail it? Where I fucking like. When? Every fucking weekend. Who with? Josephine and whomsoever I fucking like – rest assured it won't be you or Looksmart Kumalo.' He pointed to the door. 'Now please leave.'

Clements smiled. 'As you wish, sir.' He walked to the door. 'Goodnight, don't bother seeing me across the courtyard.' He grinned back and tapped his jacket pocket. 'By the way, everything we've discussed has been recorded. Sleep well, sir . . .'

Harker wanted to hurl his glass at the closing door.

Just then the telephone rang. He snatched it up. 'Yes?'

'Good evening, sir,' an American voice intoned, 'this is Detective Morgan of the New York Police Department's Homicide Division . . .'

33

That long night was very bad. Driving down to Fort
Lauderdale, turning over and over the events of the last
few days, the Platplaas Five breaking ranks and pointing
the finger at the Commissioner of Police himself, forcing
him to confess or damn himself to life imprisonment;
the sinister disappearance of Ferdi Spicer, the frightening
reappearance of Looksmart Kumalo, the dreadful murder of Stella, the phone call from the police, the shock
of finding Clements in his apartment, the cold-blooded
discussion of murder plots, the threats if he failed them.
And who were 'they'? Was the CCB still functioning under
another name? Controlled by whom? Right-wing politicians for a coup d'état one day? When Mandela retired,
the world's honeymoon with South Africa over? Or were
'they' just some beat-up ex-CCB operatives in America,
guys like Ricardo, Clements, Dupont and the numerous
other characters Dupont controlled? Guys shit-scared of
this Truth Commission?

Harker tried half a dozen times that night to call Redfern
on his car-phone but he only got his answering machine.
It wasn't until after midnight that Redfern called back.
Tearing down the shafts of light carved by his old Mercedes
on the turnpike, Harker told his lawyer what had happened
over the last few days.

'So this Detective Morgan,' Redfern said, 'indicated that
his only reason for contacting you was that he had found
Hogan's name in Stella's appointment book – and found
your cellphone number in Ferdi's telephone book under
that name?'

Harker said grimly: 'Plus the girls probably remember me

276

from my odd visit. They know me as Spicer's friend Hogan.'

'And this Detective Morgan didn't mention Looksmart Kumalo?'

'No.'

'And all you said was that you knew Ferdi and Stella because you occasionally patronized his fine establishment?'

'Yes,' Harker sighed.

'Well,' Redfern said, 'I don't think you need worry about Detective Morgan for the time being – sounds like a routine enquiry. And when you said you couldn't come in to the station to make a statement tomorrow because you were off to Fort Lauderdale he didn't get uptight?'

'No. But what worries me is the immunity from prosecution that Looksmart Kumalo says the DA will give to whoever agrees to give evidence against the rest of the CCB operatives who did the Long Island job. That means that Ferdi, or Clements, or Dupont himself could make a deal with the DA for immunity, then dash to the Truth Commission and get amnesty in South Africa, then give evidence against us in the American courts.'

'Yes,' Redfern agreed.

'And there's fuck-all I can do about that. We're all defenceless against that treachery.'

'No you're not,' Redfern said. '*You* could be the one to get immunity from the DA and amnesty from the Truth Commission.' He added: 'And a million bucks from Looksmart.'

Harker snorted, staring down the beam of his headlights. 'No way.'

'Why not?'

Harker said: 'I was the commanding officer, for God's sake. A commanding officer should not drop his comrades in the shit like that. Unthinkable.'

'But they're threatening you.'

'Clements is, yes. And that comes from Dupont, no doubt. But Ferdi? He's never done me any harm – on the contrary, he's been very loyal to me.'

277

'But if he murdered Stella he could easily change his mind about you.'

'But I think that was Dupont's and Clements' work, to stop her blabbing.'

'They've probably murdered Ferdi as well and sunk him in the Hudson, in which case you won't be dropping him in the shit if you testify for the DA.'

Harker shook his head, the cellphone clutched to his ear.

'Look, Jack,' Redfern said, 'let me approach the DA on the old-boy network. His name's Hughie Maisels, a tough Jewish leftie but a nice enough guy – and honest. I'll sound him out – *without* divulging who my client is. We want to know whether Looksmart Kumalo is really telling the truth or whether he was just trying to snag you by saying the DA is offering immunity. If it's true, we want to know what the conditions are. So? Do I have your permission to approach him?'

Harker was aghast. 'Christ, he'll find out who your client is!'

'He won't, I'll do it on the honour system, he won't ask who you are and I certainly won't tell him.'

'But then he sends his sleuths to sniff around you and find out who I might be.'

'No he won't.'

'No? Never heard of Watergate?'

'But that's not real life any more.'

'Look, the CCB is real life, and the CIA, even the KGB under another name – that type of skulduggery was my business, don't imagine that your offices can't be broken into, your filing cabinets microfilmed until the name Jack Harker shows up.'

'Jack, on the old-boy network, lawyers don't do that sort of thing to each other.'

Harker shook his head. 'I wouldn't know a moment's rest. And even if the DA were to offer me immunity I wouldn't testify against my comrades. And if I did Josephine would leave me like a shot when she heard the truth. Forget it.'

'Well, if you won't cover your ass, you'd better get it down to Fort Lauderdale and buy that boat,' Redfern said soberly. 'Jack, Stella is dead. And she sure didn't commit suicide. Ferdi has disappeared, and I have a feeling he's dead too; but if he isn't, he's going to be soon. And all because Looksmart Kumalo has come to town. So, who's knocking off the witnesses? And who's the next target? Jack, your ex-comrades are warning you that you're next if you don't keep your mouth shut.' Redfern sighed. 'And what about Josephine? They're scared that she is going to come back from South Africa with a bag full of facts and publish them. Through you.' Redfern snorted. 'Jack, on the face of it you two look like very obvious targets. So my advice is buy this boat and go on a long, long sail, get away from these bastards who're deciding whether to kill you. Will Josephine go along with that? Can you persuade her to pack up and leave immediately?'

Harker sighed. 'In six months' time she'll go for it with a whoop and a holler. Right now her head's full of this new book; when she comes back she'll be hot to settle down and work, not sail the high seas.'

'You haven't got six months to spare,' Redfern said. 'Do it now. Josephine can work on the boat. The most important thing is to get as far away as possible and as untraceable as possible – by the Truth Commission *and* by Dupont and company. Which brings me to the next point.' He paused. 'To be untraceable you must sell Harvest House.' He added, 'You can sell it to another offshore company which you create for the purpose, which you control. In that way you get Harvest out of your name but still control it, you own it indirectly but nobody knows it. I can set up a totally question-proof company for you in the Cayman Islands for a few thousand dollars. It'll take a few phone calls, a few signatures and everybody will believe you've sold Harvest House.'

Harker stared down the beam of his headlights, his mind trying to deal with overdrafts and percentages.

'Or, if you need the money for your round-the-world voyage,' Redfern continued, 'you can sell your shares to a publisher who wants your authors. I know of several who would probably snap up Harvest House if the price was right.'

Oh God, selling Harvest . . .' And what should I do about my apartment? You'll remember that it's only leased to me, and the lease will expire in December.'

'Excellent,' Redfern said. 'Just write a letter to the landlord informing him that you will be leaving when the lease expires. Perfect. So when the Truth Commission tries to serve a subpoena on you – or if the DA comes looking for you – you've clearly left town. For good.' He paused. 'So what I recommend is that I set up that company for you in the Cayman Islands. Let's say we call it the Neptune Company. You transfer your personal fifty-one per cent shareholding in Harvest to Neptune and *you* own all the shares. That way you're technically no longer a Harvest shareholder and can't be traced. But you'll still control Harvest, anonymously, through Neptune.'

34

The next two weeks were hectic: buying a boat, preparing to sell Harvest House, packing up a whole life so he could hit the high seas and *run* for his life.

It was a fifty-two-foot ketch, built in Hong Kong, called *Rosemary*. She was sound but she had been neglected and Harker beat down the price to $140,000. She was built of fibreglass, had teak decks, lots of fancy woodwork, three cabins, two bathrooms, a large saloon, an excellent galley, a spacious wheelhouse, a second steering wheel aft. Harker took an album of photographs of her out to the airport when he went to meet Josephine on her return from South Africa. He also took two air tickets. They rushed into each other's arms, then he thrust the tickets at her.

'Where are these to?' she demanded.

'To Las Vegas,' Harker said. 'We're getting married, whether you agree or not. And this –' he put the album of photographs into her hand – 'is your beautiful new matrimonial home . . .'

Josephine stared at the topmost photograph of the handsome yacht.

'Oh *wow* . . .' she said.

And so Jack Harker and Josephine Valentine got married. Josephine hurriedly began to pack up all her ornaments and pictures and paintings for storage to enable Harker to let the apartment: she thought he was the owner and that a tenant would be occupying it for the next three years. Jack Harker was lucky that he could so easily persuade his bride to disappear with him like this: the only unpleasantness came from her father. After the ceremony in The True

Love Wedding Chapel, Josephine telephoned her father in Boston from their hotel room. Harker listened on the extension in the bathroom.

'Dad,' Josephine said, 'I'm calling you from Las Vegas. First of all, to tell you I love you.'

'Las *Vegas*? I thought you were in South Africa.'

'I got back to New York this morning. Jack met me at the airport, and we flew straight on to Las Vegas. Dad? Jack and I are married.'

There was a stunned silence. Then: 'So you've done it, huh?'

'Dad,' Josephine said, 'we want your blessing.'

There was another silence. Then a bitter sigh. 'Against my wishes . . . Against my advice, you have rushed off and committed the *folly* of marrying that man.'

'Dad, he's a good man and I love him.'

'That soldier of fortune.'

'Dad. Believe me, I know him better than you.'

'You think you do,' the old man said bitterly. 'So tell me, what time today did you go through this so-called marriage ceremony?'

'Half an hour ago. Why?'

Harker was amazed to hear the old man say, 'So you have not yet consummated the marriage?'

Josephine half-laughed, embarrassed. 'Dad, I'm sure you're worldly-wise enough to imagine that our relationship has been consummated many times over the last several years.'

'I said *marriage*! You haven't, have you – consummated the marriage in the last half-hour?'

'Dad, if you must know, the answer is no – but what the hell has it got to do with you?'

'It has,' the old man said, 'a great deal to do with me. As your trustee. And with *us*, as father and daughter.' He paused, then pronounced: 'Josie, you can take it from me, as a lawyer, that you can walk out of that hotel room right now and your so-called marriage can be declared null and

282

void by the courts, *because* it has not been consummated *since* the marriage!'

There was a shocked silence. Then: '*Father* – do you realize what you're saying?'

'I realize perfectly, I'm telling you to escape this folly – all you've got to do is catch a taxi to the airport and a plane to Boston. I'll meet you and take care of everything.'

'Dad, does it not occur to you that I *want* to be married to Jack? And he to me?'

'Because you imagine that you're in love with him. Josephine, the man is a soldier of fortune, it's your wealth that he's in love with. He knows you inherit over two million dollars on your marriage. Josephine – if you go ahead with this marriage, I will not give you the time of day. I cannot prevent you getting your entitlement in terms of your grandfather's trust, but I will disown you. I will cut you out of my own will and bequeath my entire estate to charity. I refuse to let that so-called husband get his hands on our hard-earned wealth.'

'Dad,' Josephine said softly, 'you can stick your wealth right up your sweater, all I want from you is your blessing. And Dad? You'd better give it soon because we're going to go away for a long, long time, on a lovely yacht we've just bought, we're going to sail right around the world, starting next month.' Her voice caught. 'We'd like your blessing, Dad, but if you don't want to give it you can go to hell!'

Josephine banged down the telephone and burst into tears.

Harker came through from the bathroom, sat down on the bed beside her and took her in his arms.

'It'll be okay,' he said, 'he'll come around.'

'Oh,' she sobbed, 'I'm so sorry you heard all that.'

'He'll come around when he sees how happy we are.'

'He doesn't mean it,' she sobbed, 'he's just . . . desperate.'

283

Oh, he means it all right, Harker thought. He lifted her chin. 'Now, about this consummation of the marriage business he was talking about . . .' He toppled her over on to her back.

It was half an hour later, when they were sprawled out on the bed, naked, sweating, exhausted, that the telephone rang.

'It's got to be him,' Harker said. 'Nobody else knows we're in Las Vegas.'

Josephine reached to answer it, then stopped herself. 'You speak to him,' she said.

Harker reached for the phone. 'Hullo?'

'Is that Jack Harker?'

'It is.'

'Let me speak to Josephine, please.'

Jesus. 'Who,' Harker asked, 'is speaking?'

'Her father, Denys Valentine.'

Harker closed his eyes in anger – the man's arrogance, not introducing himself upfront. He held the telephone out to Josephine.

Josephine hesitated, then said, 'Tell him,' she said loudly so Valentine could hear, 'we have consummated the marriage!'

Harker returned the telephone to his ear. 'Denys, my wife sends you her love and hopes for your blessing. She asks you please to telephone her at home tomorrow as she is indisposed at the moment.'

Valentine snorted bitterly. 'I heard what she said. So, I understand you are to be congratulated.'

'Thank you,' Harker said.

'On marrying the best girl in the world,' Valentine said.

'Yes, that's absolutely true.' Harker was grinning. He added: 'The best young *woman* in the world. And one of the world's most talented writers.'

The old man snorted again. Then: 'Well, just you look after her, Mr Harker. If you don't, I'll hound you to the ends of the earth. Now, is it true that you intend

284

taking my daughter off around the world in a small sailboat?'

Harker smiled. 'In a big, strong, fifty-two-foot ketch with a Lloyd's A1 survey certificate.'

'Mr Harker, are you completely selfish? Are you completely reckless of my daughter's life?'

'On the contrary, I am devoted to my wife's well-being, Denys. This round-the-world adventure is the fulfilment of a lifetime's dream for both of us. And, as I am sure you're aware, your daughter has a legendary reputation as an adventurer in umpteen war-zones.'

'Mr Harker –'

'Please,' Harker said crisply, 'call me Jack.'

'Mr Harker,' Valentine continued, 'what about my daughter's literary career while you take her off gallivanting around the globe?'

'Josephine's literary career is also my professional business. But the fact is, Josephine can work anywhere in the world. She will continue to write and Harvest House will continue to publish her to the best of its ability. To our mutual profitability.'

'And how,' Valentine enquired, 'will you run Harvest House – and thus my daughter's career – when you are on the high seas?'

'I'll be appointing a managing director.'

'Who?'

Harker frowned. 'Forgive me, but that's none of your business.'

'On the contrary, as my daughter's husband you have a responsibility not only for her happiness, for her spiritual and physical well-being, but also for her literary career, and I as her trustee and father certainly have a moral right to know how you propose discharging that responsibility when you're endangering her life on the high seas. Now I've just spoken to Josephine's agent about this problem, and she tells me she's heard a rumour that you propose selling Harvest House. Is this true?'

Harker didn't want Josephine to know this yet. 'Untrue, Mr Valentine. And now, if you'll excuse me, I would like to be with my wife. It is our honeymoon, after all.'

Valentine snorted. 'Your wife . . .' he said bitterly.

Before he could continue Harker said quietly, 'Yes, Mr Valentine, and I want you to know that I will always do my utmost to be a good husband to her, as I am confident she will be a good wife to me. And I want you to know that she very much wants your blessing. And now *goodnight*, sir. Please feel free to telephone us in New York tomorrow evening.'

He hung up.

It was a time of mixed emotions: the happiness of being married at last and the excitement of preparing for the adventure of sailing off into the wide blue yonder; the sadness of packing up a whole life, pictures and ornaments and paintings and china packed into crates, their furniture prepared for storage so that Harker could pretend to put the place on the market for rental. He dearly wished he had told her long ago that the property was only leased. And he was exhausted: the tension of the preceding months, the deafening ticking of the amnesty clock had robbed him of much sleep, made him drink too much, had dogged his every waking thought. But now, with Josephine back from Africa, in his bed every night and morning, with the boat now waiting for them, it seemed he was getting some control over his crisis: he was very relieved that he had persuaded her so easily to help him disappear. He was very lucky that Josephine was mad-keen about sailing. Oh yes, he liked his boat and he was excited too about the adventures ahead, but relief was his uppermost emotion.

And he was very lucky about the Gramercy Mews apartment too. Josephine loved the place and if she had found out the truth about it she might have discovered the whole truth about him. Josephine did not expect to see the apartment for the next three years – he had that long before having to explain to her that the apartment was no more. Cross the bridges when you come to them.

And there were many other things to be done.

He said: 'It's only sensible that we should both take out some more life insurance. How much have you got? You told me once but I've forgotten.'

'Only forty thousand. Took it out years ago just as a form of saving, don't know what it's worth today.'

'Which company?'

'Manufacturers Life.'

'Okay, I'll telephone 'em and ask a salesman to call. You need at least a hundred thousand dollars' worth these days. I've only got fifty, I'll get another fifty.' He added: 'We both appoint each other as beneficiary. That way if one of us dies the survivor doesn't have to wait for probate of the estate. And we should both make new wills.'

'Doing the same? Both leave our estates to the other?'

'If that's what you want to do.'

'Of course. I've got no siblings. So, what else have we got to do, partner?'

Sell Harvest House, that's what. He did not want to mention that subject to Josephine, he did not want a crisis, but sell he must, to pay off his debts, to pay for the boat, to pay for this voyage around the world, to do a total disappearing trick. It broke Harker's heart to think of selling his beloved Harvest House but it had to be done. Harker hoped that Redfern would quietly sell it after they had left. Redfern had discreetly put the word out that Harvest might be for sale at the right price and there had been interest from Terence Packard, the British media mogul who was said to be looking for a good little publishing house. And then, when Harker got back to Gramercy Mews from work one evening, Josephine confronted him at the front door.

'What's this about you selling Harvest to that bandit Terence Packard?'

Harker was taken unawares.

'I haven't sold anything, Josie. All I've done is set up an

offshore company in the Cayman Islands and transferred my fifty-one per cent share in Harvest to that holding company. It's called Neptune.'

'Why?'

'Because we're going away for years. It's easier to administer and there are certain tax advantages. And if I ever decide to sell, I'll only have to sell Neptune.'

'And – *have* you decided to sell?'

Harker sighed. 'Who told you about Packard?'

'The venerable Priscilla Fischer herself. She says the word's out that Harvest is up for grabs and that Terence Packard has offered nine-dollars-sixty a share!' She stared at him. 'Why didn't you tell me about all this?'

Harker sighed grimly. 'I didn't want to upset you.' He added untruthfully: 'And I didn't set out to look for a buyer – the word got out and Packard's men approached *me*.'

'Of course I'm upset! God, my publisher – who also just happens to be my husband – is about to sell his soul *and* his best author to the biggest predator in publishing.'

Oh, he wished he could tell the truth. He went into his long-rehearsed speech: 'Josie, I'm forty-six years old. I've worked hard. We're going off around the world on our yacht – and I want the money. We don't know how long we'll be away. We may not want to come back at all. So if I get a good offer now, why not take the money and invest it? Anyway, I can't administer Harvest when I'm on the high seas, can I?'

Josephine looked at him. 'And what,' she demanded, 'about me?'

'You'll still get paid your normal royalties by Harvest, no matter who owns the shares, me or Packard.'

'But I don't *want* to write for Packard – that megalomaniac.'

'Well,' Harker said, 'your next book, after this one you're writing now, you can take to any publisher you like – and probably be paid a higher advance than Harvest will pay you.'

Josie frowned. '*But,*' she objected, 'I don't *want* to be published by just anybody else.' She pointed across Gramercy Park. 'I *like* the gang over at Harvest. Most of them will leave if Packard takes over. I *like* the building. I like your office, which is my territory, not just yours. I'm not only one of your authors, I'm the boss's pillow companion.'

Harker sighed. 'When we're back from our travels I can start a new publishing house. With you as my star author, I'll have no trouble getting off the ground.'

Josephine turned away. 'Bull*shit* . . .' She turned back to him: 'Look, you've got the best little publishing house in New York just over there. Up and running, an established name, a good list of authors, excellent sales team.' She spread her hands. 'And you *love* publishing. And your ever-loving wife is your star author who earns you lots of money.' She frowned. 'And you want to give all this away to a scoundrel like Packard? For what – a couple of million dollars?'

'When you've been paying yourself the minimum salary for years that is a lot of money. And,' he ended, 'I'm sick of you earning more than me.'

Josephine looked mystified. She waved her hand. 'But you provide this apartment. And the living costs. And our holiday expenses. *And* Harvest provides all the money I earn – *you're* the guy who sells my books, not me. Christ, what more does a damsel want in a husband?'

'Josephine –'

'Okay – what's Packard offering you? Nine bucks-sixty a share? I offer nine-seventy!'

Harker sighed. 'Josie –'

'You don't think it's worth it? I do – every goddam penny. Especially if Packard thinks so! In fact it's a bargain, because I know I'm going to write such marvellous books Harvest is going to treble in value over the next three years – *I'm* going to make the killing, not Mr bloody Packard! And that way we keep Harvest in the family. And when we come back we can reappoint you managing director.'

She held up both hands: 'My money is as good as Terence Packard's.'

Harker sighed. Oh, he would love to do the deal – love to have his cake and eat it. But no – too risky. Before he could respond Josephine planted herself in front of him.

'Jack, this is very important to me. *Very* important. And I demand, as your wife, a proper say in this matter, which affects not only you but our livelihood. *And* affects me as a writer – writers like to feel comfortable with their publishers. The personality of the publisher, his character, his . . . sense of humour, his artistic sense, his vision – and above all his *integrity* is terribly important to an author. The author's only partner is his publisher. So if the author suspects his publisher is a bullshitter, or insincere, that would be deeply disturbing.' She looked at him. 'And that's exactly how I feel about Terence Packard. He's a steel-hearted blackguard dressed up in publisher's clothing. In fact I hereby advise you that if you sell to Packard I am off – to Doubleday or Dutton or somebody like that. *Which* detail will doubtless reduce the value of Harvest's shares.' She glared at him. 'So, my darling? You sell your shareholding in Harvest House to me for nine-dollars-seventy a throw, or,' she pointed at the door, 'I am off . . .'

And so Josephine paid Harker somewhat over two million dollars – a sum agreed by both her accountant and his as fair – for Neptune, which owned fifty-one per cent of Harvest House. The other forty-nine per cent remained in the ownership of Westminster NV, the registered offices of which were in Curacao, which unknown to anybody except the Curacao International Trust Company was formerly owned by the South African Defence Force but was now owned by Jack Harker. Harker then bought back a two per cent shareholding in Harvest from Neptune: 'Just to retain a stake in the company, a small say in the voting.' And so Harker both had his cake and could eat it: he had two million dollars and he still retained secret control of

Harvest with his total of fifty-one per cent shareholding – Westminster's forty-nine and his own two per cent. With enormous relief he paid off his personal debt to the bank and invested the remainder. He told Josephine that he had invested in gilt bonds averaging seven per cent: in fact he invested in high-yield mutual funds whose track record for a long time was over fifteen per cent.

And so, piecemeal, Harker wound up his affairs, while all the time the amnesty clock ticked deafeningly loud. Now it was one hundred days away, now ninety, now eighty.

It was their last day in New York. The Gramercy Mews apartment was stripped of all its paintings, flowerpots, rugs, books, ornaments, all packed into crates ready to go into storage when the furniture removers arrived the following day. Harker stood in the living room. He was very sad to leave this apartment, knowing he was never coming back to it. He had been happy here. There had been many good times. Josephine was not sad because she believed they were coming back to it in a few years. Harker sighed: God, the web of lies he was caught up in . . . And at stake was his very life.

That evening there was a farewell party at Harvest House. Harker felt emotional. He loved these people, most of whom had been with Harvest since its inception, he loved this old brownstone house, its big windows and faded carpeting and marble fireplaces, its creaking floors, and he hoped that one day he would come back to it after this Truth Commission crisis was dead and buried. He made a brief farewell speech but by agreement with Josephine he did not announce that she had invested in the company: he intended dropping that news by letter from some faraway place, with no return address. That was also the way he intended closing down his American bank account, operating thereafter exclusively on a numbered Swiss account. It was a pleasant little party until, right at the end, the telephone rang. It was for Harker. He took it in his secretary's cubicle. 'Hullo?'

'So,' Dupont said, 'doing a disappearing trick, are we? Just as long as you don't go anywhere near the Truth Commission. Or you'll end up in that big publishing house in the sky. In Head Office we do hope that you're mindful of that little detail as the countdown to the fifteenth of December approaches.'

Head office? Christ, this was 1996, five years since F.W. de Klerk had disbanded the CCB – and there was still a Head Office! 'Where the hell are you speaking from? Washington?'

'My dear fellow, I'm calling you from the *old* Head Office.'

Harker stared. He was calling from Pretoria? The old Military Intelligence *still* functioned? For whose benefit – the old guard of the apartheid regime? It was terrifying. He said:

'My lawyer will send you a letter advising that I haven't got a fucking clue what you're talking about and that if you trouble me again you'll have a writ slapped on you! Now go to hell!' He slammed down the telephone.

He was shaking. Christ, he couldn't wait to get out of this town, right out of this country.

And then, as they entered their apartment after the party, the telephone was ringing. Josephine picked up the receiver. 'Hullo?' Then, 'Hullo, Looksmart!'

Harker froze. He turned into the bedroom and picked up the telephone extension.

Josephine was saying, '. . . were talking about you, I thought about trying to get in touch with you but we didn't know where you were staying and it's been all go go go since I got back from South Africa last month.' She added: 'Jack and I are married now.'

'Congratulations!' Looksmart exclaimed. 'All the more reason for me to buy you guys a drink tonight – make that a bottle of champagne!'

'I'm sorry, Looksmart, but we really can't; we're leaving tomorrow morning crack of dawn for the Bahamas and we've still got a lot of packing to do – we've bought a boat, you see, and we're setting off around the world.'

'Yes, so I've heard, but I didn't realize you were leaving so soon.'

Harker's heart lurched. *How did he know that?* Looksmart continued, 'Can't I pop around with a bottle for a few minutes right now to see you before you disappear?'

'Well . . .' Josephine hesitated. Harker stepped hurriedly into the corridor and shook his finger at her. 'Well, I don't think so,' Josephine said, 'I'm undressed already and Jack's soaking in the bath right now, we're both really tired.' She changed the subject. 'So how's your investigation into the Long Island massacre progressing?'

Harker tensed.

'That's one of the things I wanted to tell you about.' Harker held his breath. 'My detective is progressing well. For obvious reasons I'm told not to discuss details but I can say that we are now absolutely certain that the massacre was not committed by the Cuban exiles – it was definitely the South Africans. We've now got the DA convinced too.'

'*Wonderful*,' Josephine enthused. 'Oh, I really want to hear all about this, I need this for my book. Would you be so kind as to dictate it all – or as much as your detectives permit – on to a tape and post it to me?'

Harker could imagine the wolfish smile on Looksmart's face.

'Sure,' he said. 'What address?'

'Address it to yacht *Rosemary*, Post Restante, Nassau, Bahamas, until I advise you that we're moving on to some other port. What's your phone number?'

'Will do,' Looksmart said, 'and please send me any comments or clues you may have.' He gave her his telephone number and fax number.

When she hung up Josephine went through to the bedroom and said, 'Isn't that exciting news?'

Harker ripped off his tie shakily. 'But it's bullshit, darling.'

'How can you say that without seeing the evidence?' Josephine demanded.

The next morning they woke early. The apartment seemed abandoned: their bags stood ready, awaiting the final garments before being zipped up. Josephine stripped the bed. The taxi arrived as they finished dressing. As they left the apartment Josephine looked around.

'Goodbye, Gramercy Mews.' She crossed the living room and kissed the wall. 'If you kiss a house it knows you're coming back.' She called down the staircase: 'Goodbye, Madam Velvet, see you in three years, don't do anything we wouldn't!' She turned to Harker. 'Okay, let's go, Captain.'

It was noon when the turquoise waters of the Bahamas unfolded below them. Down there the deep blue water of the Gulf Stream suddenly turned to the silvery clear shallows of the Bahama Sea, sparkling clear, the sand just a couple of metres below the surface, the fringes of Bahama's hundreds of islands easing into view through the haze.

'It's beautiful.' Josie squeezed his hand. 'Do you think there's any truth in the Bermuda Triangle theory?'

Harker was a superstitious man: yes, he believed. 'No,' he said.

'Oh,' Josie said, 'we're going to have a lovely time . . .'

PART V

35

The boat lay at the end of the jetty, fifty-two feet long not counting her bowsprit, her woodwork dull, her fibreglass unkempt, strands of weeds awash below her waterline: but she was a handsome, strong, sleek, comfortable round-the-worlder and Josephine was thrilled.

'A gas oven *and* a microwave. A big refrigerator *and* a big deep-freeze!'

Harker slid back a panel of the engine room. 'And a separate generator to run them. And a desalination plant so we need never worry about fresh water crossing oceans.'

'Oh, darling, she's beautiful. And a third cabin for me to work in!'

That was a most important feature – a study in which she could write. It had a table and two bunks, one above the other. 'Absolutely *ideal* . . . Oh, we did do well for a hundred and forty thousand.' She looked around the spacious saloon. 'All this lovely teak. And those super brass lamps.'

Harker led her down the companionway to the aft section. 'Our master-cabin.'

'Oh boy . . .' She looked around happily. 'All this space. And that sexy double bunk. And our own en-suite bathroom. And our own living room when we get sick of our guests.'

'And,' Harker pointed to the corner, 'our own fridge for our booze.' He opened it.

'Now you're talking! Oh, I'm so thrilled. Such *space*. And *glamour*. All this teak and brass is a lot of work but it's going to be a labour of love.'

And she loved Nassau, the quaint little colonial capital with the subtropical flowers and trees, historic buildings drenched in shade, the old cathedral, the supreme court, the library, the Victorian shops and cafés along the water-front, the markets and jetties and bars, the long bridge over the shipping channel to Paradise Island with its row of tour-ist hotels opening on to the white beaches and coral reefs of the Atlantic. And out there were hundreds of islands with little sprinklings of villages, the shallow waters crystal clear, the coral heads growing up like flowers, the multi-coloured fish swimming amongst them. Every day at noon, when they stopped work, Harker and Josephine went out in their dinghy with their lunch and snorkelled along the reefs.

There were dozens of yachts in the marina, more anchored outside in the channel. There was a bar overlooking the marina and Paradise Island beyond. Many yachts came and went during the time that Harker and Josephine prepared their vessel, and they met many people. Most of them were Americans who regularly sailed the Caribbean but a good number were Europeans, Australians and New Zealanders sailing their way around the world: some were retired people but many were young, making ends meet by doing odd jobs. There were a lot of tales around the bar of faraway places, good ports and bad, safe places and treacherous places, good seas and dangerous ones, pirates and ghost ships.

'Have *you* ever seen a ghost ship?' Josie demanded.

'Yes,' said the skipper of *Mermaid*, the guy with the pony-tail. 'Right here in the middle of the Bermuda Triangle. Large as life she was, two hundred metres away on my port side. The sun on her sails. Nobody on deck. "Where the hell did you come from?" I thought. Astonished, I was. Then I thought, "Are we on a collision course?" So I watched her closely. I noted the angle between us on the compass for two or three minutes. When I was satisfied we were not going to collide I went below to the galley. Came back up three minutes later and – *poof* – she was gone.'

'What were you drinking?' Josephine grinned.

'Coffee. It was only sunrise.'

'Had you been keeping a good lookout?'

'Every fifteen minutes I stood up and did a three-sixty, looked around in a full circle. So she had appeared from nowhere. And disappeared into nowhere.'

'But,' Josephine said, 'as it had appeared from nowhere why did you go below?'

'Well,' the young pony-tailed skipper said, 'afterwards I asked myself that same question. And the only answer I can give is that that ghost ship made me stop being astonished, made me like having her there, she was kind of comforting.'

'She bewitched you?' Harker said.

'Maybe. Like that US Air Force squad that all disappeared over the Bermuda Triangle. They flew out over the Atlantic in formation one sunrise then suddenly the leader radioed back to base that their compasses had all gone haywire. So their base commander instructed them to fly west, back towards America. And the leader said, "Which direction is west?" Although the sun was just up he was so disorientated that he couldn't even decide where west was.'

'So what happened to them?'

'Whole squadron just disappeared,' the skipper said. 'Never seen again. No radio contact, nothin'. So, maybe something like that happened to me. I *liked* that ghost ship being there.'

And they heard many tales of pirates. There was a converted trawler manned by four young Americans armed with guitars and rings in their ears heading north and living life on the ocean wave as if these were their last days on earth, drinking and singing and wenching – do not imagine it is not hard work to enjoy yourself so much. They had been attacked by pirates.

'Mostly they're drug runners,' said Pete, the trawler's owner, who looked like a drug-runner himself. 'They rush up to you in the middle of the night, swarm aboard, kill you, use your boat for one or two drug runs between Colombia and Florida, then they sink it and steal another one.'

Josephine was riveted. 'Why do they sink the boat?'

'To destroy the evidence. Shit, that Gulf Stream over there is full of yachts that've been sunk by those bastards. If they use the same boat their pattern will be noticed by the US Coast Guard. So it's better and cheaper just to sink her and steal another one.'

'And murder another boatload of people.'

'Nice guys, aren't they?'

Josephine's writer's blood was stirring. 'Who *are* these guys?'

'Ask the Coast Guard. Ask the Drugs Enforcement Agency. They all know who the big bad guys are in America and the Caribbean but they can't prove it.'

'How did you escape when you were attacked?'

'Two blasts from my shotgun. They fell back.'

'God. Did you kill anybody?'

'Don't know for sure, it was night. But I sure made a mess of his wheelhouse.'

'Where do these people operate?'

'All over the western Caribbean. But right here in the Bahamas is bad. Particularly near the island of Andros. Don't go anywhere near Andros. Big island, full of creeks and reefs. And the weirdest people who still talk Elizabethan English – "thee" and "thou". If you go near those guys come zooming out and you're a goner.'

'But why doesn't the US Coast Guard go in there and root the bastards out?'

'Andros is in the Bahamas, the US Coast Guard has no jurisdiction there. And the Bahama government ain't going in there because of corruption – some politicians are in cahoots with those pirates. The Bahamas is a nation for sale.' He snorted. 'See that long speedboat there?' He pointed at a sleek vessel forty feet long anchored in the channel. 'That's called a cigarette boat, because it looks like one. Boats like that belong to smugglers. They load them up with drugs, crank up those two engines on the stern, and set off at night, screaming across the Caribbean heading for Florida. No Coast Guard vessel can catch them. They hit the Florida coast where their buddies are waiting for them, throw the drugs ashore, grab their money, zoom back deep-sea and head flat-out for home. The next week they take a new load.' He shook his head. 'They make a lot of money. But if they're caught they're in jail for a long time.'

And then there were tales about the 'floaters', refugees from Cuba and Haiti who try to make it to Florida on rafts and in overloaded old boats.

'They can be just as dangerous if they get near enough because they're desperate,' Clive said. He was the captain of a charter yacht that took tourists around the islands. 'So if you see a bunch of people waving from a raft pleading for help just look the other way. Don't be tempted to be a Good Samaritan.'

Harker shook his head and sighed. 'I couldn't do that.'

'Nor could I,' Josie said.

'Well,' Clive said, 'it's you or them . . .'

For the first couple of weeks it was hard to believe, in this exotic setting, that way down there in South Africa the amnesty clock was ticking. Josephine had arranged with her friends in the Anti-Apartheid League to send her regular digests of developments in the Truth Commission but nothing arrived in Nassau during their first fortnight. The radio on which Harker would have listened to the South African news was undergoing repairs and the marina bar had no television. Every day Harker bought the *Miami Herald*, but there was little international news. He telephoned Luke Mahoney but only got his answering machine; Redfern was away from New York on vacation; every morning Harker jogged to the post office to intercept any letter or tape from Looksmart Kumalo to Josephine. But there was nothing; and in the languor of the Bahamas with their turquoise waters, coral reefs, balmy beaches and pubs and restaurants it was hard to imagine that the harsh world of the Truth Commission was grinding away relentlessly on the other side of the Atlantic; that down there matters of life and death were being bitterly argued, remorse and fear and indecision running rampant, the panic mounting as the amnesty cut-off date loomed. Most of the time in the balmy Bahamas it was hard for Harker to realize that all that drama was actually relevant to him. Indeed it applied to him more than to most of those bastards over there shaking in their old apartheid boots because most of them had committed their crimes inside South Africa and they could get a cast-iron indemnity – whereas Major Jack Harker could be sent to Sing-Sing for the rest of his days for his contribution to the defeat of communism. Most of the time when he was working on his boat, putting in new plumbing, rewiring, replacing parts of the rigging, he was able to shove the Truth Commission out of his mind, and when at midday they climbed into their dinghy and went chugging out to the coral reefs to explore their underwater wonderworld it seemed impossible that he could be in deadly trouble. Then one day his cellphone rang. It was Luke Mahoney.

'Remember General Malan, the former Minister of Defence who was charged with a dozen others with the massacre of ANC people in Natal? Well, they were all acquitted this morning for want of reliable evidence.'

Harker stared across the marina. 'Yes?'

'This is good news for you,' Luke said, 'because I think a lot of people who've been considering confessing to the Truth Commission will now feel they would rather take their chances in court. So less information is going to come to light. However, next week those five policemen from Platplaas are going to give full details of their crimes. There're a lot of worried cops waiting to hear what these five guys say. Indeed they could drop so many people in the shit that they've been closeted overseas somewhere in the Truth Commission's witness protection programme in case they're bumped off. You'll remember that they've sub-poenaed General van der Merwe, the former Commissioner of Police, to give evidence – to get him to admit that he knew all about Platplaas and therefore politicians like the president must have known and approved. And next week the army must make its submissions to the Truth Commission.'

Oh Jesus, Harker was worried about what the army would say. 'So what do I do?'

'Just lie low. I'll keep you in the picture, I'll telephone again in a week. How long will you be in Nassau?'

'We need another month here to get absolutely sea-worthy.'

'Well, the sooner you get going the better.'

The Truth Commission had become a remote phantom until this telephone call; now once again it was screamingly real. The next day a wad of newspaper cuttings arrived from Josephine's friends in South Africa, and a faxed newsletter from the League. It all brought Harker back to earth. It was a long seven days waiting for Luke to call back. It was noon in the Bahamas when he did. Harker was sitting in his dinghy drinking a beer while Josephine snorkelled along a reef.

'Well,' Luke said soberly, 'it's been a big day for the Truth Commission. What do you want first, the good news or the bad news?'

'For Christ's sake, Luke!' Harker glanced over the water for Josie.

'Well,' Luke said, 'the army made its submission to the Truth Commission today, through General Mortimer as its spokesman. The good news, from your point of view, is that the general got on his high horse and virtually told the Truth Commission to mind its own bloody business – war is war, which softie civilians sitting in their snug suburbs know nothing about, so don't dare to presume to tell us officers and gentlemen how to run our business.'

'Mortimer said all that?'

'That was his line, I believe. The army confessed to nothing, by gad sir. But the bad news is that Archbishop Tutu sent him packing with a flea in his ear. The newspapers described his one-sided submission as "quite breathtaking" in its arrogance. The Truth Commission refused to accept his blanket denials and told him to go back to HQ and have another damn think on-the-double before the Truth Commission loses patience and subpoenas the whole damn General Staff. But most Military Intelligence files have been "lost", and raids on military bases haven't come up with anything, so I don't think the army is going to admit to much.'

Thank God for that.

Luke continued: 'But the cops from Platplaas may be a problem.'

'Why?' Harker demanded. 'The army hasn't got anything to do with the police.'

'Well, these five Platplaas officers have now given their evidence, admitting to forty high-profile political murders. They have spilt the beans on their superiors, and they publicly urged the relevant politicians to own up. All very humble and contrite. General van der Merwe, the last Commissioner of Police, had to appear on their behalf, and he not only corroborated their evidence, he also admitted again to being responsible for bombing Khotso House, headquarters of the South African Council of Churches and of the ANC, and for the first time he told us where he got his orders from! From the former President of South Africa himself, P.W. Botha! How do you like them apples?'

Harker stared across the water. *Christ . . .* 'How does this affect Military Intelligence. And me?'

Luke sighed. 'Well, these five cops and the Commissioner of Police have revealed that in addition to the CCB there was a kind of combined police and military operation called CRITT – the Counter-Revolutionary Task Team – which decided on targets for their hit-men. CRITT held monthly meetings where police and Military Intelligence sat down together over coffee and biscuits at a nice big varnished table and solemnly compared lists of political opponents and discussed who should be assassinated for the good of the apartheid government. In other words, *official* Murder Incorporated. And they "prioritized" these names – they made solemn decisions as to who should be hunted down and killed first. Having made those decisions, CRITT in collaboration with the army and police would hunt their targets. But they had to be killed in such a way that the government was not suspected – or at least so that nothing could be proved.' Luke snorted. 'The Commissioner of Police and the five Platplaas cops explained that they murdered their victims rather than detain them under the state of emergency legislation because, firstly, it was easier and secondly, murder was a permanent solution. And thirdly, in the madness of the Total Onslaught Total Strategy era, any tactic was acceptable.'

Harker felt sick in his guts; this was what he had been mixed up in? 'I assure you I knew nothing about CRITT.'

'I believe you, but we know that President P.W. Botha knew because CRITT reported daily to the State Security Council, and that means that F.W. de Klerk also must have known because he was also a member of the Council.'

'*Christ* . . . So, do you have any different advice for me?'

'Have you had any contact from your former colleagues?'

'No.'

'Well, they may come looking for you now to get reassurance that you're not going to squeal on them. If that happens say as little as possible as they'll probably be tape-recording the conversation.'

Josephine was snorkelling back towards the dinghy. Harker said: 'Luke, I'd better go.'

And then, that very afternoon, when Harker returned to the boat from jogging, he saw a man sitting on the deck of his yacht talking to Josephine, a bottle of beer in his hand, a white Panama hat on his head. The man had his back to him and Harker did not realize until he was clambering aboard that he was black. And that he had only one hand.

'Darling,' Josephine said, 'you remember Looksmart Kumalo . . .'

36

With a wave of his claw, Looksmart said easily, 'I thought what the hell, I deserve a few days' break in the sun. I'd promised to send Josie an update to my investigations, so I thought, why don't I just flip down to the Bahamas and tell her the latest developments in person?' He smiled wolfishly at Harker.

'Why not indeed?' Harker said.

'And what *are* the latest developments?' Josephine demanded.

Looksmart took a swig of beer, waved his claw again and smiled at Harker. 'I believe I told you that we have now convinced the DA that the Long Island massacre was definitely committed by the CCB?'

Josephine was hanging on his words. Harker nodded curtly, his ears ringing. Josephine demanded: 'What's the evidence that proves that?'

'Afraid I can't get too detailed but, yeah, we've got proof.' He smiled briefly at Harker. 'And the DA is not an easy man to convince.'

'And?' said Josephine.

'And,' Looksmart said, 'the police have been looking for somebody in the CCB who can testify in exchange for immunity from prosecution.' He looked at Harker significantly. 'And they think they have found such a witness.'

Harker's heart lurched. 'Really?' Josephine said. 'Who?'

Looksmart smiled. 'Afraid I'm not allowed to say. Except that the CIA is proving very helpful.'

Harker felt sick. *Who in the fucking CIA was talking to the DA?*

306

'In what way are the CIA being helpful?' Josephine asked.

'Not allowed to say, but they have strong contacts with the South African army. People who can be tapped for information.' He turned to Harker: 'And of course they have a vast network of agents who are helping us trace Ferdi Spicer.'

'Who's Ferdi Spicer?' Josephine asked Harker.

Harker cleared his throat. 'A guy who was in the Rhodesian army with me. And later in the South African army. American, ex-US marine. When the Angolan war ended he came back here and set up a brothel in Manhattan.'

'A brothel?' Josephine repeated. 'How exotic. You've never mentioned him before.'

Harker tried to smile. 'Haven't seen him for a long time.'

Josephine said with a twinkle in her eye, 'I hope he gave you a discount, darling. But what's he got to do with this Long Island massacre?'

'Looksmart thinks he was a member of the CCB so he went to Ferdi's brothel to talk to him. Now Ferdi's disappeared.'

'I *know* he worked for the South Africans,' Looksmart said, 'because he regularly paid a certain black diplomat in the United Nations to give him information about the Cubans and the ANC. And as soon as I tried to speak to Ferdi, he disappeared. And his girlfriend was promptly murdered.'

Josephine was astonished. *'Murdered!'*

'Strangled. In her apartment – *their* apartment – which was at the back of the brothel.'

'Good God . . .' Josephine turned to Harker. 'Did you know her, Jack?'

'Only met her a couple of times, through Ferdi.'

'But,' Josephine demanded, 'why haven't you ever mentioned this to me? This is riveting stuff. And you *knew* her. But why was she murdered?'

'Because,' Looksmart said, 'Ferdi Spicer had probably told

307

her who was involved in the Long Island massacre. Or she could have been murdered by one of his former comrades in the CCB to stop her talking to the DA. Or to me.'

'If,' Harker said grimly, 'Ferdi knew anything. I doubt Ferdi was in the CCB. He was just a solid, dumb marine.'

'Well,' Looksmart said with ill-concealed smugness, 'the DA disagrees with you.' He gave a small wave of his claw. 'What did the police say when they interviewed you, Jack?'

Josephine turned to Harker, astonished. 'The police came to *you*?'

Harker concealed his fury. How did Looksmart know this detail?

'No policeman came to see me – I was telephoned by a certain Detective Morgan. Evidently Ferdi had mentioned it around the brothel that we had been in the wars together; when Stella was murdered and Ferdi did a disappearing trick the police followed every possible lead. I told them the little I knew.'

Josephine was staring at him. And Harker hated Looksmart. 'But you told me nothing of this,' Josephine protested.

Harker barely controlled his anger. 'What's there to tell? I told them I knew Ferdi in the old days. The police didn't even want to take a statement from me.'

'But . . . I'm amazed you didn't mention any of this.' She turned to Looksmart. 'So what other exciting developments have you come down to the Bahamas to tell me?'

Harker got up. He could not bear to sit still and let this Looksmart bastard taunt him with his veiled threats. 'Another drink, anybody?'

Looksmart said, 'Not for me, I must go, I've got some urgent phone calls to make. But to put the latest developments in South Africa in a nutshell, you've heard of the recent discovery of CRITT, haven't you?'

'No,' Josephine said.

Looksmart stood up to leave. He put his dark glasses on again, his Panama hat tilted just so. 'The world will be hearing a lot more about CRITT in the next few months.

Anyway, the Truth Commission has just learned that CRITT was a bunch of police and army hit-squad people who met regularly to decide who had to be assassinated next.' He smiled. 'CRITT reported directly to the State President and his State Security Council. So all the top brass knew and approved of all these murders.' He smiled again. 'Well, you can imagine the reaction in South Africa. Panic reigns, while ex-president P.W. Botha is hotly denying he has anything to be in the slightest ashamed of. And F.W. de Klerk is strenuously maintaining he knew nothing. But you can be sure that the tempo of applications for amnesty is going to hot up now. The flood is about to start as the villains realize that the Truth Commission is their only escape from Nuremberg-style trials.' He turned to Josephine. 'Well, I must away.'

Josephine protested: 'But this is getting so interesting. Will you drop around tomorrow?'

'Thank you, I will.'

Harker said he would walk up the jetty with Looksmart. When they were out of sight of the boat Harker stopped, turned to the man and said quietly, 'You will not drop by the boat tomorrow, Looksmart.' He glared. 'You obviously suspect me of knowing something about this massacre. I do not, repeat *not*. I deeply resent your innuendoes. And if you come near my boat or my wife or me again I will knock your fucking head off.' He grimaced a smile. 'Is any part of that unclear, Looksmart?'

Looksmart Kumalo gave a broad white grin. 'All perfectly clear, Major. But I must say I'd like you to know where I'm staying, in case you change your mind and want to see me. It's a little private lodging house called Ma Jenkins's.'

'I won't change my mind!' Harker turned and strode back down the jetty to the yacht. He was trembling.

By God, he was getting out of this place fast . . .

As he clambered aboard, Josephine called from below, 'Wasn't that fascinating?'

* * *

That evening Harker went for a walk, telephoned Redfern on his cellphone and told the lawyer about Looksmart's visit.

Redfern said: 'Yeah, the man clearly suspects you, but don't panic – unless he finds Ferdi and forces him to give evidence against you – or persuades Clements to do so, or Dupont himself, all of which are highly, *highly* unlikely. Everything that Looksmart Kumalo has said is only conjecture and hearsay. He's just trying to intimidate you. But unless you confess, I assure you the DA knows that he hasn't got a chance of even getting you into court, let alone securing a conviction.'

'Damn right he's intimidating me,' Harker said. 'And I'm terrified he'll poison Josephine's mind. Make her smell a rat.'

'Are you still adamant about not testifying for the prosecution?'

'Christ, yes. Apart from losing all military honour I'd lose Josephine.'

'Then,' Redfern said, 'you should get away from there as soon as possible. When could you put to sea?'

'Not for several weeks – I've still got to strip down the engine. But I'll move the yacht off the jetty and anchor out in the channel so that Looksmart can't stroll aboard so easily.'

That month the Truth Commission issued subpoenas against seven police generals to answer allegations of murder and torture and mayhem – and against former President P.W. Botha, to answer for his role in apartheid. The Big Crocodile had loudly vowed never to apply for amnesty. 'I do not perform in circuses,' he said. 'What I did I did for God, for my country, for all my people . . .' Now the Big Crocodile was going to be forced to answer allegations that he and his securocrats sanctioned countless specifiable crimes against humanity: most of the world were rubbing their hands in glee.

'Oh boy, oh boy, oh boy . . .' Josephine exulted.

Then it was announced that the various political parties would have to appear before the Truth Commission to answer for their role in the era of apartheid: the churches would also be called upon to explain how they tolerated such debasement, and Big Business would be required to explain their acquiescence. The Zulus' Inkatha Freedom Party loudly retorted that they would prove that the ANC murdered countless Zulus in their quest for power. The AWB, the Afrikaner Resistance Movement, had long proclaimed that it 'refused to be absorbed into the most bizarre democracy in the world, where the unemployed ruled the productive, the ineducable the educated, where squatters govern the suburbs'. Then the National Party, which created apartheid and ruled the country for forty awful years, appeared before the Truth Commission.

F.W. de Klerk, former president, accepted responsibility for some of his party's repressive measures and admitted that these may have created circumstances conducive to human rights abuses. But 'no president can know everything that takes place under his management . . .' He sanctioned 'unconventional strategies' but never authorized murder, torture, rape, assault. Such abuses were the work of 'bad apples' in the security forces. However, he said: 'I want to reiterate my deepest sympathy to those who suffered.' He was given a hard time in cross-examination.

'Bull*shit*!' Josephine cried when she read the faxed report sent by the Anti-Apartheid League. 'Do you believe he didn't know? Calling serial mass murder "unacceptable things"! And how many bad apples does he expect the world to swallow? Everybody from the Big Crocodile down! Is F.W. de Klerk such a stupid bad apple himself that he expects us to swallow his claim that he *"didn't know"*? The man is adding insult to injury by abusing our collective intelligence! Boy, am I going to tear him to shreds in my book!'

That fucking book must never see the light of day . . . 'Give

311

some credit where it's due,' Harker said. 'He's the guy who disbanded apartheid, remember, let Nelson out of jail.'

'*Bi-i-g fucking deal!* He finally acknowledged the writing on the wall the world had been seeing for forty years!'

The ANC's submission to the Truth Commission was all about the tyrant's terror, not its own: During the previous decade, Vice President Mbeki told the Commission, the apartheid forces had invaded three countries, hitting the three capitals, had tried to assassinate two black prime ministers, backed rebels that brought chaos to Angola and Mozambique, disrupted oil supplies to six countries, sabotaged the railway lines to seven. As a result over one million people had been displaced and more than one hundred thousand had died, mostly from famine; the total damage exceeded sixty-two billion dollars. The ANC, he claimed, had fought a 'just war'. The horrific 'necklace', killing someone with a burning tyre around the neck, was never official ANC policy.

'But the ANC leadership never *denounced* necklacing!' Harker said. 'They never issued instructions that its enemies were *not* to be put to death like that! Over five hundred and forty blacks were executed by necklacing! Make that clear in your goddam book!'

'I thought,' Josephine grinned, 'that you didn't want me to write this goddam book?'

'I goddam don't – but if you do I want to see the *truth*, not fiction as sanctified by the goddam ANC!'

The ANC had loudly proclaimed, like P.W. Botha, Winnie Mandela et al, that none of their members would be applying for amnesty. 'Should Churchill,' the ANC's legal adviser said, 'have asked for amnesty at the end of World War II? Should Roosevelt? Should Moses?'

'Quite right!' Josephine said emphatically. 'How can you equate the horrific violence of the apartheid tyrant with the struggle by the oppressed to resist apartheid?'

'Resist?' Harker echoed. 'Is the horrific necklacing of over five hundred blacks on suspicion of not supporting the ANC "resisting" apartheid? Is the torture of their own soldiers in the Angolan training camps "resisting" – starving them, torturing them with red ants and stinging nettles and floggings and other sophisticated agonies. And all the executions by firing-squad without trial on mere suspicion? And the widespread raping of their own female recruits – is rape galore "resisting"? And what about all the violence inflicted on their own people for breaking boycotts – forcing women and old men to eat soap and drink detergent while beating them senseless, is that "resisting"? And what about the reign of terror by the ANC's so-called Self Defence Units, the bands of thugs armed with AK47s and spears and axes terrorizing and murdering anybody they suspect of not being an ANC supporter? Call that "resisting"?' Harker jabbed a finger. 'Make goddam sure you put all *that* stuff about your Holier-than-Thou ANC in your book. That's what we want the ANC leadership to confess to, tell us who was responsible for allowing such terrible things to happen, and we need to be sure that such people never hold public office in the new South Africa. And the victims have a right to be compensated – that is the purpose of the law creating the Truth Commission. But no, the ANC considers itself above the law – even though it was the ANC itself which insisted on creating the Truth Commission! This is typical African political thinking!'

But the ANC did not get away with it – Archbishop Desmond Tutu threatened to resign from the Truth Commission if the ANC persisted in its lopsided view of the law and 'granted itself amnesty', until President Nelson Mandela had to tell his party to change their blundering tune. Then the ANC put the word out that any member wishing to claim amnesty had to have his statement checked by the party.

'In case they tell too *much* truth?' Harker snorted. 'The ANC only wants the Truth Commission to hear the truth the ANC approves of – history as sanctified by them!'

The Truth Commission declared itself astounded. And

when the time came for cross-examination the ANC delegation was taken offguard by the commissioners' hard-nosed
questions about the murder of black policemen, necklacing,
slogans inciting people to kill, the violence of the ANC's Self
Defence Units, the torture and executions in ANC military
camps, to the point where Deputy President Mbeki finally
admitted that the ANC's violations of human rights were
wrong; yes it was 'a mistake' to issue firearms to the
rabble of the Self Defence Units; yes, their military tribunals had 'serious flaws'; yes, confessions were extracted
under torture; yes, cadres were tried and executed without
legal representation. They agreed that they should have
condemned the dreadful necklace murders, and that the
slogan 'Kill the Boers, Kill the Farmer' was a vicious, indis-
criminate incitement to murder which could not qualify as
a 'political statement' and therefore qualify for amnesty –
and that the ANC's death-squad activities against Inkatha
members were wrong.

'At fucking last!' Harker said. 'But it's just an exercise
in political damage control after stupidly proclaiming itself
above the law. And they never told us who did what, who
authorized which atrocity. For example, who authorized
the bombing of those three Wimpy Bars? And Magoo's
Bar – where those three young women died. The ANC
delegation is not telling. So no amnesty can be claimed,
therefore the victims of those bombs can sue the ANC to
Kingdom Come, for millions – I wonder if the ANC has
thought about *that* little problem?'

'You're very uptight about this Truth Commission, aren't
you, darling?' Josephine said. 'You're very antagonistic
toward the ANC. Why?'

'The ANC is in unabashed alliance with the South African
Communist Party. The communists intend to ride to power
on the coat-tails of the ANC. And communism has fucked
up the world. For seventy terrible years communism has
murdered millions and millions of people, deprived millions
and millions of their freedom, thrown them into dreadful

314

prisons, reduced them to poverty – communism has utterly ruined the whole of Africa, most of Asia and all of Eastern Europe. And yet the ANC *still* makes bedfellows with the murderous bastards! How can anyone not be antagonistic to double-speak like that?' He jabbed a finger. 'Make sure you put that in your book!'

Then came 'The Winnie Mandela Hearing' or, as it was officially known, 'A Human Rights Violation Hearing into the Activities of the Mandela United Football Club'. Like the Big Crocodile, P.W. Botha, Winnie had refused to apply for amnesty for anything so she had been subpoenaed by the Truth Commission to answer allegations made against her. Two hundred journalists from sixteen countries were crammed into the seedy hall set aside for her hearing, twenty foreign television crews, stringers for over a hundred news agencies, all come to see the burning of a martyr on one hand, or a Lady Macbeth on the other. Winnie was the queen of all those millions of black South Africans for whom the ANC had failed miserably to deliver; to Afro-Americans she was the incarnation of solidarity with the mother-continent and the mystique of being black. She was a siren, Caesar's divorced wife, a dangerous warlord, seething with conspiracy, a ruthless menace to South Africa's new democracy. As Winnie Mandela arrived at the hearing, a daunting, imperious figure surrounded by her bodyguards carrying her cooler-box of refreshments, a bevy of women chanted:

'Winnie had a mandate from us to kill!'

Winnie Mandela was linked to numerous human rights abuses by witnesses but the Truth Commission concentrated on only three murders. For two weeks the world saw her former 'football team' members, bosom friends and admirers testify to her crimes, watched Winnie pooh-pooh, scorn and deride her accusers, denouncing their evidence as 'ludicrous' and 'ridiculous'. But the evidence was overwhelming that she ordered her so-called football team, which terrorized Soweto in her name, to kidnap little

Stompie Seipei from the Methodist manse where he had fled to escape her abuses, overwhelming that she had him fatally beaten, that he was stabbed twice before she ordered his throat cut and his body dumped in the veldt. The evidence was irresistible that the next day she had her football team shoot dead Dr Asvat, her personal physician, because he was a witness to Stompei's brutalized condition; the evidence was incontrovertible that she personally, with her henchmen, kidnapped young Lolo Sono, another youthful follower who had fallen from favour, who was never seen again. The former friends, bodyguards and football team members who testified against her admitted they were still in thrall to her, still adored her although they feared her. The proof of her turpitude was overwhelming yet at the end Archbishop Tutu addressed the unrepentant woman pleadingly.

'I acknowledge Winnie Mandela's role in the history of our struggle. And yet something went horribly, badly wrong . . . Many, *many* love you. Many, *many* say you should be First Lady of the country. I speak to you as someone who loves you deeply . . . I want you to stand up and say: "There are things that went wrong . . ." If you were able to bring yourself to say "I am sorry, I am sorry for my part in what went wrong . . ." I beg you. I beg you please . . . You are a great person . . . your greatness would be enhanced if you were to say: "I'm sorry, things went wrong, forgive me".'

The good archbishop's plea to one of the toughest women in the world hung in the air; then Winnie Mandela said, with *élan*: 'It is true: things went horribly wrong and we were aware that there were factors that led to that. For that I am deeply sorry.'

'Bullshit!' Harker cried. 'She's not sorry, she did it for the television cameras! Archbishop Tutu has just thrown a bucket of whitewash over her which purportedly absolves her sufficiently to enable her to pursue her terrifying ambition of becoming president one day – and when that happens God help South Africa!'

Josephine frowned. 'Jack,' she said, 'I don't understand. What's worrying you so much about this Truth Commission?'

There was plenty to worry about. For one thing, the army was now run by the ANC. If all the old files had not been destroyed, how long would it be before somebody discovered a file pertaining to Major Jack Harker and his Harvest House operation? And collective confessions had been ruled out so that meant the Chairman, General Tanner, would have to front up himself if he wanted amnesty – how much would he reveal under cross-examination? And P.W. Botha himself, the emperor of all securocrats: he had dodged the Truth Commission's first subpoena on the grounds of ill health, the second on a technicality, the third he had ignored; now he had been summonsed to appear in court on a criminal charge for this defiance. Sooner or later he was going to be forced to talk to escape going to jail and then anything could happen.

'Yes, of course it's worrying,' Luke Mahoney said on the telephone. 'And the sooner you get to sea the better. When can you do that?'

'In a couple of days. I've just finished rebuilding the engine.'

'Well, get going. And you still haven't seen anything of your former colleagues?'

But then the very next evening, when Harker was having his usual jog along the waterfront, a stranger fell in beside him and said in an American accent, 'Just keep going, Major.'

Harker stopped, his fists bunched. 'Who the hell are you?'

'I said keep going.'

'And I said who the hell are you?'

317

'I am a friend of your friends in the former CCB. They would like to have a chat with you.'

Harker stared. 'I don't know what you're talking about. And now, if you'll excuse me.' He turned and began to cross the road. A car suddenly appeared from behind him and swung across to block him. Harker whirled around, fists clenched; he began to run and the American hit him from behind. Harker saw stars as he sprawled on to the asphalt. Then all he knew was the bastard's foot thudding into his ribs, and he grabbed it, and slung him. The man went reeling across the sidewalk. He crashed on to the sea parapet. Harker scrambled up furiously, ran at him and kicked. He heard the man's arm snap, then he saw Derek Clements getting out of the car. Harker bounded at him, grabbed him by the shirt, rolled back on to his spine, got his foot in his guts and kicked. Clements went flying through the air. Harker jumped up frantically. Clements was on his knees, pulling a knife from his pocket. Harker leapt at him, seized his wrist and bent it backwards. The knife clattered into the gutter. Harker snatched it up and kneed Clements savagely on the side of the head. Clements went down and Harker dropped his knee into his back, one hand twisting Clements' hair, the other pressing the knife against his neck.

'What the fuck are you doing?' Harker hissed. The American was picking himself up off the pavement, his broken arm distorted. 'Tell him to cool it or your knife goes through your jugular.'

Derek Clements rasped: 'Cool it, Mac.'

'Tell him to fuck off,' Harker hissed.

'Fuck off, Mac.'

The American turned and limped away, nursing his injury. Harker held the knife at Clements' throat and frisked him for tape-recorders. He found one strapped to his hip, he wrenched it off, grabbed Clements' hair again and twisted it. He rammed the man's face hard against the asphalt. 'So what's your problem, asshole? What the hell are you doing here?'

'The Director sent me,' Clements gasped.

'Dupont is nobody's director any more! So what does he want?'

Clements swallowed. 'Some cops from Platplaas are singing like canaries to the Truth Commission.'

'So?'

'They're admitting they were hit-men – and members of CRITT. That they often collaborated with Military Intelligence and the CCB to make their hits.'

'So, what does Dupont want me to do, publish a sonnet about it?'

'He wants to be sure you don't confess to the Truth Commission about the Long Island operation.'

'So you were sent here to kill me!'

'I was sent to warn you.'

'Bull*shit* – you pulled out this knife! So why shouldn't I kill you?' He jabbed the knife harder against Clements' throat and twisted his hair savagely.

Clements jerked, trying to look up at Harker out of the corner of his eye. 'Because I'm just the messenger. And it's not your style to kill an old comrade in cold blood.'

'I'm in fucking hot blood, comrade!' Harker jerked the knife again and Clements flinched.

'And because you know you'll never get away with it, sir. You're on an island. And you don't want another murder on your hands.'

'I'll be killing you in self-defence!'

Clements rasped: 'That means explaining to the police. You don't want to go anywhere near any policemen.'

'And nor do you, comrade!'

'Exactly, sir. We're really looking for Ferdi Spicer.'

'And I look like Ferdi?'

'I mean we believe he may be hiding somewhere in the Bahamas.'

'What makes you think that?'

'Because Looksmart Kumalo's here. We got a tip-off that he arrived here last month. Have you seen him?'

'So when did you get here?'

'This afternoon.'

'No, I haven't seen Looksmart Kumalo and I don't fucking want to! Why do you think I might have seen the bastard?'

'Because we don't believe he's here for his health. He's either looking for Ferdi or for you. And Josephine.'

'Why?'

'Because he wants to offer you – or one of you – a deal, to testify for him in his civil action against us for damages. And for the DA when he prosecutes us.'

Harker jabbed the knife harder against Clements' neck. 'So Dupont sent you to kill me to make sure I don't co-operate, huh?'

Clements flinched. 'No, sir, to warn you.'

'That I'm dead meat if I either apply to the Truth Commission for amnesty or make a deal with Looksmart and the DA! And what about Josephine?'

Clements said, 'Head office is only worried that she'll find out about us from you and Looksmart and publish damaging material, sir.'

'Jesus . . .' Harker jabbed the knife harder. 'I don't believe you. Not even Dupont is so stupid as to think that I would publish a book that lands me in jail for life! Dupont sent you here to kill me, didn't he?'

'No, sir, only to intimidate you.'

'And to kill Josephine!'

'*No*, sir.' Clements looked at Harker out of the corner of his eye. He rasped: 'You need me. To find Looksmart Kumalo and Ferdi, and get rid of both of them. For your sake and ours. We're really on the same side, sir. It's in all our interests that Looksmart and Ferdi keep their big mouths shut.' He paused, gasping, then went on: 'So just tell us where Looksmart's staying, and we'll take care of the rest. He'll never testify against any of us, ever.'

320

Harker glared at the man. And oh God, wouldn't it be wonderful if Looksmart disappeared?

Clements continued: 'We know that you know where he is, sir, which hotel he's staying at, because he came to see you aboard your yacht recently. We've made a few enquiries, sir – a black man was seen drinking aboard your boat.'

'The Bahamas is full of black men!'

'But very few of them have had their right forearm amputated. All you've got to do is tell us where he's staying, sir. And you'll never have to worry about him again. No legal action for damages, no prosecution, no Truth Commission, no nothing. The same applies to Ferdi.' He paused, then added: 'We'll find Looksmart, sir, with or without your cooperation, it'll just take a bit longer without.'

Harker crouched over Clements, the knife at his neck; he hesitated, then made a decision. 'Get this straight: I haven't seen or spoken to anybody called Looksmart Kumalo. Nor Ferdi Spicer. Stay out of my life, and I'll stay out of yours. And tell Felix fucking Dupont this, verbatim: "I have no earthly reason to go to this so-called Truth Commission because I have never, in my entire military career, done anything criminal to warrant doing so".' He glared. '*Reassure* him. And yourself. Got that?'

Clements flinched at the knife. 'Yes, sir.'

'Stay there.' Harker slowly stood up. He put his foot on Clements' neck, reached down, picked up the tape-recorder and stuffed it in his pocket. 'Where're your car keys?'

'In the ignition.'

'Get up,' Harker rasped.

Clements clambered to his feet.

Harker pressed the knife in his ribs. 'Get up on the parapet.'

Clements climbed up on to the low sea wall.

'Have a nice swim,' Harker said, and shoved him. Clements fell six feet into the sea.

Harker turned, ran to the car and scrambled in. He twisted the ignition, let out the clutch and roared off, the wheels spinning.

37

Harker abandoned the car in a side road. He ran into the marina complex, down the jetty, clambered into his dinghy, wrenched the outboard motor to life and swept out of the marina's entrance into the channel.

He looked back. Nobody seemed to be chasing him. He opened the throttle and sped towards his yacht.

Lights were shining in the porthole of the master-cabin's bathroom. He churned up to the stern and grabbed the swimming platform. He cut the engine and grabbed the davit's cables. He hooked them on to the dinghy's cradle-wires, scrambled up the swimming ladder on to the transom, hit the button of the davit winch. There was a whirring noise, and the dinghy began to lift out of the water.

'Jack?' Josephine called from below. 'That you?'

'Yes.' He winched the dinghy up to the davits, lashed it into position. He hurried into the wheelhouse. He pressed the glow-button, counted twenty seconds, twisted the ignition. Under his feet the engine cranked into life.

'Jack,' Josie called from the bathroom, 'what're you doing?'

Harker called down the hatch: 'The harbour master has asked us to move a couple of kilometres downchannel to make way for a big incoming ship. I can handle it by myself, take your time.'

He eased the gear lever and the boat began to churn forward. He stabbed the windlass button and the anchor chain began to come clanking aboard. He felt the anchor break out of the sand. Then up it came. As it clanked into its cradle on the bows he opened the throttle wide and swung the wheel. The yacht went into a turn, then began moving south into the dark, shallow Bahamian sea. He put the helm to automatic pilot, then dashed below to their cabin. Josephine was still in the bathroom. He pulled open his bedside drawer, grabbed his .38 Smith & Wesson pistol and rammed it in his waistband under his shirt. He stuffed Clements' tape-recorder in the drawer, alongside his .25 Browning pistol. He hurried back to the wheelhouse.

The lights of Nassau were several miles astern when Josephine came up into the wheelhouse. She was carrying a glass of gin and tonic. She paused in the hatchway, looked around and said, 'Hey, where are we? This is dangerous, these shallow waters at night.'

Harker said grimly: 'It's time to get out of the Bahamas, I've just been mugged.'

Josephine stared. '*Mugged?* Who by?'

Harker snorted. 'Actually they tried to murder me. Came at me with a knife. Fortunately I got the knife away.'

Josephine was staring. 'Good God . . . Who were these guys?'

'Pirates. They were going to steal this boat after they'd got rid of you and me.'

Josephine slapped her brow. 'How do you know they wanted the boat?'

'They told me!'

'But we must report this to the police! Would you recognize them again? How many were there?'

'Two. No, I wouldn't recognize them again. It was dusk.'

'White or black?'

'Black.'

'How old?'

'Who can tell in the dark?'

'Clothing?'

'Jeans and T-shirts. I tell you, I wouldn't recognize them again. And I'm getting you and me out of their clutches. They'll come after me again because they'll be scared I *will* go to the police. And they'll kill you too!'

'Don't be angry with *me*!' Josephine cried. 'It's damn

dangerous to sail over these shallows at night, with coral heads everywhere, there's only seven or eight feet of water over these flats! Why did you tell me you were just moving anchorage?'

'In order to avoid this very argument taking place in the Nassau channel where the bastards could see and board us! And please don't raise your voice at me.'

Josephine waved her hand. 'But I'm horrified at what's happened to you! Look at you, all bruised. And I'm terrified what might happen now in these shallows!'

'These shallows are the least of our worries. The more shallows we put between us and those bastards the better.'

'Not if we run aground! We must report them to the police; they'll hit somebody else if we don't!'

'We are *not* going back to Nassau, we're going into the Gulf Stream and getting the hell out of here.'

'Then for God's sake let's anchor right here for the night and push on in the morning when we can see the coral! We're miles away from Nassau now. Why can't we report to the police by radio?'

'No!'

'I said by *radio* – we don't have to return to Nassau to do that!'

'And I said I'm not going to report anything to the police because then we'll have to go back to identify them and give evidence and God knows what. It could tie us up for months!'

'But . . .' Josephine waved a hand incredulously. 'But it's our civic duty to report dangerous criminals before they kill other people! I don't care if it does tie us up, we can afford to fly back to Nassau from wherever to give evidence!' She scrutinized him closely. 'You're concealing something from me.'

Jesus . . . 'Yes – I haven't mentioned that I'm shit-scared. And the best way to get unscared is to get as far away as fast as possible!'

Josephine took a grim breath. 'It's our moral duty to report those guys to the police. This is *our* boat, remember, not just yours and I am not just your damn crew member! If you won't report it to the police I damn-well will!' She snatched up the handset of the two-way radio: 'Nassau Police, Nassau Police, this is yacht *Rosemary*.'

Harker tried to snatch the handset from her but she jerked backwards. '*Jesus.*' He lunged at the radio and pulled the cable out of the machine.

Josephine glared, holding the handset with the transmission cable dangling. Then she hurled it across the wheelhouse. It smashed against the bulkhead, cracking the transmitter. She turned, clattered furiously down the companionway and strode through the saloon. He heard their cabin door slam.

Harker took a deep breath. He reached for the whisky bottle and poured a big slug into his glass. His hands were shaking.

A minute later he heard the cabin door burst open. Josie crossed the saloon and wrenched open the booze cabinet. He heard the refrigerator door open and close again. Then she strode into her writing cabin. The door slammed.

38

It was shortly before dawn when Harker swung the yacht from the shallow waters of the Bahamas into the deep Gulf Stream just north of the island of Andros, and turned her bows south, directly into the trade winds.

He had been drinking all night and had consumed half a dozen beers and more than half a bottle of whisky. When he had been below for something to eat and to change into warmer clothing he had heard Josephine moving around, but he had not seen her all night. She had closeted herself in her writing cabin. But now, bashing into the trade winds, the boat began to pitch, the spray flying like grapeshot. He heard her cabin door open. She came into the saloon, lurching into bulkheads, then started up the companionway into the wheelhouse. She was tousled, she looked drunk. She was clutching her cellular telephone and Clements' little tape-recorder in one hand; in her other hand was Harker's .25 Browning pistol. Josephine lurched up into the wheelhouse, her face ashen.

'You've lied to me . . . All the years we've been together you've lied to me.' She stared at him furiously, then held up Clements' tape-recorder. 'It's all on here. You were in the CCB. You were part of that dreadful Long Island massacre . . .'

Harker was aghast. He held out a shaky hand. He whispered: 'Give me that pistol and that tape-recorder.'

Josephine took a step backwards, and thrust the recorder behind her back. 'It is vital and conclusive evidence that you –' she pointed the pistol at him dramatically – '*you* committed that atrocity which killed four people and blew Looksmart's hand off.' She shook the recorder at him. 'I'm giving this to the police. And it's doubtless *you* –' her eyes narrowed in contempt – '*you*, you bastard, who committed the burglary of the Anti-Apartheid League's offices all those years ago! While all the time pretending that you were on our side.'

'We *were* on the same side,' Harker said wildly. 'Still are.' He kept his hand out. 'Give me that gun, Josie. And the tape.'

Her eyes slitted. 'Me on the same side as the thugs who committed cold-blooded murder of those anti-apartheid activists on Long Island?'

Harker rasped desperately: 'They weren't anti-apartheid *activists*, they were full-blooded terrorists plotting the butchery of innocent women and children. Two Cuban military officers – big bad bastards in the espionage business! And two ANC bastards, *all* communists, all plotting the murder of civilians!'

A salvo of spray hit the wheelhouse. Josephine lurched against the chart-table and sneered, full of hate, 'ANC *officials*. Not *soldiers*!'

'They were MK!' Harker roared. 'And a soldier does not challenge orders he gets from headquarters! He does not say "Please, sir, are you sure these Stalinist murderers with their Gulag Archipelagos and their KGB death chambers and all their Cold War surrogates like Cuba and North Korea and Vietnam – are you absolutely sure that these chaps are really plotting to blow up women and children in downtown Pretoria because I'm a bit squeamish, sir, maybe they're jolly good sorts just getting together for a game of poker in Long Island, sir!"' He glared at her furiously, panting.

Josephine closed her eyes. 'The Long Island massacre . . .' she whispered witheringly, 'God, that was the week we first met.' She looked at him, her eyes suddenly bright with tears. 'You were a wing-ding publisher and I was a young writer with stars in her eyes. That night we made love for the first time. And you had committed the Long

328

Island massacre just the week before . . .' She looked at him, horrified. *'You committed cold-blooded murder the week before you made love to me . . . One week after committing a hideous crime you lay in my arms and made love to me!'*

'Give me that recorder!'

'Oh no, you bastard . . .'

That night was bad, crazy-making. The boat pitching, the sky black as ink, lightning flashing, spray flying, the drink, the anger, the outrage, the fear, the shouting.

'I'm horrified! Mortified. Not only have I discovered my husband is a cold-blooded murderer but he's an *apartheid* hit-man! And I have been deceived into marrying this monster! So you were only "obeying orders"? That's what the Nazi war criminals said!'

'They were legitimate military targets for the South African army!'

'You murdered them in America!'

'Total War is the Law of War, like the allies bombing Dresden in World War Two! Whether I shot those bastards in Angola or Pretoria or Washington makes no moral difference!'

'The Allies were bombing the Nazis whereas the CCB *were* the Nazis! And now I learn that my whole literary career has been built on blood-soaked feet of clay! My fame built on a front-business for apartheid's killing machine! Which I now *own*!' Her horrified tears were brimming. 'You've made a laughing stock of me!' She shook her tearful head: 'Well, I've got some very bad news for you, Major Jack Harker of the CCB! I'm going to *denounce* you to the whole world!'

Harker shouted, 'Those guys who were trying to silence me this evening will silence you if you start shouting your fucking mouth off!'

'I'm going to tell the world the truth and see you in jail for life!'

'A wife cannot testify against her husband! Save your breath – *and* your life!'

329

Josephine snatched up the *Nautical Almanac* and hurled it at him. Harker dodged and the big book shattered the dial of the speedometer. She shrieked: 'You only married me for my money! Well tough luck, Major.' She shook the tape-recorder aloft. 'The evidence is all on here!'

'Give that to me!'

'Like hell!'

Harker bounded at her, grabbed both her wrists. He wrenched them backwards and the tape-recorder and pistol fell out of her hands. They clattered to the deck. Harker snatched up the tape-recorder, blundered out to the rail and hurled it into the black night-sea.

Josephine shrieked with laughter. She had picked up the small pistol and it was pointed at him.

'No luck, Major – I made a copy of that tape and you will never find it!' She shook her cellphone at him maliciously. 'And I am going to telephone the police right now!'

Harker knew she would not shoot and he bounded back into the wheelhouse to take the cellphone from her. She turned and scrambled down the companionway into the saloon. She lunged across it, flung herself into her writing cabin, slammed the door and bolted it. She leant back against it and cried out, 'You're going to jail for the rest of your life, you murderous bastard!'

Harker grabbed the handle and shook it. *'Open up!'*

'Like hell!'

Harker stepped backwards then rammed the door furiously with his shoulder.

Josephine shrieked: *'I'll shoot you through the door, you bastard!'*

PART VI

The trial of Sinclair Jonathan Harker on the charge of murdering his wife, Josephine Valentine Harker.

39

Edward Vance was a very tough, very handsome Assistant District Attorney, and he had ambition. He wanted to be elected the District Attorney, thereafter a congressman, then Governor of the State of Florida, and finally the first black President of the United States of America. Not that he was black in colour. He looked as Caucasian as anybody else in Florida with a deep suntan. His great grandmother had been a mulatto slave, but the rest of his progenitors were lily-white – though there was a questionable Spaniard in there somewhere. That was good enough for Vance. 'I've a foot in all camps,' he was fond of saying, 'white, black, Hispanic.' Edward Vance reckoned that his political future mostly lay with the black and Hispanic vote. (Ed Vance was known in Miami legal circles as Advance.) The liberal, arty vote, and the female vote generally was also very important to him, and Josephine Valentine Harker, the deceased in this murder trial, fell nicely into all categories. Not only was she very liberal and highly arty but she was famous as a novelist, a household name to most of middle-class America. And very beautiful – or she had been until her husband murdered her on the high seas in order to collect the insurance she had taken out on her life, plus the shares in Harvest House which he had sold to her just before they had set out on their expedition around the world. If Josephine were to perish on that hazardous journey, who would collect that life insurance, who would inherit all those shares that the defendant had so recently sold to her? And why had he sold those shares to her at all but to get the money before regaining them costlessly through her will?

That was the substance of the Assistant District Attorney's excited reasoning after receiving the file from investigating officer Commander Orwell Jackson of the US Coast Guard. This Major Harker was clearly as guilty as sin – the only problem was proving it beyond reasonable doubt to twelve assholes plucked from the telephone directory and turned into a jury who might shrink from convicting a man of murder in a case where there was no corpse. Because, as Ed Vance put it a dozen times to his tripod-mounted video camera before the critical eyes of his prosecution team – and to his full-length mirror at home – when rehearsing his opening address in the case of The People of Florida versus Sinclair Jonathan Harker:

'There is a popular misconception, members of the jury, that there cannot be a conviction for the capital crime of murder unless there is a body, a corpse to prove that the victim is in fact dead, to show how he or she came to die. In other words, there is a popular misconception that murder cannot be proved by circumstantial evidence alone. And I am sure that defence counsel is going to try to worry you with this question: *How can we be sure that Josephine Valentine Harker is in fact dead?*' Vance shook his head at his video camera. 'This strategy, this argument, will be nonsense: death *can* be proved beyond reasonable doubt by the surrounding circumstances, by irresistible inference, as I shall do in this case.

'Ah, but proving actual murder – *intentional*, unlawful killing – is more difficult if there are no witnesses. If the defendant says he does not know what happened, how can we gainsay that?' Vance smiled at his camera. 'That scenario appears to be a perfect murder: no corpse, no witnesses.' Then he turned and pointed dramatically at an imaginary Harker. 'And that is what this defendant thought he had achieved, members of the jury – a perfect murder! Ah,' (perfect smile) 'but he is so wrong! Because in this case the fact that he murdered his wife can be proved irresistibly by all the threads of circumstantial evidence surrounding the case – his behaviour before and after her disappearance, the numerous falsehoods inherent in his story! In short, I am going to prove to you that those gossamer threads of circumstantial evidence hang as heavy as a millstone around his neck.'

When Ian Redfern learned that Ed Vance was going to be prosecuting counsel he said to Harker, 'Jack, I'm not the right guy to defend you at the trial. Vance is a rabid leftie, half your jury is likely to be black. Vance is young and good-lookin' whereas I'm not. And you, my friend, are a white man who fought in the apartheid army. What you need for this trial is . . . are you ready for it? A black lawyer. Now, do you have any problem with that?'

Harker's heart sank. 'No, provided he's good.'

They were sitting in a white-painted conference room in Miami Prison. Redfern said: 'It may be *she*. There're two black lawyers here I'd recommend. One is a grand old guy of about seventy, snow-white hair and a courtly manner, but rather slow and doddery in appearance. The other is a smart chick of about thirty-five called Esme. Gorgeous, big eyes, big tits, long, plaited hair, smart as a whip and hard as nails. Always dresses in white and drives a white Cadillac with white upholstery – stops a lot of traffic. But I recommend the old guy for this case.'

Harker didn't want a black lawyer of any description. 'Why?'

'Because half your jury may be white males and they may find Esme a turn-off because she looks like a ball-breaker who knows she's good-looking. Whereas old Charlie Benson, he's the opposite, the sort of guy who is always untidy, looks a benevolent type who would never mislead anybody. He's kind of slow but he's smart, he won't miss any tricks. Everybody will like him, the whites because he looks like the traditional Uncle Tom, and the blacks because he's one of their own who's come up the hard way. Whereas, by comparison, Ed Vance will appear brash and harsh.'

Harker sighed. 'If I must have a black, let's have the old guy. Will you be there beside him?'

'No. You'd not only have to pay my fees, you'd have to pay my travel expenses from New York, my hotel. A local attorney is going to be much cheaper.'

Harker shook his head. 'I want you there.'

'Why? Because I'm white? Look, much as I hate to admit it, both those attorneys are just as good as me.'

'I want you because you know my whole background.'

'Expensive,' Redfern warned. 'How about your cousin, Luke Mahoney? Hey, maybe this is a good idea. Luke would have no right of audience in a Florida court, but he'd be a big asset to old Charlie. And it could be good race relations. Shall I give him a call? He'd surely do it cheap, for family. Maybe for only the price of his air-ticket?'

Harker sighed grimly. 'I've never even met him.'

'I'll sound him out anyway,' Redfern said. He ran his eye over his notes, then cleared his throat. 'Okay, now there's something we must settle once and for all, before I brief Charlie Benson.' He paused significantly. 'Correct me if I have misunderstood anything.' He glanced at his notes again. 'Your case is that you know nothing about Josephine's disappearance. You simply left her on watch, went to bed, woke up and found her missing.' He looked at Harker.

'Correct,' Harker said.

'You searched the sea for two days but saw no trace,' Redfern continued. 'But you knew she was wearing a life-jacket because that was standard procedure when on watch alone. And there is one life-jacket missing from the locker. Correct?'

Harker's throat was dry. 'Correct.'

'You had no quarrels with her, everything was normal when you went to bed?'

'Correct.'

'And nothing untoward had happened in Nassau before you left?'

'Correct.'

'You've heard stories of pirates but nothing of that nature happened to you?'

'Correct.'

Redfern leant forward. 'This won't be mentioned to the jury, of course, nor will I tell Charlie Benson, but the fact is Josephine knew nothing about your CCB past? She knew nothing about the Long Island operation or Operation Heartbeat. Right?'

Harker closed his eyes. 'Right.'

Redfern sighed and Harker said, 'You don't believe me, huh?'

'Jack, it doesn't matter whether I believe you or not, as long as you don't tell me you're lying. I'm your lawyer, not your judge, and you're entitled to your defence, to have any set of facts put forward by your lawyer. If you say something did or did not happen that's good enough for me and Charlie Benson. Just don't change your story once the trial begins – if you want to change anything, or add anything, tell me now. Or tell Charlie, when you meet him.' He added, 'Just don't tell him anything about the CCB, that'll open a can of worms.'

'But do you believe me?'

Redfern smiled. 'Yes, as it happens,' he lied. 'And in my opinion you're putting forward the best defence, in the circumstances.'

'What are my chances?' Harker demanded grimly.

Redfern took an unhappy breath. 'Well, I'm pretty damn sure we're going to win this case. There's no corpse. It is entirely credible that Josie fell overboard in the middle of the night because the boat pitched in that wind. And I'm not worried about that bloodstain on the transom. Okay, it's Group B and we know from Josie's life insurance application that she was also Group B, but so are millions of people. It's a secondhand boat, that stain could have been there for years. The same applies to the bullet hole in the saloon upholstery . . .'

40

The Miami courthouse is a massive stone edifice called the Richard C. Epstein Justice Building. It sits atop expansive stone steps, adjacent to the huge building housing the District Attorney's offices. Surrounding both are acres of parking areas under the sweeping, roaring, elevated road system of central Miami. Inside the portals of the courthouse is a big marbled atrium dominated by airport-style metal detectors and baggage X-ray machines manned by numerous bored policemen; beyond, elevators and escalators and staircases lead upwards to dozens of offices for court staff, police, probation officers, shorthand writers, and several floors of courtrooms and chambers of the judges.

Jack Harker met his cousin for the first time on the day the trial began. Luke Mahoney came down to the holding cells in the bowels of the courthouse. There were many prisoners and they all seemed to be talking at once. Like a zoo, Luke thought.

'Terribly good of you to come,' Harker said through the bars. He was pale, his face gaunt.

The policeman unlocked the cell door and let Harker out: he pointed at a wooden door marked *Conference*. As they walked towards it Harker said self-consciously: 'Is your hotel okay?'

'How're you is more to the point?'

'I've been in tight corners but never like this.' Harker's hands were trembling. 'And the company was more congenial on the battlefield.'

'Is there anything you need? Cigarettes? Chocolate?'

'If there's one thing the Yanks do well it's feed you. And I gave up smoking long ago, unfortunately.' They entered the small conference room. 'Good to meet you at last. I've read about you over the years.'

'I've heard a lot about you too on the family grapevine,' Luke said. 'Have you had any contact with the Harkers of Harker-Mahoney Shipping fame in New Orleans?'

'No. You?'

They sat down at the bare table. 'Not for years. I was engaged to one of the daughters once. Did you ever meet our other cousin in Rhodesia, Joe Mahoney?'

'He was in the Rhodesian army with me during the war.' Harker cleared his throat. 'So what's the situation with the Truth Commission? I've hardly heard anything since I've been in prison.'

'Well, the floodgates are open now, villains are stampeding to confess before the deadline next week, almost seven thousand applications so far. It'll take years to sort out. Now a lot of ANC villains are running scared too, seeking amnesty for necklacings and bombings, and the abuse in their military camps. Even senior people like Vice President Mbeki are filing applications.' Luke glanced at his wristwatch. 'But then big guns like General Magnus Malan were subpoenaed and admitted he had authorized the creation of the CCB for spying purposes but he baldly denied he had ever authorized anything illegal like assassination.'

Harker closed his eyes. *Thank God* . . .

'And Big Business – and the Dutch Reformed Church. Both have had to appear before the Truth Commission and explain why they worked with apartheid. Of course, the Church pointed to the Bible, how the sons of Ham were damned by God to be black, hewers of wood and drawers of water, but they *did* admit they were wrong, and apologized, as Big Business eventually did. The breathtakingly wealthy captains of industry started off protesting their innocence, claiming they were hampered by apartheid because it prevented the blacks from becoming a strong buying force. They produced all kinds of statistics but it sounded very hollow and by the third day they were all admitting that they did benefit, and apologizing.'

Harker snorted tensely, 'And what's happened to P.W. Botha?'

Luke smiled. 'Botha is still defying the Truth Commission. He was summonsed to the magistrate's court in his hometown on the charge of ignoring the Commission's subpoena – and the magistrate was black! The international media were there in force. But the trial was postponed for a month. However, afterwards he gave a press conference in the courtroom. What a circus. I brought you a newspaper cutting.' Luke unfolded the piece of newspaper and read aloud. ' "I stand by my principles. I believe in God, I believe in Jesus, I believe in the Holy Ghost, and I pray that they take control of this country and this world! I told Mandela to his face – yes, I treated him like a gentleman in jail – I told him anarchy and the forces of communism will destroy you! I've said many times that the word apartheid means good neighbourliness." '

Luke smirked. Harker shook his head. ' "Good neighbourliness"? But what's going to happen to him? He must surely be prosecuted, and then the whole CCB story could emerge, including my part in it.'

Luke said: 'Not necessarily. You can bet your boots he will confess to nothing. The guy thinks he's bullet-proof.'

'Yeah,' Harker said, 'but what about when one of his former subordinates gets scared and runs for amnesty?'

'Jack,' Luke said, 'there's less than a week to go before the amnesty deadline, after that nobody's going to confess, are they? So hold fast – you've got enough to worry about here.' He glanced at his wristwatch. 'Now, Charlie Benson and Redfern have sent me summaries of all the evidence. I had dinner last night with Charlie, and clearly he knows nothing about your former connection to the CCB.'

Harker dragged his hands down his face. 'Right.'

'Don't under any circumstances tell him, or break down

in the witness box, or nobody will believe anything you've ever said.'

'And what did you think of Charlie?'

'He's going to be all right.'

'I don't want him to be "all right", I want him to be first-rate! And I don't think he is. He's . . . doddery. He ums and ahs.'

'He knows his law. And he has a big asset – his charm. He's a charming old guy. And he's got a long track record of defending civil-rights activists – so that should help dissipate prejudice against you for being a South African.'

Oh Jesus, being a South African. 'Jurors may be prejudiced because of that, huh?'

Luke shook his head. 'Who knows? Juries can be the dumbest, most prejudiced, most inefficient of creatures. However, that's the luck of the draw. You're in good hands with old Charlie, and I agree with him that you stand a very good chance of getting off because there's no corpse. Even if the jury is suspicious, there's insufficient evidence for a conviction.' He glanced significantly at Harker. 'However, I must say I wish we could blame Josephine's disappearance on something more specific. Like an attack by pirates. That way we could account for that bloodstain on the transom. And the shattered speedometer dial. And the bullet in the saloon upholstery.' He paused expectantly.

Harker dragged his hands down his face again. 'Nothing like that happened.' He added, to change the subject: 'Do you know about the judge? Has Charlie told you anything?'

'Judge Wally Ludman. Charlie says he's a character, a bit of an eccentric, but a good judge. Hates juries. Usually has a few caustic words to say about the system, especially in high-profile cases, plays to the gallery. Looks daunting, but his bark is worse than his bite.' He added: 'However, he's strict on sentencing. Strong sense of duty.' Luke glanced at his watch again. 'Okay, I'll go up to the courtroom to join Charlie, but once jury-selection starts I'll push off and have some breakfast and come back later. I'll be sitting directly behind Charlie. If you have any questions, pass me a note.' Luke stood up, and put out his hand. 'Good luck.'

Harker took his hand. 'Thanks again for coming. Deeply appreciate it. But, please tell me: do you believe me? That I'm innocent?'

Luke smiled. Wearily. 'Jack, it does not matter whether I believe you or not: you are presumed by law to be innocent until the prosecution proves you guilty. So, yes, Jack, as far as I'm concerned you are innocent. But in addition to that, yes, I also *person*ally believe you are innocent.' He dearly wished that last sentence were true.

Harker was still holding his hand. 'Thank you,' he said grimly. 'And Charlie?'

'Charlie feels the same,' Luke said. He wished this to be true too. He dropped his hand on Harker's shoulder. 'See you in court. And don't worry, you're in the best hands with old Charlie.'

He wished he believed that too.

Court 4B was crowded to capacity when Luke Mahoney entered.

Every seat in the gallery was occupied, people were lining the walls, and in the corner beside the jury box there were two television crews. In the well of the court were the tables of the prosecution and the defence. The jury stand was empty at this stage but the two long press tables opposite were crowded. Below the bench sat the clerk of court at his table, a large balding man; next to him, at her own desk, sat the stenographer. She was a young woman in a red dress with spectacles and flowing blonde hair. Beside her sat a large black policewoman in blue uniform, while another even larger law officer, a black man, was bustling around looking busy. At the defence table, his back to the public gallery, sat old Charlie Benson in a rumpled black pinstripe suit with a black bow-tie with big white daisies on it. At the prosecution table sat Edward Vance, Assistant

District Attorney: beside him was a very striking woman in her mid-thirties, a redhead in a dark two-piece suit; she was Sheila Devereaux, an Assistant District Attorney, known around the Miami legal fraternity as probably one of the best criminal-law minds in town and certainly one of the best lays.

In the foyer outside the courtroom several hundred people were awaiting their chance to get in to watch one of America's great trials. The courtroom was abuzz as Luke Mahoney entered. He made his way to the gate behind the bar. Behind the defence table were two chairs. Luke dropped his hand on Charlie's shoulder and sat in one of the chairs. Charlie turned, with a smile. It was a wide, charming smile, white dentures gleaming in his weathered old face.

'Good morning, Luke, what's the crowd like outside?'

'Hundreds. Had to work hard to get through them.'

'Probably the most notorious case this neck of the woods has seen in several decades,' old Charlie said happily. 'Josephine was a popular figure.'

Luke thought, I wish you wouldn't look so pleased about it. 'Are these TV crews all local?'

'Local, national, CNN, the works,' Charlie said cheerfully. 'Worldwide audience, O.J. Simpson level.'

Luke looked around the courtroom. He was not impressed. It totally lacked grandeur. Where were the oak-panelled walls of most British and colonial courtrooms? The bench, where the judge would sit, was not high enough, and his chair was not wooden or carved, but vinyl. The bench itself, the clerk's desk, the witness stand, all appeared to be made of varnished plywood. The wall immediately behind the bench had no coat of arms: the two end-sections had transparent plastic panels of different colours electrically illuminated from behind creating an incongruous art-deco effect. Maybe, Luke thought, the architect hoped to create a sepulchral or cathedral effect. Anyway, it didn't work.

Just then a door opened and the buzz of voices subsided

as Jack Harker entered, escorted by two burly policemen. He was dressed in a grey pinstripe suit and a regimental tie. He walked grimly across the courtroom to the defence table, his face gaunt. Luke heard a woman behind him whisper to her companion, 'Good-lookin' brute, isn't he?'

Harker sat down next to Charlie at the defence table, the television cameras following him all the way. Luke leant forward and patted him on the shoulder. 'Good luck.'

Harker took a trembling breath. 'Thanks.'

Then there was a rap on the door and one of the police orderlies shouted, 'All rise!'

Everybody shuffled to their feet, and His Honour Judge Walter Ludman entered the courtroom. He stalked to his vinyl chair on the plywood bench beneath the art-deco plastic panels. He was a grey-haired, square-faced, bad-tempered-looking little man with hooded eyes. He wore a black judicial gown and a floral bow-tie. He stopped at his chair, glared around his courtroom, picked up his gavel, rapped it and sat down.

'Okay,' Judge Ludman said grimly, 'let's go.'

Luke wondered whether he had heard right.

Everybody sat. The fat clerk remained on his feet and intoned: 'In the circuit court of Florida, His Honour Judge Walter Ludman presiding. The People of the State of Florida versus Sinclair Jonathan Harker charged with the crime of murder in the first degree.'

Judge Ludman glowered: 'Okay, bring the jurors in.'

They were as mixed a bag as ever Luke Mahoney had seen, a couple of dozen people of all shapes, sizes, ages, races and genders. Only one, a middle-aged bespectacled gentleman, wore a suit; all the other men wore open-neck shirts or T-shirts, jeans, running shoes or loafers. Several badly needed a shave, two had lavish pony-tails, one was a Rastafarian with long black tresses. The women were reasonably dressed except for one with no brassière and a T-shirt proclaiming *Life's a Beach*. In Hong Kong and Rhodesia, where Luke was accustomed to practising law, the judge would have sent them out with a flea in the ear 'to dress'. Judge Ludman looked at them with a jaundiced eye, but then his eye was always jaundiced.

'Good mornin',' he growled.

Luke stared, as did the jurors, who shuffled more uncertainly and murmured a ragged something.

The judge continued, 'But twelve of you *ain't* going to have a good day for some time, folks. Because twelve of you unfortunates are finally going to be selected for the jury, and you can betcha it's going to give you a sick headache. However, that's your problem – me, I'm just the referee in this black gown who's going to see fair play. These gennelmen,' he waved his hand dismissively at the prosecution and defence tables, 'are the protagonists who're going to tire you out; me, I'm here to answer any legal questions you have. You, and only you – not me, not those lawyers sitting over there – *you* are the judges and whatever *you* decide is entirely your business.' He gave a toothy grimace, meant to pass as a smile, then continued: 'You are not as good as your dentist when it comes to teeth, as your doctor when it comes to medicine, as your optometrist when it comes to your eyesight, as your motor mechanic when it comes to your car, as your plumber when it comes to your lavatory, and you probably wouldn't know if your backsides were on fire when it comes to filling in a form as simple as your income-tax return – but for some extraordinary reason which has escaped me for over forty years of courtroom experience you are deemed as good as me when it comes to deciding matters of life and death.' Judge Ludman paused, looking at his jury unpleasantly. 'And to make confusion even more confounded, I, a full-blown judge, am not allowed to address you at the end of this trial, to sum up and thereby try to help justice to be done by you. Counsel –' he waved a disparaging hand at the prosecution and defence tables – 'will stuff your heads with their histrionic view of the facts but not I. You will retire to that uncomfortable little jury room, to decide life or death, without the benefit of my wisdom.' His finger shot up. 'Elsewhere, where British law prevails, the judge gives a summing up to the jury after the counsel, thus giving a more sober interpretation than their inflated oratory.' He looked at the counsel malevolently. 'But not in America. For some reason, I, the wisest person in this courtroom, am not allowed to give you any advice about the case beyond an explanation of the law involved.' He glared at them. 'Can you imagine a judicial system more wacky than that?'

The jurors looked at him, wide-eyed. Some, the smarter ones, shook their heads with nervous politeness. Judge Ludman frowned at them all, then continued: 'Well, that's what we're stuck with, ladies and gentlemen, so let's get on with it. Now we're going to select a jury out of you hapless folk from the telephone directory with no greater qualification than you ain't got a criminal conviction to your discredit. But before we embark on that let's put you wise about who's who in this Floridian court of ours.' He pointed at the back of the stenographer's head: 'That's Wendy Long, our shorthand-writer. Every word that's uttered in this courtroom, wise or stupid, often stupid, she writes down on that little machine of hers.'

Wendy raised a hand to the jury. 'Hi,' she smiled.

Judge Ludman continued: 'The big fella next to her is Mervin Phipps, who handles all the files and such.'

Mr Phipps nodded importantly at the jury. 'Mornin'.'

'And that big guy in uniform over there is Earl.'

Earl was busy handing a file to the prosecutors' table and waved over his shoulder. 'Hi,' he called.

'Earl is like an extension of myself, any problems you have tell Earl and he'll tell me if necessary.' Judge Ludman turned his glower on to the counsels' tables. 'Introduce yourselves, please,' he growled.

Ed Vance stood up and faced the television cameras. This was worth millions of dollars in free publicity come election time. He was a picture of groomed elegance in his immaculate suit, a handsome face to remember. He gave his perfect smile.

'My name is Edward Vance, I am a Senior Assistant District Attorney, and I am the prosecutor in this case. This good lady,' he indicated to his left, 'is Miss Sheila Devereaux, Assistant District Attorney. The gentleman next to her is Commander Orwell Jackson of the United States Coast Guard, an investigating officer in this case. Next to him is Captain Vincent Orlando of the police, also an investigating officer.'

Vance flashed the cameras a brilliant smile and sat elegantly.

The cameras turned to the defence table. Old Charlie stood up. His black suit was rumpled and his bow-tie awry, his shirt and beaming false-teeth smile very white against his genial black face. He gave a little courtly bow.

'Good morning, ladies and gentlemen, lovely morning for such sombre business as putting a man on trial for life or death in the electric chair –'

Vance got to his feet. 'Objection,' he intoned wearily.

Charlie spread his hands in wounded wonder: 'If my learned friend objects to simple, courteous comments like that, imagine how objectionable he's going to be when we get going!'

'Get on with it, Charlie,' Judge Ludman growled; 'I said introduce yourself, not make your opening speech.'

'As your honour pleases,' Charlie murmured. Luke smiled inwardly: Charlie had won some sympathy at the outset for appearing to be an underdog. 'I am Charlie Benson, a humble attorney-at-law in this vast, cosmopolitan, dog-eat-dog Miami of ours where polyglot America meets Spain, Africa and the marvellous mixture of them all that is called the Caribbean. I represent this fine man,' he dropped a black hand on Harker's shoulder. 'Jack Harker, a foreigner to our shores, a South African gentleman who, as a matter of conscience, fled his country to escape the dreadful apartheid era and came to live in our Land of the Free as a publisher some nine years ago, where he met, published and eventually married his beloved wife, Josephine, the tragic deceased in this case.'

'Objection,' Vance sighed.

'Come on, Charlie!' Judge Ludman snapped.

'As your honour pleases.' Charlie beamed apologetically. 'I apologize for getting carried away.' He turned back to the jury. 'Unlike my learned friend Mr Vance the prosecutor I do not have the resources of the entire State of Florida behind me to enable me to have –' he pointed at the prosecution table – 'expensive investigation officers to help me or to engage the services of another attorney like the beautiful Miss Sheila Devereaux over there, one of the smartest attorneys in Florida, if not in the whole of America –'

'Charlie . . .' Judge Ludman warned.

'We have none of the advantages of the mighty District Attorney's department, in fact my poor client is in such financial circumstances that he has to employ *me* to defend him, one of the humble black lawyers in town.'

'Mr Benson!'

'But,' Charlie's finger shot up brightly, 'we are very, very fortunate to have the help, *without charge*, of the defendant's cousin, a fine lawyer –' he pointed – 'Mr Luke Mahoney QC, Queen's Counsel, formerly in Her Majesty's legal service in Hong Kong. He has now retired but has come all the way here to try to help me see that justice is done. I am deeply grateful for his assistance. Of course, being a British lawyer he cannot speak in our American court but –' Charlie turned to the bench with a hang-dog smile – 'your honour, may Mr Mahoney be permitted to sit beside us at the defence table so that we can confer more easily?'

Ed Vance rose. 'No objection, your honour. And I would like to make it clear that the prosecution is also anxious to see *justice* done. We represent the people, the taxpayers who want their streets safe.' He sat down with a photogenic, righteous glare.

'Very well,' Judge Ludman said. 'Mr Mahoney, is it? He can sit with you.'

Old Charlie beamed at Vance, then at the judge. 'I am deeply indebted. This reduces slightly the great disadvantage under which the defence labours.' He sat down quickly before Judge Ludman could give him an earful. Luke moved to sit at the defence table.

The judge glowered around. 'Okay, so let's get going on jury selection.' He turned to the jury stand. 'Earl tells me you've all filled in your questionnaires, right? So stand up now, one at a time, and read out your answers. Starting with you, sir.'

He pointed at a pimply young white man with a Jewish skullcap, a mop of frizzy black hair. As the young man stood up, his hands in his trousers, Charlie whispered to Mahoney, 'Go'n get some breakfast. But make it look like I've sent you out on some important mission, like to the Law Library. Come back in two hours with a few law books under your arm. There's a good fast-food joint on the ground floor called the Pickle Barrel. Excellent burgers.'

Luke suppressed a smile. 'Any particular books you'd like me to bring from the library?'

'Any damn law books will do; just look *earnest* . . .'

41

The Pickle Barrel provided the best hamburger Luke Mahoney, no stranger to America, had ever eaten. So impressed was he that he went back into the queue and ordered another. (*'Luke,'* the black cashier bellowed when his burger was ready *'rare but not unusual . . .'*) Thereafter he took the elevator up to the library armed with Charlie's card. He emerged ten minutes later with two tomes plucked at random off the shelves and returned to the fourth floor. The foyer was still packed with hundreds of people hoping to get into Court 4B. Luke shoved his way through them.

Ed Vance was closing his opening speech as Luke solemnly sat down next to Charlie. Charlie's eyes were closed as if in sleep. 'Good burger, huh?' he murmured.

'Excellent. How's Vance doing?'

'His usual electioneering stuff.'

Vance was pacing up and down, using his hands, cocking an eyebrow, giving his perfect smiles and dramatic scowls, his resonant voice rising and falling, just like actors do when playing in courtroom dramas. Luke had never believed that American lawyers behaved like film directors imagine they do – a lawyer behaving like that in a British court would soon get a flea in his ear from His Lordship. And when he had watched the dignified behaviour of the lawyers in the O.J. Simpson trial his opinion was confirmed – American film directors had never been inside a real courtroom. But now here was Ed Vance behaving just like a soap opera star, and Judge Ludman, who looked as if he ate barbed wire and lawyers for breakfast, was letting him get away with it. And the jury appeared spellbound.

Luke looked at the twelve jurors. They looked as mediocre a bunch as he had ever seen. There were five whites, three of them female, and seven blacks, three female. Two of the whites looked like grandmothers who would believe anything nice Mr Vance told them, the third looked like a gum-chewing hat-check girl who would do anything to get out of here, including sending a man to the electric chair if that's what everybody wanted. All three of the black females were large scowling matrons. All the men except one looked like construction workers, big tough guys with arms like hams and bellies like barrels, who took no shit from nobody, especially South Africans. The exception was a prim little white man with wire-rim spectacles and a forelock slicked over a balding pate. He was the foreman of the jury: he was the man to win over, the one who might sway the others in the jury room. Indeed it was this little man that Vance had his eyes on as he wound up his theatrical address, forefinger on high.

'. . . and I will prove that those gossamer threads of circumstantial evidence hang –' he pointed at Harker dramatically – 'hang as heavy as a millstone around the defendant's neck!'

He paused, his face flushed with righteousness; then he turned and strode back to his table, a fine figure of a man.

'I call my first witness, your honour, Dennis Mayton.'

Mr Dennis Mayton was a bespectacled, chubby-cheeked man in a dark suit, every inch a respectable witness. He took the oath and sat importantly.

Vance oiled up to the witness box and said, 'Are you a chartered life underwriter for Manufacturers Life Insurance Company in New York?'

'I am, sir.' Mayton touched his spectacles.

'Do you know the defendant?'

'I do. I visited his apartment in New York about six months ago, on the fifth of June to be exact, to write an insurance policy on the life of his wife, Josephine Harker, the deceased in this case.'

'Did you know Josephine before this?'

'Yes. My company had insured her life for a small amount about ten years ago. The defendant telephoned me to secure some more insurance for her. I arranged to have Josephine medically examined, then I went to their apartment to do the necessary paperwork. There I met the defendant for the first time.' Mr Mayton touched the bridge of his glasses.

'How much life insurance was the deceased seeking?'

Mr Mayton opened his file. 'Two hundred and fifty thousand dollars.'

'A quarter of a *million* . . .' Vance echoed. He waved his hand. 'Continue, please.'

'I asked Josephine Harker the usual questions and completed the application form for her.' He produced the document and added, 'The defendant was present throughout, assisting the deceased in answering certain questions.'

'I put that application form in as Exhibit One, your honour.' Vance turned back to Mayton with a very puzzled frown. 'But with what sort of questions did Josephine need the defendant's assistance?'

Mr Mayton said primly: 'Generally he was taking a great interest in the proceedings. As if to ensure there was no hitch in getting the insurance.'

'Objection!' Charlie Benson rose to his feet creakily, theatrical injury on his face. He scowled at the witness, then at the judge. 'Your honour, we're not interested in this man's *impressions* of what was going on in somebody's mind. He's not a thought-reader, is he?'

'Sustained,' Judge Ludman said. He turned to the jury: 'You will disregard the witness's last answer because it is only his opinion.'

Vance was quite happy – the jury would not disregard it. He said to Mr Mayton: 'Now, who did the deceased specify was to be the beneficiary of this life insurance policy?'

'The defendant.'

'And this policy was for two hundred and fifty thousand dollars.' Vance gave the jury a significant look. 'Did you ask the defendant about his own life insurance needs?'

'I did. And he said that he was taking out an additional two hundred thousand dollars' worth of cover with Sun Life, who had insured him before.'

'Did you ever hear from the defendant again?'

Mr Mayton adjusted his spectacles with a dab of his forefinger. 'I did. On the seventh of September this year he telephoned me. He said he was calling from Road Town, Tortola, British Virgin Islands. He sounded agitated. He said, "I have to report the death of my wife".' Mayton paused dramatically. 'I was astonished, your honour, as this was only a few months after the policy had been taken out.'

Vance shook his handsome head and murmured, 'And what did you say?'

'I said, "How did she die, Mr Harker?" And he said, "She was drowned, fell overboard." Before I could ask any more questions he said, "Please fax me all instructions about what I've got to do concerning the policy, care of American Express, Tortola." Then he hung up.'

Vance strolled along the edge of the jury stand and repeated softly, '"Instructions concerning the policy" . . .' He sighed sadly. 'So what did you do?'

'I sent Mr Jefferson, one of our insurance assessors, down to Tortola to investigate. But the next thing I heard was that the defendant had promptly been arrested for murder.'

'Objection,' Charlie Benson said with long-suffering weariness. '"Promptly"? Hearsay. And untrue.' He shook his head sadly at the jury with an apologetic smile.

'Sustained,' the judge said.

Vance smiled unctuously. The answer was disallowed but the jury had got the message that the defendant's guilt had been apparent to the authorities from the outset. He continued: 'Finally, Mr Mayton: has your company paid out the two hundred and fifty thousand dollars assured under the policy?'

Mr Mayton touched his spectacles. 'Certainly not, sir,' he said. 'My company's policy is – and indeed the *law* is – that nobody can be allowed to profit from his crime. Therefore, if a man insures his wife's life and then murders –'

'*Objection*, your honour!' Charlie looked like an old war-horse whose patience had been sorely tried. 'Objection,' he repeated. 'The prosecutor knows perfectly well he can't sneak in so-called evidence like this!'

'Why, your honour?' Vance appealed. 'The witness is only telling us what his company's policy is; he's not telling us what his opinion of this case is. He is simply saying that his company's policy is that no man may legally benefit from his crime – that is a *fact*, not an opinion.'

'That,' Charlie said, 'is exactly the same as saying that the company's board of directors are of the opinion that a crime has been committed, your honour. And my young friend knows it!'

'Objection overruled,' the judge said.

Charlie sat down and whispered to Harker: 'Good. A good hiccup, good point for appeal.'

'No further questions, your honour,' Vance said smugly.

Old Charlie sighed and got to his feet to cross-examine. 'Mr Mayton, good morning to you.'

Mayton looked taken aback. 'Good morning.'

Charlie smiled. 'Mr Mayton, please don't think I'm being unpleasant if I ask you some difficult questions – I'm just doing my solemn duty to the cause of justice. You understand?'

'Of course.'

'Mr Mayton, you don't like the defendant, do you?'

Mayton seemed disconcerted. 'I neither like him nor dislike him, sir,' he said primly. 'I feel entirely neutral.'

'Good. So when you say he sounded agitated when he telephoned you from Tortola, you mean he sounded *upset*, how you'd expect a man to feel when he'd just lost his wife overboard accidentally at sea?'

Mayton shifted fussily on his chair. '*If* he had just lost his wife accidentally.'

'Exactly. So his behaviour was precisely what you'd expect in those circumstances. And similarly his behaviour when Josephine applied for insurance was what you'd expect from a husband being helpful to his wife.'

'Well, he seemed anxious that the application be successful.'

'Of course, they both wanted the application to be successful, that's why they were applying. And you – don't you get a commission on every policy you write?'

'Yes.'

'So you were also anxious that the application be successful? Or is money a matter of supreme indifference to you?'

Mayton smirked. 'No, it's not a matter of indifference.'

'Then you *also* were anxious that the application be successful? And,' Charlie frowned, 'the deceased was a perfectly healthy young woman. So there would be absolutely no difficulty in her getting insurance? So you're imagining it when you say the defendant appeared anxious! Surely you, a neutral, unprejudiced, honest witness will concede that?'

Mayton looked uncomfortable. 'I suppose so.'

'Thank you,' Charlie beamed. 'Now, when a policy holder dies, you *expect* to be informed at the earliest opportunity, don't you? So that if somebody is to blame for the death – as may happen in a car accident, for example – your company has the opportunity to investigate in case you decide to sue that person. Correct?'

'Correct,' Mayton admitted.

'So there was nothing sinister in the defendant telephoning you with the sad news of his wife's death, was there?'

'No, not really,' Mayton agreed.

'"Not really"?' Charlie echoed. 'And you say you're not prejudiced? And because the deceased had died under

355

unusual circumstances, you sent an investigator down to the Caribbean to check it out. But that is your company's standard practice in unusual cases, isn't it?'

'Yes,' Mayton admitted.

'Yes. So there was nothing sinister in Mr Jefferson, your investigator, being sent to investigate. And similarly when the defendant asked you what procedures he had to follow to claim the insurance, there was nothing sinister in that either, it was a perfectly normal question? He was far from home, he was upset – as you've said you would expect – something had to be done about this insurance and he simply wanted to know, as a responsible person, what he had to do about it. Not so?'

'I suppose so,' Mr Mayton said uncomfortably.

'Thank you,' old Charlie beamed. He sat down.

Ed Vance stood up.

'No re-examination, your honour. I call my next witness, Doctor Lawrence Ross.'

Dr Lawrence Ross was a large man with thinning red hair, friendly blue eyes and freckles. Led by Vance, he told the court that he was one of the medical doctors retained by Manufacturers Life Insurance Company in New York, and that on June 6 1996 he medically examined Josephine Valentine Harker and found her in perfect health. He produced his written report as Exhibit Two. He analysed her blood and found that she belonged to Group B.

Charlie Benson rose stiffly to cross-examine. 'Doctor Ross,' he smiled, 'good morning, and thank you for coming all the way from New York to assist us.'

'You're welcome.'

'Doctor,' Charlie said, 'just in case the jury don't know: Group B is a very common blood group, isn't it?'

'Very common.'

'In fact, possibly half the people in this courtroom are Group B, even our friend Mr Vance?'

'Quite possibly.'

'Thank you,' Charlie beamed. He sat down.

Edgar Goldman was a compact, neat, Jewish gentleman in a dark suit. 'Mr Goldman,' Vance said, 'are you an attorney practising law in New York?'

'I am.'

'Did you know the deceased in this case, Josephine Valentine Harker?'

'I did. She was a client of mine. I last saw her on the sixth of June when she came to my office accompanied by her husband, the defendant. The deceased said she and the defendant wanted to make new wills. I did hers first. It left certain small specific bequests to certain friends, the balance of her estate to her new husband, the defendant. I prepared the will there and then and she signed it in the presence of two witnesses, members of my staff.' He opened a file and produced a sheaf of papers. 'This is the will in question.'

Vance said, 'I put that in as Exhibit Three. Then what happened?'

'I then prepared the defendant's will. He left everything to Josephine.' He produced a document from his file. 'This is the defendant's will.'

'I put that in as Exhibit Four, your honour. Now, did you see the defendant and the deceased again?'

'I did, some three weeks later. The defendant explained that he owned fifty-one per cent of the shares in Harvest House, those shares being in a holding company called Neptune, registered in the Cayman Islands, and that Josephine wished to buy most of them, namely forty-nine per cent, leaving him owning only two per cent of Harvest. They had agreed on a price. So for simplicity I drew up two contracts of sale: in the first contract the defendant sold Neptune to Josephine for two million two hundred thousand dollars; in the second, Josephine sold to the defendant two per cent of Harvest House shares.' He held up two documents. 'These are the contracts.'

Vance said, 'I put those in as Exhibits Five and Six, your

honour. So the result was that Josephine now owned forty-nine per cent of Harvest, the defendant two per cent. But who owned the other forty-nine per cent?'

'The defendant explained that the other forty-nine per cent was owned by a trust company called Westminster NV registered in the Netherlands' Antilles, which as you know, is a tax haven jurisdiction that maintains strict secrecy. The shareholders in Westminster are anonymous.'

'But the defendant and Josephine between them, with their respective shareholdings, controlled Harvest.'

'Correct.'

'And now Josephine is dead, the defendant inherits her shares and he will control Harvest all over again.'

'Correct.'

'Thank you.' Vance sat down.

Charlie stood up and turned to the witness. 'Good morning, Mr Goldman. Now, as a lawyer, please explain to the jury what effect marriage has upon a will.'

Goldman turned to the jury. 'When somebody marries, his or her will is automatically revoked. So, to avoid intestacy, people should make a new will immediately after their marriage. If he or she fails to do so they will die intestate.'

'So there was nothing unusual about the deceased and the defendant coming along to you and making new wills in each other's favour as they had just got married, was there?'

'Nothing at all,' Goldman agreed.

'Nothing sinister.'

'Nothing sinister at all.'

'And the same applies to the question of the sale of Harvest shares to Josephine doesn't it, Mr Goldman? There is nothing unusual in a businessman placing some or even all of his assets in his wife's name, is there?'

'No,' Goldman agreed.

'It's quite normal for a man to rearrange his estate after marriage, isn't it?'

'Yes, that's correct.'

'Even,' Charlie said, 'if the wife buys the assets that the husband transfers to her, to enable him to do other important things with the money. Nothing unusual or sinister in that, is there?'

'No,' Goldman agreed.

'And, in fact, isn't it true that Josephine was eager to buy those Harvest shares because the defendant had decided to sell to an outsider and she had persuaded the defendant to sell to her instead because she wanted Harvest to remain in the family, as a family business?'

'I believe that's so.'

'And Harvest is a very sound family business, isn't it?'

'Very sound.'

'So Josephine made a perfectly good investment?'

'Perfectly good.'

'Nothing underhand at all about the defendant's behaviour?'

'Nothing.'

'And similarly,' Charlie said, 'there is nothing unusual or sinister in this offshore trust company called Westminster owning the other forty-nine per cent of Harvest. Nothing sinister in the Westminster shareholders being anonymous. That sort of thing happens all the time, perfectly legally, doesn't it?'

'All the time,' Goldman agreed.

'And if my *young* learned friend –' Charlie pointed at Vance – 'suggests otherwise he is talking balderdash and displaying his abysmal ignorance?'

'Your honour!' Vance appealed, leaping to his feet.

'Thank you.' Charlie smiled at the witness and sat down happily.

Judge Ludman glowered around. 'Time for lunch. Court will adjourn until two p.m. sharp.' He added: 'And I mean *sharp*.'

'All rise,' the court orderly intoned.

Everyone stood as the old man stomped out irritably.

*   *   *

Charlie and Luke took three of the Pickle Barrel's excellent hamburgers down to the holding cells below the courthouse. They ate them with Harker in one of the consultation rooms.

'What do you think?' Harker demanded.

Old Charlie unwrapped his hamburger. 'Harmless stuff so far,' he said with his reassuring smile. 'Formalities. I got rid of the bullshit, that's all. Advance's innuendoes that taking out insurance and making new wills was sinister.' Charlie bit into his hamburger and continued, with his mouth full, 'But now the heavier evidence begins. But,' he put his hand on Harker's wrist, 'it won't add up to a conviction. Or if it does, it'll go out the window on appeal. Luke?'

Luke nodded as he chewed.

'And what do you think of this jury?' Harker demanded.

Old Charlie chewed. 'Most juries are fools,' he said. 'That's the beauty of our justice system – the decisions are taken out of the hands of lawyers and placed in the hands of fools. Hallelujah! If you did the same thing with the medical profession, half the world would be dead, but we trust juries with the electric chair.' He grinned. 'I wouldn't change it for worlds. It makes the practice of law such fun.' He pointed upwards at the courtrooms. 'Those people up there are such *fun* . . .'

42

'I call Doris Johnston, your honour,' Vance intoned.

Doris Johnston, a large, black woman with an enormous bosom, dressed in heavy navy-blue uniform, entered the courtroom like a galleon in full sail. She billowed across to the witness box and sat down. She took the oath.

'Mrs Johnston,' Vance began, 'are you a superintendent in the Immigration Department of the British Virgin Islands, in Road Town, Tortola?'

'I am *the* superintendent.'

'Thank you. What time do you start work in the mornings?'

'Eight o'clock sharp.'

'Now, where were you just before eight o'clock on seventh of September this year?'

'I was walkin' along the bayfront road towards my office, when I noticed a yacht at anchor about sixty yards off. I noticed it because it was the only vessel in the bay, all the rest being moored in the marina.'

'Now, can you see the bay from your personal office in the Immigration building?'

'Yessir, best office in the buildin', your honour. An' I continued to notice said boat at anchor during the mornin', an' at times I noticed a man movin' about on her.'

'What time was it when you first noticed a man moving about on her?'

'About noon, sir. An' at two o'clock I saw him come to shore in his dinghy. I expected him to walk straight to my building to check in but he didn't. He disappeared from view. It was about an hour later, at three o'clock, that he came to my department with his ship's documents and checks in. I asks him how come he took so long and he said he'd been sleepin'. But I notice the smell of liquor on his breath, your honour.'

'And who was this man?'

Doris Johnston pointed dramatically across the court-room. 'Him. The defendant.'

'Very well,' Vance said. 'Now did he have to fill in some kind of arrival form, giving his details?'

'Yessir. This is it.' She held it up importantly. 'Under his signature.'

'I put that in as Exhibit Seven, your honour. Now, what did he give as his last port of call?'

'Nassau, Bahamas. Said he left there seven days earlier.'

'Did you ask him for his Departure Form, the port clearance form from the Nassau authorities?'

'I sure did, sir. He said he did not know he had to have one. So, as standin' orders require, I ordered him to return to Nassau to get aforesaid document. He appeared very surprised, then said okay, he would fly back there to get it. So I stamped him in, on his passport, but the legality of his boat was subject to aforesaid condition.'

'Is this his passport, with your stamp in it?'

'Yessir.'

'I put that in as Exhibit Eight, your honour. Now, did he also have to fill in a form called a Crew List, providing the names of all crew aboard?'

'He did.' Doris Johnston held up another document. 'In his own handwritin'.'

'I put that in as Exhibit Nine. Read that crew list, please, and tell us the names on it.'

'Just his own name, as captain. And Josephine Valentine Harker, as mate.'

'Josephine was on as mate,' Vance repeated. 'As if she was aboard. Now, did you ask him where Josephine was?'

'I did. 'Cos all crew gotta report to me, with their pass-ports. The defendant –' she pointed – 'presented Josephine's passport along with his, for stamping. I said, "Where's Josephine?" He said, "Must she come in person?" I said, "Yes!" So I stamped his passport and told him to bring Josephine.'

'And, did he ever come back?'

'No, he did not.'

'He never came back . . .' Vance mused softly for the jury's benefit. 'Thank you.' He sat down.

Charlie stood up to cross-examine.

'Mrs Johnston, good afternoon to you.'

Mrs Johnston looked suspicious. 'What?'

'Never mind. Now, when the defendant came into your office to report you were annoyed with him for not coming earlier, not so?'

'His legal duty is first to report to me, not go gallivantin' roun' town.'

'Quite,' Charlie said. 'So, when he came to check in with you, late, you were annoyed?'

'Me, annoyed? Never. Why should I be?'

'Because he had been disrespectful by not coming straight to you.'

'Nope.'

'You thought he had been *gallivanting* around town when he should have come straight to your department?'

Mrs Johnston snorted. 'Of course he shoulda come straight to me! It's the law.'

'Right. Same as any airport – you have to check through Immigration first, before you go'n do your gallivanting. Right?'

'Right,' Mrs Johnston agreed suspiciously.

'Especially in Road Town, Tortola, British Virgin Islands?'

'Right,' Mrs Johnston said suspiciously.

'Right. And that's why you subsequently telephoned your cousin, Police Commissioner Joshua Humphrey, to discuss the matter in depth, when the defendant never came back to you *despite* your orders.'

Mrs Johnston looked at Charlie. 'Anythin' wrong with that?'

Charlie gave his perfect enamel smile. 'And when you heard that Josephine was missing you told your cousin you were *sure* the defendant was guilty as sin, didn't you?'

Mrs Johnston scowled. 'What of it?' she demanded.

'In fact you told many people your opinion.'

'What of it?'

'In fact the whole town was talking about it?'

'So?'

'It was hot gossip.'

'Weren't gossip – it was *fact*,' Mrs Johnston proclaimed.

'Ah. Your opinion was fact? And you told 'em the *fact* that the defendant had no port clearance from Nassau?'

'So?'

'Yes or no, please.'

'Yes. So?'

'And you told 'em, and your cousin, Joshua Humphrey, the *fact* that you had ordered the defendant to return to Nassau to get the port clearance document.'

'Sure. That a crime?'

Charlie smiled widely. 'Now, turning to this crew list, Exhibit Nine: you've told us that he presented Josephine's passport but you told him that she had to come in person. Right?'

'Right.'

'But you had also told him that he had to go back to the Bahamas to get his port clearance papers. Right?'

'Right.'

'Now,' Charlie said, smiling, changing tack, 'you said you smelt liquor on the defendant's breath. Must have smelt strongly, huh?'

'Yeah.'

'Strong smell of drink. And did he not also appear exhausted? Red-eyed? Haggard?'

'His eyes were red some,' Mrs Johnston said guardedly. 'And he sure needed a shave. Dunno about the haggard.'

'Exhausted?'

'Dunno. Maybe.'

'Drunk? Would you have let him drive your car?'

Mrs Johnston shifted in her chair. 'Guess not.'

Charlie smiled. 'Very well. Last question. Despite your opinion of him, and your irritation that he had been gallivanting around town before checking in with you, he was polite and cooperative with you, wasn't he, even if he was drunk?'

Mrs Johnston looked at him sulkily. 'Cain't say he wasn't,' she conceded reluctantly.

Charlie beamed. 'Thank you. No further questions, your honour.' He sat down.

Harker whispered, 'How did you know Humphrey is her cousin?'

'I didn't. But everybody's related to everybody else down there.'

Miss Violet Huggins was a pretty girl of about nineteen in a white summery frock which set off her mulatto complexion very well.

'Miss Huggins,' Vance said, 'are you an employee of American Express in Road Town, Tortola?'

'Yes, sir,' Miss Huggins said nervously.

'Do you work in the front office, dealing directly with the public?'

'I do, sir.'

'Do you remember the seventh of September this year?'

'Yes, sir.'

'Do you know the defendant?'

'Yes, sir.'

'How?'

Miss Huggins wriggled, then said, 'He came into American Express and told me he wanted to make a phone call to the US. He wrote down the number and I dialled it for him. He received the call in our sound-proof kiosk.'

'Okay. What time was this?'

'It was at seven minutes past two in the afternoon, sir. The number he called was Manufacturers Life Insurance Company in New York.'

'What happened then?'

'Then he came back to the counter and said he wanted to send a fax. He wrote it out, and I sent it for him. It was to a lawyer in New York, I think his name was Goldman or Goldstein. I didn't read it. While I was sending it he wrote out another fax, I didn't mean to read it but it was so short I couldn't help it. It was to a Mr Valentine, it said words to the effect, "I regret to tell you that Josie has disappeared overboard, I will call you when I feel better."'

Vance repeated, pacing elegantly: '"I will call you . . ."' He raised his eyebrows at Miss Huggins. 'What happened then?'

'Well, sir, the defendant then left. He returned the next morning at eight o'clock and asked if a fax had arrived for him from Manufacturers Life Insurance Company. I said no. He then asked for a list of flights leaving the island that day. I gave him a list and he left the office.'

'Was there a flight to America that day?'

'Yes, sir, to Miami. At midday.'

'And was there another flight to the French Island of Guadeloupe?'

'Yes, sir, at ten o'clock.'

Vance smiled. 'Thank you. No further questions.'

Old Charlie stood up to cross-examine.

'Good afternoon, Miss Huggins, welcome to Miami.'

Miss Huggins squirmed prettily. 'Thank you, sir.'

Charlie said abruptly: 'There's no direct flight from Tortola to Nassau, the capital of the Bahamas, is there?'

Miss Huggins looked taken aback by the change of tone. 'No, sir,' she said anxiously.

'Is there a direct flight from Guadeloupe to Nassau?'

Miss Huggins looked worried. 'I don't know for sure.'

'And there is a direct flight from Guadeloupe to Miami?'

'Yes, sir.'

'And from Miami there are frequent flights to Nassau?'

'Yes, sir.'

Charlie gave his pearly-white smile. 'Thank you. Now, the defendant came in and asked for this flight information quite openly, didn't he?'

'Yes, sir.'

'And at this stage you knew who he was – that he was the person who had been interrogated by Commissioner Humphrey the day before in connection with his wife's death. Not so?'

Miss Huggins looked nervous. 'Yes, sir.'

Charlie punched the air with his finger: 'And you knew that Mrs Johnston had used her authority to order him to return to Nassau to get his port clearance papers?'

'Yes,' Miss Huggins said worriedly.

Charlie smiled benevolently. 'And in fact Mrs Johnston is your cousin. Or is she your aunt?'

Miss Huggins said nervously, 'Aunt.'

'And what relation to you is Joshua Humphrey, the Commissioner of Police?'

'My cousin. But I call him uncle.'

'Yes, uncle. Because of his age – and his importance.' Charlie smiled. 'In fact, most people in Tortola are related one way or another, aren't they?'

Miss Huggins looked very worried about all this. 'I guess so, sir.'

Old Charlie nodded, and smiled at the pretty girl paternally: 'And after the defendant asked about the flights off the island, you phoned your uncle and told him, didn't you, Violet?'

Miss Huggins nodded. 'Yes, sir.' She added, 'I thought I should.'

'You thought you should because the whole island was talking about him.'

'Yes,' she agreed apologetically.

'Quite. And your uncle was very grateful for your tip-off.'

'Yes, sir,' Miss Huggins admitted.

'Thank you,' Charlie said gently. 'Have a nice day, Miss Huggins.'

Old Charlie sat down happily. Vance rose and said, 'I call Police Commissioner Joshua Humphrey, your honour.'

But Judge Ludman looked at the clock and growled, 'I think that's enough for one day.' He turned to the jury. 'Okay, we're going to knock off until tomorrow. Now, I've decided that you folk must be sequestered in a hotel for the duration of this trial. Sorry about that, but this case is attracting huge international attention and I must ensure that you speak to nobody about it. A hotel has been arranged, you'll be taken there by bus, you'll be guarded all the time, not allowed to go anywhere. Your family will bring you clothes and toiletries but you will not be allowed to speak to them.' He held up a finger. 'You are not allowed – by *law* – to discuss this case with anyone, d'you hear? And you do not read the press or listen to the television about the case. Do you hear me?'

The members of the jury nodded self-consciously. Judge Ludman's gnarled finger shot up and he cried, 'Because today you are *judges*, ladies and gentlemen! Not house-wives and butchers and bakers and candlestick makers but judges! Entrusted with matters of life and death!' He grimaced then pointed at Harker. 'You have the terrifying responsibility of deciding whether or not this man goes to the electric chair! And you have taken a solemn oath to God Almighty to discharge that responsibility without fear, favour or prejudice!'

Ludman glared at the jury. Everybody shifted, looking embarrassed. Judge Ludman picked up his gavel. 'Okay, so we'll knock off for the day. Goodnight!'

He banged his gavel.

Luke and Charlie accompanied Harker back down to the cells.

'Vintage Ludman,' Charlie said. 'Hates juries.'

'Seems to be a strong character,' Luke said. 'How's his law?'

'He used to be an excellent advocate.'

They entered the human zoo of the cells. As they waited for the warder to unlock the holding cells Harker said, white-faced, 'How's it going in your opinion, Luke?'

Luke was embarrassed that Harker had consulted him first. He held out his hand to Charlie in deference.

'Good,' Charlie said. 'It's going fine so far.'

Luke said to Harker above the hubbub: 'It's going very well. Charlie has neutralized all Vance's innuendoes pertaining to your possible motive.' He added, 'You can afford to sleep better tonight.'

Harker stepped through the gate into the human zoo. 'Sleep?'

As they emerged from the building into the late afternoon, Charlie said, 'I'm going to Beauty's Paradise, just down the road.'

'What do you think?' Luke asked.

'As you say, we've done okay so far,' Charlie said, striding along, head down. 'But don't count your chickens . . .'

43

It was another beautiful Floridian day. When Luke Mahoney arrived at the courthouse the crowds on the fourth floor extended down the stairs, out down the stone steps into the sunshine of the parking area. Luke was a little late. Court had already begun.

'I call Joshua Humphrey, your honour,' Edward Vance was saying.

Luke sat down next to a pale-faced Harker. Joshua Humphrey strode to the witness stand, portly and resplendent in his uniform. His gold-braided cap was tucked under his arm, as regulations required, his swagger stick and white gloves were in his hand. He took the oath at attention, glaring into the middle distance. Then he sat, also at attention.

'Are you the Commissioner of Police in the British Virgin Islands, stationed in Road Town, Tortola?' Vance said.

Humphrey said to the middle distance: 'I am, my lord.'

'Please,' Vance said, 'address your answers to His Honour. Now, did you ever know the deceased in this case?'

Humphrey said to the far wall: 'No, my lord. Not in the flesh. But I sure read her book, *Outrage*.'

Vance pointed at Harker dramatically. 'And do you know the defendant?'

Humphrey's eyes darted at Harker, then reverted to the wall. 'Certainly do, my lord. I mean your honour. I arrested him in connection with this here case.'

Vance said, pacing across the courtroom. 'And where did you do that, Commissioner?'

'At Tortola airport, my lord, on ninth September. He was trying to leave the island on an *expired* passport. Whereas I had his valid one in my possession. I looked in his baggage. I found a pistol. I seized same.'

'Is this it?' Vance held up a Browning .25 pistol.

'It is, my lord. I mean your honour.'

'I put that in as Exhibit Ten, your honour,' Vance said. 'Was it loaded?'

'It was, my lord. The bullets are in that plastic bag attached to the trigger.'

'Very well. Now you've told us that you had his valid passport in your possession. Why was this?'

Commissioner Joshua Humphrey said stolidly, 'Because the day before he was being questioned concerning the murder of his wife, Josephine Valentine Harker, the deceased in this case. I had tol' him to return the following day at noon for further questioning and to ensure the above I took possession of his said passport. But the next morning he tried to leave using his expired one, plus smuggling said pistol, so he was arrested.'

'Very well,' Vance said. 'Pause there. Now, when and where did you first meet the defendant?'

Humphrey stiffly launched into his serious evidence. 'At four o'clock in the afternoon of Thursday eighth September, 1996, my lord. Acting on information received I proceeded in the police launch out to the defendant's yacht which was at anchor in Road Town bay. I boarded and entered the wheelhouse. I looked down the hatch into the saloon. There I saw the defendant, my lord. Evidently he had not heard me. He was sitting at the table opening a bottle of rum. He was wearing only short trousers. He was unshaven.'

'So what happened?' Vance said.

'I told him he was in the British Virgin Islands illegally on account of he did not have port clearance papers from Nassau, his last port of call. An' because his wife, Josephine Valentine Harker, the mate according to his crew list, had not reported to the Immigration Department as required by law.'

'Very well, Commissioner Humphrey, what happened then?'

Humphrey shifted his ample buttocks. 'I told the defendant I wanted him to accompany me to the police station. He said, "I was about to come to see you anyway because I want to report the death of my wife."'

'Indeed?' Vance said. 'So then what happened?'

'We went to the police station. There I questioned him about his wife. Finally I recorded a statement from him. I cautioned him that he was not obliged to say anything but if he did it may be used in evidence. He then made a statement, freely and voluntarily. I typed it and read it back to him. He signed it.'

Vance said, 'I tender this statement in evidence, your honour.'

Old Charlie stood up, his hands spread in sweet reasonableness. 'No objection, it's God's own truth.'

'Read the statement please,' Vance said.

Humphrey cleared his throat, then read in ringing Caribbean tones: 'I was on watch in the wheelhouse until midnight when my wife came up from our cabin to take over. I had been drinking quite a lot, about half a bottle of whisky. We were in the Gulf Stream, battling into the trade winds on the engine, on automatic pilot. It was a dark night. No moon, overcast. I handed over to my wife and went below to sleep. I expected her to wake me in six hours to take over again. I woke up naturally and found it was half past four. I went up to the wheelhouse. My wife was not there. I looked out on deck, I couldn't see her. I went below to the forward cabins. Not there. I looked in the toilet. I was worried now. I dashed back to the wheelhouse, took the helm off automatic, turned the yacht around and went steaming back the way we had come. I put on all lights. I blew my foghorn. I put the helm on automatic and dashed out on deck with binoculars. I knew she had a life-jacket on. I searched for her all night. I threw two life-rings and the yacht's life-raft overboard at different intervals. I fired off flares. When daylight came I widened my search. I was frantic. I saw nothing all day. At nightfall I decided it was hopeless. I turned around and set off for the Virgin Islands to report to the authorities. That is all.'

'I put that statement in as Exhibit Eleven, your honour.' Vance turned back to Humphrey. 'Then what happened, Commissioner?'

'I told the defendant he could not sleep on his boat because I had impounded it for forensic examination. I took possession of his passport. And I told him I wanted to resume questioning at noon the next day.'

Vance said, strolling towards the witness stand, 'Now, the next morning did Dr Smythe, a forensic scientist with the US government, come over from St Thomas to examine the boat with you?'

'Yes,' Humphrey said stoically. 'I pointed out a cracked glass on the speedometer, a broken handset on the radio, a bullet mark in the saloon upholstery, and bloodstains on the transom.'

'Thank you,' Vance said, 'we'll get that evidence from Dr Smythe. Now, you told us at the outset that you arrested the defendant at the airfield the next morning. Did you caution him?'

'I warned him that he was not obliged to say anything but anything he did say could be used in evidence. He made a verbal statement.'

'I tender this statement in evidence, your honour.'

Charlie raised his palms at the bench. 'No objection,' he beamed. 'We've got nothing to hide.'

Vance nodded and Humphrey continued: 'He said, "Leave me alone, I am returning to Nassau to get my port clearance documents, for Christ's sake".'

'I *see* . . .' Vance said to the jury with a disbelieving smile. 'He said he was returning to the Bahamas. But did you look at his ticket?'

'Yes, my lord, I took possession of said ticket in his pocket.' Vance passed him a document. 'Yes, this is it.'

'I put that in as Exhibit Twelve, your honour. What is the destination printed on that ticket?'

'Guadeloupe, my lord. I mean, your honour.'

'Is there no onward destination after Guadeloupe?'

'No, nothing. Ticket ends in Guadeloupe.'

Vance smiled at the jury. 'Strange . . .' he said. 'Now, did you ask the defendant if he had a licence for this gun you found in his possession?'

'I did. He took an American licence from his wallet – but, of course, that don't give him no right to smuggle it aboard an aircraft.'

'Is this the licence?' Vance passed him a document.

'It is.'

'I put that in as Exhibit Thirteen, your honour. Now, did you find anything else in his wallet?'

'I did. I found another American licence for a .38 Smith & Wesson pistol. I asked the defendant where it was. He said it was stolen some time ago from his car in New York.'

'I *see*,' Vance said. 'Stolen? So then what happened?'

'I returned to my police station with the defendant, and put him in the cells. I then returned to his yacht where Dr Smythe was still doing his forensic examination.' Humphrey paused dramatically. 'That afternoon, I decided to charge the defendant with the murder of his wife, Josephine, the deceased in this case.'

'Thank you,' Vance said. He sat down.

There was a silence. Charlie stared at the witness, his mouth open; then he stared at the judge, amazed. Then he stared at the jury. Then, still seated, he turned to the prosecution table.

'Is that *it*?' he demanded of Vance incredulously. 'You ain't going to let the jury know what the defendant *said* in answer to the charge of murder?' Charlie stood up, seething with indignation. He threw his pen down on the table so hard it bounced. '*Well*,' he said, his benevolent old face creased in disgust, 'we're sure going to get to the bottom of *this* in my cross-examination!'

He strode from his table up to the witness box. He put his foot on the dais, his elbow on his knee and glared at Humphrey, black lawman confronting black lawman. He waited a dramatic moment, then hissed sarcastically, '*You don't say . . .*'

Humphrey looked at old Charlie worriedly, eyes wide. Then he smirked unhappily. 'I don't say what, sir?'

Charlie leant towards him. '*Bi-i-i-g* deal . . .' He thrust out his arms wide. 'Bi-i-i-i-i-g deal, the Commissioner of Police of the BVI, Joshua Humphrey *himself*, tells this honourable court that after his discussion with the forensic scientist *he* decides, in his *infinite* police wisdom, to charge the defendant with . . . wait for it . . . *murder!*'

Humphrey swallowed. 'Yes, sir. That's what I done.'

Charlie looked at him with withering contempt. 'And you thereby hope to leave this jury –' he pointed at the twelve bemused folk – 'these good honest Americans you hope to leave with the *impression* that if *you* saw fit to charge the defendant with murder then he must be guilty!' His finger shot up as he turned to the jury. 'You do not have the *fairness* to tell this jury what the defendant *replied*!'

Humphrey protested, bug-eyed, pointing at Vance. 'The District Attorney decided, not me, my lord.'

'Aha!' old Charlie cried, 'you say the District *Attorney* is up to something? It's *he* who wants to leave the jury with that fallacious, *unfair* impression!'

'Your honour,' Vance cried, leaping to his feet. 'I strenuously object to the allegation!'

Old Charlie cried triumphantly, pointing at Humphrey, 'Your witness said it, not me! He doesn't want us to know what the defendant said when he was charged with murder. Because –' he suddenly whirled and glared at Humphrey – 'because the defendant said, didn't he: "For the umpteenth time I deny the charge, you silly old *fart*!"'

There was a shocked silence. Then a titter ran through the

375

courtroom, smothered laughter. 'Isn't that what he said?' Charlie thundered.

Humphrey had his eyes downcast, intensely embarrassed. He muttered: 'Somethin' like that.'

'Something like that?' Charlie echoed. Then he cried, 'Didn't you write it down and ask him to sign it?'

Humphrey shifted. 'No,' he muttered.

'*Why not?*' Charlie persisted. 'Why not? The law says you must write down his answer!' He paused, then went on, 'Because you didn't want the jury to know that he thought you a silly old *fart*!'

Commissioner Humphrey was slumped in embarrassment. Vance rose. '*Please*, your honour, Mr Benson is deliberately embarrassing the witness!'

'Darn right I am,' Charlie cried, all smiles. 'Because I intend to prove what a bully he is, your honour! I put it to you, Commissioner Humphrey, sir, that you didn't write it down because you didn't want the jury to know that the defendant had vehemently denied the charge umpteen times, and you didn't want the jury to know he became so angry with you because you were *persecuting* him!'

Humphrey shifted his buttocks, sitting at attention again. 'I wasn't persecutin' him, my lord. I didn't write down his reply because I didn't think his insulting answer was relevant, my lord.'

'But what about his denial?' Charlie cried incredulously. 'The defendant denies the charge and you don't think that's *relevant*?' Charlie stared, then jabbed with his finger. 'Surely to God the jury *should* know that he denied it!'

Humphrey shifted. 'Guess so.'

'So it *was*, and *is*, relevant! So why did you say it wasn't? And why didn't you write it down?' Before the unhappy witness could reply, Charlie continued: '*Do* tell us – is there anything else that you're concealing from this court?'

'I ain't concealin' nothing,' Humphrey muttered.

'That's a lie!' Charlie beamed. 'Because when you recorded

that long, cautioned statement from the defendant, you deliberately left out something that he said!'

Humphrey shook his head nervously. 'No I didn't.'

'Yes, you did!' Charlie turned to the jury and spread his hands. 'His very first words when you started typing were "I hope this is the last damn time I have to say this". But you didn't type it, did you?'

Humphrey shifted. 'I don't remember him saying that.'

'No? Well, the defendant *does* remember! So if you can't remember, you can't argue with him when he says he does remember! Thank you!' He smiled. 'The fact is you didn't type it because you didn't want the jury to know you were persecuting him!'

'I wasn't persecutin' him,' Commissioner Humphrey insisted uncomfortably.

'No? Let's see.' Charlie turned and paced. 'You're a great admirer of the deceased and her books, aren't you?'

'So?' Commissioner Humphrey glowered unhappily.

'And you're a great admirer of Nelson Mandela.'

'Ain't everybody?'

'Oh yes. But you're an Africanist, aren't you? You believe Africa should be for the Africans, don't you?'

'France is for the French, ain't it? Spain for the Spanish.'

'You think the African got a raw deal during the colonial era.'

Humphrey mounted his hobby-horse. 'They sure did. My great-grand-pappy was a slave, brought from Africa to break his back in the sugar plantations!'

'Quite,' Charlie said solemnly. 'My great-grandfather was also a slave; we all understand your feelings. But the fact is you feel very strongly against South Africans?'

'Not against South Africans, but against the apartheid government, sir.'

Charlie smiled. 'Good. So am I correct in assuming that when the defendant told you that he was a publisher in New York, and that his wife had been lost overboard, you must have been very sympathetic.'

'Sure.' Humphrey looked suspicious. 'I was sympathetic.'

Charlie frowned. 'But why had you gone out to the defendant's boat?'

'Because,' Humphrey said, 'he did not have port clearance papers from the Bahamas. And his wife, Josephine, had not reported to Immigration as required by law. I had been told that by the Immigration Department.'

'So it was a routine matter, to go to his boat?'

Humphrey looked suspicious. 'Yes.'

Old Charlie gave his beatific smile. 'Why are you lying to us, Commissioner?'

Humphrey scowled. Big eyes wide. 'How am I lying?'

Charlie smiled. 'You *knew*, before going out to the defendant's boat, that his wife Josephine, who had failed to report to Immigration, was dead. Because your niece, Miss Huggins of American Express, had told you about his fax to Josephine's father.'

Humphrey blinked. 'Oh yes. I remember now.'

'Oh, *now* you remember. How can you forget such a detail? And so it was *not* a routine visit to his boat, it was because you were suspicious. Not sympathetic. And when he told you that he had been a professional soldier who fought for the then-Rhodesian government against the so-called terrorists, you became persecutory!'

Joshua Humphrey glowered. 'Not at all, my lord.'

Charlie looked astonished. '*No?* A man like you, a glowing Africanist, a man who hates colonialism. *Amazing* . . . But when he went on to tell you that after the Rhodesian war ended he joined the South African army in their bush war in Angola, you must have been antagonized?' He frowned.

Humphrey looked at Charlie uncomfortably. On the horns of a policeman's dilemma: admit his prejudice, or deny it and be disbelieved. Commissioner Humphrey chose the lesser of two evils: 'Suppose I was a bit resentful when he tol' me he was an officer in the South African army.'

Charlie cried, '*Thank* you, Mr Humphrey! At *last* we have some truth from you!' He beamed at the jury, then abruptly turned back to Humphrey with a scowl. 'So it's obvious, Commissioner, that you're a communist! At last we have the truth about you. Thank you.'

'Me?'

'Yes!' Charlie cried. 'Because everybody knows that the communist Cubans were fighting for the communist government of Angola against the South African army, who were desperately trying to save the continent from being over-run by Russia and China! And that the United States of America was helping South Africa in that war! So don't try to kid us, Commissioner Humphrey, that you're not a closet communist!'

'I deny –'

'I put it to you, Commissioner Humphrey, that if you weren't a closet communist at least, maybe even working for the overthrow of the United States government, if you weren't a prejudiced, Africanist communist, you would not have been so persecutory against my client – who had risked his life fighting communism – and you would not have been in such a hurry to arrest him. He would have been able to fly back to Nassau as Doris Johnston ordered, get his port clearance papers, return to Tortola and continue to cooperate fully in your investigation into the tragic death of his wife. But, no – you blundered in like a bull in a china shop and arrested him, with the result that here he is today. All because of your persecutory silliness.'

Humphrey looked thoroughly disconcerted. He groped for words, then: 'I deny it, sir.'

'Of course you deny it . . .' Charlie grinned widely. Then he changed the subject abruptly – and startled Harker with the question: 'So tell me, as a senior policeman you have heard of many cases over the years of piracy in the Caribbean area, haven't you?'

Everybody in the courtroom looked interested.

Humphrey was relieved to change topics. He said, 'I've *heard*, but that don't necessarily mean it's *true*.'

Charlie smiled maliciously. 'You are very determined not to admit anything that may possibly be favourable to the defendant, aren't you?' He paused. 'But as a policeman are you interested in what you've heard about piracy?'

'Interested, yes.'

'Ah! So tell me: Is it true that most cases of piracy are drug-related in that the pirates want the boat to run drugs?'

'So they say,' Humphrey admitted.

'So they board the victim's boat, kill the crew, steal the boat and after they've used it a few times they sink it to get rid of the evidence and then they steal another boat.'

'So they say.'

Charlie sighed. 'Mr Humphrey – yes or no?'

'What's the question?'

Charlie grinned. 'Oh, never mind . . .' He sighed theatrically and ended: 'Finally, Mr Humphrey, let's go back to the circumstances of the defendant's arrest.' He paused. 'When you parted company with the defendant the night before, he was not under arrest, was he? Because you didn't have enough evidence to charge him, right? So as you had not arrested him you had no legal power whatsoever to deprive him of his passport – had you?'

Humphrey looked disconcerted again. 'Didn' I?'

'*No*!' Charlie cried. 'Don't you know the law? Read the preamble on the inside cover. Her Majesty commands everybody – *even* Commissioner Joshua Humphrey of the British Virgin Islands – to allow the bearer to pass without let or hindrance. So you had no right to seize his passport.' Charlie glared, then pointed accusingly. 'You exposed yourself to a civil damages suit, sir.' Before the man could argue Charlie pressed on: 'And your cousin, Doris Johnston, had *ordered* him to return to Nassau to get his port clearance papers!'

'He was trying to escape, sir,' Humphrey insisted. 'He wasn't going to get no port clearance papers . . .'

Charlie cried, 'Oh? So he was going to sacrifice his boat, was he? Sacrifice everything and be a fugitive from the law for the rest of his life?' Charlie snorted and turned to the jury with amused disbelief, then he sat down with contempt all over his face.

There was silence. Then Judge Ludman growled, 'Think we'll adjourn for lunch.'

44

Court resumed at two p.m. Vance called his next witness, Dr Peter Smythe. He was a neat man with a precise manner. He was also a professional witness: he spent much of his working life testifying in courtrooms for the prosecution.

Led by Vance, he told the court that he was a forensic scientist employed by the US government, stationed in St Thomas, US Virgin Islands. On the ninth of October he had examined the yacht named *Rosemary* at the request of Commissioner Joshua Humphrey and prepared a report, which he produced as Exhibit Thirteen. Referring to it, he testified that a thorough examination of the yacht had revealed one bullet hole in the upholstery of the bench in the saloon. He produced the cushion as Exhibit Fourteen. Inside the cushion he had found a bullet, which he produced as Exhibit Fifteen. He subsequently examined it microscopically, and fired test shots with the .25 Browning pistol, Exhibit Ten. This ballistic test proved that the bullet was *not* fired by the gun. He found no other bullet marks anywhere on the boat. However, in the wheelhouse the glass of the speed-counter had been shattered. He produced a photograph of it, which became Exhibit Sixteen. He collected the shattered glass and subjected it to microscopic examination and found traces of paper, which he produced as Exhibit Seventeen. He then examined all the books in the wheelhouse and found that the *Nautical Almanac* had damage to the lower corner of its spine – he produced it as Exhibit Eighteen. He found tiny fragments of glass which matched exactly the glass in the speedometer. Similarly the paper of the *Almanac* matched the traces of paper found on the glass. From this he concluded that the *Nautical Almanac* had broken the glass. He then saw that the two-way radio had a broken handset, the transmitter and receiver being cracked. The radio could not work because of this. He produced it as Exhibit Nineteen.

He then examined the whole boat thoroughly for blood-stains. He found quite a large stain, about the size of a man's hand, on the teak deck on the transom. It was barely visible. He scraped up a sample. The bloodstain had obviously been washed off because traces of soap were also found. He tested the blood particles collected and determined they were Group B. He also found two specks of blood in the actual cockpit, on the floorboards, behind the wheelhouse, also almost invisible. He found them to be Group A.

'Thank you, Doctor.' Vance sat down.

Charlie rose to cross-examine.

'Doctor Smythe,' he beamed, 'good afternoon.'

'Good afternoon,' the scientist said pleasantly.

'I want to thank you for the careful, clear way you explained it all to us simple laymen.'

'Thank you.' The scientist smiled.

'Mr Benson,' Judge Ludman said testily, 'I've asked you to cut out these pleasantries. Get on with the case!'

Charlie looked at the judge as if he had been whipped. 'As your honour pleases, but I was only being polite to a very helpful witness who has come a long way to assist us. Unlike Joshua Humphrey, *he* hasn't exaggerated and persecuted the defendant.'

'Get on with it, Charlie!'

'As your honour pleases,' old Charlie murmured. He turned back to the forensic scientist. 'Doctor, you found the faint bloodstain on the transom – that is the stern, immediately behind the *aft* steering wheel, not so? More or less where somebody would be standing, or sitting, if he was using the aft steering wheel.'

'Correct.'

'Now, immediately in *front* of that steering wheel is the mizzen mast?'

'Correct.'

'And the boom of that mast is about seven feet above the deck?'

'About that.'

'Are you a sailor by any chance, Doctor?'

'As a matter of fact I am,' the scientist said.

'I bet,' Charlie said conversationally. 'Living in those lovely Virgin Islands.' He sighed wistfully. 'Anyway, tell the jury: the mizzen mast's boom has a rope that runs along its underside whereby the sailor tightens the sail – is that so?'

'Correct.'

'And it sometimes happens, doesn't it, that that rope hangs sloppily, in a loop.'

'Correct.'

'Now if someone were standing at that aft wheel, and the boom swung a little, the rope could catch the helmsman's neck and knock him down, could it not?'

The scientist nodded. 'Quite possible.'

'And the human scalp bleeds profusely when cut, doesn't it?'

'Yes.'

'And you found that bloodstain in approximately the position you would expect if Josephine were knocked off-balance by the rope?'

'Yes. More or less.'

'Yes,' Charlie agreed pensively. Then he raised his finger as if an idea had just struck him. '*And*, of course, if a pirate were to have come up the swimming ladder at the stern of the boat, and Josephine was standing at the wheel, with her back to him, it would have been a simple matter for him to have hit her over the head, from behind, and knock her down, bleeding. Not so?'

The scientist nodded. 'Yes, I suppose so.'

Charlie nodded to himself, then ended brightly: 'Thank

you, Doctor Smythe! Have a nice evening. And give my love to St Thomas, lovely island.' He sat.

Dr Cedric Holmes took the oath. He was a young Englishman with a lock of hair falling across his brow and a deep-red suntan.

'Are you a medical doctor employed by Road Town General Hospital in Tortola?' Vance asked.

'I am.'

'On the ninth of September did you examine the defendant at the request of the Commissioner of Police, Joshua Humphrey, and prepare this report?' Vance handed him a document.

'I did.'

'I put that in as Exhibit Twenty. Tell us what you found.'

'On the defendant's right hip I found a cut six and a half inches long. It was about a week old, and healing, so I was unable to probe it to find out its depth but I would describe it as a superficial wound.'

'What was the angle of the cut?'

'It began at the bottom end of the hip, towards the back, and ran upwards at about forty-five degrees towards his waist. It was consistent with a slash made by a sharp knife.'

'What degree of force was required to inflict this injury?'

'A moderate degree, your honour, assuming the defendant was naked or clad only in shorts at the time.'

'Did you find any other wounds?'

'I did. On the underside of his left forearm there was a shallow slash wound about two inches long. It was also healing so I could not probe its depth. Depending on the shape of the blade of the knife, and its sharpness, I would say a moderate degree of force was required to inflict it.'

'What was its angle?'

'Almost exactly at right-angles to the arm.'

'Thank you.' Vance sat down.

Old Charlie rose to cross-examine.

'Dr Holmes, good afternoon and welcome to sunny Miami.'

'Mr Benson,' Judge Ludman snapped, 'I've asked you –'

'So you have, your honour, I'm sorry. Ignore that, Dr Holmes, and let's get to work. So tell me, Doctor, how old are you?'

'Twenty-seven, your honour,' Holmes said.

'My word. So you have only recently qualified?'

'Last year, your honour.'

'And all your postgraduate experience has been in Tortola?'

'Yes, your honour.'

'And tell me: are the people of Tortola a *very* dangerous bunch?'

Dr Holmes frowned earnestly. 'Dangerous in what way?'

'I mean,' Charlie said, equally earnestly, 'do they go around stabbing each other *very* often?'

Dr Holmes smiled. 'Not so far as I'm aware.'

'Indeed if they did you *would* be aware because your hospital would have to patch them up?'

'Yes.'

'Yes. So tell me, how many stabbings have you dealt with in your long service as a doctor?'

Dr Holmes smiled. 'Two,' he said.

'Ah. So your evidence is not based on much experience. I see. So I presume you concede that the wounds could have been inflicted in a number of ways. For example, if the defendant had a sheath hanging on his hip, he could have cut himself when he hurriedly thrust the knife back into its sheath – missing the sheath and cutting himself?'

'Possibly.'

'And he could have cut his left forearm when he was cutting the rope that secured the life-raft – if he held the rope up in his left hand and from underneath cut the rope too vigorously, he could have carelessly given himself the wound you saw?'

'Possibly,' Dr Holmes said.

'Thank you,' old Charlie said. 'Have a nice day, and give my salaams to Tortola.' He sat.

Donald Ferguson was a large man with a balding head. 'Are you,' Vance said, 'the general manager of the First National City Bank in New York?'

'I am.'

'In that capacity do you have access to all your bank's records?'

'I do.'

'Do you know the defendant?'

'Yes, he is a client of my bank.'

'Have you extracted a printout of the defendant's personal account over the last four years?'

'I have.' Vance passed him a document. 'Yes, this is it.'

'I put that in as Exhibit Twenty-one, your honour. Now, looking at that printout, what is the defendant's balance?'

'Today he is in credit in the sum of nine thousand four hundred dollars.'

'Now look back to the end of June.'

'At the end of June, 1996, he owed the bank one million, nine hundred and seventy thousand dollars.'

'How did that debt come about?'

'Several years ago the defendant asked the bank to lend him over two million dollars to purchase a majority shareholding in his company, Harvest House – fifty-one per cent of the shares. The bank agreed. Over the next few years the defendant more or less kept pace only with the interest payments. However, in June, he told us he was selling his shares to his wife, Josephine, and he paid in her cheque for over two million, which put him back in credit. He told us that he was keeping two per cent and selling forty-nine per cent to Josephine.'

'So he paid off his overdraft by selling most of his shares to his wife, the deceased?'

'Correct.'

'So now Josephine owned forty-nine per cent and he

387

owned two per cent. Did he ever tell you who owned the other forty-nine per cent?'

'He told us they were owned by a holding company in the Caribbean called Westminster NV on behalf of other shareholders whom he did not know.'

'Now, looking at his account I see that *before* he paid off his overdraft he went into deeper debt by issuing a cheque for a hundred and forty thousand dollars. But the next week somebody paid *in* a cheque for a hundred and forty thousand dollars. Know anything about that?'

'Yes. The defendant telephoned us saying he had bought a boat for a hundred and forty thousand dollars, and issued a cheque. He asked us to cover it, saying he would pay in enough money in the next few weeks. He did, depositing his wife's cheque for that amount.'

'So in effect he paid for the boat with his wife's money?'

'Correct,' Ferguson said.

Vance leered at the jury. 'Thank you,' he said. He sat down with satisfaction.

Old Charlie rose creakily to cross-examine.

'Mr Ferguson, I won't wish you good afternoon because I'm not allowed to, but thank you for coming down from New York to assist us. However, I'm afraid that your testimony is useless.'

The courtroom tittered. 'Mr Benson,' Judge Ludman sighed.

'Not this time, your honour, you can't tick me off this time,' old Charlie said brightly, 'because I am about to explain to this honourable court that this witness's evidence is inadmissible!'

'Nonsense!' Vance groaned.

'This better be good,' Judge Ludman warned.

'Oh it is, your honour, it is. Mr Ferguson,' Charlie said, turning to the witness cheerfully, 'you've told us that you're general manager and you therefore have *access* to all your bank's records, and that empowers you to produce the printout of the defendant's account as proof of the facts mentioned therein. Right?'

'Correct,' Mr Ferguson said, mystified.

'Mr Ferguson,' old Charlie enquired happily, 'have you read Charles Dickens's *Oliver Twist*?'

'This better be good,' Judge Ludman repeated. Vance snickered.

'I have, your honour,' Mr Ferguson said. 'But long ago.'

'And do you remember the character Bill Sikes, the burglar?'

'I do.'

'Well,' Charlie smiled, 'my young friend the Assistant DA need not have bothered an important banker like you, he might just as well have called Bill Sikes as a witness, and said:

'"Bill Sikes, are you a burglar?"

'"Yes, I am, your honour," says Bill Sikes, wiping his nose on his sleeve.

'"And in your capacity as a burglar do you have *access* to the records of the First National City Bank?"

'"Oh yes, your honour," says Bill Sikes, "banks are no problem to a good burglar like me."

'"So do you now produce a printout of the defendant's account as an exhibit?"' Charlie turned to Vance with a smile. 'Do you spot your glaring blunder, young fella?'

Ed Vance was angry. 'Your honour, I'll thank Mr Benson to stop calling me young fella.'

'Do you spot your blunder?' Judge Ludman asked. 'Because I do!'

'"Custody"!' old Charlie cried happily. 'Not "access"! Only the *custodian* of bank records has the right to produce them in court, not people like Bill Sikes who have *access*!'

Ed Vance glowered at the judge: 'Very well, I'll establish that in re-examination.'

'Do you think you'll remember?' Charlie asked kindly. 'No, I better do it for you, it's safer and we've got nothing to hide. Mr Ferguson, as well as having access to the bank's records, like Bill Sikes and Al Capone, are you also the overall custodian?'

'I am, your honour,' Mr Ferguson said.

'Bravo. Now, Mr Ferguson, banks make their money by *lending* money, don't they?'

'Yes.'

'If you didn't lend money to people like the defendant, you'd go out of business, wouldn't you?'

'Yes.'

'And you were perfectly happy to lend two million dollars to the defendant because he was a good customer who never let you down, not so?'

'Correct,' Mr Ferguson said.

'And in your vast experience as a banker you can confirm that there is nothing unusual in businessmen selling shares to members of their family in order to pay off their debts – correct?'

'Correct.'

'So please,' Charlie smiled, 'face the jury and tell them that there is nothing sinister in that. And repeat after me: If our *young* friend the Assistant District Attorney tries to tell you otherwise he's talking absolute balderdash!'

'*Objection!*' Ed Vance thundered, scrambling to his feet.

'Oh very well,' Charlie beamed at Mr Ferguson. 'Have a safe journey home.'

Ed Vance had kept his best witness until last. 'I call Mr Denys Valentine, your honour,' he intoned sombrely.

Denys Valentine was dressed in a grey pinstripe suit and it seemed his face was the same colour, the same as his mane of hair. He was a very dignified, tragic figure, pain etched on his face.

'Mr Valentine,' Vance began, 'are you the father of the deceased in this case, Josephine Valentine Harker?'

'I am.'

Vance pointed dramatically at Harker: 'And the defendant is therefore your son-in-law?'

Valentine looked at Harker with unconcealed hatred.
Harker flinched inwardly, but returned the eye-lock. 'He
is,' Valentine said.

'Are you a lawyer, the senior partner of a firm in Boston?'

'I am.'

'And are you also the trustee in what is called the
Valentine Trust?'

'I am.'

'Tell us about the Valentine Trust, please.'

Denys Valentine faced the jury. He said quietly, 'My father
– who was a judge – set up the trust when Josephine was
born. The objective of the trust was to pay for Josephine's
education and to ensure she became an all-rounder. There
was a special emphasis on sport – my father was a very keen
sportsman and the trust had to give her the best training in
athletics generally, hockey, skiing, tennis, and sailing. She
had to be given every encouragement to learn to play the
piano or another musical instrument, and she should be
taught ballet and singing. In addition –'

'Pause there,' Vance said. 'How much of it did Josephine
manage?'

'Almost all of it. She took intensive courses and became
proficient at all the things I've mentioned with the exception of ballet. The trust also required that Josephine get
at least one university degree – this she did at Berkeley,
majoring in Political Philosophy and English Literature.
In addition, the trust required her to spend at least two
years travelling round the world with a backpack, writing
a detailed journal of her adventures.'

'Did she do that?'

'She did, for three years. Extracts from her journals were
published in newspapers. And, as you know, she has since
written three books. She was writing her fourth book when
she died.'

'We'll come to that. Now in addition to paying for all her

education, sports training and travels, did the trust give her anything else?'

'Yes,' Mr Valentine said grimly. 'She was to receive the capital of the trust, over two million dollars, on her thirty-fifth birthday or on the event of her marriage, whichever came first.'

'I *see*,' Vance said thoughtfully. 'On her marriage. And when did she get married?'

'In May, 1996, about six months ago. To the defendant.' He pointed accusingly at Harker. 'She phoned me from Las Vegas where they got married and told me they were about to start packing up in order to run off to Nassau to board her boat. Repeat *her* boat, which she paid for. She telephoned me –'

'You can't tell us what she said to you because that would be hearsay, but you can tell us what you said to her.'

'I begged her to cancel this proposed sailing trip around the world with the defendant because it was highly dangerous and because –'

'No opinion evidence, please,' old Charlie croaked, half-rising.

'Very well, so what happened?' Vance said to Valentine.

'My daughter subsequently gave me banking instructions, as a result of which I transferred the two million dollars to her account with Barclays Bank.'

'Now,' Vance said with satisfaction, 'we've heard evidence that Josephine bought forty-nine per cent of the shares in Harvest House from the defendant for a little over two million dollars. Did she consult you on this transaction – just answer yes or no, please.'

'No. But when I heard about it I was alarmed because –'

Charlie was on his feet. 'Your honour, I hate to interrupt my learned friend, and I certainly don't want to upset the poor witness who has lost his daughter, but I really must object to all this prejudicial, semi-opinion, semi-hearsay evidence. The prosecution is leaving the jury with the impression that in this witness's opinion the deal between the defendant and Josephine was inadvisable – and that is getting opinion evidence in by the back door and it's grossly unfair.'

'Well, you can cross-examine!' Vance snapped.

Charlie smiled sadly. 'You betcha I'm going to cross-examine, Ed, but it's a great pity for all of us, for this poor witness who's lost his daughter, for the defendant who's lost his dear wife, for dear Josephine herself who was a lovely, sensible, sensitive woman that you try to drag in this *inadmissible* opinion evidence. And thus drag her good sense and her good marriage through the mud –'

Vance cried, 'Now it's Mr Benson who is trying to drag inadmissible opinion evidence in by the back door!'

'Your honour!' old Charlie whined incredulously. 'To describe the deceased Josephine as a fine and sensible young woman is wrong? Has the young Assistant District Attorney lost *all* his marbles? Because it's poor Josephine's death he's supposed to be prosecuting!'

'I object –' Vance began.

'Yes,' Judge Ludman sighed. 'Sit down, Mr Benson.'

Charlie sat angrily. 'Get on with it, Ed!' he said in a stage whisper to Vance.

Vance glowered at him, then said: 'No further questions, your honour!'

Charlie rose aggressively to cross-examine but Judge Ludman looked at the clock.

'I think court should adjourn until tomorrow morning, Mr Benson.'

He banged his gavel. Everybody rose and he stalked out of the courtroom bad-temperedly.

As Harker was led away he glanced at the public benches: his heart lurched as he locked eyes with Looksmart Kumalo. Looksmart gave him a wide malicious smile.

45

Harker waited anxiously for Charlie to telephone him at the prison to review the situation so far, but it was Luke Mahoney who did so. Harker was relieved – he could tell Luke about Looksmart but Charlie knew nothing about that aspect of the case.

'But why do you say it was a malicious smile, not a friendly one,' Luke asked.

Harker was standing at a row of telephones in the noisy corridor outside the prison kitchens.

'I know malice when I see it,' he said tensely. 'He threatened me the last time I saw him in Nassau and this time his smile was saying, "I've got more in store for you for Long Island".'

'Okay, so maybe he's trying to intimidate you into giving evidence for him when he sues the South African government, but he's no threat to you in this trial now, there's nothing he can say or do to endanger you, so put him out of your mind for the time being – you've got to be on the ball tomorrow when you give evidence.'

Harker had his eyes closed in the plastic bubble of the kiosk, his nerves screaming as prison life swirled about him. 'Have you and Charlie now decided that I'm going to give sworn evidence? You said maybe I should make an unsworn statement?'

'Charlie and I will decide over dinner tonight. You just get a good night's sleep.'

Sleep? With the dread of going on to that witness stand tomorrow? 'And how do you think it went today? How's Charlie doing?'

'Don't worry about old Charlie, he's doing a good job, the jury likes him.'

'But why hasn't he telephoned?' Harker could hear music in the background.

'I'm keeping an eye on him, he'll be okay.'

'What do you mean – he's hitting the bottle?'

'Don't worry, I'll see he has something to eat and goes home to bed early, he's just unwinding.' There was a girlish shriek followed by howls of male laughter. 'Jack, I'd better go.'

'What's he doing, for Christ's sake?'

'It's all right, he's only joined the chorus line, everybody's enjoying it. Okay, this is just to tell you not to worry, we think everything is going well. Tomorrow Charlie will undo any damage caused by Mr Valentine's evidence. Then he'll probably call you as a witness and this time tomorrow you should be a free man.'

Oh Jesus, the dread of giving evidence, of being cross-examined. 'But I thought you said we had such a strong defence I would not have to testify?'

'We'll decide that tonight. Now get some sleep, it's important that you be calm tomorrow.'

Calm? When you are on trial for your life, for that three-legged wooden electric chair called Old Sparky up there on Death Row at the Florida State Prison outside Starke – *be calm . . . ?*

Inside the CNN studio in Miami the anchorman reviewed the day's proceedings in ringing tones with clips of scenes within courtroom 4B.

'So we bring you now our legal expert, Professor Sydney Gregorowski. Good evening, Professor, what do you make of today's events?'

Professor Sydney A. Gregorowski said, 'Good evening, Hal. Yes, very interesting. The case against the defendant is getting more and more suspicious, but so far, in my opinion, it does not add up to a case upon which "a reasonable jury" should convict as proven beyond reasonable doubt. On the other hand there is enough evidence, in my opinion, upon which a reasonable jury *might* convict – not *should* but *might* – so the defendant has got a case to answer. In my view the outcome of this trial depends on how satisfactorily he handles that. Should he give sworn evidence, which will be tested by cross-examination, or should he make an unsworn statement, which is not subject to cross-examination, but which therefore naturally carries less weight? Personally, if I were the sole judge, and the defendant made an unsworn statement, I would acquit him – because, although all the details add up to strong suspicion, they are not in my view as a lawyer strong enough to add up to proof beyond reasonable doubt. But you can never tell with juries – they could well convict him and on appeal could it be said that the evidence was such that *no* reasonable jury could convict, which is the legal test on appeal?'

'So if you were his lawyer you would advise him to give sworn evidence?'

'I think so. And hope that he makes a good witness.'

Across town, in Beauty's Paradise, Luke Mahoney watched that interview on television while Charlie whooped it up with the chorus girls at the other end of the bar.

Yes, he thought grimly – he would love to keep Jack Harker out of the witness stand tomorrow; in that event he really should be acquitted, but you never can tell with fucking juries . . .

It was another beautiful day. The crowds milled outside court 4B.

Judge Ludman said, 'Mr Valentine, I remind you that you are still under oath.'

'I understand, your honour.'

Old Charlie rose slowly to his feet. His eyes were bloodshot and his hangover was etched on his black brow but his smile was as beatific as ever.

'Mr Valentine, I have to ask you a few questions, but please understand that I am in no way being disrespectful, neither as to your integrity nor to you as a father who has lost his beloved daughter. As a lawyer, I'm sure you understand that I am only trying to get to the truth.'

'I understand that, Mr Benson,' Valentine said grimly, 'and I have given you the truth.'

'And I beg you,' Charlie said, '*beg* you to understand, to make allowance for, even if you won't admit it, that the defendant loved – *loves* – your daughter every bit as much as you do, and is as bereft by her tragic disappearance as you are.'

Valentine gave a small bitter smirk that was seen on millions of television screens around the world; he was about to respond but Ed Vance was on his feet. 'Mr Benson is giving evidence!'

Charlie turned slowly towards Ed Vance with theatrical incredulity all over his long-suffering face. 'You deny my client loved the deceased? What impertinence, sir!' Before Vance could muster a response, Charlie turned back to Valentine witheringly: 'And you, sir. Did I hear you snort, Mr Valentine?'

Valentine looked at Charlie stonily. 'I'm sorry.'

'*Thank* you,' Charlie said. Pause. 'Tell me: How many times did you meet the defendant before this unfortunate trial began?'

Valentine shifted on his chair, then cleared his throat. 'Once.'

Charlie's eyes opened wide. 'Oh, only *once*?' Then his finger shot up, as if he had just remembered a distant detail: 'Ah yes, that would have been eight years ago when Josephine brought the defendant to Boston in 1988, especially to meet you.'

Valentine looked grim. 'Correct.'

Charlie enquired in wonder: 'And you haven't seen him since, until this trial began three days ago?'

'Correct.'

'But your daughter? *Surely* you've seen Josephine since 1988?'

Valentine shifted. 'No.'

397

Charlie looked astonished. 'No? You mean you never went to visit her in New York?'

Valentine shifted. 'No.'

'No? But . . .' Charlie waved a hand. 'I'm sure you asked her to visit you in Boston?'

Valentine cleared his throat. 'No,' he said grimly.

Charlie stared at the man, then shook his wise old head. 'How sad . . .'

There was silence in the courtroom. Charlie stared at the floor, deeply saddened by a father's rejection of his deceased daughter. 'How sad . . .' he repeated. Silence. Then he gave a sniff and said, 'And now it's too late . . .'

Everybody in the courtroom was looking very sombre, except Ed Vance who got to his feet. 'What's the question, please?'

Charlie glanced at him sorrowfully, then wiped the corner of his eye. He sniffed and said to Valentine, 'In fact, Josie brought Jack to Boston for your approval in 1988, didn't she? Because she was in love with him, already living with him.'

Valentine said grimly: 'Correct.'

'And how did you get on with him?' Charlie enquired gently.

Valentine cleared his throat, then said stiffly, 'We were on . . . polite terms.'

'Polite?' Charlie said pensively. 'Is that the same as "cordial" in Boston-speak?'

Valentine looked at him. 'Polite.'

'Not cordial?' Charlie sighed sadly. 'And isn't it true, Mr Valentine, that you got the defendant alone in your library and told him, politely enough, that you are a pacifist, that you disapproved of both his military background and the apartheid regime, that as a Christian you thoroughly disapproved of his living with Josephine out of wedlock, that you asked Jack to separate from Josephine for six months in the hopes that their relationship would die out?' Charlie looked at Valentine soulfully. 'True?'

Valentine cleared his throat again. 'True enough, I suppose.'

'*Enough* . . . ? And you told Jack – and later Josephine – that if they did not carry out this wish of yours, you would disown Josephine for ever. And disinherit her.'

Valentine said stiffly, 'True.'

'And is it not also true that you told her that if she did not obey you as trustee, you would cut off her allowance of fifty thousand dollars a year?'

'True.'

Charlie nodded sadly. 'And is it not also true that both Jack and Josephine, independently of each other, indignantly refused your ultimatum and Josephine, in so many words, told you to go to hell?'

'Yes,' Valentine admitted.

'And,' Charlie said, 'you *did* cut off her allowance, and you *did* cut her out of your will?'

Valentine nodded. 'I did.'

Old Charlie shook his head in sad wonder at his fellow man.

'And,' he continued sadly, remorselessly, 'is it not also true that since that first meeting you have refused several invitations to visit Jack and your daughter in New York?'

Valentine cleared his throat. 'True.'

'Even though you were actually in New York on business, you refused to have even a drink at their apartment?'

'Yes.'

'And isn't it true that when Josephine telephoned you from Las Vegas to tell you that she and the defendant were married, she asked for your blessing, but you refused to give it?'

'True.'

'In fact, you urged her not to consummate the marriage with him, so that you could have it declared void, and she told you to go to hell. And thereafter the defendant spoke to you and told you that Josephine loved you and wanted you two to make it up?'

'Yes,' Valentine admitted uncomfortably.

Charlie nodded, and looked at the lawyer soulfully. He shook his head and said, 'But you never saw her again . . . Never, since that far-off visit eight years ago when she first brought the defendant home to meet you.' Charlie sighed. 'Josephine contacted you on several occasions to try to heal the rift between you?'

'Yes,' Valentine admitted.

'But you never did . . .' Charlie gave a slow, sad sigh, then took a big breath and soldiered on to a new topic. 'Now, some months ago Josephine telephoned you and mentioned that she was buying Jack's shares in Harvest House. You told her not to touch the deal. Correct?'

'Correct,' Valentine said grimly.

'But, it's a perfectly respectable investment. Harvest is regarded as a very successful publishing house. And it is not unusual for a businessman to place whole or part of his business in his wife's name, is it?'

'But the defendant didn't *place* his business in Josephine's name, he *sold* it to her. For more than two million dollars. And that is exactly what I was always afraid of, that the defendant would somehow get his hands on my daughter's money.'

'"Get his hands on . . ."' old Charlie repeated. 'That implies dishonesty. Nasty stuff. But there was nothing dishonest about the transaction, your daughter got her money's worth of shares – possibly more than her money's worth. And she would control Harvest. She would get her advances and her royalties *and* she would get the dividends on her shares. So in effect she would probably double or even treble her income from her books, and she'd get her share of the profits in all the other books Harvest publishes.' Charlie raised his eyebrows and gave his enamel smile. 'Nice work if you can get it.'

'May I point out to you, sir,' Valentine said, 'that two million dollars invested at ten per cent is two hundred thousand dollars a year. *That* is nice, *without* work. And without risk.'

Charlie smiled. 'Indeed,' he agreed. 'But her investment in Harvest would yield much more than two hundred thousand, and the American Dream was not built on risk-free, work-free, cushy investments. However . . .' Charlie waved his hand, dismissing that subject. 'Let's turn to your attitude towards the defendant.' He frowned: 'I believe you're a religious man?'

Valentine cleared his throat. 'I try to be.'

'And,' Charlie said, 'as a consequence of your religious beliefs you're a pacifist. In the sense that you were a conscientious objector when you were called up for service in the Korean War – although you indeed served in a non-combatant role.'

Mr Valentine cleared his throat. 'The war was a scandalous American mistake, sir. But I don't approve of war, no. The taking of human life is never acceptable.'

'Oh, none of us *do* approve of war,' old Charlie agreed, 'we would all rather there was no war –'

'That's where you're wrong,' Valentine interrupted. 'There is a warrior-class of person who *likes* war. And I refuse to cooperate with them.'

'And, as a Christian, you didn't like the defendant living with your daughter?'

Valentine looked angry. 'I don't think any father likes that.'

'Despite the fact that she was a grown woman who had achieved everything your father had stipulated in the trust and had made her own way round the world for three years, risked her life often as a renowned war correspondent, written a bestselling book which,' Charlie pointed at Harker, 'the defendant had published so successfully – despite all that you didn't feel she was morally entitled to choose how she lived?'

'Morally?' Valentine said doggedly. '*Legally*, yes, but morally fornication is a mortal sin.'

Charlie nodded sagely. 'And you also feel that being a professional soldier is morally unacceptable – so you found the defendant unacceptable?'

'And because he was a professional soldier in the South African army. The army of the racial oppressor.'

Charlie stroked his chin pensively. Then he enquired, 'Tell us, Mr Valentine, are you a communist?'

Valentine looked astonished. 'No!'

'You are loyal to the American constitution, the right to the pursuit of wealth and happiness?'

'Yes.'

'Democracy? Freedom of speech? Freedom of worship?'

'Of course.'

'You sure? Sure you're not a closet communist?'

'Don't be absurd.'

Charlie nodded. 'And the reason for your vehemence is because communism is an atheistic political creed that enforces a one-party state, thus denying democracy, denying the worship of God, free speech and the pursuit of wealth, and so on. Not so?'

'That,' Valentine said, 'is some definition of communism, but I suppose it will do.'

'Well, can you answer this, with a simple yes or no? Are you aware, as an educated man, that the defendant devoted his entire military life to defending those aspects of the American constitution that we all – yes, including you – hold dear? That he fought against communism in Zimbabwe and Angola, that he daily risked his life in defence of *your* ultimate liberty.' Charlie paused. 'Do you appreciate that?'

Valentine looked at him. 'That,' he said, 'is a matter of interpretation.'

Charlie looked back at him, and let that answer hang. Then he said quietly, 'Let me put the question this way. If the defendant *was* fighting for your liberty against communism, would you approve? Or not?'

Valentine looked at Charlie. He knew he could not win in

402

this confrontation – either answer destroyed his credibility. He said instead, uncomfortably, 'That would depend on the interpretation.'

Charlie looked at him, eyes hooded. 'Very well, we'll let the jury place *their* interpretation on that answer.' He shook his head. 'And yet Josephine became well known in the country as a journalist and photographer who made wars and soldiering her specialty –'

Valentine interrupted: 'Josephine didn't specialize in wars, she specialized in the truth about the horrors of war, the evil of politicians and economics that cause war, injustices like apartheid that cause such suffering not only in South Africa but amongst the black frontline states whom the South African government destabilized with sabotage and cross-border raids and cold-blooded murder. That's what my daughter specialized in, sir! Not war. The truth.'

Charlie nodded. 'Oh, Josephine was an excellent journalist and a wonderful girl, we all agree on that. But surely it was obvious to you that this intelligent woman, who devoted her life to the pursuit of truth, understood the truth about the defendant, the truth that he was an honourable soldier fighting against communism.'

Valentine said stiffly, 'She thought that, but it was far from obvious that she was right.'

'Far from obvious? Aren't you being *very* prejudiced, sir? You only met the defendant once. Josephine lived with him for years! And you had almost no conversations with her after she'd met the defendant.'

'It is possible for the smartest people to make huge mistakes in their personal lives,' Valentine retorted. 'Love can be blind!'

Charlie stared at him. 'Love can be blind?' he whispered. Then he exploded: 'That's rich, coming from you, sir! *You* –' he stabbed with his finger – 'who are so *hard-hearted* as to refuse to visit your own daughter, refuse to invite her to visit you, who vowed to disown her, disinherit her if she married the man she loved, you who refused to give her your blessing after she had married him. *You* have the utter gall to advise this court that love is blind . . . ?'

The rhetorical question hung in the silent courtroom. It was embarrassing, almost cruel. Valentine looked at Charlie and for the first time his mask seemed to slip; his lip trembled. Luke Mahoney closed his eyes, *Enough, Charlie, now you're evoking the jury's sympathy for him.* But Charlie continued relentlessly, softly:

'Tell me, sir, if you had the opportunity over again, would you treat your daughter Josephine like that?'

For another long moment the question hung in the silent courtroom: Luke prayed *Enough for Chrissake!* Vance began to get to his feet to defend his witness by objecting to a hypothetical question but then Denys Valentine broke down. He was staring at Charlie, then suddenly his eyes filled with tears and his chin trembled, and he dropped his face into his hands and sobbed.

Vance subsided back into his seat, his face solemn but his heart joyful. *Oh for Christ's sake Charlie*, Luke groaned to himself. The jury shifted, eyes downcast.

Then Charlie tried to undo his overkill. 'No, I see now you wouldn't be so heartless as to treat her like that again. Thank you sir, that is all.'

Not to be outdone, Charlie pulled out his big white handkerchief and dabbed his eyes as he sat.

'The People rest, your honour,' Vance said solemnly.

'I think,' Judge Ludman growled, 'we'll adjourn now . . .'

46

Luke told Charlie he had blown it by excessively cross-examining Valentine, reducing him to tears and thus evoking the jury's sympathy. Harker agreed but grimly held his tongue. Charlie stoutly disagreed with the criticism: 'I showed the man up for a stone-hearted bigot who unfairly rejects both his daughter and Jack. Who is therefore not to be believed when he puts a sinister interpretation on the financial aspects of his daughter's dealings with Jack!'

'Sure, you did a great job at that, the jury were with you. Then you overdid it and reduced him to tears and their sympathy swung to him.'

'Look,' Charlie said dismissively, 'what were the main points of Valentine's evidence? The only points were the financial ones that the prosecution relies upon as a motive for murder – Josephine's purchase of Harvest shares for two million dollars which Jack will get back under Josie's will, plus her life insurance, all of which Jack will inherit under her will. To reinforce that motive Vance tried to sneak in prejudicial details in the form of Valentine's opinion of Jack as an unscrupulous soldier of fortune and an apartheid-monger who cynically stole his daughter's heart to get his hands on her money. To destroy the perception he had erected in the jury's mind I really had to sock it to him. It's a pity he ended up crying, I agree – but *you*, Jack –' he wagged his finger – 'will do the same when you give evidence. Your voice is going to catch when you describe your love for Josie, you are going to sniff and dab your eyes. And when you get around to describing the night she disappeared you're going to burst into tears. Right?'

Harker sighed, then nodded.

'And when I ask you how you felt about Josie's father, your heart will be full of pain. Pain at being rejected, at being misunderstood, being damned as a soldier of fortune when you are an officer and a gentleman in all the best traditions of Sandhurst and West Point. Right?'

Harker took a deep breath. 'So you've definitely decided I should give sworn evidence? Not just make an unsworn statement?'

'Correct,' Charlie said. 'Luke and I were up till late last night discussing it. There's too much suspicious circumstantial evidence against you – a judge would probably acquit you but a goddam jury will reckon you're hiding something terrible if you don't give sworn evidence and submit to cross-examination.'

Harker dragged his hands down his face. 'Not today, please. I didn't sleep last night, my nerves are shattered. Can't you ask for an adjournment until tomorrow?'

Charlie looked at him, then glanced at Luke. 'Sure, I can say I don't feel well – which I don't. I could do with a hair of the dog.'

The discussion of the case, the review of the evidence, continued in Beauty's Paradise Grill & Revue Bar after Harker had disappeared in the truck back to the prison. Luke sat at the bar with Charlie, while girls did their lunch-hour number on the stage. 'But how can you expect the man to sob and cry on cue? Unless he's a very good actor the jury will see through him and he'll be a very dead man.'

'He *is* a good actor,' Charlie said flatly.

Luke glanced at him. Up on the stage the naked girls were gyrating to the music. 'Meaning?'

'Nerves of steel,' Charlie said, watching the girls. He added: 'You'd have to have in his business, wouldn't you? Professional soldier in Africa, for Christ's sake, at war for almost twenty years, facing death for a living. What kind of nerves do you expect him to have?'

Luke looked at the old man. 'You don't think he's innocent, do you?'

Old Charlie took a sip of his *piña colada*, still looking at the girls. 'One wouldn't push any of them out of bed, would one?'

'You don't think he's innocent, do you?' Luke repeated.

Charlie's eyes didn't waver from the girls. 'Do you?' He added: 'The one fourth from the left with the thighs.'

Luke grinned despite himself. 'A bit young for you, Charlie.'

'Like fifty years too young.' He added reasonably: 'Maybe only forty.'

'You think he's guilty?'

Charlie took a long suck of his drink.

'As *sin* . . .'

47

Jack Harker had been into battle exactly one hundred times. 'You get used to it,' he had once said to Josephine, 'but you never lose your fear – you only become accustomed to it. With battlefield experience your wits sharpen, your panic-factor diminishes, your military judgement improves and it's easier to keep your morale up and get the adrenaline flowing, but underneath all that you're still scared . . .' But going into battle was easy for Harker compared with going on to the witness stand to testify in his own defence, on trial for his life. He had hardly slept since the trial began, his mind turning over and over the courtroom scenes, and the night before he testified he did not sleep at all. His face was grey, his eyes dark and he could feel his legs trembling as he took the oath to tell the truth, the whole truth and nothing but the truth. It was a good thing that he could sit down.

Luke Mahoney thought that Charlie did not look much better – and he did not feel much better himself. He had spent most of the previous night following Charlie from bar to bar, trying to ensure that the old man did not land up in hospital or jail. It was one o'clock in the morning when he had persuaded Charlie to go home.

'Mr Harker,' Charlie began with the delicate, sepulchral voice of an undertaker, 'where were you born?'

Harker cleared his throat and nervously began his evidence. Led by Charlie he told the court his background: born in England, brought up in Rhodesia, went to Sandhurst, won the sword of honour, joined the Rhodesian army, fought for the next five years in their bush war against the communist terrrorists sponsored by Russia and China.

When that war ended in 1979 because the Rhodesians were unable to sustain the war effort in the face of economic sanctions imposed by Britain, he was recruited by the South African army to fight in their border war on the Angolan front.

'Did you feel,' Charlie asked, 'that you were fighting for apartheid?'

Harker frowned nervously again. 'Absolutely not. I have never supported apartheid. In fact, I joined the Anti-Apartheid League in New York. I regarded apartheid as not only cruel but doomed to failure. No, I regarded South Africa's war as an extension of Rhodesia's war – we were fighting the communist enemy. In South Africa's war we were fighting the Cuban army whom Russia had sent to help the illegal communist government of Angola fight the capitalist UNITA. Russia intended that Cuba would there-after overrun the whole of southern Africa.' He added: 'The American government was helping us fight the Cubans.'

Harker told the court that in 1986 he was wounded in combat. After recuperation he was not up to the long physical endurance that bush combat requires, so he was offered a post in Military Intelligence, or a disability pension. He decided he wanted to go into publishing. He initially got a job in England as a trainee executive; in 1987 he was appointed managing director of a small new company start-ing up in New York, called Harvest House. He subsequently bought a majority shareholding in the company.

'Now, when and how did you meet the deceased, Josephine?'

Harker described a chance meeting at the New York Rackets Club, how he offered to consider the book she was writing, how they became lovers, how he successfully published the book, *Outrage*, which became a bestseller.

'And what was your relationship with Josephine like?' Charlie asked.

Harker cleared his throat. 'Very happy.'

'Did you quarrel?'

Harker glanced at Judge Ludman. 'Rarely, your honour.'

'When you did, what sort of things was it about?'

Harker hesitated. 'Hard to generalize. But both of us worked hard and sometimes one or other of us was a bit irritable. She felt passionately about her writing, and she didn't take very well to criticism. But I think spats like that happen in most relationships.' He glanced nervously at the jury.

'Very well. Now in May this year what did you and Josie decide to do? And why?'

'We got married. And bought a yacht. Both Josephine and I are keen yachtsmen. It was our dream to sail around the world one day, so in May this year we decided to get married and do it.' He coughed. 'I am now forty-six. Harvest House was worth quite a lot if I sold it, and Josie would continue to make money as a writer. So why wait any longer? I put Harvest House up for sale. Then Josie decided that she would buy my shareholding in Harvest – she didn't like the thought of it slipping out of the family. So, she bought my shares for 2.2 million dollars. Or rather she bought most of them, totalling forty-nine per cent. I held on to two per cent. That way, between us, we continued to control the company.'

'Now, apart from buying the boat, what else did you do?'

Harker described how they made new wills in each other's favour and took out more insurance on Josephine's life – he had intended taking out more on his own life, but decided that premiums were too high for a man of his age.

'Very well,' Charlie said, 'so you put your affairs in order – then what?'

Harker recounted their departure to Nassau, described how they set to work making the yacht seaworthy for a circumnavigation, whilst enjoying the Bahamas. Led by Charlie, Harker said that having studied charts and taken advice from yachtsmen, he considered that the biggest dangers ahead were coral reefs and pirates.

'Objection!' Vance cried. 'This is hearsay and opinion!'

'Nonsense,' Charlie groaned. 'The witness is about to tell us what *he* decided the dangers ahead were. That's no more hearsay than if he said "I consulted my stockbroker and then I decided to buy shares in American Airlines".'

Judge Ludman said, 'The line dividing direct evidence of the defendant's state of mind and the hearsay that engendered that state of mind is blurred and we have reached it. No more, please.'

'As your honour pleases,' Charlie sighed. He did not mind – the jury had got the message. 'Now,' he continued, 'what happened next?'

Harker told the court that he and Josephine decided to leave the Bahamas on August 31 1996 because the hurricane season was ending and they wanted to push on to the British Virgin Islands where they had been so happy.

'Now,' Charlie said, 'what happened on this voyage?'

Harker took a tense breath. 'Well, we reached the outer fringe of the Bahamas and entered the Gulf Stream, more or less opposite Miami. Then we swung south east, towards the Virgin Islands. The trade winds were dead against us, so we had to motor. The sea was very choppy, there was a lot of spray – very uncomfortable, particularly in the dark when you can't see the water flying at you until it's too late.'

'I can imagine,' Charlie said, full of wonder for his client's courage. 'Now, we know that something terrible happened on this voyage because Josephine is no longer with us. Please tell us what you know.'

Harker's face clouded over – momentarily he closed his eyes, but Luke was not sure it was genuine. He took a breath and quietly began his rehearsed evidence.

'On September the first, I did the six-to-midnight watch. Josie went down below, to sleep. We had both had a lot to drink over lunch. I continued drinking. The boat was

411

on automatic pilot so all I had to do was keep a lookout for other shipping. I saw the lights of a number of vessels, and I could see them on my radar screen.'

'Very well. What happened?'

'At midnight, Josie came up to take over. I went below to bed.'

'When you went to bed, how did you feel?'

'I have a strong tolerance of alcohol. I was in control of myself, but tipsy.'

'So, what happened next?'

'I fell into a deep sleep. I awoke some hours later – before dawn. I think it was the bang of a wave hitting the hull. I was very hung over. But something told me to go up top and investigate.'

'How were you dressed?'

'I got into shorts. And I had my knife on my waist, in its sheath.' Harker swallowed. 'The boat was pitching. I made my way up into the wheelhouse. Josie wasn't there. I yelled for her, but there was no response. The spray was flying. I went out on deck and shouted. No reply. I went below to check the forward toilet – looked in both forward cabins, no Josie. Then I panicked.' Harker's voice caught, and he dropped his face and sobbed once.

Luke Mahoney closed his eyes. He didn't know whether to believe that show of emotion. There was silence in the courtroom as Harker tried to compose himself. Finally he looked up at Charlie, and nodded.

Charlie said gently, 'Then what happened?'

'I realized she must have fallen overboard,' Harker said thickly. 'And . . . oh God, it was terrible. I ran to the controls, took the wheel off automatic and swung the boat around. I slammed the automatic pilot back on the reciprocal course, and went steaming back the way we had come. I grabbed my big Aldis lamp and shone it over the sea, looking for her. I sounded long blasts on the horn, and I grabbed the radio transmitter, to ask all vessels in the area to help me – but I lurched with the boat and I wrenched the transmitter out of the radio, bending the plug and I slammed the receiver against the bulkhead, cracking it. So I couldn't use the radio. I steamed back several miles, then I began to circle. I steamed slowly round and round in ever-widening circles all night, all lights blazing, blowing the horn. I threw two life-rings and the life-raft overboard. I was frantic. Then I thought it best if I stopped my engines and drifted, so that if she was afloat out there she could swim to me.' He swallowed. 'I did this all night. When dawn came I began to circle again. I circled all day, searching, blowing the horn.' He paused and wiped his eyes with the back of his wrist. 'When darkness fell I gave up. I was exhausted. I turned the boat back on to its original course for the Virgin Islands, put the helm on automatic and collapsed on my bunk. And slept. I didn't wake up until dawn.'

'Okay,' Charlie said. 'Now, how many days later was it that you arrived at the Virgins?'

'Six. I slept in snatches, mostly in the day.'

'Now, where was your first stop?'

'St Thomas, capital of the American Virgin Islands. I got there about midnight, dropped my anchor and slept for a few hours. Before dawn I woke up and sailed on to the British Virgin Islands, to Road Town. I got there at about eight a.m. I went to sleep again. Woke up about noon. Had a few drinks, then went ashore to check in with the immigration authorities.'

'And what happened at immigration?'

'The officer in charge, Doris Johnston, ordered me to go back to Nassau to get my port clearance papers.'

'Why hadn't you got clearance papers when you left Nassau?'

'I simply forgot. I forgot you needed such documents.'

'Very well. So what did you intend to do?'

'I intended to fly back to Nassau, get the clearance papers and return to Tortola. But first I telephoned Josie's insurance company, as I presumed I was required to do,

413

reporting her death. Then I sent a fax to her lawyer and to her father. Then I went back to my boat to eat before reporting Josephine's death to the police.' Harker shifted on the chair. 'I must have fallen asleep again. I woke up to find it was the middle of the night. I had something to eat, had a few more drinks, and fell asleep again just about dawn. I woke up mid-morning. I was getting myself together to go to the police when they came to me.'

Harker paused, haggard, and took a sip of water. He continued: 'I immediately told the officer, Commissioner Humphrey, I wanted to report Josephine's disappearance. He ordered me to go with him to the police station for questioning. Which I did, while detectives combed my boat looking for evidence.' Harker took another sip of water. 'At about ten o'clock that night Humphrey said we would continue with the interrogation another day. He ordered me to surrender my passport, which I regarded as illegal, but I didn't argue because I had another one, although it had expired. The next day I tried to fly back to Nassau to get my port clearance papers, as ordered by Mrs Johnston, but I was detained at the airport by Commissioner Humphrey.'

'Pause there,' Charlie said. 'And let's go back to the evidence these detectives were looking at on your boat. First of all, the bullet in the saloon cushion. Do you know how that came about?'

Harker cleared his throat. 'The hole was there when I bought the boat. When I viewed the boat only the broker was there. I never met the seller to ask him.'

'Did you ever look for the bullet that caused the hole?'

'I didn't know a bullet had caused it. There were two or three old tears in the saloon upholstery which Josephine patched but I did not associate any of them with bullets.'

'Now,' Charlie said, 'let's talk about your firearm. Mr Humphrey said he found two licences in your name, but he found only the small Browning, when he arrested you at the aerodrome. The forensic scientist found a bullet in the saloon cushion and it was a .38 bullet, not a .25. Now, where is your Smith and Wesson .38 pistol?'

Harker said, haggard, 'Sorry, I don't know. I last saw it in my car's glove compartment in New York. When I was packing up to go to the boat I noticed it was missing. I found the smaller Browning, at home, and packed it.'

'Why? Why did you want a gun on the boat?'

'Josie and I were travelling round the world, we might have needed a gun for self-defence against people like pirates.'

'Did you report the missing gun to the police?'

Harker coughed. He said: 'No. I should have, but in the hurly-burly of packing up I simply forgot.'

Sitting beside Charlie, Luke had great difficulty believing that. Evidently Charlie did too because he quickly moved on to the next subject:

'Turning now to the broken glass of the speed-counter in the wheelhouse. How did that happen?'

Harker said: 'I must have caused that. When I dashed back up into the wheelhouse when I realized Josie was missing I half-tripped over the *Nautical Almanac* lying on the wheelhouse floor. I flung it up on to the instrument console. I guess it hit the speedo; it's a heavy book.'

Luke sighed to himself. He hardly believed that either. Charlie continued: 'Now, tell us how you came by the cuts the doctor found on you.'

Harker sighed grimly. He took another sip of water.

'The life-raft was tied down to the deck. When I cut the rope I grabbed it up in my left hand and slashed underneath it with the knife, like this. I did it too forcefully because I not only cut the rope but slashed my forearm. I remember that but I don't remember cutting my hip. But after freeing the life-raft I rammed my knife back into its sheath. I must have missed the sheath the first time and cut my hip. I only noticed the blood afterwards.' He added, 'I was frantic. Panicked. In the dark.'

Charlie nodded sympathetically. 'I can imagine. Now

let's turn to the last bit of so-called evidence that the prosecution makes such a song and dance about – namely the bloodstain.'

'Objection.' Vance was on his feet, weary with indignation. 'Not only is Mr Benson being downright insulting, he's giving judgement himself!'

'Mr Benson,' Judge Ludman growled, 'keep your argumentative opinions to yourself for the time being.'

Charlie held up his hands in long-suffering resignation. '*As* your honour pleases.' He continued: 'About this bloodstain on the transom or stern of the boat: do you know how it was caused?'

Harker swallowed. 'I remember Josie saying one day when she was scrubbing down the decks that it looked like there was a bloodstain on the transom, but I never looked at it myself, I just presumed it was a bit of fish blood and that Josie had got rid of it. It must have been very faint because I never noticed it when I was examining the boat prior to buying her.'

'Quite,' Charlie said, 'quite. Now, let's get back to your arrest at the aerodrome when you were about to catch the flights back to Nassau. Firstly: Why did you try to take your pistol to Nassau with you?'

Harker gave a shrug. 'As a soldier I always carried a gun. It's just something I'm used to.'

Luke sighed: the answer sounded very unconvincing. Charlie continued: 'And you were using an expired passport, because your valid one had been seized by Mr Humphrey. Did it worry you, offering an expired passport?'

Harker shrugged again. 'The worst that could happen was that I would be turned back. Mr Humphrey had no right to confiscate my passport, I was in turmoil over Josie and my bloody-minded attitude towards Humphrey and his island was, "To hell with you, you silly old self-important codger, I'm going to Nassau to get those damn port clearance papers."'

It sounded very rehearsed. But old Charlie nodded earnestly. 'No wonder you felt bloody-minded –'

'Objection!' Vance sighed.

Charlie held up his palms again. 'Sorry, your honour, but I think it's fair comment, anybody would be bloody-minded after what the poor man had been through –'

'Objection!'

'Okay, but tell us, Mr Harker: as a soldier did you ever operate behind enemy lines?'

'Yes,' Harker said.

'Did you carry a valid passport entitling you to enter enemy territory?'

A titter ran through the court. 'No, your honour.' Harker smiled wanly.

'And while we're on the subject of soldiering, can you tell us, Mr Harker, how many battles you've been in.'

Harker cleared his throat. 'I have been in exactly one hundred "contacts". A contact meaning you encounter the enemy and a gunfight follows, an exchange of fire.' He added, 'Soldiers keep personal records of details like that. Anyway, it was on my hundredth contact that I was badly wounded and pensioned out of the army as a result.'

The jury were looking impressed. Charlie shook his sore head in wonder at his client's valour. 'Now, when you decided to return to Nassau to get your port clearance certificate – as the daunting Mrs Doris Johnston had so emphatically ordered you to do – you decided to fly there via Guadeloupe. Why?'

Harker took a breath. 'Because that was the first plane out of the island. I just wanted to get going, I was still in shock over the whole ghastly business, I just wanted to get on the next plane off the island and get to Nassau.' He sighed. 'And because Guadeloupe is a French colony I presumed Air France flew there from Europe and would fly on to Miami or maybe direct to Nassau itself.' He breathed deeply. 'So, I just bought the ticket from the lady at the desk at the aerodrome, intending to buy an onward ticket when

I reached Guadeloupe and enquired as to the best way of getting to Nassau.'

Old Charlie nodded at his client with an earnest frown. 'Quite,' he said. 'Quite,' as if any sensible soul would have done exactly the same. 'Now, finally, please tell us what happened after Humphrey arrested you.'

Harker swallowed. 'I was locked in the cells,' he said grimly. 'Which infuriated me. Then he questioned me further. Over and over. Finally he charged me with murder. I was exasperated. Exhausted. Grief-stricken. I apologize, but I called him a silly old fart.'

Charlie said in a stage whisper, 'I don't blame you.' Then loudly: 'Thank you.' He sat wearily but quickly.

48

Across the world millions of television viewers saw Jack Harker give that sworn testimony, and most of them were of the opinion that he made an unimpressive witness: he shifted on his seat, he was nervous, he cleared his throat too often, he sounded rehearsed. But when Vance began to cross-examine him they were downright convinced he was lying.

The purpose of cross-examination is to test a witness's evidence by trying to expose inconsistencies, untruths, improbabilities. Where none of these features are found, sarcasm helps. Cross-examination can be an ordeal for an honest witness who is doing his best to tell the court the truth: it is usually a nightmare for a dishonest one, especially if he is on trial for his life. It was a nightmare for Jack Harker, and good sport for elegant, photogenic Ed Vance.

'So tell me,' Vance said, 'Josephine was an immensely valuable author to Harvest, was she? An author any publisher would jump at?'

'Yes.'

Vance smiled. 'The implication being: "So why would I, her publisher, murder her, why would I kill the goose that lays the golden eggs?"'

Harker looked at him bleakly. 'Correct. Why would I?'

'I'll tell you why,' Vance leered. 'Because Harvest House insured her life didn't they?'

There was a silence. Both Charlie and Luke looked at Harker with astonishment.

Harker blinked, ashen. He swallowed and said, 'But that's not unusual, Harvest had an insurable interest in her life as she was such a bestseller –'

Charlie was clambering indignantly to his feet. '*Why*, your honour,' he demanded incredulously, 'have we not heard of this aspect of the prosecution case before? *Why* didn't Mr Advance – I mean Vance – lead evidence about this earlier? He called Mr Mayton to testify about Josephine's own life insurance; why didn't he produce this other evidence earlier? Why has he taken us by surprise?'

Ed Vance was smiling, twiddling his pen while old Charlie complained. Then he raised his eyes and said to the judge, 'Because I had no evidence, your honour.' He smiled. 'I only had a *hunch* . . . But now the defendant has admitted I'm right, may I please proceed, unharassed by Mr Benson?'

Judge Ludman said: 'You had no evidence of this, Mr Vance?'

'Just a hunch, your honour,' Vance said happily, and looked at the television cameras. 'Just a good old-fashioned lawyer's suspicion that the witness was hiding something.'

Judge Ludman subsided. 'Go ahead.'

'Thank you.' Vance smiled beautifully for the cameras. He turned back to Harker. 'How much did Harvest insure Josephine for?'

Harker swallowed. 'Three million dollars.'

There was a murmur across the courtroom. Vance raised his eyebrows and gave a soft whistle. 'Lot of *money* . . . Who decided on that valuation?'

Harker swallowed. He said: 'When I contracted to publish Josie's three unwritten books I decided to insure her life to cover our costs and hoped-for profit. Please remember that in those days Josephine was very much a photo-journalist and for all we knew she might jump on a plane and zoom off to some war and get killed.' He added: 'Term insurance, your honour.'

Vance nodded deeply. 'And you say this insurance was a perfectly legitimate business investment? Then tell me,' he said conversationally, 'why, when accountants went through Harvest's affairs, they found no mention of this insurance policy, nor of premiums paid for it.'

Harker shifted in his seat. 'The premiums are included under our general business insurance costs – along with Harvest's pension scheme, general overheads, et cetera.'

'Et cetera?' Vance mimicked. 'Covers a multitude of sins. But why, under the heading of "general overheads, et cetera", is there not a simple entry saying: Insurance premiums on Josephine Valentine, so-many thousands of dollars?' Harker shifted again and Vance let the silence hang, then he cried, with a stab of his finger, 'I'll tell you why! Because you didn't want anybody to know that Harvest had insured Josephine's life! Because you intended to collect that insurance yourself!'

Harker swallowed. 'Not so,' he said huskily.

'No? Tell us – did Josephine know you had insured her life for three million?'

Harker hesitated. 'Yes.'

'You hesitated!' Vance cried accusingly. 'Why?'

'I was trying to remember. Yes, I think she knew.'

'Why only "think"? Three million is a big deal!'

Harker cleared his throat. 'It was a business matter, authors aren't usually told their publisher's business details.' He added, 'And it was only *term* insurance, it had no cash value.'

'Except on death! And Josephine was your lover – not just *an author*!'

Charlie rose angrily. 'What's the question?'

Vance glared at Harker, then said softly, 'So the purpose of this surprise-surprise insurance was to cover the costs of publishing Josie's next three books *and* your anticipated profit – plus the cost of the loss to Harvest if she died? Correct?'

'Correct,' Harker said.

Vance rocked back on his heels. 'But,' he said softly, 'Josephine's next two books did *not* make anything like three million dollars profit, did they?' He let that hang. 'Her very first book, yes, was a bestseller, but her second book was an anti-climax, wasn't it? It barely broke even.'

Harker swallowed and glanced at Charlie, then said, 'But that's not unusual. If a first book is a bestseller the second one is often a disappointment. Second books are difficult for the author because he has often burned himself out emotionally on the first one. So his second often lacks the passion, the exuberance, the . . . spontaneity of the first, and the reviewers and the reading public are disappointed. Word gets around, the books do not move out of the shops so fast. Ask any publisher.'

'I'm asking *you*, Mr Harker,' Vance said softly. 'You're the accused in this case, you're the publisher who insured the deceased's life. Now, tell us about Josephine's third book, please.' He smiled.

Harker shifted. He glanced at Charlie. Luke rubbed his brow.

'Well, an author's third book may be his hardest. His second book is quite likely a disappointment, so with his third book he must really try hard to regain the impetus and popularity he won with the first.'

'I said *tell* us about Josephine's third book, please,' Vance repeated softly.

Harker breathed deeply. 'Josephine's third book was a novel about Pinochet's totalitarian military regime in Chile.'

'This was one of the books that you had contracted to pay four million dollars for, on a three-book contract. So tell us,' Vance purred, 'how much money that book earned?'

Harker said grimly: 'It only broke even.'

'Pity!' Vance said sarcastically. 'Now tell us about her fourth book, please.'

'She hadn't yet written it when she disappeared. That was the book she was researching in South Africa – when she came back we got married immediately. She was going to write the book while we sailed round the world.'

'And how did you feel about the financial prospects of this book?' Vance enquired.

Harker cleared his throat. 'Very positive.'

'Very positive?' Vance nodded. 'You had high hopes of it being another money-spinner, another bestseller?'

Harker shifted. 'Certainly, yes.'

Vance nodded sagely. 'And what was it to be about, when she got around to writing it? About South Africa's Truth and Reconciliation Commission?'

Harker swallowed. 'Correct.'

'Exactly!' Vance held up a folder. 'I know that because these are Josephine's notes about the Truth and Reconciliation Commission, which we found on your boat! Plus her ideas for the book – a diary of her thoughts about how the book should be written. And in these notes, Major Harker, she complains that you wish she would write a different book, that you're worried about all the money you've got invested in her.'

Luke looked at Charlie. Charlie looked at him. Harker said, disconcerted, 'She says that?'

'She certainly does, I'll get you to read it out to the jury if you like! But first tell us how you reconcile that with your statement a few minutes ago that you felt "very positive" about her new South African book.'

Harker did not look at Vance. He waved his hand. Vance waited, leering. Then:

'Can't answer the question?' Vance turned to the judge. 'May the record show, your honour, that the witness appears helpless, flummoxed, nervous.'

Charlie was on his feet. 'Objection! My client looks just fine! Just considering his response to a very broad question, that's all.'

'So be it, either way,' Judge Ludman said grimly. 'Proceed, Mr Vance.'

'So, Mr Harker, you were worried about Josephine's fourth book,' Vance said. 'Her second and third books were disappointments, you had contracted to pay four million dollars for three books, so you were a worried man?'

Harker took a deep breath. 'No. Harvest had got its

423

money back on the two preceding books, despite the disappointment.'

'Not worried? Josephine was hardly the "gold mine" you had expected when you insured her life for three million dollars!'

Harker looked flustered: 'Her potential was enormous,' he insisted.

'But *now*,' Vance said brightly, 'Harvest House is due to receive three million dollars' worth of insurance money from her death! And in terms of Josephine's will – which was made only six months ago – you'll inherit her forty-nine per cent shareholding in Harvest House – which, with your own two per cent, gives you control of the lot!' Vance smiled at the jury. 'So you would benefit by her death to the tune of fifty-one per cent of that three million dollars, *plus* the value of her shares.'

Harker said thickly, '*Harvest* will benefit – but only in the short term. In the long term Harvest will be the loser because they have no more books of hers to publish.'

'And you also persuaded her to take out an additional two hundred and fifty thousand dollars' worth of insurance which you would inherit on her death.'

'I didn't "persuade" her – we discussed it and she decided she should. A sensible investment.'

Vance smiled. '*She* paid the premiums? And in terms of her will *you* inherit her estate . . .' He looked at the jury and shook his head in admiration. He continued softly, 'And you didn't *persuade* her to make the will in your favour, perhaps?'

Harker said desperately: 'We discussed what to do about our wills. And we decided, together, that we would both make each other the principal beneficiary.'

Vance smiled. 'And the first thing you did was report her death to her life insurance company.'

'But I thought that was what would be expected of me!'

'Before you even advised her father?' Vance enquired softly.

'I sent a fax to her father straight afterwards.'

'One would expect a grief-stricken husband to advise family before anybody else.'

'I *was* confused,' Harker said shakily. 'I was also exhausted. Shocked. I was dreading telling Josie's father. That's why I sent him a fax so that when I spoke to him we had had a chance to compose ourselves.'

Vance nodded disbelievingly, then smirked at the jury. 'And then you faxed her lawyer who had drawn up her will in your favour.'

'*And* my will. In her favour.'

'You wanted him to start probating the will, didn't you?' Vance murmured.

'I have no idea what's involved in probate! I was simply advising everybody who I thought should know about Josie's death!'

Vance frowned. 'So you felt it was urgent to advise people?' Then he pounced: 'So why, oh *why* had you wasted a whole week sailing *into* the wind down to the Virgin Islands when you could have turned and sailed for Florida and reached there within two days?!'

Harker swallowed. 'It simply didn't occur to me. I was exhausted after searching for a solid night and day without sleep.'

'Exhausted? All the more reason to run for the nearest land.'

'I told you, I didn't think of it.' Harker waved a hand. 'My wife was dead. I was grief-stricken. I just wanted to get on to my destination and report to the authorities.'

'But America *was* the authority. Your boat was American, flying the American flag, technically you were on a piece of America. Josephine was an American. You had been living and working in America. You were exhausted and America was just a day's sail away – two at the most. And you tell us you didn't *think* of it?' Vance snorted. 'Come, come – and you a highly experienced military man? And then?' Vance held up his finger. 'Then, when you got to your destination,

425

to the Virgins, you were at last back in *American* territory, in St Thomas. And you even anchored, and slept off at least some of your exhaustion. And yet you *still* did not report to the American authorities! The US Coast Guard was right there, a few hundred yards from where you anchored!'

Old Charlie got to his feet. 'This is rhetoric! What is the question?'

'The question, Major Harker,' Vance leered, 'is *why* didn't you report the death of your American wife off your American boat whilst in American waters to the American authorities in *American* St Thomas?'

Harker breathed. 'I was going to . . . But I wanted to report to a senior officer, not to a junior on night-shift. The senior officers would not come on duty until about nine a.m. When I woke up at four, I simply could not bear to wait five hours. So I decided to use the time by sailing to the British Virgin Isles nearby, where Josie and I had intended going anyway. So I plugged on to there.' He picked up his glass and took a gulp of water.

'And you hoped,' Vance sneered, 'that the authorities in the British Virgins would not be as sophisticated as in St Thomas, didn't you?'

'That question did not occur to me.'

Vance cried, 'You had avoided the Americans like the plague for the last week!'

'What's the question?' Charlie cried.

Vance glowered: 'I put it to you, Mr Harker, that you ran for the British Virgin Islands because you hoped that they would be less *efficient* than in St Thomas!'

Harker swallowed. 'Not so.'

'Then perhaps you can explain this to the jury . . . You arrived in Tortola; you slept; you drank; you went ashore and reported to the immigration authorities – pretending Josephine was still part of your crew; you phoned Josephine's insurers; you sent a fax to her father; you faxed her attorney – and then you returned to your yacht and proceeded to drink a lot of rum!'

426

'What's the *question*?' Charlie cried, his arms spread.

Vance ignored him. 'If you were so anxious to report to the police, why did you report to everybody *except* the police? Why, having done all that was necessary to secure Josephine's fortune, did you *not* go to the police? *Why?*'

Harker took another gulp of water. 'Because,' he said, 'I was so tense. I had been living in a nightmare for a week, I couldn't bear to face the police yet. Couldn't bear to relive the nightmare until I'd had some more rest.'

'You needed to fortify yourself before facing the police with your lies?' Vance suggested.

'With the *truth*. Which they might not believe – like you don't.'

Vance smiled maliciously. 'You can say that again.'

Charlie jumped up. 'Objection, your honour, we're not interested in what Mr Vance believes, it's a most improper remark!'

'I apologize, your honour,' Vance said. 'The remark may be stricken.' He turned back to Harker venomously. 'Now, the next day police came and took you to the police station. You were questioned while detectives examined your boat. You finally made a statement. That night Commissioner Humphrey told you to come back the next day for more questioning, and he took possession of your passport. But the next day you tried to fly off the island. Why?'

Harker said, 'Humphrey did *not* tell me to come back the next day. He said he would study the evidence and then get me back for more questions. At some time. And as he was not arresting me he had no right to deprive me of my passport – I was free to go where I liked. I had been told by Immigration to return to Nassau for my port clearance papers. Rather than hang around waiting for Mr Humphrey, I decided to *use* the time. I had to *do* something.'

'So Mr Humphrey is a liar, is he, when he says he told you to come back at noon the next day?'

Harker swallowed. 'He is mistaken. Perhaps he thinks he said that but he certainly didn't make me understand that.'

'I see . . . However, you must have understood from the fact that Mr Humphrey took your passport away that you were not allowed to leave the British Virgin Islands. That you were a suspect – that much you must have understood?'

Harker coughed. Took a sip of water. 'I understood he wanted me to remain on the island, but not necessarily that I was a suspect – he hadn't charged me, he hadn't locked me up. Maybe he thought that because he was the local top cop he could restrict the movement of whoever he pleased. Big fish in small ponds get to think their authority is unfettered, I've seen it often in Africa.'

Luke closed his eyes and Charlie groaned softly. Vance pounced. 'And Mr Humphrey's ancestors clearly come from Africa! So you made a racist judgement against him and decided to defy his orders?'

'He didn't order me to return on any specific date,' Harker insisted huskily. 'I defied his . . . *implied* order not to leave the island *not* because he's black and self-important but because he had no right to take my passport away from me. And I was very distressed and I wanted to *do* something, get away from the boat, get out of myself. I had been told by Immigration to get back to Nassau, so that's what I decided to do, Mr Humphrey or no Mr Humphrey.'

Vance smirked. 'You expect the jury to believe that? It would have been clear to a blind man in your circumstances that to run away from the island would prove guilt – but you, Major Harker, experienced senior soldier, glibly tell this jury that you didn't feel under suspicion because you considered there was no basis for anybody to be suspicious because all that had happened was that your wife – who just *happened* to have made her will in your favour leaving you her forty-nine per cent of Harvest shares *and* millions of dollars' worth of insurance – had just happened to disappear overboard!'

'In the name of Justice,' Charlie cried, '*what* is the question?!'

Vance turned to the jury theatrically. 'I would have thought my question obvious. However, I'll simplify it: I put it to you that you're shamelessly and foolishly lying. That only a *fool* would have been unaware that he was under suspicion.'

Harker took a gulp of water. He said, 'Maybe I was unwise to ignore Mr Humphrey. But I was innocent, as far as I was concerned the man had no grounds for suspecting me, he was being pompous, making snide comments about my answers. I was . . . angry that he was adding to my torment with his stupid questions.'

'Really?' Vance sneered. 'Really?' Then he asked blandly: 'So do explain again to the jury how you, so *innocently*, came to be smuggling your illegal firearm with you when you attempted – illegally, with your *expired* passport – to leave the British Virgin Islands. You've told us that you did it because, as a soldier, you were simply accustomed to carrying arms. Yes?'

Harker shifted. 'Yes.'

'But,' Vance said, 'your firearm was packed in your bag which was going into the hold. *Concealed*. A soldier carries a weapon openly for constant use. Yours was hidden for *future* use, was it not?'

Harker's mind fumbled. 'I hoped it wasn't going to be used at all.'

'So it was for emergencies? Like shooting it out with police trying to arrest you for murder? But you knew it was illegal to bring your gun ashore, illegal to smuggle it on to the aircraft. *Didn't* you?'

Harker sighed. 'Yes, I knew it was illegal.'

'Like it was illegal when you smuggled it on to the plane in New York when you went out to join the boat. And then smuggled it into the Bahamas?'

Harker said desperately, 'But that proves that my purpose was innocent, doesn't it? When we left New York, Josephine was alive so there was no question of shooting it out with police, as you suggested.'

Vance grinned. 'Josephine was alive, yes. And Josephine had just made her will in your favour. You intended to murder her, so having your gun would be handy.'

Harker closed his eyes and shook his head.

'No?' Vance leered: 'So tell me – did Josephine know you were smuggling a firearm aboard the plane to the Bahamas? Did you make her an accomplice to those crimes?'

Harker was caught off guard. He hesitated. 'Yes.'

'You hesitated again!' Vance cried. 'Why?'

'Because . . .' Harker faltered, 'I was trying to remember.'

'Trying to remember? But Josephine was a law-abiding, sensible woman, wasn't she? And she was very excited about taking off to fulfil a dream of sailing the world. So wasn't she worried when she found out you intended smuggling a firearm into the Bahamas? Wasn't she horrified at the risk that you, both of you, could be caught out, arrested at the airport and sent to jail – that your whole dream could blow up in your faces because of one stupid gun? *Wasn't* she?'

Harker swallowed. 'Yes, she was worried but –'

'*Then, why did you have to try to remember?*'

Harker sat in the witness box, pale, his heart pounding. Vance let the silence lengthen. Then he said, 'You can't answer that question, can you? Because if Josephine had known she would have made such a fuss that you would remember clearly. So it's obvious that Josephine did *not* know. So, why you are lying?'

Harker swallowed. 'I'm not lying.'

'No? Well, we'll leave that to the jury to decide – and to wonder why. But while we're talking about guns, did Josephine know about the other pistol, the Smith & Wesson .38?'

'No,' Harker said.

Vance smiled. 'Oh, you've learnt your lesson, haven't you? But when you noticed it was missing you must have been worried?'

'Yes.'

'Yes, because the police regard stolen firearms as a serious matter, you know that?'

'Yes.'

'And you kept this gun in the glove-box of your car.'

'No, not usually. But I had put it there one trip when we went skiing, I think, and forgot it. Next time I looked it was gone.'

'Gone. And you must have been mystified. And worried, because if the gun were used by the thief to commit a crime and it was traced back to you as the registered owner, you might have been suspected of committing the crime. So why in heaven's name didn't you protect yourself – and do your legal duty – by reporting to the police?'

Harker gave a deep, tense sigh. 'I've told you: in the hurly-burly of packing up I simply forgot.'

Vance smiled. 'Despite the seriousness you, a senior military officer and successful publisher, simply forgot . . .' He smiled at the jury. 'I put it to you, Major Harker, that that gun was not stolen. That you smuggled it with the other one into the Bahamas, unknown to Josephine, and the .38 bullet that was found, which made the hole in the saloon cushion, was fired from that gun.'

Harker glanced at the jury, then shook his head. 'The hole was there when I bought the boat. The gun went missing long before.'

'Then why was the licence for it found in your wallet?'

'I simply brought it along with the other licence for the smaller Browning. I kept both licences together.'

'I put it to you that the licence was found on you because the gun was aboard originally, and fired the .38 bullet found in the cushion.'

Harker swallowed. 'If the .38 was on board, why wasn't it found?'

'*I* will ask the questions, thank you. But I will make an exception and answer yours. It was not found because you, Mr Harker, threw it overboard, after you had shot Josephine with it! To get rid of the evidence.'

431

The accusation hung. The courtroom was silent. All eyes were on Harker. He was very pale, his face haggard. He said huskily, 'Not so.'

Vance continued relentlessly: 'She probably threw that heavy book, the *Nautical Almanac*, at you in self-defence and it broke the glass of the speedometer. Josephine then fled aft, to the rear wheel, where you shot her. She fell and left the bloodstain on the deck. She then either staggered up and toppled into the sea, or you weighted her body and threw it overboard.'

Harker stared at nothing. 'Not so.'

'You then tried to scrub the bloodstain off the deck, using soap powder,' Vance continued. 'You deliberately damaged the radio by ripping out the transmitter to account for why you didn't radio for help. You also threw two life-rings and the life-raft over to make it look as if she had fallen overboard accidentally.'

Harker breathed deeply. 'I deny all that,' he said huskily.

Vance jabbed his finger. 'And *that's* why you didn't dash back to America, that's why you fled south to the faraway British Virgin Islands. To put as much distance and time as practical between you and the scene of the crime in the hopes that Josephine's murdered body was not found by the authorities when you finally reported to them.'

The courtroom was hushed. All attention was on Harker. He sat rigid, his face gaunt. 'None of that is true.'

Luke Mahoney sighed; he knew Harker was lying. He glanced at old Charlie: the man's eyes were hooded.

Vance was saying, 'And now, let's just go back briefly to that little airport in the British Virgin Islands, the day you were arrested. Do tell us again, Major Harker, what the destination on your ticket was?'

Harker took a deep breath. 'Guadeloupe. I intended buying an onward ticket to the Bahamas when I got there, once I knew what my flight options were.'

Vance nodded sagely. 'Indeed? How very sensible. All of us in this courtroom do that sort of thing all the time – when we want to fly to Canada we buy an air-ticket to Bermuda because once we get to Bermuda we will find out what our flight options are . . . *Very* sensible.'

'What's the *question*?' Charlie cried.

Vance smirked piteously at the old man, then at the jury, then he said to Harker, 'Last question, Major.' He paused. 'You sold forty-nine per cent of Harvest shares to Josephine for two-point-two million dollars, and you retained two per cent. The reason for this was that, between you, you owned fifty-one per cent and so the two of you could therefore control the company. Correct?'

'Correct,' Harker said hoarsely. He took a sip of water.

'*Very* sensible,' Vance said. 'Happens all the time . . . But, who owned the other forty-nine per cent of Harvest?'

Harker swallowed. He said: 'Westminster NV. A company in the Netherlands' Antilles.'

'Yes . . .' Vance said knowingly. 'And who owns Westminster?'

'It's . . .' Harker hesitated. 'It is a holding company for a number of shareholders who wish to remain anonymous.'

'Oh, understandable,' Vance said. 'But when it came to annual general meetings, how did the Westminster shareholders cast their votes?'

Harker took a tense breath. 'Through the Westminster accountant who was given proxies.'

Vance nodded. 'And you don't *know* the identity of these Westminster shareholders?'

Harker was ashen. 'Correct.'

Vance smiled. He walked slowly to the witness box, holding a document. He handed it to Harker and said, 'Is that your signature on this deed of sale, dated 1991?'

Harker closed his eyes. He took a deep breath. Then he glanced at the document.

'Yes,' he whispered.

'I put that document in as Exhibit Twenty-two, your honour,' Vance said airily. 'Tell the jury about it, Mr Harker.'

Luke and Charlie were staring in astonishment. Harker took a trembling breath.

'This is a deed of sale which says I bought all the shares in Westminster from the original shareholders in 1991.' He closed his eyes.

There was a murmur in the courtroom.

Vance let the answer take its full effect. Then he said softly, 'So you lied to us. You *do* know who the shareholders of Westminster are. *Yourself.*'

Everybody was staring at Harker. He had his eyes closed. He nodded faintly. 'Yes.'

Again Vance let that hang. Then, softly: 'Why did you lie to us?'

Harker still had his eyes closed. He shook his head.

'I'll tell you why . . .' Vance proposed. 'Because you did not want the jury to know that you alone still controlled Harvest House, even though you had sold forty-nine per cent to Josephine. Despite that sale, *you* controlled everything, because with the two per cent you retained, plus the forty-nine you bought from Westminster, *you* controlled fifty-one per cent – even without Josie's votes. No matter what happened, you could always outvote Josephine if you wanted to!' He paused, angrily. '*Or* her heirs, if she ever changed her will.' Vance glared then jabbed his finger. 'And Josephine had no idea of this, *did* she? Because, if she had known she would not have risked her money to buy your other forty-nine per cent!' He glared, then cried: '*Isn't that so?*'

Harker had his eyes closed. He remained silent. After a moment, Vance went on, 'And you did not want the jury to know all this because with Josie's forty-nine per cent which you inherit under her will *and* your Westminster shares you own one *hundred* per cent!' He paused for effect, then he cried, 'And as you own one hundred per cent, you'll have *all* of the three million dollars insurance Harvest had on her life, plus her own insurance, plus other assets such as her apartment! *And* the boat . . .' Vance paused, his eyebrows raised; then he said quietly, 'Nice work if you can get away with it.'

Harker was looking at him now, shaking his head. He said huskily, 'Not so.'

Vance smiled. 'No? Well, I make all those details I just mentioned total about six million dollars.' He paused. 'Isn't that about right?'

Harker stared at him, his face grey.

'Yes,' Vance said languidly, 'about six million, give or take a million . . .' Then he picked up Harker's bank statement and studied it theatrically, with a frown. 'And at the moment your bank balance, after paying off all your debts is . . .' His frown deepened. 'Only a little over nine thousand dollars.' He paused and looked at the jury with a smile. '*Wow* . . . Rags to riches, huh?'

'Objection,' Charlie cried. 'What's the question?!'

Vance smiled maliciously. 'The question, Mr Harker, is, did Josephine know, when she bought forty-nine per cent of Harvest, that you had bought Westminster? Did she know you would control Harvest even without her shares?'

Harker looked faint. Luke groaned under his breath; old Charlie cursed. Then: 'Yes,' Harker said huskily.

Vance smiled. 'You hesitated again, Mr Harker. Why?'

Harker closed his eyes. 'I didn't.'

Vance's smiled widened. 'So you're going to lie about that as well, in the face of the jury? Very well, sir, continue.'

Harker said, 'Yes, Josephine knew. But she still wanted to buy my shares in case I one day decided I wanted to sell the Westminster portion. If that happened, she could still control Harvest by exercising her option to buy back my other two per cent.'

Vance smiled, nodding, playing cat and mouse. '*Really?* If that's true why didn't you just tell us in the first place?' He let that hang; then he jabbed with his finger. 'I'll tell you why. Because it *isn't* true. You're lying again, aren't you, Mr Harker?'

Harker was shaking. Ashen. He said huskily: 'I'm not.' He blundered on: 'I didn't shoot Josephine . . . I don't know how she came to disappear! And that bloodstain on the transom is not hers, it's *old*!'

Vance was smiling at him. '*Really?*' he said. 'You don't *say* . . .' He turned to the jury, smiling for the cameras. 'No further questions,' he said. He turned to old Charlie. 'Your witness. What's left of him.'

Silence hung deafeningly in the courtroom. Then Charlie rose stiffly, to try to patch up his tattered, doomed client in re-examination.

But Charlie was smiling. He had his hands thrust deep in his pockets, pensively. He said to the ceiling, 'All very interesting . . . All *very* interesting, this dramatic speculation from my young learned friend . . . and *very* entertaining.' He turned his head and beamed at the jury. Then a frown clouded his benign countenance: 'Because, of course, it's all based on assumptions.' He shook his head. 'And, as any schoolboy will tell you, the conclusion drawn from *assumptions* is only valid if *all* the assumptions are proved to be true and correct!'

Vance rose to his feet warily. He drawled, with a weary smile for the camera, 'Your honour, this is not a question in re-examination, it is rhetoric – or argument. Can my learned friend please be told to get to the point?'

'Yes, Mr Benson?' Judge Ludman scowled.

'Oh,' Charlie said, palms up, broad enamel smile, 'all will become clear if Mr Vance will curb his endearing exuberance and listen for a change.' He turned back to Harker. 'As I was saying, Major, conclusions based on assumptions are only valid if each and every assumption or premise is correct, isn't that so?'

Harker swallowed. 'Yes,' he agreed.

Old Charlie waved a hand. 'For example,' he said conversationally, 'if the basic premise is: "Canaries have two legs," the uninitiated might be tempted to argue: canaries have two legs, Mr Jones has two legs, therefore Mr Jones is a canary.' The jury smiled. 'Ah, but there is a basic error in the premise or assumption, isn't there? What is it?' His finger shot up. 'Ah – it lies in those legs. So, Mr Jones can be a canary only if you start off with the premise: "*Only* canaries have two legs"! If *that* is your basic premise, then Mr Jones must indeed be a canary.' He beamed. 'But we know Mr Jones is not in fact a canary, don't we? So? So it is clear that what is logical can be patently *untrue*.'

'What,' Vance demanded, 'is the question?'

Old Charlie raised a finger. 'Ah, the question, quite right . . .' He beamed at Vance, then turned to Harker: 'Can you, in the name of all that's holy, tell me *why*, when you were at Tortola airport, if you were trying to collect all this life insurance of Josephine's, and all her other money and shares, why you would be running away like a self-confessed criminal from all the people who you had to cooperate with in order to get it? Namely, the insurance companies, the lawyers, the police, her father, Harvest House itself?'

Vance was back on his feet. 'Objection, your honour – this isn't evidence, this is argument!'

Old Charlie looked astonished. Grieved. Hurt. Cut to the quick. He spread his pink palms.

'*Why*, your honour?' he asked plaintively. 'What's Mr Vance's problem? His weakness in Aristotelian logic? What's he afraid of? Why doesn't he want the jury to think about these obvious weaknesses in the prosecution case?' Charlie looked deeply saddened by the way the administration of justice had fallen into dubious hands of late; he shook his head. 'Doesn't he want the jury to arrive at the truth?'

'Objection,' Vance groaned.

'Sustained,' Judge Ludman sighed.

Charlie's palms went up in submission again. 'As your honour pleases . . .' He turned to Vance and added, 'Anything for a quiet life, though I don't know what you're scared of, Ed . . .'

'Objection!'

Charlie cringed, shielded his ears and looked hurt. 'Very well, no further questions, your honour,' he said, deeply mystified by the injustice of his fellow man. 'I have no further witnesses.' He added with a catch in his voice, 'Josephine, alas, having disappeared . . .'

'Court will adjourn for lunch,' Judge Ludman said bad-temperedly. He turned to the jury. 'The evidence is now over, ladies and gentlemen. After lunch you will hear argument, the closing addresses of the prosecution and the defence, whereafter you will retire to consider your verdict.'

He banged his gavel. Everybody rose. He stalked out of the courtroom.

The people in the public benches shuffled towards the doors. Harker left the witness stand. He walked back to the defence table, exhausted.

'You *bastard*,' Charlie whispered at him. 'Sit down.'

Harker sat, drawn and trembling.

Charlie fiddled with papers angrily. He waited until the courtroom was almost empty, glancing about. 'You *bastard*,' he repeated. 'Why the hell didn't you tell me about those Westminster shares?' He glared, then threw down his pen in disgust and stood up. 'Well, I'm going for a drink! A *big* drink!'

Harker tried to grab his arm. 'Charlie – it's the truth . . .'

'Oh sure.' Charlie pulled his arm free, and turned for the door. Harker scrambled up and started after him but the guard grabbed his elbow. '*Sure*,' Charlie repeated as he stopped and looked over his shoulder. 'I'm mighty glad the evidence is over and there can be no more surprises.' He stabbed the air with his finger. 'At two o'clock we start the addresses to the jury, pal. You haven't made it easy for me. And right now I'm all you've got between you and the electric chair!'

He turned and stalked out of the courtroom.

49

The final arguments began at two o'clock that afternoon. The foyer outside court 4B was jam-packed with people, hundreds more milled on the wide stone steps of the justice building hoping to get in. Across the world people watched on television as Edward Vance, pacing elegantly, addressed the jury.

'A perfect murder – that is what the defendant thought he would achieve: no corpse to leave clues as to how Josephine died, no witnesses to gainsay his story – repeat *story* – that he simply woke up and found her missing.' He stopped and looked at the jury solemnly, then raised his finger. 'Ah – but he was so wrong! Because – as I promised you in my opening speech when this trial began – I will prove to you that the gossamer threads of circumstantial evidence hang as heavy as a millstone around his neck . . .'

Vance paused, letting that image form in their minds. Then he held up a finger, 'Thread number one: this is not even gossamer, it is very, very substantial. It is this: why did the defendant, after waking up to find his wife missing, after the horror of finding an empty wheelhouse, empty decks, after the frantic business of searching the sea for her – or so he *says* – *why* did he not turn his boat back to Florida where the authorities had all the resources to deal with his crisis?' He stared at the jury, then waved his hand. 'Fast, high-powered boats! Helicopters! Radios to call up all ships and tell them to keep a lookout for poor Josephine – who, if his story is true, might well have been alive because she was wearing a life-jacket – or she might have clambered aboard the life-raft he says he threw over.' Vance paused, looking at the jury in wonder; then his face creased into scorn. 'The defendant's answer is that he simply did not think of it!' He paused. '*What?*' He pointed at Harker. 'An experienced senior military officer, accustomed to the responsibility of thousands of men, to the screaming tensions of the battlefield, says "I did not think of it"!'

Vance stared at the jury with a sarcastic smile. 'Who does he think he's kidding?' He flipped his hand dismissively. 'And isn't it a remarkable coincidence, members of the jury, that he could not use his radio because the transmitter, by the most appalling bad luck, just happened to have broken that day? *That* day of all days, when he really needed it to send an SOS to all vessels to look for his missing wife!' He frowned in mock sympathy. 'What rotten luck!'

Vance picked up his glass of water and took a big swallow, then banged the glass down and cried, 'Indeed, as his radio was disabled wasn't there all the *more* reason for him to hurry to the American authorities in Florida?' The rhetorical question seemed to echo, then Vance dropped his voice, looking soulfully at the jury. 'That was thread number two, ladies and gentlemen.' He frowned. 'Now let's look at thread number three! And it is this . . .'

Vance paused for the cameras. Then he continued: 'The defendant finally arrives in the American Virgin Islands after seven days at sea. Seven days of nightmare, as he described it.' Pause. 'But does he go ashore and report Josephine's disappearance to the authorities? To the United States Coast Guard? To the people who have boats plying all over the area where Josephine disappeared, who had the resources to look for her body, solve the question of her disappearance?' His finger shot up. 'And perhaps even find her alive on the life-raft he threw over, or on one of the hundreds of Bahamian islands!' Vance paused again, glaring at the jury in wonder, then cried, 'Does the defendant do that?' He shook his head slowly. 'No . . . What does he do instead?' Vance smiled. 'He sleeps . . . He *sleeps*, ladies and gentlemen, *sleeps* when he could have had the resources of the mightiest nation in the world helping him look for his wife!' Vance glared at Harker, then dropped his voice. 'He sleeps . . . Then he sails on, *in the dark*, to the British Virgin Islands – which is a sleepy hollow with none of the resources of the US Virgins. And what is his reason for this? He says he was too tense to wait for the new day to begin. So he used up the time steaming through rocky waters, still into the wind . . .'

Vance looked at the jury, then frowned angrily. 'Is that the behaviour of a man who lost his beloved wife overboard and is desperate to tell the authorities?' He shook his head and his voice rose. '*No!* I suggest to you, members of the jury, that he sailed away from the US Coast Guard *because* he would rather have this matter investigated by the sleepy British Virgin Islands than the efficient US Coast Guard!'

Vance paused. Then his finger shot up again. 'But even then, when he arrived in Road Town, Tortola, and the world was wide awake, did he go ashore and report Josephine's disappearance?' He snorted. '*Again, no*. He finally went ashore, yes, and reported his arrival to Immigration, yes. But did he report Josephine's disappearance to Doris Johnston when he handed in his crew list? Did he?' His eyes widened. 'Not even when Mrs Johnston said Josephine had to report in person. Did he? No! Oh, he went on to report Josephine's death to her insurers, then he reported to her attorney, reported to her father – but did he report to Mrs Johnston and the police, the thing for which he says he had just slogged through seven days and seven nights on the high seas to do?' Vance paused, a little breathless. He shook his head in disgust. 'No . . . Having done everything necessary to make sure he inherits Josephine's estate, he returns to his boat and settles down to some *drinking*. In fact it is the police who have to go to him – *the next day!*'

Vance jabbed his finger at the floor angrily. 'And I suggest to you, members of the jury, that the defendant had not the slightest intention of reporting to the police! I suggest that if

Mr Humphrey had not gone out to the boat the defendant would have sailed away into the night! And if we need any confirmation of this we only have to look at his behaviour the following day!' Vance paused, with a righteous frown. 'What did Mr Humphrey say to the defendant at the end of the first day's questioning? Mr Humphrey is a very experienced policeman, and he tells us that he clearly told the defendant – whom he suspected of murder, remember; that's why he impounded both his boat and his passport – he clearly told the defendant to come back the next day at noon for more questioning. But the defendant denies this – he claims that Humphrey said that they would continue after he had considered the evidence. But I ask you two questions, members of the jury. One: which version is most *probable*?' He frowned. 'Isn't it more probable that Humphrey specified a time and date, having regard to the *seriousness* of the matter, the quantity of evidence and the fact that the defendant had a boat? And my second question is: why should we believe the defendant when his other behaviour up to this point has been so *sinister*? Why should we believe a man who has avoided reporting to the police for seven days and nights? Why disbelieve a sensible, experienced, honourable senior police officer like Mr Humphrey?' Vance paused, letting this question sink in. 'And now add to that what the defendant did the next day! Knowing he was suspected of murdering Josephine – because his passport had been taken away – and *without* informing Mr Humphrey of his intentions – he tries to sneak off the island – using an expired passport!' Vance spread his hands in eloquent appeal. 'I ask you, why was he so anxious to leave the island that he committed the crime of using an expired passport? Is that the conduct of an innocent man?'

Vance looked at his audience with beautiful big eyes, then shook his head. 'And if you're in any doubt, look at his excuse to the police when he was arrested!' Vance put his hand on his heart. 'He says he was only following

Mrs Johnston's orders to return to the Bahamas to get his port clearance papers.' Vance's eyes hardened and his voice rose. 'Then why did he try to take the plane to Guadeloupe, the French island, in the *opposite* direction to the Bahamas? When one or two hours later there was a perfectly good flight to Puerto Rico with onward connections to Miami and the Bahamas?' He paused, his brow crinkled in amazement. '*Why*, members of the jury, did he take that *opposite* direction just two hours before he had a further appointment with the Commissioner of Police? And *why*, if he was only leaving temporarily to go to Nassau, did he find it necessary to take his gun? Why did he take the very real risk of being prosecuted?' Vance put his finger to his brow. 'I suggest you won't have much difficulty deciding the answer to those questions! Or to the next: *is that the conduct of an innocent man?*'

Vance paused again, his eyes steely.

'And that brings us to the next three threads.' He smiled and glanced at some notes. 'We know that the defendant is a man who is prepared to break the law when it suits him; he admits he committed the serious offences of smuggling firearms aboard the aircraft in New York, smuggling arms into the Bahamas, we know he is prepared to break the law by using an expired passport. And we know he is a liar – because he has been caught at it.' Vance smiled with malice, then held up one finger. 'Firstly, he lied to us when he initially said he did not know the identity of the Westminster shareholders – when he himself is the owner, and therefore continued to control Harvest House even without poor Josephine having paid him over two million hard-earned dollars to buy his forty-nine per cent!' Vance looked at the jury in wonder. 'Oh, the defendant *claims* that Josephine knew he owned the Westminster shares – but why would Josephine spend over two million dollars to keep her and her husband in control of Harvest when she knew he already controlled it anyway?'

Vance paused, staring at the jury. Then he spread his

hands and appealed to them: 'I ask you, what kind of a man is it who cheats his own wife out of two million dollars? And why did this man lie to you about this point?' Vance jabbed his finger. 'Because he did not want you to know that once he inherited back the forty-nine per cent he had sold poor Josephine he would own one hundred per cent of the three million dollars insurance that he had taken out on her life in Harvest's name.' Vance stabbed the air again. 'I suggest to you good men and women that this proven *liar* –' he pointed at the defence table – '*lied* to poor Josephine so that he could *milk* her for every cent possible . . . Milk her own insurance policies, milk Harvest's insurance policy on her . . .'

Vance paused, still pointing. Then he continued softly: 'And now, with all that in mind, consider the question of the guns, which loom large in this case – very, very large! Because I suggest that poor Josephine met her death at the end of a gun!'

The cameras rolled. Judge Ludman had his eyes downcast, as did Charlie and Luke. Harker was staring at the floor.

Vance continued: 'Of course, the important detail about the little Browning is that the defendant lied to you when he said that Josephine knew he was smuggling it.' Vance smiled. 'This is *laughable*. It is overwhelmingly probable that Josephine would have kicked up a big fuss if she learned that her husband was about to jeopardize her dreams by smuggling a stupid gun aboard an airplane . . . !' Vance shook his head. 'And now we must bear these lies in mind when we turn to look at his story – repeat *story* – about the other gun, the missing Smith and Wesson .38!'

Vance paused, raised his glass of water and took an aggressive swallow.

'What is the significance of this missing .38 pistol?' He raised his eyebrows. 'It lies in the .38 bullet that was found in the saloon upholstery! And in the bloodstain on the transom – Group B, Josephine's blood group! What a pity that this pistol is missing because if we had it the ballistic experts could tell us whether or not it was the gun that fired the .38 bullet into the saloon! If it *is* the gun, the defendant would have to explain how a shot came to be fired from the master cabin down the corridor into the saloon . . . He would have to explain who fired his gun, tell us where Josephine was when the shot was fired. He'd have to explain why the shot was fired.' Vance paused, then cried, 'Obviously they had been fighting! But what were they fighting about?' Vance glared, then smiled. 'If we had found the gun the mystery surrounding the broken glass in the speedo, the bloodstain on the transom, the cuts on the defendant's body, would all be explained . . .'

Vance paused again, eyes fixed on the jury; then he gave a theatrical sigh. 'But, unfortunately, the gun was not found.' Then he held up his finger brightly. 'But the licence for it was found! And we know, from the defendant's own lips, that he successfully smuggled the other gun, the Browning, aboard the aircraft in New York and into the Bahamas, so we know that the .38 *could* also have been successfully smuggled! And what is the defendant's explanation for this vital missing gun?' Vance snorted. 'He says it was stolen. Oh, but did he report the theft to the police – as he is required to do by law? *No.* Why not? Sorry, I forgot!' Vance smirked again. 'Well, we know that he is a *liar* . . . And we know that he avoided turning back to Florida to report Josie missing, that instead he spent seven days battling into the winds to reach the British Virgin Islands. We know that he did not report to the police straight away as any innocent man would have done. We know that the next day he tried to leave the island against the wishes of the police, knowing that he was a suspect. And we know he was so desperate to leave that he attempted to do so with an expired passport on the first available plane even though it was going in totally the wrong direction for Nassau – *and carrying an illegal gun!*'

Vance paused again, his eyes both hard and soulful.

'And *what*,' he asked softly, 'is the defendant's explanation for all this, for what happened on that fateful night? What is this self-confessed *liar*'s explanation for all these gripping questions?' Vance glared, and spread his hands. 'He says "I don't *know* what happened, I just found Josephine *missing* . . ."'

Vance looked at the jury fiercely, the repository of the public's conscience facing the people's judges, then ended: 'Ladies and gentlemen, all these threads of circumstantial evidence hang as heavy as a millstone around the neck of this proven liar. I have no doubt that you will treat his story of "I know nothing" with the contempt it deserves, and convict him of murdering Josephine!'

That address to the jury was seen by many millions of people across the world. The trial had caught the international imagination and around the globe the vast majority decided that Jack Harker was guilty. In his office at the Royalton Hotel in Washington Felix Dupont turned to the American sitting in the armchair.

'He's a goner.'

'But he still has his appeal,' the American said. 'He won't dare say anything until after that, and then only if his appeal is unsuccessful. And that's probably a year away.'

Sitting in his study in the suburbs of Pretoria, General Tanner, formerly officer commanding Military Intelligence, watched Vance's address with mounting consternation.

'He's going to be convicted,' he said to his wife.

'But he hasn't spilt any beans so far.'

'That's because he thought he was going to be acquitted, as we all did. But when he's convicted and standing in the shadow of the electric chair it'll be a different story. At least they don't have the death sentence any more in New York State. Life imprisonment is better than the Chair.' He reached across his desk and picked up his telephone. He dialled.

446

'What do you think?' he snapped when the call was answered.

'Not good, sir,' Felix Dupont said.

'Is Plan A ready to roll if necessary?'

'Yes, sir.'

'And Plan B?'

'Yes, sir.'

In Miami, Luke Mahoney telephoned Ian Redfern in New York. 'Did you watch it?' he asked.

'Most of it,' Redfern said. 'What do you think?'

'This guy Vance is good,' Luke said. 'There shouldn't be a conviction but there sure could be. Depends on how good Charlie is, of course.' He added, 'If this were England he would be acquitted because the judge in his summing-up would sway the jury that way.'

'What do you feel, Luke?' Redfern said. 'Speaking not as a lawyer but as an ordinary guy, like the jury are – did he do it?'

Luke snorted softly. 'He's hiding something – he's not telling the truth. I'm damn sure the CCB is connected to all this but he's too scared to say it.'

Redfern sighed. 'And Charlie Benson still knows nothing about all that?'

'Of course not, you can't have the guy arguing a weak line of defence when he knows there's a much better one available. Anyway it's far too late now for Jack to change his story. But old Charlie has kept open the door to the notion of pirates possibly having boarded the yacht.' Luke glanced at his watch. 'I must go'n fetch him from Beauty's.'

'Beauty's?'

'Bar down the road where old Charlie refreshes himself every day.'

50

The public seating was full, the television crews crowded in their allotted space, the press tables crammed. As Charlie and Luke came up the street from Beauty's pressmen and cameramen converged on them with questions. Old Charlie forged his way through them, beaming his perfect smile, breathing gin, Luke following. They made their way into the building to a barrage of camera flashes.

Ed Vance and his team were seated at the prosecution table. Charlie sat down at the defence table and nodded at the court orderly. A moment later Harker entered, escorted by two policemen. He looked terrible. He crossed the court-room and sat down next to Charlie woodenly. Charlie put out his hand and patted Harker's.

'Relax,' he breathed. Then: 'Excuse me . . .'

Charlie picked up his water and made his way back to the entrance. He pushed his way back down the foyer to the public toilets. He pulled a half-bottle of gin out of his pocket and emptied it into his water flask, then pulled another bottle from his briefcase. It contained lime juice. He threw a dash into the flask, swirled it around, held it up to the light. He took two sips to check the strength, then a deep swallow for confirmation. He set off back to the courtroom. He made his way up the aisle to the defence table, and sat.

'Okay,' he said to the orderly, 'let's see Hizzonner.'

Charlie emerged thoughtfully from behind the defence table and paced slowly across the courtroom to the jury stand. He stood silent, in deep thought for a moment, ensuring that he had everybody's attention; then he began, his black face solemn.

'My learned friend, the Assistant District Attorney, has waxed eloquent about gossamer threads, ladies and gentlemen. But let me remind him of another gossamer thread, which is a *golden* one and which is the fundamental principle of our criminal law – and I quote from a famous British judgement.' Charlie picked up a volume, opened it and read: '"Throughout the web of English law one golden thread is to be found: *It is for the prosecution to prove the defendant's guilt, not for the defendant to prove his innocence* . . ."'

Charlie closed the book with a snap, and looked over his spectacles at the jury.

'And there is another principle of law I would like to remind the Assistant District Attorney of – and this is a matter of the simplest arithmetic. It is this: the combined weight of a gossamer thread that weighs nothing, when put together with another gossamer thread that weighs nothing, is *nothing*. Nought, plus nought, equals nought . . .' He smiled: 'I repeat: *it is for the prosecution to prove guilt, not for the defence to prove innocence!*' Charlie spread his hands. 'But is that not exactly what the District Attorney is demanding of the defendant – that he prove his innocence? The prosecutor has not a single fact pertaining to Josephine's disappearance! No corpse! No witnesses! No weapon! Yet he demands explanations for the unexplainable, and then pours scorn on them when he gets them!' He stabbed the air with his finger and cried, 'In other words, the only weapon the District Attorney has been able to use is *sarcasm*, and *sneering*, because he has nothing else! Repeat, *nothing* else!' He punched the air again. 'He cannot even prove that Josephine is *dead*, for Heaven's sake – he can only prove that she is missing! She might have grabbed one of the life-belts or the life-raft the defendant threw overboard. Josephine might have drifted to one of the many Bahamian islands, she might have lost her memory, she may be living like Robinson Crusoe – *anything* may have happened . . .'

Charlie paused, his eyes sliding over the jury's. He took a big, slow sip of gin-spiked water.

'And the District Attorney cannot even prove *how* Josephine came to fall overboard! He cannot prove whether she tripped, whether a sudden swell took her off balance, whether she was careless – whether or not, indeed, she took it into her head to commit suicide!' Charlie shook his head. 'So what does the District Attorney do, ladies and gentlemen?' He glared, then his finger shot up and he cried, 'As he cannot prove anything he tries to convince you that the defendant had a fight with her, shot her and pushed her overboard!'

Charlie let that hang, staring at the jury in amazement. Then he cried, 'This is absolutely *astonishing*! The District Attorney, who well knows the law – or should – tries to persuade you, because he can't prove anything, that the defendant must prove that he *didn't* shoot Josie, or *didn't* throw her overboard!' Charlie laughed. 'Is this what American justice has come to? This is crazy! And the DA knows it!' He grinned widely. 'So what excuse does the DA give you for this extraordinary revamping of the law – he points to the gash on the defendant's hip! It was caused by a knife, and the DA has the vivid imagination to allege that the knife was wielded by Josephine in self-defence!' Charlie stared. '*Self defence?* He can't even prove there was a matrimonial quarrel, let alone one that involved the use of knives in self-defence . . . And yet he asks you to fly in the face of the law! The defendant's evidence about this gash is that he must have inflicted it upon himself by accident when he tried to return his knife to its sheath – and he cut his arm when slashing the rope that secured the life-raft.' Charlie spread his hands. 'That's a perfectly credible explanation! The doctor agreed that that is a perfectly credible explanation. But what does the DA do? Scorn and sarcasm are his only weapons! And then, in desperation, he points at the traces of blood on the deck.'

Charlie snorted wearily, and shook his head.

'Traces of blood, yes, but *whose* blood? Can the DA prove it's Josephine's blood? No!' Charlie paused then went on softly: 'This boat was bought secondhand, ladies and gentlemen – secondhand. And boats are machines that can draw blood easily! I ask you, members of the jury, to consider how many cut fingers and grazed knees, not to mention bloody noses and extracted teeth, how much stray blood has been shed in *your* homes over the years!' He studied them; then he turned his palm towards Vance with a sad smile. 'But my learned friend tries to insist that you defy the law, and defy logic, and decide – *beyond reasonable doubt* – that that blood is Josephine's, and furthermore shed by the defendant when he murdered her!' Charlie stared in wonder, then clapped his hand to his forehead. 'How out of touch with both the law and reality can a District Attorney get?'

Vance got to his feet. 'Your honour, I object to the improper conduct the Defence is imputing to me! I demand a retraction!'

Charlie turned to the bench with big, innocent eyes, his palms spread.

'Me, imputing improper motives, your honour? Perish the thought! All I am imputing to my learned friend the Assistant District Attorney is complete lack of acquaintance with the rules of logic, an imperfect grasp of Criminal Law and a profound ignorance of the Law of Evidence! I repeat, your honour, the age-old rule, which seems to have deserted my friend, that the defendant does not have to prove anything, and that the proof that is required of the prosecution is proof beyond reasonable doubt – not sarcasm, sneering and *clutching* at straws!'

'*Objection!*' Vance sighed.

Judge Ludman growled at Charlie, 'Proceed. More tactfully.'

Charlie smiled. 'As your honour pleases, though it will be hard.' He turned back to the jury. 'And what is the next piece of weightless gossamer thread that the District

Attorney tries to lasso the defendant with? It is the fact that he could not use the radio to notify all shipping of Josephine's disappearance.' Charlie looked at the jury in wonder. 'But how could he? The transmitter was broken! So what does the District Attorney say about this useless transmitter – he asks you to conclude that the defendant *deliberately* broke it!' Charlie looked at the jury with a wide smile. 'This is incredible! The DA can't prove how the transmitter broke so he asks you to conclude that the defendant deliberately damaged it in order to conceal a so-called murder which the DA cannot prove took place! So the DA is trying to tell you that nought plus nought equals . . .' He shrugged. 'Equals what? The electric chair?' He snorted. 'Don't make me laugh, please. And the same applies to the detail that he headed for the Virgin Islands, not back to Florida . . .' Charlie spread his hands. 'Jack was convinced Josephine was dead. He was exhausted. Grief-stricken. So, having given up the search, he simply doggedly continues on to his destination, to report to the authorities there – that is entirely credible after the ordeal he had been through! So that point is another nought. And,' Charlie sighed, 'so is the next point the District Attorney made such a song and dance about . . .'

He looked at the jury wearily.

'*Really*, ladies and gentlemen, isn't the DA being very unrealistic in the heavy weather he makes of the defendant's arrival in the Virgins? The poor defendant had been battling the high seas, for six days and nights, for heaven's sake! Single-handed! The spray flying like grapeshot! Night and day, sleeping only in snatches. So when he arrives in the American Virgins in the middle of the night, he collapses asleep. But it was the *British* Virgins he was headed for, remember – he and Josephine had intended to go to the *British* Virgins. So when he woke up at four a.m., tense and grief-stricken, he couldn't bear to sit still and so it was *natural* for him to up-anchor and press on to the British Islands a few miles on.' He shook his head.

'So the DA's argument about this also adds up to another big fat nought!'

Charlie gave a long weary sigh, then rolled his eyes heavenwards.

'And so does his next argument, about the defendant's conduct on reaching the British Virgins . . . *Really*, have the prosecution such little worldly experience that they cannot imagine an exhausted sailor finally arriving at his destination in the early morning and collapsing asleep before facing the big wide world? Are the prosecution so *unaccustomed* to physical exertion that they cannot imagine the screaming need for rest when the exhausted sailor finally makes port?! Are they so *devoid* of human understanding that it must pour scorn on the sailor when he needs a few drinks of rum to fortify himself for the heartbreaking ordeal ahead . . .' He rolled his eyes heavenwards again. 'Members of the jury, can't we have some human compassion around here, instead of the worthless vitriol that Mr Humphrey heaped upon the defendant. Mr Humphrey has the sheer gall, the towering *arrogance* to try to lead you to believe that the defendant acted in a sinister way when he slept and then drank a few rums before going ashore . . . Most sinister that he first checked in with Immigration and then advised Josephine's family and her insurers of the heartbreaking tragedy – oh dear, most sinister that the poor, exhausted, grief-stricken defendant found it necessary to return to his boat and fortify himself with some more sleep before presenting himself to the police for the further ordeal of repeating the whole dreadful story.' Charlie shook his head at the jury. 'This self-important Commissioner Humphrey tells us we must definitely believe him when he says at the end of that first day's questioning – at which Mr Humphrey scored another big fat nought – that he told the defendant to return for more questioning the next day . . .'

Charlie looked solemnly at the jury, then he rasped, 'Why should you believe Mr Humphrey, who has an axe to grind? It's only one man's word against another, so there must be a doubt and you are legally bound to give the benefit of that doubt to the defendant. And even if Mr Humphrey *did* tell the defendant he had to come back the next morning, isn't it highly possible that the defendant, because he was exhausted and heartbroken, misheard and genuinely thought Humphrey said something else? Either way the benefit of the doubt *must* be given to the defendant. So this point also adds up to another nought!' Charlie looked at the jury, then spread his hands eloquently: 'And that being so, the fact that the defendant used his expired passport when trying to leave the island does not prove a darn thing! He had been *told* by the Immigration Department to return to the Bahamas to get his port clearance papers. The fact that he did not have a valid passport would not deter a man like Major Harker. He is a man of action, a soldier who has been in a hundred battles, a man accustomed to taking risks and he was not about to let any petty detail about expiry dates stand in his way. It would be unlikely that any immigration official would check the passport date. And the worst that could happen would be that he was turned away. "What the heck" was his attitude.'

Charlie looked at the jury with big solemn eyes.

'And the same "what the heck" attitude applies to his smuggling the Browning pistol aboard the aircraft. Good heavens, we must never forget that the defendant is a hard-bitten, veteran soldier to whom guns are almost part of his clothing. He packs a gun like you and I would pack our pen and credit card. The DA's suggestion that the gun somehow proves that he intended to run away and if necessary "shoot it out with the police" is absolutely ludicrous. The DA conveniently forgets that the Immigration Department's head had *ordered* him to return to Nassau. And if he was running away he would surely take more than the small bag of clothes he took. But more than all that, *why* would he run away and thus tacitly admit that he was guilty? *Why* would he run and thus abandon his beloved yacht, and all the insurance money and shares the DA accuses him of wanting so badly that he was prepared to commit murder? *Millions* of dollars' worth! Why should he throw all that away? What utter nonsense that suggestion of the DA's is! Ridiculously improbable!'

Charlie paused and took a big swallow of his gin. He licked his lips and continued, 'And let's quickly deal with that other piece of nonsense the DA asks you to believe – that Josephine did not know he was smuggling the Browning pistol aboard the aircraft in New York because she would have made such a memorable fuss that the defendant would not have hesitated in his answer.' Charlie frowned, with a smile. 'Now the DA is also a thought-reader, is he? He has never met Josephine. Who is the only person here who knows Josephine – the defendant! And what does he say about this? He says he remembers now that when he told Josephine about the gun they were already in Nassau and while she was surprised and a bit concerned that he had taken that risk the problem was past now and she immediately dropped the subject, being a pretty laid-back gal who had gone into scores of war-zones with soldiers like the defendant.' Charlie waved a dismissive hand. 'So forget that bit of nonsense . . . And,' he sighed long-sufferingly, 'while on the subject of guns let's get rid of that other stupid missing gun the DA's been ranting on about –'

'Objection!' Vance cried. 'Mr Benson's manner towards me and my argument is most unethical. I have not been "ranting" –'

'Why is the DA so afraid of the jury hearing my arguments?' old Charlie appealed. 'Goodness me, we had to put up with enough of *his* rubbish –'

'*Objection!*'

'Mr Benson . . .' Judge Ludman rumbled.

'Oh all right,' Charlie sighed, turning to the jury wearily, 'forget I said it was rubbish. But let's look at his fallacious argument about this mysterious missing .38 Smith and

Wesson, for the absence of which he seeks to send the defendant to the electric chair on the grounds that this gun, which we have never seen, never sent to the ballistic experts, is the murder weapon which shot poor Josephine – who the DA can't prove is dead – causing the unidentifiable bloodstain on the transom . . .' Charlie looked at the jury, then his face broke into an incredulous grin. 'Have you perhaps got a better yarn to give us a laugh?' He shook his head in disbelief. 'What wonderful fairyland logic the DA uses! Because the defendant's gun cannot be found, he says it must be the murder weapon! Of course, the DA forgets it is his job to prove guilt, not mine to prove innocence.' Charlie paused, then thundered, pointing at Vance, '*His job, not mine!* But what does he do? He forgets, and says because the defendant once upon a time *owned* a .38 pistol – and because a .38 bullet was found in the saloon upholstery – of this secondhand boat – and because an old Group B bloodstain was found on the transom – and there are *millions* of people running around this topsy-turvy world the DA lives in which even he must admit have Group B blood – and because *no* .38 gun was found on the boat, therefore –' Charlie stabbed the air – '*therefore* the defendant shot Josephine with it!'

Charlie looked at the jury in wonder, then his face crumpled into his beautiful smile. 'If that's the type of evidence the DA asks you to send a man to the electric chair on, then God help America! God help Justice! And I'm a white man!'

The court erupted into titters, in which old Charlie joined heartily.

'In conclusion, ladies and gentlemen of the jury – and I thank you for your attention – let me deal with the DA's celestial choir act over the shareholdings in Harvest –'

'*Objection!*' Vance cried. 'I demand a retraction!'

Charlie turned to Judge Ludman, mystified. 'What's my learned friend's problem now, your honour? Just because I called his argument nonsense?'

'*A celestial choir act*. And I demand a retraction!'

'"A celestial choir act"?' Charlie repeated, looking around the courtroom. 'Did I say that? By golly, that's good, I must remember that. But if I said it, your honour, I certainly retract it because it is far too good a description to apply to his arguments about the shareholding in Harvest House – fallacious is a more down-to-earth word, illogical is more appropriate, perhaps, as I am no longer allowed to use the word "rubbish" –'

'Objection!'

'Yes, yes, yes,' Charlie said, holding up his hands, eyes screwed up in pain, 'yes, we've got the message, Ed, so I'll rephrase the proposition. Members of the jury,' he said, turning to them with a patient smile, 'yes, I must admit, as the defendant himself admitted to you, shame-facedly but honourably, that he initially misled you over this unimportant detail concerning the shareholding in Westminster NV.' He paused. 'Ladies and gentlemen, there is nothing sinister in a businessman concealing aspects of his finances from his family. Good heavens, there are whole nations that make a *living* out of ensuring confidentiality to businessmen – Switzerland, Isle of Man, Bermuda, several islands in the Caribbean. If you asked any businessman who had taken the trouble to be protected by the secrecy laws of those countries about his affairs he would either tell you it's none of your darn business, or he would lie – to do anything else would be *stupid*. And that surely was the situation the defendant was in: this holding company called Westminster owned forty-nine per cent of the shares of Harvest: the defendant bought Westminster *and nobody knew it* – so why tell Josephine?' Charlie glowered and waved his finger around. 'I bet there's many a man in this courtroom right now who has not told his wife everything about his financial life! The defendant was not *cheating* Josephine – when he died *she* would inherit Westminster and then own a *hundred* per cent of Harvest! The only reason why he didn't admit it to this court in the first place was because he knew the DA would make such a fuss, imputing a sinister motive to it!' Charlie looked at the jury solemnly, then shook his head and waved his hand dismissively: 'So you can forget about that shareholding nonsense.'

Charlie took a swallow of gin, then shook his head sadly.

'Ladies and gentlemen, nobody except Josephine knows what happened in the dark small hours of that fateful night in the Gulf Stream. *You* don't know, the defendant doesn't know and the District Attorney –' Charlie pointed at the man – '*certainly* doesn't know! Hasn't a *clue*, if you'll pardon a pun. All these so-called gossamer threads he boasts about add up to nothing. And let me remind you of that *golden* thread, that it is for the *prosecution* to prove guilt – *beyond reasonable doubt* – not, repeat *not* for the defendant to prove innocence, as the DA seems to suggest.' Charlie paused, then his finger rose, and his voice, 'But I submit that the defence *has* in fact proved a great deal, namely that each one of the prosecution's threads weighs nought! And nought, ladies and gentlemen, multiplied by ten is still *nought*.' Old Charlie considered the jury solemnly. 'Ladies and gentlemen, you don't know what happened that night, because the DA cannot *prove* what happened . . . It is therefore your legal *duty* to *acquit*.'

That address by Charlie Benson was seen on television across the world. Most of the people who heard it were spellbound. Almost everybody, whether for or against Jack Harker, considered it brilliant, and many of those who had been convinced of Harker's guilt were now either uncertain or persuaded of his innocence.

In Pretoria, General Tanner snatched up his telephone and dialled the Royalton Hotel in Washington. 'What do you think?' he demanded.

Dupont said: 'Our legal advisor says he should get off.

458

That nigger did a good job. But you never know with juries. It's that lie Harker told about his Westminster shareholding that worries me.'

'The stupid bastard, the jury'll see that as cheating Josephine,' General Tanner said angrily. He sighed. 'Well, we've still got Plan B if he's convicted. But Plan A would be much better. You've got all the bases covered?'

'Yes.'

Derek Clements watched Charlie's speech in the saloon of a Grand Banks motor-yacht anchored off a remote island in the Bahamas chain. When the jury was escorted out to consider their verdict he picked up his telephone and dialled Felix Dupont but found the number engaged. He dialled another number and a Hispanic man called Ricardo, sitting in a car parked outside the Miami courthouse, answered. Two men sat in the back seat.

'It looks like Plan A,' Clements said. 'One shot. That's all you can afford. Then drive like hell. Fuck it up and you'll fry.'

'But if it turns out to be Plan B, when does the bait arrive?'

'You'll be advised, don't worry.'

'Look, a guy's gotta sleep. And eat and shit and shower. Now Plan A can happen at any moment, any fucking moment the jury can walk back in. But all I know about Plan B is that it starts after midnight of fifteenth December. Day after tomorrow's the fifteenth. *When* after midnight? One minute? One hour? One day? One week?'

'Of course it won't be one week, asshole. In a week on Death Row his nerve could go, he sings and we're all in the shit. It'll be sometime on December sixteenth. Daylight. Seventeenth latest. But make sure you get a good night's sleep on the fifteenth.'

Luke Mahoney telephoned Redfern from Beauty's Paradise. Old Charlie sat down the far end of the long bar, closest to the stage, happily sucking gin through a straw while he watched the girls go through their bump-and-grind routine.

'Yeah, Charlie was good,' Redfern said, 'told you he would be. There should be an acquittal. But if he's convicted it should be a cinch on appeal.'

'If he's convicted it'll be that damn-fool lie about Westminster that sinks him.'

'Plus that damn bullet in the upholstery and that missing gun he failed to report to the police. And the fact he tried to skip the island. But that gun will be a problem for the jury. That's the murder weapon if there is one, Luke,' Redfern said. 'That's what the jury'll think. And, frankly, it's what I think – and if I secretly suspect he shot Josie with that gun, then the jury is very likely to suspect the same.' He added, 'Particularly after his lie about the shares which appears to give him a motive.'

They were very long hours waiting for the jury's verdict.

Harker was accustomed to contemplating death, accustomed to the waiting before going into battle, accustomed to fear, but he never became cavalier about it. While you waited you could play cards maybe, watch a video, write a letter, but grow blasé about the prospect of battle? Never. But while you're waiting you have the consolation that your fate is at least partly in your own hands because you're a good soldier, highly experienced, a crack shot, you're fit and for Chrissakes you intend to come out of this battle alive like you've done a hundred times. *Think positively.* High morale, that's the biggest trick. But when you're facing death at the hands of a jury, at the whim of twelve people out of the telephone directory, people who have not taken a single note of any scrap of the evidence, it is far, far worse than going into any battle.

'Try to be calm,' Luke said. 'I really don't think a reasonable jury can convict on this evidence. A judge wouldn't.'

'Then why are they taking all this time to decide?'

'Because juries are like that, they haven't got the experience to marshal facts and law rapidly.'

'Then why the hell are they sitting in judgement?'

'That's the law.'

'Some fucking law.'

Harker paced across the conference room, haggard. 'But people don't understand about proof beyond reasonable doubt. They believe any gossip. Like housewives over the backyard fence. Like troopers in their pub. You should hear the crap those guys talk – nice guys, but they'd believe just about anything I told them because I was their commanding officer.' He looked at Luke, fear in his eyes. 'People are fools And this bunch of fools wants to convict me.'

'Not true.'

Harker snorted. 'There're five blacks, they all deeply dislike my South African military background, very suspicious, you can see it in their eyes. Josephine was as American as apple-pie, and I'm a goddam Rhodesian who fought for the South Africans – which they think means fighting for apartheid. Where's Charlie?'

'Down the road,' Luke said, 'in Beauty's Paradise, unwinding. I've come over to see if you'd like something to eat.'

Harker paced. 'A bottle of rum, but as I can't have that I need a big, rare hamburger.'

'Onions? Relish? Fries?'

'The works. And a king-size cup of Coca-Cola made up of fifty per cent rum.'

'You got it,' Luke said.

As the lawyer turned to leave, Harker said, 'One question.'

Luke stopped. 'Yes?'

Harker waved a hand. 'That witness, Mr Mayton, from Manufacturers Life Insurance – he said the law is that nobody can be permitted to benefit from his crime. Is that right?'

'Yes,' Luke said.

Harker said worriedly, 'I can understand that about the life insurance, but does it also apply to Josephine's other assets, like her shares and her royalties and apartment, et cetera?'

Luke looked at him. 'Yes.'

'So if I am convicted I get absolutely nothing under her will?'

'Correct,' Luke said stonily.

'Then who inherits her estate?'

Luke said guardedly, 'In principle, Josie's estate would be distributed according to the laws of intestacy. I'm not sure about American law on this point but as she has no siblings, it seems her father will probably get most of it.'

'Her father.' Harker sighed bitterly. 'But if I'm acquitted I'll inherit everything under her will – unconditionally?'

Luke looked at his cousin, trying to keep the stoniness out of his eyes. 'Yes, except for the insurance monies. The insurance company can resist your claim in a civil court if they can prove – on "a balance of probabilities", instead of "beyond reasonable doubt" – that you murdered Josephine.'

Harker stared at him. 'You mean that if I'm acquitted, I could have to go through this all over again in a civil trial over the life insurance?'

'Yes,' Luke said.

Harker closed his eyes. He dragged his hands down his face. 'Jesus Christ,' he groaned.

Luke looked at him narrowly. 'What's so surprising about that?'

Harker took a deep breath, and turned away. He paced. 'Nothing, I suppose,' he said. Then: 'It's just that I'm wondering how the hell I'm going to pay poor old Charlie and Redfern if I'm convicted.'

Luke dearly wanted to believe the answer was genuine.

He said, 'I'll go'n get your hamburger.'

*   *   *

It was almost seven o'clock that evening when the messenger came into Beauty's Paradise to announce that the jury had reached their verdict. Simultaneously another messenger entered the Regency Bar where Vance and his team were refreshing themselves. All the lawyers hurried back to the courthouse. Old Charlie arrived five minutes after everybody else, because he had to swallow one last gin. Harker was already seated at the defence table when Charlie slumped down beside him, exhaling alcoholic fumes. Across the world people saw him beam at Harker and whisper something to him.

'Why the fuck didn't you tell me about them Westminster shares, you cowboy?'

'I'm sorry.'

Charlie smiled. 'Not as sorry as your ass is gonna be if they offer you a sit-down in Old Sparky.' Then he relented. 'But I'll get you off on appeal. Here,' Charlie slopped a big shot of his gin-water into Harker's empty glass. 'Indulge in some of this.'

Harker took a big swallow and millions of people across the world saw his eyes widen as he almost choked. 'Christ . . .'

There was a rap on the door and the orderly shouted, 'All rise.'

Everybody stood. In walked Judge Ludman. He stalked to his bench, then he nodded to the bailiff. The bailiff went to the door leading to the jury room. Everybody remained standing. There was a rap on the door; it opened and in filed the jury.

They walked self-consciously across the silent courtroom to their stand, and filed into it. They stood at their seats until everybody was in place. They looked at Judge Ludman, who then solemnly took his seat. Everybody sat.

The court clerk intoned: 'Members of the jury, have you reached a verdict?'

'We have,' the foreman with the bald pate and wire-rimmed spectacles said. He handed a folded slip of paper to the bailiff.

The bailiff walked across the courtroom with it and passed it up to the judge.

The judge read it. He glanced at the lawyers expressionlessly. Harker's heart was pounding. Judge Ludman cleared his throat, then said:

'The verdict is . . . Guilty.'

A murmur ran through the courtroom. Harker stood, staring blankly. His head was swimming. He gripped the edge of the table. Judge Ludman sat forward and looked at him.

'Mr Harker, you have been convicted of murder in the first degree. As regards sentence, that means –'

Harker blurted huskily: 'I did not murder Josephine. You are sentencing an innocent man, your honour.'

Judge Ludman made a note.

There was a ringing in Harker's ears. He went on, 'I'd like to consult my attorney, please . . .'

51

Charlie sat at the table in the conference room, a cigarette poised in front of his mouth, astonishment all over his face.

'Jesus Christ . . .' he said. 'Why didn't you tell me this before?'

Harker paced. 'How could I? I'd already told the police in Tortola that I didn't know what happened; if I changed my story nobody would believe anything I said ever again.' He took a deep breath and turned to Luke. 'And anyway, if I told the truth I would be prosecuted for the Long Island murders.'

Charlie was astounded. '*What* Long Island murders?'

Harker slumped down at the table and held his face. 'Tell him, Luke.'

Luke Mahoney clasped his hands on the table and looked at Charlie. 'You're not going to like this. But I couldn't tell you because, firstly it would have placed you in an unethical position, and secondly because Jack forbade me to tell you.'

'Forbade you to tell me *what*, for Chrissakes?' Charlie demanded.

Luke sighed again. 'Okay . . .' He briefly summarized the facts concerning the Long Island massacre.

Charlie stared at the table throughout the narrative. Then:

'Jesus Christ . . .'

Harker said: 'But the CCB was officially disbanded five years ago. And I bought out all the CCB's shares in Harvest – first the shares I nominally owned on behalf of the CCB, then Westminster's shares which were indirectly owned by

465

the South African army. That's why I thought it best to lie about my Westminster purchase, so I didn't have to explain who I bought Westminster *from*. I didn't want to open a can of worms.'

Old Charlie shook his head in exasperated wonder. 'Jesus Christ, you can say that again. *And* again . . .' He banged his hand on the table. 'And so these bastards who boarded your yacht pretending to be pirates were really CCB hit-men who intended to kill you?'

'And intended to kill Josephine,' Harker said. 'Then steal the yacht and sink it to make it look like the work of drug-runner pirates.'

Charlie shook his head. 'Jesus Christ, now you tell me . . .' He took an exasperated breath. 'But when you finally got to the British Virgin Islands, why didn't you just tell the police that you were attacked by common-or-garden pirates, whom you'd never seen before and would never recognize again?'

Harker was holding his ashen face.

'Because,' he breathed into his hands, 'I shot three of the bastards. Dead. And I *did* recognize them. Two were American CIA agents who had worked with the CCB for years – one I only knew as Fred, or Froggy Fred. The other I only knew as Beauregard. Two tough bastards. I pulled their balaclavas off after I shot them. I knew that if their bodies were found by the US Coast Guard they would be identified and definitely *not* mistaken for pirates, and if I had confessed to shooting them with my .38 – or to shooting any so-called pirates – the cat would have been out of the bag. The Coast Guard would have wondered why I described well-known CIA agents as pirates, why they were aboard my boat – and the whole CCB connection would have begun to emerge.' Harker ran his hand over his chin. 'It was much safer just to weight their bodies, heave 'em overboard and say I simply found Josie missing.'

Charlie groaned. 'Now he tells me . . .'

'For Christ's sake,' Luke said, 'if he'd told you upfront

about this you couldn't have defended him ethically. You'd have had to tell him to get another lawyer.'

Charlie said: 'I assure you I don't want to continue defending him now!' Then he closed his eyes. 'Sorry, I take that back. I'm just shell-shocked.' He looked at Harker. 'So how did you get the wounds to your hip and arm?'

Harker said: 'The arm wound was caused by Fred when he tried to stab me in my bunk. I fended the blow off and he got my arm. We wrestled for the knife, I butted his nose, I grabbed my Smith & Wesson pistol, he staggered down the corridor, I shot, missed, he stumbled up into the wheelhouse. I then shot him in the chest, he staggered to the transom and collapsed. Beauregard sprang at me and I shot him dead. Another bastard jumped at me, I shot him dead too. I saw an inflatable boat out in the darkness, at least two people in it, I fired at it – it sped away. Then I saw a big motor yacht about a mile away – the inflatable was heading towards it. I looked for Josie. Nowhere. I dashed below. Nowhere to be seen. Panic. I dashed topsides. Nowhere. I dashed below again and got my hunting rifle –'

'*What* fucking hunting rifle?' Charlie demanded incredulously.

Harker sighed. 'I should have told you. Anyway, I had a high-powered, telescopic hunting rifle, because if you're going on the high seas, around the world, you're going to need at least one rifle to deal with trouble. So I bought one in Fort Lauderdale when I bought the boat. I hid it under the deck-boards and so it arrived in Nassau when the yacht was delivered, without any trouble. Anyway, I ran below and got this rifle and blasted off at the motor yacht to intimidate it – I was frantic. Meanwhile my yacht was steaming on into the tradewinds on automatic pilot.' Harker sobbed once into his hands.

Charlie waited. 'Then?'

Harker wiped his eyes with the back of his wrist. 'Eventually I went down to the body at the transom. I pulled his balaclava off his face, saw it was Froggy Fred, CIA. I weighted him and threw the bastard overboard. That bloodstain? It's his, not Josie's. The motor-yacht and the inflatable had disappeared. I then checked the other body – it was Beauregard, also CIA. I then looked at the third bastard. And it was Ferdi Spicer. He was one of my men who disappeared shortly before Josie and I left New York. I thought he intended to run to the Truth Commission to get amnesty for the Long Island murders, then turn prosecution witness for the DA when we were prosecuted – that's one of the factors that made me decide to buy the boat and disappear.'

'So you threw all the bodies overboard. Then?'

'I turned the yacht around, to look for Josie. Threw the life-rings and life-raft over the side.'

Charlie sighed and stood up. He began to pace.

'So the CCB tried to murder you – and succeeded only in murdering Josie. They tried to kill you to stop you confessing to the Long Island murders to this Truth Commission.'

'You know about the Truth Commission, and its amnesties?'

'I've read about it.'

'Tell him, Luke,' Harker sighed grimly.

Luke briefly summarized the legal situation. He ended: 'The amnesty cut-off date is midnight tomorrow night, South Africa time.'

'But,' old Charlie said, 'did you *intend* to confess to the Truth Commission and apply for amnesty?'

'No. Because I would be prosecuted in America. But those CCB bastards thought I *would* confess to the Truth Commission, thought I would make a deal with the New York DA to testify for the prosecution in exchange for immunity, and drop them in the shit.' Harker dragged his hands down his face. 'But now that I'm about to be sentenced to death, do you think I should confess to this judge? At least there's no death sentence in New York.' He looked at Charlie, then at Luke. 'What do you advise?'

468

Luke shook his head. Charlie said, 'No. Too late – nobody will believe you now. In fact they'll probably say you did both crimes, the Long Island murders *and* Josie's murder. No, my friend, you should only change your story as the very last resort if your appeal has failed. Then we make an application to reopen your trial because of this fresh evidence and we strike a deal with the New York DA to get immunity in exchange for giving evidence for the prosecution about the Long Island murders. And you've got a *very* good chance of getting off this murder conviction on appeal, remember, because all the prosecution's evidence is circumstantial – they can't even prove definitely that Josephine is *dead*, for Christ's sake!' Charlie sighed angrily and shook his head. 'No, you don't change horses yet. Agree, Luke?'

'I agree,' Luke said grimly.

'So all you can do now, pal, is put a brave face on it. And go back up there to the court and be sentenced.'

On the steps of the courthouse James A. Hunter, CNN anchorman, stood in front of his camera and solemnly told the world:

'This is a very dramatic time. The jury have returned their verdict of guilty. The judge has discretion as to whether the sentence should be death in the electric chair or life imprisonment. But at the eleventh hour, the defendant, Jack Harker, has asked for time to consult his attorney. What is going on in the conference room can only be speculated upon, but it is certain to be charged with life-and-death drama. Amongst the public who has jam-packed the gallery for days and whom you see behind me overflowing on to these balmy streets, speculation and vicarious suffering is rife. This trial has evoked great emotion both against the defendant and in his favour. But now let's cross back to the studio . . .'

'Thank you very much indeed, James,' Donald Booker in the CNN studio said as if he had been done a great and unexpected service, 'and we have here as always over the last ten days, Professor Alex Stevens from New York University – good afternoon, Professor.'

'Good afternoon,' the podgy, middle-aged professor said. He had freckles, a youthful crewcut and a bow-tie.

'What do you make of this eleventh-hour adjournment?'

'Well, the defendant is simply instructing his attorney, Charles Benson, to make a plea in mitigation . . .'

Meanwhile the Sky TV reporter was interviewing Josephine's father at the other end of the courthouse steps. 'Mr Valentine, how do you feel about the verdict of guilty?'

'Justice has been done,' Denys Valentine said stonily.

'Did you ever have any doubt about the defendant's guilt?'

'None whatsoever.'

'And what sentence do you want to see?'

Denys Valentine said flatly, 'Life imprisonment. And I mean *life*, until his death. The taking of human life in retribution is not acceptable, but the man must rot in prison for the rest of his days.'

Those scenes were televised around the world. In Pete's Tavern off Union Square in New York where Josephine's Anti-Apartheid Leaguers held their daily vigil monitoring the television coverage there had been cheers when the jury returned their verdict. In Harvest House the staff monitored the television in the receptionist's office, people constantly sticking their heads in seeking updates: there was consternation when the word spread through the building, '*Jack's been found guilty . . .*' From the officers' mess of the South African Defence Force in Pretoria the news spread like wildfire. In the leafy suburbs of Pretoria, General Tanner cursed, snatched up his telephone and called Felix Dupont in Washington.

'So it's Plan B. You got that?'

'Yes sir.'

The general groped for words. 'What a fuck-up!'

470

'Our advisor was confident of an acquittal, sir.'

'Fucking lawyers!' Tanner said. 'And what's happening now, what's he telling his attorney? If it's what I think we're all in big trouble!'

'Plan B will straighten it out, sir.'

General Tanner said, 'It better, my friend, or you're very dead meat. So get your ass out to Nassau!'

'They're going back into court now,' Dupont said. 'I must get back to the television, sir. Good day to you, sir . . .'

Charlie paused outside the courtroom. 'Okay, stiff upper lip, as the English say. And both lips zipped: "I deny the charge, your honour." That's all. Take the sentence on the chin. Repose your confidence in the appeal court. Okay?'

Harker nodded, ashen.

They filed into court, following the bailiffs. A buzz went up as people strained to see the man who was about to be sentenced. Harker followed Charlie to the defence table.

The prosecution team were already at their table. The jury were in their stand. They flitted their eyes guiltily at Harker, then looked away. The public benches were packed. Charlie sat down at his table and nodded at the orderly.

There was a rap on the door. 'All rise!'

His Honour Judge Ludman stalked into court. He glared around, then slowly sat.

Charlie and Harker remained standing.

'Yes, Mr Harker?' Judge Ludman said. 'Having consulted your attorney, do you have anything further to say on the matter of sentence? And how – under oath or in an unsworn statement?'

Harker had a ringing in his ears. He said thickly, 'Unsworn statement, your honour.'

'Very well.'

Harker took a big, fraught breath. He said, 'I am innocent, your honour.' He swallowed. 'That is all.' He slumped down in his seat.

Judge Ludman made a note. Then he sat forward.

'Mr Harker, please stand up.'

Harker got to his feet again, shakily, and Charlie rose beside him.

Judge Ludman fiddled with his pen, then said, 'Mr Harker, whether or not I agree with the jury's verdict is beside the point. By law, I have to accept their judgement, as you do. I must assume that they are absolutely right in convicting you of the cold-blooded murder of your wife, Josephine.

'I repeat, cold-blooded, because the only possible motive for this murder is money. So, that said, what is the appropriate sentence for a man who cold-bloodedly murders his innocent bride for her money?'

Judge Ludman sat back. He looked at Harker.

'You,' he said grimly, 'murdered your lovely bride for filthy lucre ... You succumbed to lust for millions of dollars ...' He shook his head. 'That is what the jury convicted you of, and that is a horrific, dastardly crime. To deter others who may feel tempted to murder their spouses for gain, and in order to satisfy society's sense of outrage at such a crime, the appropriate sentence is death.'

There was silence in the courtroom. Harker's ears were ringing.

Judge Ludman glowered at them all, then said, 'The sentence of the court is that you suffer death by electrocution in the Florida State Prison ...'

A section of the gallery broke into spontaneous applause.

PART VII

52

A man being sentenced to death is a dramatic spectacle – the expression on the judge's face as he passes sentence, the expression on the condemned man's face, the flicker of an eye, a flinch, the reaction of the lawyers – all these are matters of intense, morbid interest as the public experiences, vicariously, the horror of the death sentence.

Jack Harker's sentencing was seen and enjoyed around the world, live, and it was replayed many times in many languages over the next forty-eight hours, from Scandinavia and Russia in the north down to Patagonia in the south; from Japan in the east to Greenland in the west. Around the world journalists sat poised in front of their computers as sentence was passed, to dash down their impressions of the dramatic moment; within seconds wires and the stratosphere were streaming with images of Jack Harker's shocked countenance, abuzz with the learned pronouncements of law professors, criminologists, journalists and lawyers commenting on the justice or otherwise of the dramatic ruling that had just been made. Within minutes of the sentence of death being passed television anchormen and newspaper editors around the world, in dozens of languages, were unburdening themselves of profound pre-prepared pronouncements on the merits of the verdict and the uncertain future of the condemned man's chances on appeal.

The spectacle of Jack Harker being sentenced to death was seen on the television set of a big, white motor-yacht that was anchored off deserted Leonard Island, one of many in the Bahamas archipelago. Derek Clements shook his head as he watched Harker being led away. Almost immediately afterwards his telephone rang.

'Yes,' he said, 'I saw it. Thank Christ he kept his mouth shut.'

'Only for now,' Dupont said. 'If his appeal fails, he's got nothing to lose. So it's all stations go on Plan B. Have the goods on the jetty in Nassau by dawn the day after tomorrow.' He added: 'Does she know the result?'

'She thinks the jury is still out,' Clements said. 'She's on the beach right now.'

'Well, get going. And make damn sure she doesn't say anything about us.'

Clements left the wheelhouse. He scanned the long white beach through binoculars. At the far end he saw Josephine jogging along the waterline in the sunset. The dinghy was beached a hundred yards away. Sitting on a sand dune watching her was an American called Donald, with a pistol and a radio-telephone.

Clements spoke into his transmitter.

'Bring her aboard,' he said. 'It's Plan B.'

53

Death Row, where Old Sparky the electric chair lives, is in the Florida State Prison near the town of Starke, several hundred kilometres north of Miami. The prison is in rolling, farming country carved out of forests. It is flanked on either side by two other prisons, euphemistically called correctional institutions: Broward, for females, and Pinewoods for lesser male felons. All three prisons are surrounded by pastures full of fat cattle, lands farmed by the inmates. There is an abattoir with huge freezing capabilities, and extensive vegetable fields. Florida State Prison is for the real bad boys for whom maximum security is necessary, minimum rehabilitation expected. It was to this daunting array of three-storey buildings, surrounded by double rows of high security electric fencing topped with razor wire, which were themselves surrounded by double rows of high security electrified fencing, that Jack Harker was driven, from faraway Miami, the day after he was sentenced to death.

It was nine o'clock in the evening when the cars escorting him to Death Row pulled up outside the gates of Florida State Prison. Lights were burning in the pleasant administrative building outside those gates, for staff had stayed back to receive the new prisoner, now a famous name. It was with considerable interest that Jack Harker was processed into custody; his body searched, his possessions catalogued and signed for, his health determined by the prison doctor. He was issued with the distinctive orange clothing of the condemned inmate, and heavily escorted up a bewildering array of staircases and corridors, a process involving much opening and clanging of iron doors, to

Death Row. Finally he was escorted down a long corridor of barred cells, from which the snores of condemned men emanated. A fat, white, unshaven face appeared at one set of bars, eyes blank.

'Welcome to Hell, pardner.'

Harker was led into the adjoining cell. It was six feet wide and nine feet long. There was a bed, a washbasin, a toilet-bowl, a shelf, a small table.

The black warder unlocked his handcuffs. 'Breakfast at five a.m. You'll be told your rights after that.' He walked out, the door clanged shut, the keys turned.

A voice said, 'Lunch at ten-thirty, supper at four.'

Harker turned. He could not see the fat young man standing at his bars, spectacles on the end of his nose.

The voice continued in a monotone: 'Two hours' exercise twice a week. The yard has basketball facilities, volleyball, weights. Otherwise inmates are confined to their cells at all times, except for medical and legal consultations and social visits. Visitors allowed every weekend from nine a.m. to three, all visitors must be approved by prison authorities, members of the media may request interviews with Death Row inmates through the office of Information Services. Shower every second day. Mail every day except holidays, a limited number of magazine subscriptions allowed but no pornography. As many cigarettes as you like, plus a radio and television – but black and white only, no colour in case you get excited. No cable TV, but inmates can tune into church services on closed-circuit television. Chaplain consultations arranged on request.'

'Please.' Harker slumped down on to the bed and held his face. 'Please leave me alone.'

'Those, more or less, are your rights. Now for the bad news. Down the end of this line of cells is the Death Watch cell. Beyond that is the execution chamber. The Death Watch cell is where they take you after the governor has signed your death warrant, usually about six hours before your execution. It is slightly more comfortable than your common-or-garden Death Row cell – it is twelve feet long by seven feet wide, so that you can have your priest and your lawyer beside you to hold your hand. But your television is outside your cell, you can only watch through the bars.'

'Please,' Harker whispered, 'shut up.'

'Beyond the Death Watch cell,' the fat young man continued in his monotone, 'is the room where your actual electric chair sits, Old Sparky as it is affectionately known. Before electrocution became the preferred method in 1923, execution was by public hanging. Old Sparky is a three-legged oak chair built by inmates in 1923 and still going strong if a trifle erratically – a guy who was executed last year burst into flames, took a long time to die. Give me hanging every time. But the electricians say they have sorted out the problem now. The electrocution cycle is two minutes in duration, voltage and amperage levels peak three times, maximum current is two thousand volts and fourteen amps. The executioner who pulls the levers is a private citizen who is paid a hundred and fifty bucks a throw. He is anonymous but reputed to be a perfectly nice Joe who just needs the money.'

'For Christ's sake,' Harker whispered, 'leave me alone.'

'Do you play chess?'

'No, for Christ's sake.'

'You'll have plenty of time to learn, nine-point nine years is the average length of stay on Death Row before execution, what with appeals and all that jazz. Of course, it could be longer – Gary Alvord, just a few doors down, he's been on the Row since 1974, over twenty-two fucking years. I've only been here seven. I'm writing a book about some of the fruitcakes I've seen come and go down the corridor to Old Sparky. Maybe you'd like to publish it.'

'*Shuttup, Mervyn,*' somebody hollered down the corridor.

'It's nearly breakfast time, Al,' Mervyn said flatly.

'*Shuttup or I'll break your goddam neck.*'

'Yeah? You'll have to break a few bars first . . .'

54

In the nightmarish dawn, his first on Death Row, Jack Harker, exhausted and in shock, fell into a stunned, feverish sleep. He was whirled in a dreadful vortex of courtrooms, gallows, electric chairs. Then he dreamed an angel was shaking him and telling him that Josephine was alive, *alive* . . . The wonderful words were echoing and swirling, and Harker tried desperately to fight his way up out of the dreadful vortex to reach the angel, kicking and thrashing and clawing himself upwards, but the more he tried the faster the vortex whirled, sucking him down, down, and the angel in white was shouting and trying to grab him, to pull him up and free him from the dreadful suction of the vortex. Then the wonderful angel seized his upstretched hand and started to heave him upwards, all the time his mouth echoing the resounding words that Josephine was alive, *alive* – but then the angel could not hold him any longer and Harker was falling back into the dreadful vortex, falling and crying out for Josephine – and he crashed onto the floor beside his bunk.

He scrambled up wildly, stunned, shocked, his fists bunched, chest heaving – and there stood the prison governor in a white suit, saying, 'Easy, Mr Harker, take it easy. You're a free man. Josephine is *alive*. Take it easy . . .'

Harker stared at the angel, gasping, heart pounding, wild eyes wide. 'Alive?' he whispered. '*Alive? Is this true* . . . ?'

The governor was grinning, nodding, as were the warders beside him. 'Yes, she's alive; you're a free man, Mr Harker. The Justice Department has called me and it's been on the news. All we're waiting for is the official order written to release you . . .'

Harker stared at the wonderful man, wild eyes welling with joy. Then he dropped his face into his hands and he slowly sank to his knees.

'*Thank God . . .*' he sobbed. '*Thank God you're alive, Josie . . .*'

It was headline news on almost every newspaper of the western world, the top story on almost every television and radio station.

Only the Nassau newspapers and Bahama TV got the story of Josephine arriving at the American consul's residence, looking like a castaway, the pictures of her with long hair matted, the later photographs of her departing in the consular limousine, arriving at Nassau's little airport in a pretty dress provided by Hassim's Fashions, her long blonde hair now washed and shiny. But a mob of media people were at Miami International Airport to meet her, the arrivals gate besieged by television crews and pressmen, and there were many, many more on their way to Miami from all over the world.

Charlie Benson was there to greet Josephine, with Luke Mahoney and a junior representative of the District Attorney's office: Ed Vance, in a telephone interview, had explained that he was too busy with other weighty matters to attend, though he wished both 'the defendant' and Josephine well. (It was leaked by some member of his staff that he spent the whole day in front of his television in his office.) When Josephine came walking down the wide corridor to the arrivals barrier with no luggage whatsoever, not even a handbag, her skin golden-brown, her long hair bleached by the sun, the camera bulbs flashed and the barrage of questions began. But Charlie hurried forward to greet her and she only gave the media men a wide smile and answered, once, '*Yes, it's great to be alive!*'

The three lawyers hustled Josephine across the marbled foyers of the airport, chased by cameras and clamorous questions all the way. Outside a hired limousine was waiting. They scrambled in, and sped off towards the city. They were heading for the courthouse where Judge Ludman was waiting to hear evidence as to the identity of Josephine Valentine Harker before issuing a court order.

The Governor of Florida State Prison could not release a condemned man on the strength of a telephone call from the Justice Department or the State Governor's residence; he could not even let a condemned man out of the Maximum Security section until he had the official order in his hand. That document was being carried by helicopter from Miami up to Starke: and in that helicopter, courtesy of the governor, were Josephine Harker and old Charlie Benson.

The roads approaching Florida State Prison and its two sister institutions were clogged with traffic when Josephine's helicopter came whirring over the forests that surround the prisons' pastures. A murmur went up from hundreds of throats, arms pointing. There were half a dozen helicopters parked in the fields, chartered by the media, a dozen police cars with lights flashing trying to control the congestion, on alert for any attempted jailbreaks during the excitement. Reporters and television crews from around the world were gathered there at three o'clock that afternoon of December 16th, 1996.

As Josephine's helicopter came clattering over the pastures beside the administration block, James A. Hunter, CNN anchorman, stood in front of his camera and said, 'What can it feel like to wake up on Death Row this morning with the awful knowledge that you were convicted of murder and sentenced to death the day before yesterday – then learn that your loved one, whom you've been convicted of murdering, is alive and that you've been reprieved? It is hard to imagine the boundless joy, the . . . *mind*-blowing joy of knowing not only that you are to be spared death in that dreadful electric chair but that your darling wife, the woman you were accused of vilely murdering, was not dead after all but had drifted for days before being washed up on a deserted island on the edge of the Gulf Stream. But we'll let her tell her extraordinary story when she emerges through these prison gates on the arm of the man she loves . . .' Then the clatter of the landing helicopter drowned his voice, his hair flew in the rotor's downblast. He shouted into his microphone, *'And now here they are . . .'*

The mob of media people and spectators surged across the parking lot but the line of policemen and warders held them back. The helicopter touched down, then the passenger door opened and old Charlie clambered out. He was in his crumpled black suit, his halo of white hair resplendent, his enamel smile gleaming. He held out his hand gallantly; Josephine took it and climbed out, her hair and dress flying in the rotor's turbulence. A car was approaching across the pasture; in it was the prison's governor. It pulled up as the rotor's blasts subsided, the governor stepped out, strode towards Josephine and clasped her hand. He shook Charlie's hand, then hurried them back to the car. They all scrambled in. The car turned and, to the dismay of all the media people, sped off for a distant corner of the field. It turned and drove up to the back entrance of the prison where nobody was waiting. A gate in the high fence opened and the car disappeared from sight into the prison complex. A frustrated cry went up from the assembled media.

But they did not have to wait long. Fifteen minutes later the big front doors of the main building opened, facing the administrators' parking lot beyond the double security fences. Jack Harker stepped out, into the Florida sunshine. The crowd surged up against the outer fence, cameras rolling, all the television anchor people started talking to their cameras at once, all the reporters speaking into their radios and tape-recorders and scribbling notes.

Josephine was beside Harker, holding his hand. Smiling broadly but tearfully. Old Charlie Benson was behind them, beaming all over his benevolent face. Beside him was the prison governor. They walked together down the paved path, and came to the first perimeter gate. Guards opened it and they passed through on to the wide path down to the gate in the outer fence. The eyes of the world were upon them, the cameras rolling and clicking.

Three hundred yards away Ricardo sat behind the wheel of a Ford car with false numberplates; in the back seat sat two Cubans.

'Impossible . . .' Ricardo picked up his mobile telephone and dialled. In Fort Lauderdale Clements answered.

'Impossible. Too many people; we come badly unstuck. And a dozen cop cars. We'd get caught, sure.'

'Okay, don't risk it,' Clements said. 'If they leave by car follow and report your situation. If they leave by helicopter get the hell back here.'

The governor stopped a few paces from the main gates as the cameras zoomed in. He shook hands with Josephine, and with Charlie. Then he shook hands with Harker warmly, congratulated him again and wished him every happiness. Then Charlie turned to the mass of cameras and faces beyond the gate. He produced a sheet of paper from his pocket, put on his reading spectacles and smiled. He held up a hand for silence. It came instantly.

'Ladies and gentlemen,' Charlie said. 'Jack and Josephine Harker have prepared press releases, as neither of them feels up to saying much, and they certainly don't want to answer questions after the ordeals they have been through. Now, these gates are going to be opened and we'll pass through and I'll read their statements. Please don't interrupt and please give us breathing space.'

The guards swung open the gates and the crowd fell back a little as they walked through. Guards closed the gates again and Charlie stopped. He smiled, raised his voice and read loudly:

'Ladies and gentlemen, Jack and Josephine Harker want to thank the media for their interest and sympathy. Josephine wants the public, and particularly the justice system, to know that the account that Jack gave concerning her

484

disappearance is substantially correct. She fell overboard when she was alone on watch – Jack was asleep below at the time. She fell overboard as she was adjusting the aft mizzen sail. The vessel rolled suddenly, she was caught off balance, bumped into the handrail and toppled over. She was not wearing a safety harness – which she should have done – but fortunately she was wearing a life-jacket. In the water she helplessly watched the yacht motoring away from her into the night: she shouted and screamed but her cries went unheard against the boat's engine and the whistling trade winds.'

Charlie adjusted his spectacles, smiled widely at the crowd, then continued:

'So the boat disappeared into the night, and Josephine floated. It was some hours later when she saw the boat return on a reciprocal course. But it was going to pass hundreds of yards from where she was. She could see Jack on board, shining his light over the sea, searching for her. She waved and shouted but, alas, he did not hear her or see her, and he disappeared again. She never saw the yacht again but she did see its life-raft which Jack had thrown overboard. She managed to swim to it and clamber aboard. She was exhausted, of course, having been battling the water for about four hours at this stage. Mercifully the life-raft – like all such craft – had a container of water, some hard rations and fishing lines, and it is covered by a canopy. Josephine collapsed asleep as soon as she had eaten something and drunk some water. She slept for some ten hours.'

Charlie looked up from his notes. 'She was wearing a sea-man's waterproof wristwatch, which gave her the date as well as the time.' He continued: 'Josephine had no control over the life-raft's direction, of course, it drifted northwards with the trade winds and the Gulf Stream current. She tried to keep a lookout for vessels to hail but the wind, sea and heat soon drove her back inside her canopy. She knows that she drifted for four days, before being shaken awake by her life-raft washing up on to a beach. She found she was on a flat island. She presumed she was on one of the hundreds of Bahamian islands. And she was right – it was the island of Leonard, which is unpopulated. It does, however, have a small fresh-water spring which mercifully she found.'

Charlie looked up and smiled happily. Then he continued: 'And there Josephine stayed for the next several months. Like Robinson Crusoe, living off shellfish and fish which she caught with the equipment from her life-raft. There was a packet of matches amongst that equipment and she was able to keep a fire going. On several occasions she saw passing boats in the distance, and she tried to hail these by waving and shouting and by building up her fire, but nobody noticed her. Until the day before yesterday.

'On December fifteenth a Bahamian fishing boat passed the island. Josephine's frantic efforts succeeded in attracting the crew's attention. They kindly agreed to take her to civilization, to the capital, Nassau, arriving there today. There she learned the fate of Jack. She hurried to the American consul's office. Contact was made with the Miami court authorities and thus with me.' Old Charlie looked up and gave his enamelled beam. 'And here she is, overjoyed to be reunited with Jack, overjoyed that she has gotten him out of prison, off Death Row, overjoyed to be alive . . .'

Charlie wiped his eye with his knuckle.

'That concludes Josephine's statement. I turn now to Jack's.' Charlie unfolded another sheet of paper. 'All Jack wants to say is this: "I am overjoyed that Josephine is alive, overjoyed to be reunited with her, and, of course, to be vindicated, to have it proved that I was telling the court the truth. And overjoyed that the nightmare of living in the shadow of the electric chair is over."'

Charlie folded the paper and thrust it in his pocket. 'That's all, ladies and gentlemen. Thank you. Now, if you'll be so kind as to let us get to our car . . .'

Then the questions started. '*Excuse us . . .*' Charlie cried, happily forcing his way through the jostling crowd to the prison's car, Josephine and Harker following. '*Excuse us . . .*' They clambered into the vehicle. A warder had the car moving before the door slammed against the reporters. He drove off, some of the media running alongside the car shouting questions. The driver forged through the crowd, hooting, through the parking lot, then into the field beyond where the helicopter stood. He drove up to it between the prison guards. The doors opened and Jack, Josephine and Charlie climbed out. They ran for the helicopter and clambered into it. They put on headphones. The door slammed, the guards withdrew, the rotors began to turn. The helicopter rocked, then rose. The ground began to drop away. Down there the media were running for their cars and chartered helicopters.

'Well,' the pilot said over the headphones, 'back to Miami? That's where I'm flight-planned, but I can change it.'

'Fort Lauderdale, please,' Charlie said. He turned to Jack. 'I've had your boat moved to the police jetty there because it's much nicer than Miami, and I've booked you into a good hotel on the beach.'

Josephine said, 'I think we should go straight to the police jetty.'

'Like hell!' Harker said. 'The hotel. The best damn hotel in town, with the best restaurant and the best bar serving the best damn champagne.' He added: 'Your father's not waiting at the hotel, is he?'

Josephine said, 'No. But I've seen him. He flew down from Boston this morning. He's overjoyed, of course. Sends his congratulations to you and his apologies. Says he's writing to you.'

He snorted cheerfully. 'Oh, I can't wait. Does he now think I'm a great son-in-law?' He added, 'What's happened to Luke?'

'He's waiting for us at the hotel,' Charlie said.

Josephine squeezed Harker's hand hard. '*Listen* to me. You'll be safer on the police jetty, believe me.'

Harker frowned at her. 'Meaning?'

Josephine pointed at the back of the pilot's head, then pulled off her earphones. She reached into her pocket and pulled out a piece of paper and a pen. She scribbled, *We can't talk now. But your CCB friends are after you I am sure.*

'Well, I think we can start our celebration right now,' Charlie said brightly. 'I just happen to have brought along a little picnic basket containing a bottle or three of champagne and a selection of other libations. And as it happens, the hotel where I've booked you in has a helicopter pad on the roof. It's very secure . . .'

55

The Edgewater is a pleasant hotel on the suburban beachfront where the canals of Fort Lauderdale, Venice of America, flow out into the blue Gulf Stream. It is a pretty hotel, ten storeys high, bounded on the south side by the wide canal-mouth, on the east side by palms, the white beach and the sea. It has a thatched bar out in the gardens, a five-star restaurant with another bar on the rooftop below the helipad. The view is spectacular: on a clear day you can see down to Miami, and behind is a lovely view of the meandering canals and waterfront homes of Fort Lauderdale. The corner suite allocated to Harker and Josephine had a balcony view of both the sea and the canals.

Josephine said, 'I didn't hear them approach because the wind was against us and our engine was on. I was sitting at the aft wheel, on automatic pilot, my back to the stern. I got up to adjust the mizzen because it was flapping, when suddenly I saw four men scrambling up over the stern rail from a speedboat. They were all wearing balaclavas. I screamed and two of them lunged at me. I lashed out as I tried to get back to the cockpit, I got one of them in the face and he tripped or crashed into the rail and fell overboard. And then the others were on to me. I can't remember what happened exactly but I tried to kick, then suddenly I got a tremendous blow to the chest. I staggered backwards against the stern rail, then another blow, to the head. I crashed on to the deck behind the wheel and the next thing I knew there was blood in my eyes. I scrambled up and I saw the bastard coming at me again. I lunged backwards, and I must have hit the rail because the next thing I knew I was crashing into the sea, water in my gullet, choking. Thank God I was wearing my life-jacket. When I got my breath back all I saw was the boat a hundred yards away, heading into the wind. The speedboat was following it. I yelled and yelled, but it just kept on going. Then I heard a shot, maybe two. Then another two or three shots. Then more. Then the speedboat turned and came straight towards me.'

Josephine breathed deeply. She took a tasteless sip of champagne, then continued, 'I was terrified but I desperately hoped they weren't going to let me drown. Even if they shot me it would be better than drowning.'

Harker squeezed her hand.

'But they didn't shoot me, they hauled me aboard. I was crying. One of them was badly wounded, blood all over his chest. There was an argument – two of them wanted to shoot me and sink my body but the driver – his name was Derek – he said I was more useful alive.' She snorted. '"For the moment." Quote, unquote.'

'Jesus,' Harker said. 'What did this Derek look like?'

'Smallish. Wiry, tough. Blue eyes.'

Harker said, 'That's him, Clements. So?'

'So they took me back to their motor-yacht. I hadn't noticed it before, it was about two miles away. The one who was badly wounded had to be taken to a doctor. They started off north-eastwards, into the Bahamas at full throttle. They locked me below in a cabin. I was frantic about you – I asked what had happened to you, but they said you were okay. I didn't believe them, of course. I asked what they wanted and Derek just said they only wanted the boat – implying that they were just pirates.' She looked at Harker. 'But I didn't believe that after what I had just discovered about your CCB past. And one of them had a distinct South African accent. And I'm sure I caught a few words in Afrikaans. The only reason they weren't rushing after you to kill you was because one of them was badly wounded.' She took a deep breath. 'So we motored all that night and eventually I fell asleep. When I woke up I was let out to shower and eat, and I was told that the wounded man had been put ashore, handed over to a doctor.'

'And his name was?' Luke asked.

'I subsequently overheard it was Dupont.'

Harker nodded. 'So then what happened?'

'For the next two weeks we looked for you. Tried to catch up with you.'

'Where did they look?'

'The Virgin Islands. That was my fault. I let slip the very first day that you and I had intended going to the Virgins. They figured you wouldn't go north, turn back towards Florida, in case you bumped into them again.'

'They were right.'

'So they went flat out for the Virgins. But you had at least a two-day lead on them, we never even saw you on radar.'

'That's because I swung east, into the Atlantic. Their boat couldn't follow me there because they would not have the fuel-range, whereas I had sails.'

'Of *course*.' Josephine nodded. 'Didn't think of that. Anyway, we finally found *Rosemary* in the British Virgin Islands. I was locked up all the time, only let out of my cabin to eat. Anyway, they found our boat but by that time you had already been arrested and flown off back to Florida. The boys got the story from the locals. They were terrified that you would tell the court about the whole CCB business and put the finger on them. So they hightailed it back up towards Florida, to a deserted island in the Bahamas. Evidently the idea was to use me as a hostage: Derek was going to get word to you to keep your mouth shut about the CCB and about the Long Island murder or unspeakable things would happen to me. *And* you, if you were ever free again.' She sighed deeply. 'Oh God, I was sick with fear. For you and me.' She looked at Charlie. 'Either way we were doomed – if Jack was acquitted they would murder him to make sure he didn't spill the beans on them. And of course they were terrified that if Jack was convicted he would blurt out the truth to try to save himself from the electric chair. And whatever happened, they would have to kill me to stop me running to the police.'

Harker squeezed her hand. Jesus. 'Jesus. Go on.'

Josephine took a big swallow of champagne. 'And then,' she said, 'your trial started. The boys watched it all day, every day, every minute of the live coverage. They videoed it and re-watched it over and over. And they let me watch it. And,' she sighed, 'I was horrified. Horrified for you, horrified for me. Because the boys were sure you were about to tell the court the truth to save yourself from the electric chair. And that meant the whole CCB connection and the Long Island business would emerge.'

Harker sighed grimly. 'So what happened?'

'So,' Josephine said, 'every day we watched your trial.' She looked at him. 'God it was awful to watch you being tried for murdering me when I was alive but unable to jump up and shout, "*Here I am!*"' She wiped her eyes. 'And your cross-examination was terrible. You *looked* so goddam guilty. Anyway, they were expecting you to be acquitted. So was I. In which case, they would murder you if you were released before fifteenth of December, the last day for amnesty applications. And, of course, they would have to then murder me too, to stop me talking. And then on the fourteenth of December you were convicted. They were frantic you would spill the beans on them. And so was I because then I was going to be murdered.' Josephine closed her eyes. She took a moment, before continuing. 'And then Derek came to me. He pretended to befriend me. To offer me a deal. He said that the fifteenth of December was the last day anyone could apply to the Truth Commission for amnesty. If you were going to spill the beans it would have to be the next day in order to qualify for South African amnesty – so Jack only had another twenty-four hours or so in which to confess to the Truth Commission, if he didn't do it before then he would never do it, Derek said. He said he had contacts in the Truth Commission secretariat who would advise him whether or not you had confessed in time. So, Derek said, after midnight the next day, South African time, there was no further reason to worry about you and therefore no further reason to keep me hostage – because surely I would keep my mouth shut, wouldn't I? Obviously, if I were freed I would immediately get you released from Death Row and I would hardly then send you straight back into jail by telling about my captivity and your CCB background, would I? That was logical. So, Derek said, the day after tomorrow they would release me, but if I ever changed my mind for any reason and decided to report them to the police I would be "blown away". *And* you, Jack. We would be hunted down to the ends of the earth, we would be fugitives for the rest of our lives.' She took a deep breath. 'And I believe them.'

Harker stood up and began to pace. 'But your pal Derek is also right when he says we'll keep our mouths shut. Because, no way do I want to go back to jail for Long Island, and I'm sure you don't want to be a fugitive for life either.'

Josephine rubbed her eyebrows.

'Except,' she said tensely, 'I'm quite sure that it was all a trick.' She looked up at Harker. 'I'm quite sure that their strategy was to release me so that I could get you released, and then they would have the chance to murder you – and me – in case you broke down and confessed to the Truth Commission.' She looked at him.

Harker said, 'But that doesn't make sense – why would I confess to the Truth Commission now that the amnesty cut-off date has passed? I'd be prosecuted.'

Josephine said, 'Because of Looksmart Kumalo. They're scared you'll make a deal with the DA and give evidence against them, then give evidence for Looksmart in his civil action when he sues the South African army for millions. Then give evidence for the DA against the boys, Derek, Dupont and company, at their criminal trial. And for the attorney general in South Africa if they were prosecuted there.' She closed her eyes. 'Looksmart suddenly appearing on the scene, vowing to sue, really worried them – that's why they went after you, Jack, because they feared you'd team up with Looksmart.' She sighed tensely, then ended: 'Believe me, they're after you, Jack. I am quite sure that they were waiting for you outside the prison this morning. And that they've followed us to this hotel – they're waiting for us somewhere right now.'

Charlie and Harker were frowning at her. Luke said, 'Then you guys need protection. I mean bodyguards – not the police. Hired muscle. Until you're safely out of this town.'

Harker asked Charlie, 'D'you know a reliable security firm?'

'Sure,' Charlie said. 'Don't come cheap, however.'

'Hell,' Harker said, 'we'll only need them for a few days. For as long as it takes us to get the boat cranked up.'

'The police assured me that the boat is in good condition,' Charlie said. 'She's clean and the engine's fine. You could go straight to sea if you wanted to.'

'I think,' Harker said, 'we both need a few days' rest in this nice hotel.'

Josephine glanced at him, anguished. Then she turned to Charlie and Luke. 'Would you mind leaving us alone for a short while?'

'Sure,' Luke said. He stood up.

Charlie looked taken aback. Then he stood up stiffly. 'Of course. We'll be in the bar downstairs.' He added, 'As if you couldn't guess.'

Harker frowned. The two men crossed the room.

The door clicked closed behind them. Josephine sighed. Suddenly her eyes were tearful.

'I love you, Jack,' she whispered. 'But I cannot live with you. I cannot sleep with you tonight. I cannot sail away with you.'

* * *

494

Harker stared at her, disbelief on his face. Josephine held his eye, her tears glistening.

'I love you but I do not want to love you, Jack. I want the man I first fell in love with. The go-ahead publisher, the honourable soldier, all that lovely stuff. I do not want to love the man who was an assassin. Who deceived me for years about his political associations. Who pretended to support my political beliefs – who even *published* my political beliefs, whilst all the time working for my sworn political enemy.'

Harker stared at her, his mind stumbling. 'For Christ's sake, I've explained all that –'

Josephine interrupted desperately: 'Oh, I remember! I've had almost four months' imprisonment to remember, and to weigh every word. And to *reconsider*. For months I've talked to you in my head about it all – and nothing that you say can change my mind, Jack. Because you deceived me for years and I don't think I can trust you again.'

'For Christ's sake,' Harker cried incredulously. 'Espionage is *based* on deception! I was in the game before I met you!'

'The fact remains I was totally deceived by the man I love! Right now I do not know whether I can ever trust you again.' She looked at him, tremulously. 'And,' she said, 'you deceived me about the shares in Harvest.' She looked at him. 'I was horrified when I saw you admit that under cross-examination. *Horrified*.'

Harker closed his eyes. 'Please listen to me. Don't interrupt.' He looked at her. She looked back at him grimly. He said, '*I* didn't ask you to buy my fifty-one per cent shareholding in Harvest – *you* did. I intended to sell on the open market to Packard, but *you* insisted – you refused to let Packard get control of "your" publisher. I tried to dissuade you, but you insisted. You even agreed that I keep two per cent of the shares so that we controlled the company *between* us.' He glared. 'If you had not insisted I would have sold to Packard or somebody else, and had the same

495

amount of money. And *you would* have the same amount of money invested elsewhere – if you hadn't invested in Harvest you would have bought some other company's shares.'

Josephine's eyes were moist. 'You deceived me into thinking you and I controlled Harvest, between us.'

'But we *do* control Harvest between us!'

'Sure, with your two per cent and my forty-nine we control Harvest! Great! That's what I bargained for. But the truth is that with your two per cent and Westminster's forty-nine per cent *you* control Harvest *without* me! You can do what you like, *despite* my expensive forty-nine per cent!'

Harker said angrily, 'So you don't trust me to run Harvest in our best interests? Mine *and* yours? Fine – you want your money back? I'll give you your money back!' He jumped up and strode across the room to his bag. He unzipped it and snatched out his cheque book.

Josephine said sullenly, 'A two-point-two-million-dollar cheque? I know how much money you've got in that account, the whole world knows because it was on television – nine thousand dollars.'

'And the rest,' Harker said angrily. 'Because, *darling*, I'm going to sell my *Westminster* shares to Mr goddam *Packard* for two-point-two million dollars and –' his eyes flashed at Josie – 'nice Mr *Packard* and I will control Harvest with our joint fifty-one per cent, and *you*, my darling – as you spurn my lousy two per cent – you can scream your head off at annual general meetings and nobody will take the slightest fucking notice!'

Josephine glared at him. Furiously astounded. Then she whispered, 'You wouldn't do that to me.'

Harker cried, 'Oh wouldn't I?' He tapped his breast. 'Listen, baby, I've just got off Death Row, and you've just got off CCB's death row, and if you don't mind me saying so I think you're being a trifle fucking precious! You can control Harvest through me, or *Packard* can control Harvest through me. It's up to you!' His eyebrows shot up. 'Or I can control Harvest, *all by myself* – through Westminster!'

Josephine glared. 'With nine thousand dollars in the bank?'

'You think I can't find a bank to lend me money against the security of Harvest and Westminster?'

Josephine looked at him angrily. Then she repeated, 'You didn't tell me about Westminster, that you owned it.'

Harker cried, 'How could I have told you about Westminster? If I had you would have asked all kinds of questions and the fact that the CCB had owned Westminster might have emerged – as it has now! Then you would have exploded and deserted me! As you have now.'

Josephine looked at him, her eyes hard. She repeated doggedly, 'You deceived me.'

'Right, I deceived you! And so you'll never trust me again. Okay, so I'll now leave. But before I do let me just set the record straight.' He strode to the writing desk, snatched up a sheet of paper and wrote: *I, Sinclair Jonathan Harker, hereby sell to my wife, Josephine Valentine Harker, my two per cent shareholding in Harvest House, Inc, for the sum of one dollar, value received.*

He signed it and strode back to Josephine. He thrust it at her. 'There. You now control Harvest House. Give me a dollar!'

Josephine read the brief contract. She glanced up at him.

'I don't want it.'

'Oh yes you do!' Harker strode to her handbag, snatched out her purse, extracted a dollar note. He held it up to her. 'Want a receipt?'

Josephine looked at him tearfully.

'Good.' He glared at her. 'Thank you. I'm leaving now, in accordance with your wishes. I'm going to the boat, to crank her up and put to sea, seeing that the honeymoon I had in mind is not forthcoming.' He paused. 'Any chance of you changing your exquisite mind?'

Josephine's big blue eyes were full of tears. Then she shook her head slightly, her lip trembling.

'You go, Jack,' she whispered. 'Go and disappear into the wide blue yonder. These guys are after us, Jack. After you and me. I do not wish to spend the rest of my life on the run, a fugitive from your terrible people.'

Harker strode back and dropped to his knee beside her. 'But we won't be!' He shook his head. 'I don't believe you're right in your assessment of the situation. The deadline for amnesty was midnight *yesterday*. If I were to confess now I would be mad – even if the DA in New York gives me immunity to testify against the CCB, and for Looksmart, I'd be prosecuted in South Africa!' He spread his hands. 'Why on earth would I do that? I've just got off Death Row! And why did the CCB wait until the sixteenth of December – the day *after* the expiration of the amnesty cut-off date – before releasing you?' He spread his hands again. 'Because *after* that date I am no threat to them, and therefore nor are you.' He squeezed her arms urgently. 'Josie, I doubt anybody's out there waiting to kill us.' He took both her hands. 'Josie, let's forget about all that – all that dreadful past. *Josie* –' he squeezed her hands hard – 'we've both just got off Death Row, for Christ's sake!' He looked at her in tearful wonder. 'That is an event so joyous, so extraordinary that we should be dancing in the streets.' He shook his head at her: 'We can't split up now after all we've been through – we've just been reunited! Besides, if what you say is true you need me to *protect* you!'

Josephine's eyes were brimming. 'On the contrary, the greater the distance between us the safer I'll be.'

Harker closed his eyes. 'For Christ's sake, realize that there is no danger now that amnesty deadline is past!'

Just then the telephone rang. 'Leave it,' Harker commanded, but Josie reached out and picked it up. 'Hullo?'

'Sorry to disturb you,' Luke said, 'but I thought you should know it's just been announced on television that President Nelson Mandela has extended the deadline for amnesty applications by another six months.'

56

Harker rode down in the elevator with the bodyguard Charlie had arranged.

It was all unreal. Unreal that he was free. Unreal that Josie was alive. Unreal that he was leaving her. And it was all screamingly real. And his heart was breaking. The tears were burning in his eyes.

The elevator doors opened in the parking basement. The bodyguard, name of Mike, stepped out, gun ready. He peered all around, then led the way through the gloom to his vehicle. Their footsteps echoing. Another bodyguard was waiting behind the wheel. Harker climbed into the back seat. Mike walked up the exit ramp and peered out into the sunshine. He beckoned. When the vehicle drew up he got in beside Harker.

'Where to?' the driver said.

'Police jetty, please.'

And the drive there was unreal. Traffic and palm trees flashing past, suburbs, condominiums, canals, yachts. And all the time back there in the Edgewater Hotel was Josephine, weeping. Also unreal. *Go now, go and save your life, go and sail away over the horizon and disappear like you were going to do . . .*

Please come with me.
Please go now before they find you.
Then meet me in St Thomas.
I don't want to love you any more.
But you do love me?
Please go now, and never come back.
Meet me in Jamaica. It's lovely there.
Please go now.

I'll phone you from Jamaica.
No, it'll break my heart . . .

There were all kinds of vessels moored stern-to along the police jetty. They were mostly boats that had been seized for involvement in smuggling offences. Yacht *Rosemary* was right down at the far end.

Harker went into the police station, followed by his bodyguards. He signed some forms, took possession of the boat's keys and papers. The policeman on duty was very nice to him; he had followed the trial on television avidly. 'Good luck to you, sir!' Harker thanked him and walked down the concrete quay to his boat.

And there she was. So beautiful. And so heartbreaking.

He clambered aboard, over the transom, and threw his bag down at the aft helm. He went forward and unlocked the wheelhouse door. He turned to his bodyguards who were still standing on the jetty.

'Thank you, you can go now.'

Mike shook his head. 'Our orders are to stay by you until you sail.'

Harker smiled bleakly. 'Then, come aboard out of the sun. Have something to drink.'

'No drinking on duty, sir. We'll sit under the awning.'

Harker opened the door to the wheelhouse. It was stuffy, hot and humid. And, oh God, all those dreadful nights and days after the attack came flooding back at him. Dreadful and heartbreaking. There was the broken glass on the speedometer dial, the broken radio.

He opened the windows, and the overhead hatch. Then he clattered down the steps into the saloon.

He went into the galley and hit the electric-generator switch. The little machine thudded to life. He turned on the refrigerator, then he slid back the engine-room door.

There was the big red engine, gleaming at him. He pulled out the dipstick: plenty of oil. He unscrewed the radiator cap: the system had fresh water. He tugged the fan belts: they were tight. He checked the batteries: they had water.

So, the police had looked after her. He slid the door closed.

He opened the overhead lockers in the galley. There was plenty of canned food. He knew there was booze aboard. He went back up into the wheelhouse. He pressed the glow-switch for twenty seconds, then twisted the ignition; beneath his feet Big Red thudded sweetly to life.

He left the engine idling and clattered below again before he could start thinking. He went down the companionway to his aft cabin to change clothes. And, oh, the big panelled cabin cried *Josie* at him . . .

He opened her lockers. And there were her pretty dresses and skirts and blouses. Harker looked at them, his heart breaking – he wanted to slam the closet shut to stop himself hurting, but he could not. He reached out and fingered the first dress. Feeling its soft femaleness. He brought it to his face and smelt it – and yes, he could smell her scent.

Then he pulled open her lingerie drawer.

And there they all were in a silky, multi-coloured jumble: her scanty panties, her stockings, the ones with seams that led all the way up her beautiful legs, her suspender belts . . . Harker's eyes were brimming, his heart breaking. He wanted to clutch them all to his face, to feel her intimacy, to breathe her scent deep. Instead he banged the drawer closed and pulled open the closet that contained his clothes. He snatched up a T-shirt and shorts.

The engine was idling sweetly under his feet when he clambered back up into the wheelhouse. The two bodyguards were sitting under the aft awning.

'Okay, I'm about to cast off,' he told them. 'You can go now, many thanks.'

Mike stood up. 'Okay, sir,' he said. 'Have a good trip.' He put out his hand. 'And congratulations again.'

'Thank you.' Harker shook hands with both of them.

'Would you mind throwing off those two stern lines on the jetty?' He pointed.

The bodyguards clambered ashore. They threw the stern lines off their bollards, and Harker pulled them aboard. 'Thanks.' He turned to the wheel.

He pressed the electrical windlass switch, and the anchor chain began to come clanking aboard. The yacht eased forward out of her berth as the chain came up. He felt the anchor break out of the mud: half a minute later it inched up into its cradle in the bows, and clanked into position. Harker eased the gear lever into forward, opened the throttle a little. The propeller bit the water. And the good ship *Rosemary* began to ease out into the canal.

Harker took a deep breath and held it.

This was it . . . This was the moment he had dreamed about in his cell. The moment so wonderful that it had been impossible to believe it could happen, the day he would be finally adjudged innocent and set free, walk away out of the shadow of that dreadful electric chair, out of that dreadful prison, out into God's sweet sunshine . . .

It had been a dream so impossibly wonderful that it couldn't ever happen. And now here it was, happening. And not only was the impossible happening, the doubly impossible had happened because his dearest darling Josephine, the love of his life whom he had been convicted of murdering, his dearest person whom his broken heart had believed was dead, was not only alive and well but just a mile away across this beautiful city – but she would not come with him. She did not want to live with him any more because she did not want to love a murderer, and now he was sailing away from her for ever with a broken heart. But somehow all that was unreal too, unreal and untrue that she did not want to love him, untrue that he was sailing away from her for ever, untrue that he was a murderer, it was even untrue that he was sailing away at all. He was sailing *towards* her, she was waiting for him at her hotel balcony . . . Harker guided *Rosemary* down the winding canal between the lovely waterfront houses, and his tears were glistening, and his heart was breaking.

And then the canals widened out at their confluence, and there ahead was Pier 66. The Immigration jetty on one side, the big bridge, the Edgewater Hotel towering up beyond it, the open Gulf Stream and then the wide blue ocean.

Harker steered slowly towards the bridge, tears in his eyes. He lifted the binoculars and looked at the row of balconies of the Edgewater just below the penthouse roof.

It was unreal that he expected to see Josephine up there on her balcony. He steamed slowly towards the bridge; and then it began to open up for him. Slowly the two halves began to part in the middle, rise slowly up on end just for him. Harker steamed slowly underneath, and out the other side. On his left was the Marina Inn complex, jetties and boatsheds and hotel and chandlers and boat brokers, beyond that the lovely canalside homes again. Harker carried on past them. Around the big bend in the canal. And then there, five hundred yards ahead, was the mouth, and the wide open sea, the Gulf Stream, the beaches stretching away to the north and south. And there, rearing up, was the Edgewater Hotel.

Harker looked up desperately at the hotel as he motored slowly towards it. There was no face in the windows of their suite, no figure on the balcony. The tears were running down his face. Closer and closer he slowly approached, and still there was no face at those windows. Then he was at the hotel's flank, the canal's mouth opening out into the sea. Then he was passing out of the mouth into the Gulf Stream, the hotel's gardens and beach dropping behind, and his broken heart leapt as he saw her.

Suddenly Josephine was standing on the balcony, her long hair cascading down her shoulders. 'Josie!' Harker shouted. 'Josie!' He leapt and waved, a tearful laugh all over his face. He waved and waved and laughed, then he snatched up his binoculars. And his overjoyed heart was breaking. He thought he saw her try to smile for him; then he saw her mouth form some words – and with all his heart he believed they were 'I love you . . .' He dropped his head and wept for joy. Then he swung the helm.

He was well past the mouth of the canal now; he swung the helm around, towards the hotel's beaches.

The yacht was about eighty yards from the shore, the sea almost flat. Harker rammed the engine into neutral, then flicked the switch and the anchor dropped into the sea, the chain rattling out. He was grinning all over his face. The water was only twenty feet deep here: he waited until sixty feet of chain was out, then he shoved the engine astern. The boat went surging backwards; then he felt the anchor bite into the sand.

Harker's heart was pounding deliciously as he lowered the dinghy from the davits. He clambered down into it. He unhooked the couplings, then started the outboard motor. It purred into life. He swung the tiller, and the dinghy turned her nose towards the hotel.

Harker put the binoculars to his eyes. He found her: she was still on the balcony, a smile on her tearful face. His broken heart seemed to turn over, he threw up his arm and waved and waved. And he laughed when he saw her wave back.

'*I love you!*' he bellowed. '*I love you . . .*'

He was thirty yards away from the hotel's beach now: the yacht was anchored about fifty yards behind him. Josephine was still standing on her balcony. Harker bellowed: '*I love you!*' He saw Josephine smile, then she turned and disappeared.

He was about ten yards from the beach when the bomb went off, and the yacht erupted in flames.

The boat exploded with a crack like thunder. It exploded in a mass of flying fibreglass and wood and steel, balls of yellow flame and black smoke billowing out and upwards. Then there was another thud as the fuel tanks exploded, another mass of flying debris amidst barrelling smoke and flame.

Harker slammed the nose of the dinghy into the sand. He stared back, astonished, horrified.

Josephine burst out of the hotel. She ran across the gardens, then down onto the beach.

Harker clambered out of the boat. Josephine was running across the sand, aghast. Harker started towards her. She ran into his arms, and they clutched each other, staring back at the conflagration.

Then she looked at him, her eyes full of shock, and she dropped her head on his chest and wept.